# GARDEN
## *of*
# THORNS

# GARDEN
## of
# THORNS

## AMBER MITCHELL

Entangled Publishing, LLC
2614 South Timberline Road
Suite 109
Fort Collins, CO 80525
Visit our website at www.entangledpublishing.com.

Entangled Teen is an imprint of Entangled Publishing, LLC.

Edited by Lydia Sharp
Cover design by Erin Dameron-Hill
Cover art from iStock

Manufactured in the United States of America

First Edition March 2017

*To Brian*
*For always being my light in the dark.*

# Chapter One

Needle-thin spikes line the shackles that bite into my wrists and ankles. Blood crusts between my fingers and toes, but my chapped skin stopped throbbing sometime last night. I've learned that the less I move, the less they dig. Stiffness creeps up my back, growing out from my bones like branches.

"We're almost there now," Fern whispers next to me, her voice my only comfort in the never-ending darkness.

"I wish we weren't." Fear slips into my stomach like a stone, remembering where we're heading.

I lean my head back against Fern's, her long black hair tickling my bare arms. Maybe some of her courage will soak into me as she peers out of the tiny peephole we widened on our cart to sneak a view of her old home.

For as long as we've been paired in the Garden, she's told me stories of Imperial City's grandeur, of the cobblestoned streets that shine like honey during midday, of the four multiroofed temples that shoot up so high they look like pillars supporting the bright blue sky, and hidden gardens tucked between buildings, where you can duck under a blossoming dogwood tree to escape the heat.

Most nights, after I stumbled on stage and she bore the bruises or broken bones caused by my clumsy feet, we would lie head to head on top of the dirty straw lining our cage, and she'd spin golden webs from her memories of the Imperial City to get us by. Her whispers allowed me to forget, until I turned to look at her smiling face and watched a trail of fresh blood drip down her cracked lip. As a Flower, it's my job to dance. As a Wilted, hers is to keep me in line by paying for my mistakes with her skin. In the Garden, Flowers are low, but Wilteds are the dirt beneath our petals, silently keeping our roots alive.

"Do you want to look?" she asks, pulling me back to the present.

A beam of light spills into the cart, its weak ray like gentle fingers on my face. It gives the illusion of hope. I turn away before that seed can root into my chest.

"Sure," I say, and the spikes of my shackles bite as I move toward the hole.

My eyes fight to adjust to the glaring brightness, but once they do, I gasp in awe.

A white wooden building lined in red trim appears in my line of vision, shooting up farther than I can see through our peephole, and I can just make out the edge of its slanted red roof. Everywhere I look, I catch color—a blue stream slicing through the city, green bamboo shoots groomed artfully next to an arched golden bridge. I drink it all in, letting the scenery fill my soul after the endless stream of bland grays and browns of the small towns we usually visit.

"Beautiful, isn't it?" Fern says, her voice tinged with longing.

She hasn't seen her home in nearly ten years. We were stolen into this horror show within a month of each other. When the Gardener stuck us in the same cage, I assumed it was an act of kindness, so we wouldn't wither under the weight of our capture. I didn't know until later that allowing us to bond the first four years would be his cruelest trick. That he would twist that bond to keep both of us in line or else we would both end up hurt—her flesh a physical manifestation of the mental scars I bear.

I pull my face away from the slit in the wood, ready to comfort Fern, but I don't see a trace of the sorrow on her face I thought I heard in her voice. She motions for me to return my gaze outside.

During our parade through town, we've attracted quite a crowd. The people in their plain linen clothes gawk at our processional, shock straining their pale faces as they witness the first public entertainment to enter Imperial City in over ten years. As our caravan bumps through the streets, women grab their husbands' hands tighter, guards in their shiny metal uniforms pretend not to stare as they herd people off the streets, and children weave in between the carts, playing a game of chicken with the horses' hooves.

At a glance, the bright colors painted on our carriages make it seem like the show is meant for children. When I first saw them, I was reminded of the grandiose red and golden tops of the Wonder Emporium from my homeland. Behind those walls lie men who could swallow whole swords and women who rode elephants.

But our carts depict what the Gardener sells: his thirteen Dancing Flowers. And we aren't meant for children's eyes. The paintings on the sides of our carts tantalize. Each dress brighter than the last, accentuating the curves of our forms as we dance, forced to lose one petal at a time, exposing our souls.

I twist my body so I can peek ahead. The ornate blue gate has been swung wide to let us pass unencumbered, and about ten men flank it, their woven chain armor as silver as the walls they guard. My heart squeezes, and panic swells my veins.

"Can you see the palace?" Fern asks, the familiar weight of her hand on my shoulder.

Before I can answer, our cage jolts to a stop and we fly off the bench, crashing in a pile of limbs. The splintered floor underneath the straw stings my knees. As I look up at Fern, I catch the thick scar twisting down her shoulder blade—a reminder of the first time I talked back to the Gardener—and keep my discomfort silent. She catches me staring and playfully sticks her tongue out at me.

I meet her gesture with a smile, like always. The word "sorry" hangs unspoken around us in the air. We both know that no matter how many times I say it and no matter how many times she whispers that it isn't my fault, it won't change the fact that she suffers every time I make a wrong move. All the scars and bumps and cuts littering her body are because of me. Though I didn't wield the weapon or the fist, they always fall on her because of my imperfections.

And yet, she still tries to make me smile.

We remain motionless until sounds spill from the crack in our wooden cage: men shouting orders, wood banging against the ground as cart doors are thrown open, and the shrill sound of giggling. All the noises feel so familiar I can almost trick myself into forgetting that tonight we'll be performing at the first Spring Ceremony in ten years since the border to the neighboring kingdom was shut down. My gut twists thinking about what that day meant for me, and I push it from my mind.

Fern's fingers pick through my hair, yanking out pieces of straw, while I crawl back toward the peephole. Every bit she drops to the floor will be one less she'll have to pluck later when helping me dress.

"I lived here for nine years and I've never once seen the palace gates open," Fern says, longing coloring her voice. "I used to wonder what the inside looked like, how the cherry blossom trees were arranged, what their benches were made of."

"Then you should look," I say, scooting out of her way. Fern peeks outside. As she does, a loud *bang* sounds to our left and, despite my best effort, excitement grows in my chest. My shackles won't be on for much longer.

One of the Gardener's lackeys has begun releasing us. They always start with Clover's cart at the front of the line, since her throwing knives aren't going to sharpen themselves. The heavy door at the back of the cage is yanked up, and we're temporarily blinded by sunlight then ripped out onto the grass. Torn from our cage and planted into the Garden for a one-night show.

And tonight's spectacle is the one our ringleader has been scheming since the idea of the Garden developed in his head. The emperor of Delmar personally requested our show to entertain him and a hundred of his highest-ranking soldiers, celebrating in the name of the Delmarions' earth goddess, Lin.

With the particularly grueling winter and shortage of crops, rumors of how important this festival is to the people have even spread into the Garden. I overheard several lackeys talking around the campfire three nights ago about a town near the Blue Wall where bowls are even emptier than they are here after a bad performance.

That's the only reason I can think why the Gardener packed up our show before we'd even performed at the last city when a scroll with the imperial seal was dropped at his feet. And just like that, we're back at Fern's home, in the heart of Delmar, where rumors of glowing men and weapons that can freeze a man's movement run rampant. The Garden's lackeys whisper of magic, but I know too well that magic can't exist in the same world as our show.

"I can't believe I'm back here," Fern says. "I never thought

I'd get to see these streets again."

We don't talk about her family or the house she used to live in. She only ever told me once, right before we fell asleep a few years ago, that her father traded her to the Gardener for the price of a cow. That her head literally has a price on it. That she has nowhere to go back to.

"I didn't think we'd *ever* see the palace," I whisper.

Fern pulls away from the peephole, and we meet each other's gazes. My worry is reflected in her face. For as long as I can remember, our nightmare show has been flitting on the outskirts of the emperor's watchful eye, his heavy ban against any form of entertainment casting the shadow of an ax over all of our heads. The entirety of the land knew about our traveling band but turned a blind eye, because it was one of the only things that kept the soldiers happy.

But now the emperor is publicly acknowledging our existence, inviting us into his home and openly allowing us to perform behind his gates, which can only mean one thing: he's planning on legalizing the Garden. If that's really true, then we will never be able to leave.

And our master will get everything he has ever dreamed of.

I have to do something, *anything*, to make sure that doesn't happen.

Fern pulls her hair behind her back, revealing a jagged scar across her collarbone, the very first lesson of what my disobedience would cost us.

If I make a move, if I try to stop whatever it is this invitation means, Fern will pay for it in blood.

"When you were looking out earlier, did you notice the new lackey that gave Clover a blanket back in Lao Zun?" Fern asks. "I didn't see him out among the rest."

Our show picks up a few new lackeys at almost every stop we make, men not deemed fit for the emperor's army or the odd single man who spends all his spare coin underneath our silken tent flaps while we're in town. But the particular lackey Fern mentioned has made waves through the Garden with every spare piece of bread he sneaks for Juniper, every kind word he whispers when the others aren't looking, and every clean bandage that passes through his hands.

"No, I didn't," I say.

She leans up to look out the peephole again.

"We should have seen him by now," she mutters under her breath. "He said he would check in when we arrived."

"What're you talking about?" I ask, crawling up beside her.

I place a hand on her back as the muscles in her shoulders stiffen.

"What is *he* doing here?" she asks.

Before I can ask who she's talking about, something heavy slams into the side of our cart, the wood creaking with the weight of it. "Rose, there's something I need to tell you," Fern says, pushing off from the wall of our cart.

"One second," I say, taking her place to see what the commotion is.

"No, this can't wait." Panic colors her voice, and she wraps both hands around my arms, trying to pull me back to her.

I catch the back of Shears's head. He's the Gardener's right hand. He bangs a stick on the wheel spokes of our cart. The infamous set of gardening shears that gave him his nickname poke out of the back pocket of his ratty pants. The Gardener collects many things, but Shears is by far the worst of his collection. No one really knows where he came from, but that hasn't stopped the myriad of rumors spreading like weeds throughout the Garden about how many people he killed and how many body parts he separated before signing on to do the Gardener's dirty work.

I shoot back from our peephole, into Fern's waiting

arms, and try to breathe. No one ever wants to catch Shears's attention. The Gardener is cruel, but Shears is twisted. He cuts with a smile on his face and a twinkle in his eyes that activates only when his blade carves flesh.

"I didn't do anything," I say as the sound of another person banging against our cart echoes. "I swear I didn't."

"I know, I know." Fern presses me against her chest, rocking us back and forth.

A third set of *bangs*, then a fourth. The number keeps rising with every pound of my heart. They're surrounding us like a herd of swarming beasts.

Somewhere in the distance, the airy sound of a flute slithers through the air like a snake in the grass, one of the musicians probably practicing for our performance tonight in a nearby tent.

"I just *thought* about disobeying him," I say over and over again. "I wasn't going to do anything. I'd never let them hurt you again, I swear!"

"They must have discovered who Bái really was," Fern says, her hands shaking underneath mine.

She pulls away from me and leans down so we're eye to eye. Every ounce of ease has left her face, and her mouth draws into a serious line. I've never seen her look at me like this, and it scares me more than the banging outside ever could. Her brown eyes are saying the one thing I could never survive: good-bye.

"Now listen to me," Fern says, holding my face in both of her hands. "You know I'll always do my best to protect you, right?"

"And I'd do the same for you."

Her words send a sharp jolt of panic through me. Why would she bring this up now, with Shears right outside our cart?

She nods. "Just like we promised."

We were two little girls clinging to a splash of stars between wooden planks, whispering the only words that could ever truly mean anything to us: no matter how dark the night, we will always be there for each other.

"Whatever happens next, remember that we have to stop him."

"What are you talking about?" I demand, clutching her hands.

"Something's happening," she says. "Something between the Gardener and the emperor, and we can't let it—do you understand me?"

The latch to our cart releases with a loud *pop*. Soon light will flood inside and I won't be able to see her.

"I don't—"

"It has something to do with you, Rose," she says. "You and that glowing rock they found a few towns back."

She's speaking so fast that it's hard to stay focused, but I remember the chunk of jagged brown rock that glows green every time the Gardener presses his fat fingers to it. He brought it to his personal trailer where he keeps all of his favorite trinkets.

"I know you have your secrets; we all do," Fern continues. "But you can't let it happen. No matter what, you can't let that bastard get what he wants, or none of the Flowers and Wilteds will ever be free."

"I don't understand what's going on. I didn't *do* anything."

Her brow furrows, and the ghost of a smile plays on her face. "You're right, you didn't," she says. "Let him think you're scared. Don't let him think there's anything different about your behavior, and during tonight's performance get every step perfect. When the time is right, when the lights are low, escape and don't look back until you can free the others."

Her words flood my mind as I try to figure out how many broken bones and bruises my escape would cost her, but before I can ask what she means, light pours in from our open door.

Four dark silhouettes block the pristine white square as they jump into our cart, the floor shaking with their weight.

Fern squeezes my cheeks.

And then we are ripped from each other, the shackle spikes digging into my flesh as I'm thrown from the cart onto the grass inside the palace gates.

My head spins from the combination of bright light and the impact of hitting the ground. One of the lackeys yanks up the chain connecting my shackles and unlocks them. Warm air attacks my chapped wrists.

I turn on my side, pain shooting up my shoulder, and see Fern's ocean of black hair spilling out around her a few feet away. I reach for her, my fingertips brushing the ends of her hair, but another hand beats me to it, grabbing a fistful and holding her up off the grass.

Though pain must be shooting across her scalp, she doesn't scream.

I follow the arm to the shoulder and see Shears, his unnaturally wide grin revealing a row of shiny white teeth before he turns away from me.

And I realize we're lying like plucked flowers at our master's feet, in the perfect position to be stomped back into the earth that we came from.

# Chapter Two

My body immediately seizes as I stare up at the Gardener's bulbous stomach, my limbs turning to rock. All the fear and anxiety swirling inside me bubbles to the surface, leaving me defenseless.

Fern's whispered words bounce around in my head, but they slip through my fingers like sand when I try to grasp them.

I look around desperately for some kind of help, even though it's never come before. We've stopped somewhere deep inside the palace walls, in a secluded courtyard.

The forty lackeys in charge of setup have already erected the largest tower of the elaborate purple silken tent that we'll perform in tonight, blocking off all prying eyes from the north. Our carts have been positioned in a semicircle to the south, with the changing tents and housing for the rest of the troupe filling in the empty spaces. The Gardener's brutality isn't unknown, but it's like death, something people prefer to step around.

"Ah, my Fern," he croons in his deep voice. I'd recognize

that accent anywhere, listening to him draw out the *F* sound. The Gardener's strange pronunciation haunts my dreams. "You're looking lovely as ever, my leetle Wilted one."

The Gardener pauses in front of Fern, his girth jiggling underneath his tight red silk shirt for a second after he stops. He lined his tiny eyes with kohl and donned the pair of pointy-toed golden Varshan boots he'll perform in later.

He leers down at her, his sun-spotted skin stretching tight over his chubby face as his mouth splits into a smile, revealing a crooked row of yellowing teeth. Sweat plasters what's left of his dark hair to his face and leaves stains under his arms.

He's as cruel as he is round. Both features grow daily.

"But you see," the Gardener says, reaching behind his back to clasp his hands together, even though his arms are too short, "I've heard some distressing rumors." He rolls each *R* on his tongue like a cat's purr.

The four men that were banging on our cart with Shears tighten the circle around us, their heavy footfalls loud on the packed earth. My heart pounds in my chest. Everything in me begs to cry out, but Fern's shoulders tense and I realize she already knows they're surrounding us. I fight against my aching limbs to sit up, but the lackey nearest me plants a foot on my back, sending my face crashing into the prickly grass.

"One of my leetle buds has been talking to a spy," the Gardener says. "You don't happen to know anything about that, do you?"

The weight on my back disappears, and I lift my head, watching Fern. *A spy in the Garden? Why?* Questions flood my mind, and I nearly miss her answer.

"I have no idea what you're talking about," Fern says. Even though I can't see her face and her voice doesn't shake, I catch her pointer finger curling ever so slightly. She's lying.

The Gardener reaches up and threads his fingers around the links of his necklace as though he's checking to see if it's still there. It's a habit he's had since I was a Seedling, and I've come to understand it's what he does when he's thinking.

For his heft, he's surprisingly quick. His tiny hand shoots underneath Fern's chin, and he jerks her face upward at an unnatural angle so they're staring at each other.

"You know *nothing* of this?" he asks.

"Of course not," she replies, her voice dangerously low.

His lip curls into a frustrated snarl, and as much as I want to enjoy his annoyance, fear sends ice pumping through my veins. I haven't seen him this way since a rare Varshan sapphire went missing from his personal collection and he couldn't get anyone to confess they took it. Instead of trying to figure out who took it, the four lackeys and three Wilteds he randomly selected as culprits were slaughtered.

I'm safe, thanks to the secret the Gardener and I share that makes me his star. But Fern has nothing. The girl who got me through those first four years, who taught me to keep my head down in order to stay alive, has nothing to bargain with. She's just a prop for his plan, a means to his end. But I can't let him hurt her.

"I didn't do anything!" I shout, my voice sounding high-pitched even to my own ears. "Don't hurt her, *please*."

The spine-tingling way his gaze crawls over me feels like skittering cockroaches, but I muster up the courage to look into his eyes. Everything around us has frozen with my words. Except the flute plays on.

"No?" the Gardener asks, his voice as sweet as the moment after you've eaten too much cake. "But are you certain *she* is innocent, leetle Flower?"

His question swirls around me. A few minutes ago, I would have been certain, but now... How could Fern have been up to so much without me knowing? And how could she have put her trust in a man? A pang of guilt creeps through me.

He snaps his fat fingers, and a tall lackey walks out of the tent behind us, holding a burlap sack out in front of him. Something dark drips from both corners and has stained the fabric a few inches up from the seam. He stops a few feet away from the Gardener, who gestures for him to remove whatever he's holding. The lackey sticks his crooked nose up in disgust while reaching into the bag.

He yanks out the severed head of a man by his short black hair. That's the man Fern was looking for! The lackey throws the head at Fern, the place where his neck was cut making a sickening *squish* as it hits the ground next to her knee.

"Unfortunately for you, Wilted one, this one was more willing to talk after Shears had him for a few days," the Gardener says.

Shears lets out a chuckle, admiring his handiwork. "He was a screamer," Shears says, tightening his grip around Fern's hair. "But he did tell me all his secrets."

My stomach shifts as the dead man's lifeless black eyes stare at me from the ground, and if there were anything in it, it would have spilled onto the grass right then.

"So you see," the Gardener says, studying his fingernails, "we already know you've been talking with the rebellion."

Whispers of a rebellion fighting against the current emperor have leaked into the Garden, but why would they have a spy tucked among us? The more the Gardener speaks, the less this entire situation makes sense.

But then I remember Fern's words right before we were ripped out of our cage. She told me not to do anything, to act scared and then run because she knew they were coming for her. She'd probably known from the moment she spoke to that headless man that she would die for anything she said, and she did it anyway, to keep that tiny seed of hope alive, even if I no longer could.

"Do you know what I do to traitors?" the Gardener asks,

leaning down to Fern's level.

"No!" I shout, grabbing a fistful of grass to try to crawl closer.

The man's dead eyes mock me.

A silver chain around the Gardener's neck slips out as he leans forward, the large ruby attached to it gleaming in the sunlight. The same ruby I used to wear. The only thing left of my home.

The Gardener's lips press to her ear, washing her in a wave of his putrid breath, and he says over the rising sound of the flute in the distance, "I cleep them."

Pruning means losing an ear or finger, something easily concealed. But clipping… Clipping means the whole head is severed.

I won't let that happen to her. I swore I would protect her.

The metal handle of Shears's cutting blades protrudes from his back pocket. With all the strength I have left, I push up from the ground and run for them, with the practiced grace from a thousand nights of performing helping me move steadily. I slip past the nearest lackey and grab for the handle.

It's rough against my skin and far too big for my hands.

Shears's eyes widen in surprise, and he releases his grasp on Fern's hair to hold up his hands in some kind of defense as I snatch the weapon from his pocket.

"Should we go see the emperor?" the Gardener shouts, his voice tightening around me like ropes, stopping me. "What would he do, I wonder, if he knew your secret? Do you think he'd let you come back and see this leetle family you've created here?"

"No," I whisper.

My heart nearly stops. No one besides the Gardener can know my secret. Even being stuck here in the Garden would be less dangerous than if another soul found out.

Taking advantage of my momentary panic, the lackey I

dodged before slips his arms around me, and Shears rips his weapon from my fingers.

"Silly little Flower," Shears says, scraping a fingernail across my cheek. "If you're going to kill someone, you have to mean it."

My gaze falls to Fern, her brow furrowed somewhere between shock and fear.

"We'll see soon enough what the emperor decides for you," the Gardener says to me. He flicks his hand toward Shears. "Do it."

Shears kicks Fern, and she topples over like a rag doll. She lands hard on her back with a scream, all four limbs spread out, as the three men surround her. Shears is front and center, his tanned face pulled tight in a twisted smile.

"No, stop!" I yell, twisting against the lackey's grip, but his arms are like iron, the muscles in them barely straining to contain me. I could have saved her. The moment was right there and I let the Gardener's words control me.

The Gardener yanks out a silk handkerchief and meticulously wipes each of his fingers clean of Fern's skin. My eyes fall to Fern, her face twisted in fear. I still remember her weaving me a bracelet out of straw as she told me how her family sold her to the Garden, how safe I felt when she slipped the bracelet on my wrist and told me that we had to be each other's family now.

Shears takes a step toward her; the hedge shears gleam in the waning sunlight. I kick out, trying to free myself, but the man holding me just laughs, his chest rumbling against my back. Fern crawls toward me, a broken thing treading water until her limbs give out. "Run!" I scream to her. "Run!"

But there is nowhere to go. Nothing I do can stop this, but still I try. The only act of defiance I have left.

Before I came here, fear was a four-letter word that had nothing to do with me. My mind struggles to get back to that place where warm hands greeted me every morning and music meant dancing only when you wanted to.

Now Fern's screams mingle with the coiling melody of the flute, challenging each other for dominance in a dance that keeps twisting over a private stage where no one can help us. The awful symphony assaults me, pouring into my skin and soaking into my bones until we are all rolled into one—the flute, Fern's death, and me. Her screams weaken into whimpering, and finally, silence...leaving me alone in a darkness I'm not equipped to face without her.

They leave the door to our cage open after they throw me back in, and I curl into myself, trying to block out the sound of her death.

*How could I let my fear stop me from saving her? Even after we promised each other.*

The shame stays with me, like a thousand needles pricking all over my skin.

Several people return later, along with the shuffling sound of them dragging her lifeless body through the grass and their guesses as to what made the Gardener take action.

And they will be coming for me again soon.

Fern's final words shift around in the darkness, her plea not to let this moment slip away lighting up the roof of our cage. Now is the only time I will ever get to escape. There's no one left to pay for my crime. I couldn't save her, but I *will* save the others.

Other thoughts buzz around me, too—who was that man Fern spoke to, and was he really on our side—but I push them aside. That doesn't matter now. They're both dead.

My fear hardens into something not even I could anticipate. I rest my head on the same straw Fern and I were lying in only a few hours ago and push the hair off my face. Fern's whispered plan slides through the heartbreak of her screams and the painful realization that I let her die echoing in my head, and the thread of an idea forms. I can't just sit still and wait to see who's next. I have to get free and rescue the others. The Gardener might have meant for Fern's death to keep me rooted, but she has shown me that now, more than ever, I need to fly. I wasn't strong enough to save her, but I won't waste this precious gift she gave me, that she paid for with her life.

I don't know how, but I have to escape tonight. Like she told me to.

It's night by the time they usher me out of my cage, snot stained and drained. There shouldn't be any lights near our carts, but it seems the Gardener has left me a gift. A burning torch attached to the side of our cart casts enough light to reveal Fern's blood watering the grass a deep red.

# Chapter Three

I tremble against the night air, the breeze winding around my long hair and slithering up my limbs. But my will won't be shaken by terror. The Gardener's words that froze my limbs long enough for Fern to be killed stick to my neck like sweat.

But I won't be swayed by his threats again. Not tonight, not ever. One way or another, I'm leaving, and I'm taking every single girl here with me.

After a stop in the wardrobe tent, I enter the small emerald tent tucked into the corner of the courtyard, freshly scrubbed, bandaged, primped, and clothed in a plunging top and long skirt dripping with sparkling crystals. The deep ruby fabric pops against the warm tones of my Varshan skin, the color echoing the hills of desert sand that surround my home. I'm the only one permitted to wear this color, the Gardener's sign of "his deepest respect for my heritage," as I'm reminded every night in his introduction before I take the stage.

While I walk, the ties holding up the layers of fabric bounce against my legs and bared stomach, begging to be tugged so the heavy clothing can fall away in pieces. I pick through the crowd—Flowers, Wilteds, and lackeys, all rushing around to prepare last-minute details before the show begins—searching for the twins, Calla and Lily. This tent barely holds us all, and stuffed in any empty places are wooden benches and long mirrors lining the side.

The longer it takes me to find them, the more I feel my earlier resolve faltering. Every ounce of my being longs for comfort, for conversation, for a second when my mind doesn't replay my mistake over and over again. Fern would know exactly how to ease the pain somersaulting through my stomach.

My hair tickles my elbows as I search for them, falling in straw-colored ringlets down my back. The Wilteds, unlucky girls who pay for our misdeeds with their beaten flesh, left my hair down like always. The costumes and sets change, the silken drapes are switched out, and even the dance routines are scrapped for new ones, but my hair has always remained loose to accentuate my Varshan heritage.

The distinction used to bother me when I was younger, especially in the first few years when the Delmarions would look at anyone with light hair as someone who betrayed their kingdom.

And I guess in some ways, it's true. When news of the traitor taking over the Varshan throne reached me, my caretaker and I fled west with hordes of other sympathizers for the old regime before the Delmarion gates were barred shut. We escaped persecution, but I wound up in a place much worse than where we were running from. Now I've grown numb to the looks thrown my way, and the whispers that used to grate against my back fall on deaf ears. Though Varsha and Delmar have been at war for hundreds of years, an uneasy stalemate has settled between the neighboring kingdoms. That and the treacherous desert stretching between them has reduced the war to nothing more than words.

Not that any of it matters to my sisters here. Even though I am the only Varshan Flower, the others have never treated me differently. I slip past another set of Wilteds, their heads pressed together as they desperately stitch up a small tear in Violet's skirt. If they don't finish by the time she is called, Violet's punishment for wearing a tattered costume will come back onto them. All of our mishaps become bruises on the Wilteds.

Calla and Lily, clad in petal blue and purple, whisper to themselves in the middle of the room as their Wilteds, Star and Sickle, adjust the intricate silks twisting up their arms. The twins catch sight of me and wave me over in unison.

Every Flower turns to look at me with bleeding eyes as I pass. They all know the pain of hurting their Wilted, the girl who stays with them in the dark. But only Tulip, who plays with her straw doll in the back of the tent and never speaks, has felt the ache of losing her Wilted. Before today.

"You aren't hurt!" the twins say, worry mirrored in both sets of their dark brown eyes.

Though I've known them for seven years, their strange way of speaking, especially in unison, never grows any less odd.

Calla grabs my right hand and Lily takes my left. Though my hands aren't large, they feel huge clasped between their tiny ones.

"No, I'm not hurt," I say, my voice surprisingly soft.

The concern radiating from the twins' tight grip almost makes me smile. I know that every girl in here cares for me, even if prying eyes keep them all from showing it, but to have Calla and Lily show me this small kindness is enough.

I nod a hello to their Wilteds, unwilling to risk acknowledging them aloud. I won't be the cause of more pain tonight. At this point, Fern should be fluffing out my chiffon skirt and sticking out her tongue when my worried eyes meet hers. The empty space where she should be knocks the wind from my lungs, and tears form.

"There were rumors," Lily says, letting go of my hand.

"Vicious rumors," Calla adds, following her sister's lead.

"But you're here now," they both finish.

They each tuck a strand of black hair behind their ears simultaneously.

"*Only* me," I say.

We stare at one another for a moment as the implication of my words passes through them. Even Star and Sickle's fingers pause on the bustle of Calla's skirt. I don't need to hear them speak to know they're wondering what I did to cause such a drastic punishment. I can see the twins calculating each mistake they'd made that hurt Star and Sickle and exactly what it costs them.

Even though I know it wasn't my fault, shame heats my cheeks.

A nine-year-old girl crashes into my side, nearly sending me flying into Calla and Lily. She blurts out a hasty apology and darts behind my voluminous skirt. One of the Seedlings, trained to replace us. Their presence is a constant reminder that any one of us can disappear in an instant. The Gardener always keeps at least six spares ready in case of an accident, or when one of us grows too old.

I twist around to ask her why she's hiding, and a hush falls over the tent. The little girl presses her lips together, her brow furrowing as she focuses on something behind me.

"As you can see, we take painstaking measures to make sure the Flowers are in top shape for each performance," comes the voice from my nightmares.

Turning back around, I see the crowd in front of me parting like a river around a boulder. Nothing good can come of the Gardener visiting our tent. The more cynical part of me wonders what else he could possibly do, since he already did the unthinkable just a few hours ago. Fern's scream still echoes in my head, and I grit my teeth against the pain of loss that makes it hard to breathe. I was supposed to have her back.

The few girls in front of me move to the side to reveal our master dressed in his black silk stage costume as he approaches me. The only pops of color on him besides his yellowed teeth and golden shoes are the plethora of thick golden chains around his neck, the countless golden and jeweled bands around his arms, and the army of rings jammed on every finger. Since our last meeting, the thick kohl around his eyes has been reapplied and his hair has been combed over in a feeble attempt to cover the bald patches.

Standing a good foot taller than him is a trim man I've never seen before, in a simple blue ceremonial robe crafted out of very fine silk. White thread in a swirling pattern of jagged suns lines his long sleeves and the opening of the wrap around his chest. His impeccably trimmed goatee is in the short fashion of most Delmarion men and his sharp gray eyes scan the room, striking the perfect balance of annoyance and disgust. Though his lips are downturned, he possesses the strong jawline of a man whose age is impossible to wager.

He strides several inches away from the Gardener at an even pace, with his hands placed rigidly behind his back. The silver hilt of a sword, in the shape of a dragon's head, peeks out from his side.

At least fifteen Sun soldiers cram inside the tiny tent behind them, pushing girls and lackeys outside. Their chinked silver armor glitters like fish scales in the warm glow of the yellow lanterns.

"And this is the one I've been tellin' you about, Your Imperial Majesty," the Gardener says, bowing his head and extending a hand toward me.

The Gardener's words send a shock wave through me.

Everything Fern feared is true. If the Delmarion emperor really stands here inside our shabby holding tent, the Gardener must be negotiating some sort of treaty with him to sanction his horror show. If the Garden is legalized, how many more girls will he be allowed to steal? How many others will become my sisters through their blood and tears? The air flies out from my body as the realization comes crashing down on me.

Behind me, the Seedling gives out a tiny squeak then darts outside the tent.

The emperor takes his time turning his eyes to me, and the moment he does, I feel the weight of his assessment. He presses his lips together at whatever he sees before I bow my head.

All the air seems to have left the tent as the emperor marches in my direction. There isn't a single sound to distract me from what's happening. His presence overwhelms me, pinning my feet to the ground in a way the Gardener never has. When the Gardener commands we look down, I fight the urge to raise my head, but the emperor's devastating air of oppression leaves no choice.

The intricately lined edge of his robe comes into view, and panic quickens my pulse. What do common Delmarions even do in their ruler's presence?

A Varshan curtsy comes to mind, but considering this is the man who barred the passage between here and my home, I doubt he'd find any honor in it.

The emperor's hand hooks underneath my chin quicker than a snake's strike and wrenches my face up. His gaze cuts into me, sharper than the blade at his side, but beyond the ferocity in his eyes is a question I can't interrupt. Or rather, one I don't want to. His intensity nearly brings me to my knees.

He lets go of my chin. "This is your star?" he asks, his voice low. "Spin."

I clench my jaw at his clipped order but remember Fern's warning to act scared and obey without question. Even though she isn't with me any longer, she still had the foresight to help me.

Not that fear isn't coming easily. It takes every ounce of my will to control my limbs so they don't shake under the harshness of the emperor's gaze.

I spin very slowly, fighting the sickness that washes over me at knowing I'm being appraised like cattle.

"How utterly disappointing," he says when I come full circle.

He continues to stare directly into my eyes as he speaks to the Gardener.

"She better be worth what you say, peddler." The emperor turns away from me. "Otherwise, every single participant in this criminal band will pay with their heads."

For the first time ever, a flash of fear colors the Gardener's face red, and he levels me with a glare that threatens to split me in two. If Fern were alive, it would have been enough to scare me, for her sake.

"You've nothing to fear, Your Imperial Majesty," the Gardener says, waddling after the emperor to catch up with him. "Everything will be perfect tonight, and your people will be talking about this Spring Ceremony for years to come. Now let us continue on to my quarters so you can see with your own eyes the other part of our beautiful arrangement. It won't disappoint."

"It better not," the emperor says.

The soldiers clear out behind their leader, leaving the tent nearly empty. My legs give out and I drop in a pile of silk and chiffon, trying to catch my breath. The buzz of people whispering, the ripping of combs running through hair, and the lackeys shouting orders with extra vigor filter through my daze.

I'm not sure how long I sit there, trying to erase the feeling of the emperor's gaze from my skin. None of my sisters bother me as I fight my fear.

Finally, two pairs of hands rouse me from my panic, and I look up into identical faces fixed in concern. Calla and Lily lean down next to me, resting their heads against mine.

Fern's death and the emperor's warning about my sisters paying with their lives for the Gardener's ambition pulse through me, and I want more than anything to tell the twins I will free everyone tonight. But this knowledge would kill them if anyone overheard us, and if something happens to me, I won't let them pay for my mistakes.

"Listen," I whisper, looking each of them in the eyes. "No matter what happens, you know I'll always come back to all of you, right?"

They glance at each other, talking without ever moving their lips, and shift to the right. Everything about tonight has made us uneasy, and I know my question isn't helping.

"Of course," they say in unison.

One of the younger lackeys signals with his four-fingered left hand for the twins to head to the front of the tent.

"Sprout well," I say.

Both of their mouths split into stage smiles, but their dark eyes simmer as they follow the lackey into the music-soaked night.

I sit on the nearest bench, not even feeling the splintered wood catch against my skirt, and barely notice as each Flower is called away to the stage like plucked petals in a game of "he loves me, he loves me not." The questions running through my mind blur together in a confusing jumble, each one screaming for attention: What's the emperor getting out of a treaty with the Gardener, and why did Fern think it was so important to stop that she'd risk dying for it? Louder than everything else is the single thought that allows me to stand up when the four lackeys charged with escorting me to the main tent signal me forward.

The thought aids me as we walk toward the Garden. It follows me as we step over a beautiful blue carpet that lines the opening of the palace directly up to the mouth of the Garden, sparkling like a river. It dances between the glowing lanterns shaped like bubbles that hang suspended at different heights on either side of the carpet on invisible wire and infuses the cherry blossom petals painstakingly arranged around the tent to depict images of the Delmarion goddess Lin with an otherworldly beauty. Even the luxurious top of the plum tent that peeks out over the grand castle wall locking it inside doesn't scare me.

Nestled among the burning white stars littering the night sky is my truth. The thing that keeps me moving: tonight is the last night I will see any of it. Whether I live and escape or die fighting for my freedom, I will never make this walk again.

# Chapter Four

Though the entrance beckons us forward, my four escorts make a hard right, skirting along the side of the tent fabric. The lilting sound of a violin floats out into the star-soaked night. Accompanying it like a dancer to the melody is the soft sound of chatter and bell-like clinking of glasses from the audience.

I keep pace with the front two lackeys, my head bowed in perfect submission. The other two box me in from behind, whispering back and forth as we make our way to a wooden ladder around the back.

"I heard the glowing men have been spotted in town tonight," Gen, an older lackey who's been with the Garden since before I arrived, whispers to the other one.

"My sister says they're ghosts," Fa says. "Seen them with her own eyes."

"Nah, they're just men with torches out to scare the simpletons."

"They're spirits," one of the lackeys in front of us adds. "The gods sent them down to walk the earth, displeased with the lot of us."

I curb the urge to tell them that magic doesn't exist. I'm not even sure their gods do. And if by some small chance they are actually real, they're cowards for letting us Flowers suffer at the hands of their worshippers. We reach the rickety ladder in the back, and I grab the nearest rung, feeling the wood shake as it accepts my weight.

Leaving any prying eyes on the ground, I duck into the slit in the tent near the top. The moment I break the barrier, the intoxicating mixture of roasted fish, steamed rice, and freshly baked red bean buns rises up to greet my nose.

Tiptoeing onto the platform barely wide enough to fit me in my costume, I make my way across to the center of the tent, high atop the Garden. Directly across from me, a lackey walks on a matching thin beam with a torch in his hand, fueling the limelights that create green spotlights on the stage below.

My gaze follows one of the lights down. Even now, after hundreds of performances, the beauty of the tent steals my breath.

Thousands of candlelit glass bubbles hang suspended from blue silk swathing the ceiling, casting the room below in a golden glow. Thirty musicians adorned in traditional emerald robes spin the sultry tones of Varshan music into the air like silken webs, a few well versed in the lyre and lotar from my home. Long tables circle the room, the guests sitting shoulder to shoulder on elaborate silver and blue silk pillows. Several of the Wilteds hand plucked by the Gardener for their beauty sashay around in revealing chiffon costumes with gold pitchers, filling up drinks and flirting as they go. Every form of pleasure is on full display tonight. It's hard to believe such beauty could have come from the imagination of the Gardener.

The only inclination that this night is any different than the countless others before it are the jade and gold statues depicting the goddess Lin that dot every entrance, to honor her during this first night of the Spring Ceremony. After so many years on the wrong side of the gate, I know only from snippets and whispers that this is the first of six nights of festivals. In the middle of the tent, Calla and Lily twist around the dance floor in a dizzying blur of blue and purple silks, the swathes of their dresses that they leave behind resembling plucked petals on grass. Though none of the patrons are permitted to touch us without the Gardener's permission, they have paid for the chance to look at the way our curves form and gawk at the exposed pieces of us. I turn my attention to the swathe of white silk attached to a beam in the ceiling, as more of the twins' bodies become visible, and expertly wind the fabric around my leg.

With everything in place, I push off the platform. The fabric's long tail stays secure in my fingers. After the twins are finished, I'll let it drop, a stark white ribbon in a room swallowed in black, and untwist it, the fabric unwrapping as I hurtle toward the ground. But for now, I'm suspended in midair more than three stories up. Falling right now would mean certain death.

But already, the vise that has clenched my gut since Fern's death loosens and my shoulders relax. For this moment, I'm free, and it's a feeling I plan to keep. Someone in the audience has no idea they're about to become part of the show. Part of my plan for escape.

Using my torso to get the fabric spinning, I focus on the crowd. The majority of the men sit upright, taut as an arrow against a bowstring, their eyes alert even through the haze of rice wine and women surrounding them. Unlike our usual patrons, who would be sloppy with drink and half crazed by now, this crowd remains politely subdued. Though they are all uniformed in the traditional robes this evening calls for, most wear on their right arms a blue band that signifies high rank in the emperor's army.

Their wives sitting beside them alternate between clasping their goblets a little too tightly and burying their faces in their napkins, careful not to dishevel their dark hair piled high and shaped like butterflies and spitting fountains. Their long silk robes display every shade of spring, and large flower hair combs glitter with jewels.

Every face hides behind an ornate mask, each one honoring the flora or fauna of spring, as is tradition. I can't imagine how much dust each one had after spending so long in disuse. Even though all faces are covered, it's still easy to spot Delmar's emperor, Galon, in the same simple outfit from before. Remembering his presence earlier causes the fabric in my hands to slip just slightly as I relive the way he passed judgment on me like a piece of meat.

Even he joins in on the festivities, which he's rumored to loathe, adorned in a large round mask molded into the shape of an ant head. The sharp mandibles jut out on top of the onyx headdress like twin swords. Though most of the other masks look like they've been passed down from generation to generation, his shines with a freshness that could only come from something newly crafted.

A mountain of on-duty Sun soldiers guard his back and sides, standing alert, with gleaming swords fastened to their belts. My newly formed plan requires audience participation, but I'm hard-pressed to find a suitable subject among the high-ranking warriors. Any one of them could outmaneuver me in a fight, thwarting my only chance at escape. My heart begins to pound, and desperation bleeds into my determination.

A flicker of green light catches my eye, and I look farther down the long table, searching for the source in the darkness below. But instead, I catch a figure seated near the end, his gray silk robe and carved wolf mask lacking the finer details of those around him. The blade of a knife tucked in his belt reflects light back at me. It looks nothing like the glowing green that caught my eye. A trick of the light. If I can grab the blade and throw him to the soldiers before they chase after me, I might have a chance to escape and then circle back for the others. The moment the Gardener realizes I've slipped away, he'll empty out his ranks to search for me, his star, leaving the others unguarded long enough to sneak them out. It isn't a solid plan, but it's better than waiting for the Gardener to pick a Seedling as my new Wilted to take out my fabricated misdeeds on.

The music stops before I can think any further. With a deep breath, I shift into position for my opening roll, body rigid and parallel to the ground. The shrill, snaking melody of the flute drifts up to me. It grates against my skin as my vision flashes red with Fern's blood. I can almost hear her screams mingling with the instrument as the lights dim on the world below. I fight to stay in the present and block out the music as three bright green limelights draw the crowd's attention to high above them. The tail of the silk slips from my fingers and flutters down like a waterfall for the ground.

Then, I let go.

# Chapter Five

For the audience, it looks like the ground comes toward me too fast, but I know better. Though the fall only takes seconds, when you know what you're doing, those seconds multiply like raindrops. All you have to do is trust the silk to catch you. Which is why I get to twelve inches above the ground before the fabric snaps into place.

The audience's gasps switch to oohs and aahs of delight as I twist up the silk, lacing my arms through the fabric to climb higher. Even our host sits up straighter. I start spinning with a twist, letting my body slide sensually through the air. The wind catches my hair, caresses my face in a cool kiss even as their gazes sting my body, every strip of my bare skin raw and exposed.

I go through the motions, my hands and feet recycling what they've done for years. The art of aerial dancing originates from my homeland, but few Delmarions have ever seen it live since the emperor closed the border ten years ago.

My body remains on display, but my mind strays to the blood near my cart, the only thing left of Fern. I wonder what her life might have been like if she hadn't been sold to the Gardener. What all of our lives might have been like. I know one thing for certain: Fern shouldn't be reduced to a mere stain on the grass because of one man's whim.

The thought burns itself into my movements as I finish the aerial portion of my performance and prepare for my grand exit. My heart pounds harder than my feet hitting the ground.

The music begins to swell, the drums growing louder and faster. Smoke floats into the middle of the ring, and I search the room for my captors. Three of the Gardener's lackeys guard the door and eight are positioned around the tent behind the partygoers. Once I make my move, I won't need to worry about them. The lights dim as the smoke hides me from the audience.

Time to move.

With a flick of the wrist, I unfasten the sash holding up my long, heavy skirt to reveal a shorter skirt underneath. With nothing to encumber my movement now, I rush for the audience.

My feet pound in time with the rhythm of the drum as I race in the direction of the man in the wolf mask. As I burst through the cloud of smoke, one of the lackeys shouts over the music. He's too late. They all are.

I find the man in gray and lunge for him, jumping up onto the table. A silver goblet tumbles over, spilling rice wine onto the white tablecloth, as I dodge his plate and jump over him. Twisting my body midair, I flip myself around the man and snatch a sapphire encrusted knife from his belt, then hold the blade up to the tender part of his neck. The woman next to us clutches her chest like she might faint. It's almost comical, considering five seconds ago she was watching me just as eagerly as the rest of the audience.

"Get up," I say into the man's ear, still trying to catch my breath.

The muscles in his hand tense as he tightens his grip on a pair of silver chopsticks.

"You really should pick someone else," the man says.

His wolf mask muffles him, but I swear there's a smile in his voice. My eyes flit toward the emperor, and the soldiers must realize this isn't part of the show. I have precious few seconds rolling away like the sweat trickling down my brow.

"Up! Now!" I command, pressing the blade a little harder.

"I'm telling you," my hostage says. "You really should — "

"Now!" I shout. One of the soldiers raises his crossbow. I tug the edge of Wolf Mask's robe, the fabric coarse against my fingers, and angle him so he blocks me from getting shot with an arrow.

"As you wish," he says with a sigh. "But don't say I didn't warn you."

He puts his hands out in front of him and rises painfully slowly, tucking in his chin like he's trying to rest it on the knife. I have to stand on my tiptoes to keep the blade steady when he reaches his full height.

"Now back," I say, grabbing a fistful of his robe.

He should stumble as I yank him, but his movements are smooth, like this is a practiced routine. If I can just keep a hold of him until we reach the tent flap, then I can push him into the converging swarm of men and find a place to hide until I can come back for the others. Hopefully the lackeys will already be nice and drunk so they won't put up a fight. We'll make it out of here. We have to. I'll have a head start on the Gardener. It'll have to be good enough. The Delmarion soldiers shouldn't care about a single dancer escaping, so I doubt they'll track me.

"Let's go," I scream, my voice echoing through the tent. I hadn't noticed the musicians drop their instruments.

All I can think about is Fern's death, and it rips through

me worse than a hot iron to the back of my legs.

"Don't worry," my hostage says. "In a moment, those soldiers aren't going to be worrying about you anymore."

I take a step backward, jerking him along with me, but instead of moving, he rips off his mask. The audible gasp from the audience confirms what he just said, and I nearly lose my grip as I crane my neck to see his face.

"It's the traitor!" one of the Delmarion soldiers shouts, pointing at us.

"Get the Zareeni vermin!" shouts another.

My fingers go slack on his robe.

"I did warn you to choose someone else," my hostage says, turning.

No... It *can't* be him.

Even from behind the bars of my cage, I've heard whispers of the rebellion fighting against Delmar's emperor. Sometimes when the Gardener's lackeys get really drunk, they scheme about hunting down some of the rebels for the ridiculous bounties on their head. And no one is worth more than their leader and ex-heir to the throne, Rayce Sun. I've seen his poster so much that I've come to memorize the thick scar that cuts down the left side of his face. But those pictures didn't do justice to the commanding presence of the man standing before me. Even in the glow of lanterns, his hair is as dark as the inside of my cage in the middle of the night and hangs loose over hooded, mud-brown eyes.

"Now would be a good time to light it up!" Rayce shouts to some unseen person.

Before his mouth closes again, four rockets explode into the air, ripping through the top of the tent then bursting into a million little sparks that catch the fabric. I've never seen fireworks up close, but it sounds like thunder trapped in a bottle. Screams erupt as people dive to avoid the sprinkles of flame raining down on the audience, but I'm transfixed by the fire consuming the tent fabric and wooden poles like it is the literal translation of the rage burning inside me. This is exactly what I needed to break away, and I wonder if Fern had known about the rebellion coming here tonight. Now I just need to sneak out and get lost in the crowd of panicked people.

"Time to run," Rayce says, easily twisting the knife out of my grasp. He tosses the blade into his other hand and grabs my palm, entwining our fingers tightly.

"I'm not going with *you*," I shout over the panic.

I face the leader of the Zareeni rebellion squarely. A wicked grin plays on his chiseled face, promising a thousand more reckless moments.

"You put a knife to my throat," he says. "There's no way I can let you off now, not with so much at stake. Follow me."

"Let me go," I snap. "This is my chance! You'll ruin everything."

I wrench my hand back, but our palms stay connected. Though his grip remains tight, he isn't hurting me.

"Sorry, but I did warn you," he repeats. "You should have picked someone else. Now we're in this together."

I start to protest again, but he ignores me, pulling us through the burning tent flap with a trail of soldiers shouting our exit.

# Chapter Six

Outside the tent, the tidy world of upper-class Delmar has descended into chaos. Men drag women in trailing robes out of the burning tent like it's a sinking ship, trampling the beautifully lain flowers and sparkling blue rug under their heeled feet. Fireworks explode in an array of vivid colors, lighting up the nighttime sky, while leather-clad Sun soldiers rush around, assisting guests out of the flame-engulfed Garden. So much for a cheerful welcoming of spring.

Everywhere I look there are blurs of people and shouts of panic, all submerged in a thick cloud of gray smoke. From somewhere among those screaming, the Gardener's voice rings out as the consequence of tonight's events get through his thick head: his tent is destroyed and his star is missing. Almost everything he worked for is gone. Now I just need to finish him off by freeing the rest of the girls.

My hostage-turned-captor pushes us through the crowd of panicked people, keeping his face down and his callused grip squeezing my palm. My cheeks heat at the strangely intimate contact, and I wish more than anything that he'd let me go. We pass the emerald holding tent where my sisters are waiting for me.

I can almost hear them calling out, can see their faces through the green fabric and smoke burning my eyes. This is my chance. I don't even need to wait. The Gardener and his lackeys will be more concerned with saving the main tent, not the lives of his replaceable dancers.

"I have to go," I yell over the chaos of the crowd.

I kick out my foot, connecting with the back of Rayce's knee, and he drops to the ground, letting go of my hand in his hurry to catch himself.

I don't check to make sure he isn't injured, instead plunging toward the tent, clawing through anyone who gets in my way. This is our only chance to escape. To start a new life. The memory of Fern's screams spurs me on, the comfort of her face hardening my resolve.

The crowd thins as I draw closer to the burning Garden. A giant firework explodes in the air, like a red spiderweb, and rains down more fire and smoke. I push past an older lady and can almost touch the tent flap.

A large hand wraps around my forearm and yanks me backward, just as my fingertips graze the coarse fabric. I stumble back, straining my arm toward my sisters, and crash into something rock hard. I look up to see Rayce's creased forehead and dark eyes, realizing I'm pressed up against his chest.

"What are you doing?" he yells over the people screaming. "We've got to get out of here. They'll find us."

"Let me *go*!" I jerk away from him, but it doesn't break his hold.

"Stop fighting me! You'll get caught again."

"It doesn't matter. I've got to save them."

"Who are you talking about?" he asks.

"The other dancers," I say. "The Gardener will take out

his fury on them if I don't help them escape."

He frowns, and surprise flickers in his eyes at my answer, but his hand tightens around my arm. Why won't he just let me go? This is my only chance! I throw all my weight away from him, but his arm over my shoulders doesn't budge. His eyes flash toward the tent, and I automatically follow his gaze. Inside stands the Gardener, sweat sticking his hair to his head as he screams at several lackeys running back and forth with pails of water. The Flowers aren't even there. If Rayce hadn't stopped me, I'd have run right back into the Gardener's waiting arms.

"Come on," Rayce says.

"No." I cough as smoke pours into my lungs. "I'm going to find the other Flowers."

He shakes his head and draws me closer. I struggle against his chest, twisting to break out of his grip, but before I can get free, he bends down and lifts me over his shoulder. His arms feel raw over the backs of my exposed legs. I scream and beat against his back, but he's already moving through the crowd.

I can't tell if it's from my burning eyes or from the overwhelming terror of knowing my only chance to rescue my sisters disappears behind the gate we pass through, but I'm crying. My heart is locked away with the girls back in the Garden, so how can it still be pounding in my chest?

Rayce takes a hard right and tucks us into a dark alley right outside the palace gates. It's just wide enough for us both to squeeze through. He lets me down gently, and I lean against the stone wall to hold myself up.

"Don't think about running back there," he warns, his eyes boring into mine. "You're staying with me until I know it's safe."

"And if I refuse?" I ask, my voice betraying the anger seething inside me.

"Then we'll have to do this the hard way again," he says.

I look away from him, back to the smoke cloud billowing in the sky. The pockmarks in the rocks dig into my bare legs, but I'm too numb to care. The lingering smell of several-days-old meat and sewage mix with the smoke still clinging to our clothes, making my lungs work hard to catch a breath.

He sighs. "I know you want to help the other performers, but you won't help anyone if you wander right back into the Garden's trap."

"How could you just leave them?" I ask, wrapping my arms around myself. "You're the leader of the rebellion. Aren't you supposed to help people?"

He frowns, rubbing the back of his neck.

"This is the meeting place," Rayce says, ignoring my question. "My men will be here any minute, and then we can get out of the city."

"Why not just let me go then?" I try again, looking down at my soot-covered feet. "It's not like I'm your responsibility."

I can't stay here. Not only will the others be expecting me to rescue them once word spreads that I escaped, but the most dangerous place I could be right now, even more so than the Garden, is standing next to the leader of the rebellion. If this man knew the secret the Gardener and I share about my past, it very well could spell the end of my freedom for eternity. Or my death.

"You're joking, right?" He cocks an eyebrow. "You just pressed a blade up against my throat and threatened my life in front of a room full of witnesses. How do I know you're not an assassin sent by the emperor?"

"I had to get out of there somehow," I snap. "Besides, if I were an assassin, I'm obviously not a very good one, since you managed to get the knife away from me and capture me, twice."

"Or you just want me to believe that," he says. "You have to understand, you picked me out of a crowd of a hundred people. How am I supposed to believe it was random? It'd make sense that my uncle would send someone to eliminate me, since the details of his precious treaty are being finalized tonight."

Fern mentioned something about a deal between the emperor and the Gardener, and how it had to do with me. "I have no idea what you're talking about," I say.

He shakes his head. "Yeah, realization wasn't just all over your face." He swings around to look out into the courtyard. "Besides, even if I let you dive headfirst into trouble, where do you even think you'd go?"

Now that the chaos of the tent burning has begun to die down, slipping back into the Garden unnoticed isn't an option. When I made my plan to escape, I'd imagined staying somewhere in the city, near the Garden, until an opportunity to infiltrate showed itself. And if by some miracle that worked, where would we have gone? We couldn't have made it to Varsha. Even if we managed to bribe one of the soldiers on the Blue Gate, the Gardener and I both know I'd never be safe there. Not with my past. It's the main reason our show has never crossed into Varshan land.

"A girl like you, dressed in an outfit like that," Rayce says, turning back to me. A blush sweeps my cheeks as his eyes pass over my bare stomach, tiny strip of a skirt, and low-cut top. "Well, if you didn't have anywhere to hide, you'd draw quite a bit of attention."

"I know where I'm going," I snap, unwilling to reveal just how poorly I've planned ahead.

"Yes, with me, back to Zareen." He unties the strip of fabric holding his robe together. "Until we assess whether or not you're a threat to our cause."

He shakes off all three layers of his clothes and lets them drop into a puddle of fabric, revealing a pair of black trousers underneath.

I look down at my bare feet. It's not like I've never seen a man's bare chest before. The lackeys are anything but modest, especially when they're setting up the Garden in the sweltering heat. I just haven't seen anything like Rayce's lean, muscled back as he fishes through the pile and pulls out a simple linen shirt.

"Now, take off your clothes," he commands.

"What?" I hug my bare stomach.

He straightens, a black robe hanging from his hands. "I mean no harm. As I said earlier, you stick out in your current attire."

He hands me a white robe, and I accept it without question.

"I'm Rayce, by the way," he says, clearly changing the subject.

"I know who you are. Your face is plastered on every surface in every town in Delmar. You're the leader of the rebellion."

"Almost as popular as you are, Miss Flower," he says with a mocking bow.

"My name is *Rose*."

I slide my arms through the large sleeves and wrap the opening around my body, realizing too late that this is his under robe. I spin around to face the courtyard so he doesn't see the blush creeping onto my face as I tie it closed. His warmth still clings to the fabric, seeping onto my skin.

"But you already knew my name, too," I say, "since you attended the show." I don't mean for the edge to come out in my voice.

I smooth down the robe, nearly drowning in it. This is the most covered I've been since before I was stolen to be in the Garden.

"I know your stage name," he says. "Going to give me a real one?"

I haven't been called by my real name since I was eight years old, and happy. I'm not about to pick that scab right now.

"No."

"Fair enough, Rose," he says, enunciating my pseudonym. "But your cooperation would go a long way in determining whether or not I can trust you enough to let you go."

I press my lips together to keep from snapping back at him. If he wants my cooperation, I can pretend long enough to slip away. My years in the Garden have made me very good at showing men the face they want to see.

I step out of the alleyway. Peering into the courtyard, I notice the crowd thinned out while we were changing, and a thick layer of smoke moved in to take its place. A figure breaks through the smoke, running straight for us, the shiny links of the Delmarion chest plate glinting in the firelight.

Panic seizes my chest, and I grip the top of my new robe shut.

"W-we have to run," I say.

Rayce turns toward the figure, following my line of vision. A slow smile finds its way onto his face.

"Relax," he says. "That's one of my men."

The man clambers up to us, his body covered in the brown leather uniform of a Sun soldier. He stops in front of Rayce and pops off his helmet, revealing wavy light brown hair plastered to his head and large brown eyes. He doesn't exactly look Varshan, but he's got the thick hair and round eyes that are common in my homeland. "Did you see all the fancy inside that tent?" he says, shimmying out of his armor "I can't believe your cheap jerk of an uncle spent so much on tonight's festivities."

"Nice to see you, too, Arlo," Rayce says.

Arlo gives him a sarcastic salute, and then his gaze travels to me. A toothy smile slides over his face like it was always meant to be there.

"You picked up another stray," Arlo says. "This one's pretty, especially the violet eyes."

He wears his goatee short, and it should make him look serious, but his chocolate eyes are lit with jest, and that relaxes me. He's about an inch shorter than Rayce and has the lean build and quick movements of someone who'd be good at aerial dance. If the Gardener showcased Trees instead of Flowers, Rayce and Arlo would be the first two in his collection.

"What's your assessment of her?" he asks.

"Inconclusive," Rayce answers, tossing Arlo a brown robe from the pile on the ground. "Terrible grip on my knife and hesitated on the uptake, but she also doesn't have a solid plan for escape, leaving her motives questionable."

"Excuse me?" I say, crossing my arms over my chest. "It's not like I had a lot of time to come up with a plan before I acted on it. And there hasn't been a lot of opportunity to practice with knives where I've been, either."

Arlo clicks his tongue, his smile widening. "Spirited, isn't she?"

"Arlo, this is Rose," Rayce says, ignoring his comment. "Rose, Arlo Shing."

These Delmarions and their love of short names. My father used to tell me you could judge the worth of a man by the length of his name.

"She's charmed, I'm sure," Arlo says, giving me a quick wink before throwing on the robe he was handed. He runs a hand over his short hair to smooth it down. "Since we're on formalities, I wasn't able to acquire much information on our target. Only that your uncle moved her before the ceremonies."

"Yun's beard," Rayce says, spitting out a curse at their god of death. While he's distracted, I turn back to the smoke, combing for a place to slip away.

Several glittering flashes like stars on the ground catch my attention. About ten soldiers head straight for us.

"Were you followed?" I ask Arlo, cutting into their conversation.

Arlo reads the panic in my voice and turns to see what's causing it.

"It would seem that way," he says, sliding into the alley. "We need to move."

The soldiers pick up their pace.

"Definitely." Rayce motions to the yawning mouth of the alleyway. "After you, Rose."

My feet stay rooted. If I go in now, I'll be sandwiched between Arlo and Rayce. Running from one cage straight into another.

"Please, just let me go," I say, nearly choking out the words. Begging, after just gaining my freedom, hurts more than I care to admit.

"I can't." He motions with his hand for me to go ahead of him.

"Guess I don't have a choice then," I say, my teeth clenched.

My insides rip into a thousand pieces as we part the shadows with our racing footsteps. Every inch leads me farther away from my sisters. What horrors lie at the end of the night for Calla and Lily and the others?

Over the sound of my silent shrieking, I hear Rayce whisper, "Neither do I."

# Chapter Seven

We plunge deeper into the darkness, picking our way through the maze of alleys. I can't see much of anything on either side of me, but the walls are getting closer to my shoulders. I keep my eyes focused on Arlo's back, trying to match his movement. Without the weight of the chains slowing me down, I feel like I could run forever.

But my chains are never far behind. I can hear the clinking of soldiers' armor bouncing off the tight quarters at our backs, and it pushes my feet faster. Arlo takes a hard left into another alley, and we keep running, taking turns with what seems like no reason until the chasing footsteps fade into the distance.

We finally break through the alleyway into a small marketplace. The worn cobblestone floor and paint-chipped buildings suggest this isn't a place the emperor visits often. Tents packed on top of each other line the west and east sides of the open marketplace. Night dulls the brightly colored fabric better than the rusty wrought-iron lamps can light them. The scents of sweat and animal excrement lingers in the air, even though the market has been closed since dusk.

A small group of soldiers edge toward the market from the east, probably trying to cut us off. With both passages blocked, we only have two options: south into a wall or west toward the Changhe River. Arlo opts for west and skirts away from a pool of light in our path. We run a few more feet and turn onto a dirt street.

Off to our right, a tiny stone building hunches over, its door swung wide open with an illegible sign sagging over the entrance. Judging by the laughter pouring out of the building, it's got to be some kind of brothel. Three men slump near the door, clutching half-empty mugs and arguing about something unintelligibly. Another leans against the wall, retching, and a few people with heavy, hooded cloaks tucked up over their heads walk farther up the street. I get the sense this isn't the type of place respectable citizens dwell.

Someone bundled in a pile of ratty fabric huddles near the entrance of the street. The person must be passed out, but Arlo stops in front of them and squats down. The figure pops up, the blankets falling away to reveal a completely sober man with long coal-black hair streaked with silver tied into a low ponytail at the base of his neck. His pale face doesn't show much sign of aging, except the crow's-feet that gather around his sharp eyes and his bushy eyebrows, but I can tell by the tender way his gaze passes over both my captors' faces that he has to be old enough to be my father.

"There you two are," the man says, clicking his tongue at them. "I was getting worried. Everyone else has checked in."

"Yeah, we got tied up," Rayce says.

"More like *you* got tied up," Arlo says to Rayce while extending his hand to help the man up.

The older man stands and brushes himself off. His broad shoulders take up half the narrow alley. His bulkiness feels intimidating, but there's something soft gleaming from his eyes. Almost like his oversize frame is only there to contain his kindness.

"Is this the girl the rest have been reporting tried to assassinate you?" the man asks, turning to me.

Panic shoots through my gut hearing this man accuse me of the same thing Rayce had earlier. Is that really the rumor going around? And so quickly? The weight of my predicament slams into me.

"I wasn't really going to harm him," I say, pulling my robe tighter. "What motive would I have?"

"I told you," Rayce says. "You chose me out of a crowd of a hundred. It's suspicious."

"What's your name, girl?" the older man asks, stroking his long black-and-silver beard.

His words should sound harsh, but the dead piece of leaf still stuck in his beard softens his entire appearance.

"Rose."

"After the rare Varshan desert rose, I assume," he mumbles, nodding to himself. "It'll do just fine."

"What will?" I ask, furrowing my brow at his odd assessment.

"Oren's got a thing for names," Arlo says. "Just ignore him."

"Imperial City has always held all kinds of folk," Oren says. "But lately it's been rare to come across a Varshan. It's very nice to make your acquaintance."

Something about the way he makes sure to mention I'm a foreigner sends a chill down my spine. There's no way he could know the secret of my exact heritage and yet, every time he looks at me, I feel like he's reading it on my face.

"We should get moving," Rayce says, cutting into the conversation. "It won't take long until this entire city is crawling with soldiers."

"It stands to reason they'll be headed down this particular street very soon," Oren says, rubbing a hand down his beard and finally catching the piece of leaf. "It's very near the river, and they'll most likely have set up a barricade they'll want to herd us toward."

"Which means we're going to need these." Arlo reaches into the pile of blankets Oren was wrapped in and pulls out several metal contraptions. They look a little like the base of a metal crossbow with the front chopped off and the inside hollowed out into a barrel.

Rayce takes two of the contraptions and Arlo hands Oren the third, holstering two for himself.

"And you're going to need to take this," Rayce says. He pulls out a leather cord suspending a glowing vial from under his shirt and hands it to me.

"Is this poison?" I ask, staring at the luminescent green powder. The sand-like grains sparkle in their own light.

"We aren't going to kill you. We can't question the dead," Rayce says. "And we have no reason to hurt you unless you give us one."

I frown at the vial. It's a good thing to know, I guess, that I'll be unharmed until they question me.

"Swallow it," Arlo says, tipping an imaginary vial into his mouth.

He and Oren begin walking ahead of us.

"It's going to boost your body heat," Rayce explains.

"Why should I trust you?" I ask, keeping my hands tucked firmly by my side.

In my experience, trusting a man's word ends in misery. It's the first lesson I ever learned on this side of the Blue Gate and one I swore I'd never forget.

"Neither of us has a choice, remember? We're in this together." Rayce folds the vial into my hands, the coolness bringing me back to the present. "If you want any chance at escaping the Sun soldiers, please drink it."

I glare at him and down the contents. It tastes a lot like

the paste they slop into our carts at the Garden. There's a distinct earthy note followed by a very sour finish.

I hand the empty vial back to Rayce. He motions us forward, so I start walking.

"What exactly is that thing Arlo gave you earlier?" I ask.

"Hopefully you won't have to find out," Rayce says.

We pass under the shadow of the brothel unimpeded, and I settle into our pace. We might just make it to the river safely. From there, I can split off from them and circle back around in the morning to spy on the Garden. The palace gate won't be terribly difficult to scale with all of those fancy buildings next to it that gradually grow in height, some of the nearest ones just peeking over the tops of the high wall.

Rayce leans in close to me, like he's sniffing my hair. I open my mouth to tell him to go away, but he whispers, "They're behind us."

As he finishes speaking, the clinking of metal-plated footsteps reaches my ears. He must have been pretending to get close so he could check behind us. As if Rayce can sense that I want to turn, he grabs my wrist.

"Don't turn around. Keep pace with me."

I consider making a break for it right now. If I run, I doubt they'll follow. It'd draw too much attention. But he was right before when he said I'd rather be with them than detained by Delmarion Sun soldiers. It'll be much easier to slip away from three than twenty. Besides, if I'm captured, I'll likely wind up back in the emperor's presence again. The skin on my arms prickles as I think about his overbearing gaze.

I tuck myself closer to Rayce and try to remember how the Wilteds act around the male clientele. We're near a brothel, so it wouldn't be out of place for us to be walking together.

"How am I supposed to protect myself if they discover us?" I ask. "Can't you give me that knife at least?"

"You won't need to protect yourself if we aren't spotted,"

Rayce says.

My face feels as hot as it did when we were standing next to the burning Garden. I take a few deep breaths through my nose to calm down.

Behind us, one of the soldiers shouts to "spread out." The sound of their boots echoes against the walls and paints a picture of a vast army at our backs.

"Yun's beard," Rayce hisses under his breath. He pulls out one of the contraptions he took from Arlo and slips it in my hands, feigning a couple heading into the night for a good time.

"What's this?" I whisper. "I said the knife."

"It's a stunner," he says.

I look down at the weapon joining us. His palm heats the back of my hand, in sharp contrast with the stunner's cool metal handle. It's much lighter than I imagined, and the same green powder he had me ingest fills the glass handle.

"If they do end up spotting us, it'll stop them from following." He moves my finger with his to a little switch above the handle. "This is the trigger. You pull it back when you want to shoot. And don't think about pointing it at any of us, because it won't work."

I can't say the idea didn't cross my mind.

Even though Rayce said not to, I casually tuck my hair behind my ear and peek back the way we came. A group of soldiers charges into the little brothel we just passed. Their large shadows bounce around the nearest wall. A second later, people come pouring out the door, stumbling over one another to get away from the men in metal armor. Another group of soldiers heads our way, so I turn back and bury my head in Rayce's arm to obscure my face.

"You peeked," Rayce says, though he doesn't sound angry.

I nod.

"And what did you see?"

"Five of them are coming at us quickly," I say to the ground, my voice shaking.

"Remain calm," Oren whispers from a few paces ahead. "We haven't a reason to panic."

A man staggers past, running from the brothel raid. The stench of rice wine and vomit rolls off him. A short woman with her tattered green robe around her shoulders and her crimson lip blush smeared follows behind. My mind screams that we should run, but I force myself to keep time with Rayce's steady footfalls.

"Hey! You four," one of the soldiers shouts. "Stop right there."

The weight of the stunner feels heavier the second I realize I'm going to have to use it. Even though it would probably hurt them more, I wish I had a Varshan blade instead. At least I can use one of those without worrying I'll shoot myself.

"Now," Arlo says, spinning around with a stunner in each hand.

The powder in the barrels glows bright green, but I can't tear my gaze from the glowing green lines running over his skin like veins.

Next to me, Rayce snatches his stunner, his body bursting with light. A web of green ink spreads down his left side from the base of his ear, sleeving his shoulder and trailing farther down his stomach, glowing through his light linen shirt. The intricate lines swirl like they're trying to mimic the wind.

These are the glowing men the lackeys were talking about, and it's the same color light I saw from high above the Garden when I was suspended by my silk! Could this really be magic?

I don't have time to process that before Arlo lets loose a pair of green electric waves that light up the dark street. They look as dangerous as lightning skipping from cloud to cloud on a stormy night. One beam rockets past my cheek, sending a heat wave shuddering down my body. The twin shots race toward the men chasing us, finding their target in the exposed skin of the neck, just between the helmet and the chest plate. The two lead soldiers go down.

"Over there!" one of the other soldiers shouts, his voice ringing out like a death sentence.

We dart forward down the wide street. I can see the mighty Changhe River that cuts through the western half of Delmar in the near distance. If we can make it there, maybe I can slip away in the chaos.

Oren and Rayce both turn around and take shots. I look over my shoulder as another soldier collapses. At quick glance, there have to be at least eleven. Almost an entire unit. They spread out, blocking the way back with their bodies.

I have no idea how we can outrun them, but I've got to do something. I swing around and hold out my stunner. I do my best to aim, but the running and the adrenaline aren't helping. I pull the trigger, and the kickback almost slams the metal contraption into my forehead. The bolt rockets toward the crowd and hits one of the outside guards. His shoulder twists back from the impact, but the green bolt ricochets off the tiny metal plates and into the wall, not even slowing him down.

Two of Arlo's bolts follow mine, finding their mark. I snarl at the stunner in my hands as if it's responsible for my poor aim. Increasing heat courses down my body. It feels like I'm the one burning instead of the Garden. But Rayce mentioned the powder would make me feel hot. Before I can look to see where we are, Rayce pushes me away from him. An arrow whizzes through the space my head previously occupied.

"Spread out!" Rayce orders. "They have crossbows."

I turn around again and try to aim my weapon better. Oren's shot stuns another while mine hits an armored knee. The blow causes the soldier to fall, but he scrambles back to his feet.

Arlo guns two more down, narrowing the crowd to six, a perfectly manageable number for the four of us if I had a usable weapon. I just hope these three men are as good at hand-to-hand combat as they are at shooting, because the river is coming up faster than we can fire. Another arrow cuts through the air, grazing Oren's shoulder.

The buildings break away, and the only bridge connecting the poor part of Delmar to the capital comes into view a few blocks up, but we'll never make it there with arrows flying. Which only leaves the murky black water. I recoil just thinking about jumping in and the cold attacking my body. As if it's already happening, I can feel icy water flooding my lungs, can see Rayce and the others splashing away from me as I sink to the bottom.

The ledge comes up quickly. A wrought-iron fence about the height of my hip is all that separates us and a sheer drop into the water below.

I slow as we draw nearer. If I'm going to jump, I really don't want to do it from a running start. But I hope it doesn't come to that. Rayce swings around, grabbing the blade I used to take him hostage and then kicking a soldier to the ground.

Without command, Oren and Arlo stop next to the fence and pivot, taking shots at the remaining soldiers. Rayce grabs my shoulder and pushes me behind him, blocking me from any stray arrows with his own body.

The last remaining soldier charges for us, but Rayce parries his attack, never moving from his spot in front of me, dispatching the soldier quickly with his tiny knife.

I stumble backward, leaning against the railing to stay upright. For some reason my legs shake and I'm reminded of the winter when I was eleven and caught a fever in the Garden. The Gardener had me dunked in water for tearing my dress on a nasty fall, and I was thrown into my cart overnight. At first I couldn't keep warm and I thought I might freeze to death—until the fever set in.

"Rose, you don't look well," Oren says, his voice loud next to me.

My tongue feels three sizes too big, and I fight to keep him in focus. I try to tell him I'll be fine, but words won't form.

He presses his cool hand to my forehead.

"How much Zarenite did you give her?" he asks Rayce. "She's burning up. We have to get her out of here."

*No!* I want to scream but only manage a throaty moan.

"Not enough for a reaction like this," Rayce says, his furrowed brow coming into focus.

"I need to leave," I say, trying to push off the railing. I search desperately for the puff of gray smoke in the sky to lead me back to the Garden, but everything's spinning.

Rayce sweeps his arms under my legs and picks me up. Fern's face appears in front of my eyes. Can't they understand I have to go back?

My head lolls until it rests against Rayce's cool chest. What did he give me? My flesh feels like it's melting off. Never trust the word of a man. How many times must I learn this lesson before I remember to apply it?

Then the Flowers, the Garden, the pursuing soldiers, and this vexing man who cradles me petal soft in his capable arms…everything slips away from me in the burning darkness.

# Chapter Eight

I awake inside a black darker than a starless night, the pounding in my head louder than my pulse. At least my body doesn't feel hot anymore. I try to open my eyes, but my lids feel too heavy. Instead, I focus on wiggling my toes, but they don't respond.

What did that powder do to me?

The only thing I can do right now is rely on my other senses to figure out where I am. I lie still and wait for the jolt of a cart underneath me.

*Nothing.*

Horseback would be even rougher. No bumps or jostling leads me to believe I'm stationary. The pops and crackles of a fire confirm this theory. As soon as I hear it, the smell of wood burning overruns my senses, tickling my nostrils with the smoky scent. The intensity of it brings on a wave of nausea, but my body still hasn't moved. The only thing I can accomplish is an involuntary gurgling noise.

"I think she's stirring," a male voice says, unsettlingly close to my face. The voice sounds like stones crunching under a boot. Must be Oren.

After a moment, Oren sighs, apparently satisfied I haven't woken.

"I guess the mineral powder hasn't worn off yet," he says, and there's a rustling of fabric as he slides away from me.

Finally, I can force my eyes open and catch a sliver of nighttime sky. I haven't seen this much of it in years. Judging by the thick treetops that frame my view, we must be somewhere deep in the Shulin Forests that frame the west side of Delmar. My tutor taught me a little about the Delmarion lands before I was captured by the Garden, showing me that this forest stretches as far south as the sea does north, and beyond it lie snow-dusted mountains.

It's some time past midnight; the moon has already finished painting the sky a deep shade of navy. Judging from the soreness creeping up my back, they must have dragged my unconscious body for several hours into the forest. As I stare at the stars, the patterns warp into my sisters' terrified faces. Fern's screams reverberate around me, her last words sticking to my skin like sweat. She gave her life to set me free, and I failed her by not saving the others. How many more girls will die before I can free them all?

I breathe steadily through my nostrils to stay calm. The Gardener lost his tent and his star all in the same night. There's no way he'd be crazy enough to kill any more girls right now. He might be cruel, but he's way too greedy to stop his show, even for vengeance. The other Wilteds pop into my mind. Perhaps they won't be so lucky.

"So what's the plan, then?" Arlo says, cutting into my worried thoughts. "Once we get the girl back to base."

I keep still, hanging onto the silence as I wait for an answer.

Someone clears his throat. "We're going to have to observe her," comes a commanding tone that can only belong to Rayce. "Right now she's an unknown variable, and if she really was sent by her master or my uncle to kill me, she might have information on their treaty."

"So you want to lock her up and interrogate her?" Arlo asks.

My breathing stops. Of course they would want to throw me in another cage. That's been the goal of every man I've ever dealt with. The vision of Park's smiling face and kind eyes tries to surface, but I push it away. He can't slip into my thoughts right now.

What would a Zareeni interrogation be like, especially with that powder at their disposal? And even though I was just trying to escape, what if they start asking about my past? About who my father was and when I traveled to Delmar from Varsha? They would trade me to the emperor in exchange for whatever it is they're fighting for, just like *him*. Or worse, they might try to use a position I feel I can no longer claim to their advantage. How can I convince them I'm not lying when I've been lying about my past every day since I arrived in this land?

"I don't see a better option," Rayce says. "At least not until we know where her true loyalties lie."

I've been up front about my loyalties since the beginning. I want to help my sisters. But Rayce wouldn't let me do that.

"Just use caution," Oren says, his voice almost lost to the fire's crackle. "She's already withstood the worst possible living conditions and survived better than most of our army would. I'd imagine kindness might be better received."

"I doubt she'd trust it," Rayce says. "I wouldn't, if I were her."

"Either way, I'll prepare a cell as soon as we get back," Arlo says, his voice wavering. "If she knows anything about the deal between the emperor and the Gardener, that information could be vital in turning the public's opinion. If your uncle gains enough coin to fund his campaign into the woods, we won't be able to hide for much longer."

An uneasy quiet falls over the site, like he just doused water on the fire. The weight of their separate thoughts presses down on my frozen body.

Not that it matters. The moment I'm able to move again, I'll disappear into the night, leaving their suspicions behind.

"And what about Piper?" Arlo asks. "We've got to figure out what to tell her, because she's going to be livid."

"Well, it stands to reason that we just tell her the truth," Oren says.

"We owe her that, at least," Rayce adds.

"I'm not saying you're wrong," Arlo says. "But you know Piper. How do you think she's going to react when we go back and tell her, 'Oh, we were going to rescue your sister, but then we found this girl and saved her instead'?"

What? I tilt my head toward the fire and can barely make out three figures beyond the bright glow. Guilt for not saving the other Flowers melds with the knowledge that the rebellion was trying to liberate another girl. It seems my plan to escape has left *everyone* captive.

"Well, I wasn't planning on saying it like that," Rayce says, and one of the blurs moves to throw something into the fire. "Besides, you said my uncle moved her, right?"

My body begins thawing quickly. Numbness clinging to my limbs melts away, and the aches of our escape creep up my body.

Arlo holds up his hands, palms out. "That's the report. The troop sent to infiltrate the ground-level dungeon while we lit the tent on fire as a distraction said she was no longer there, which can only mean one thing…"

"The pits," Rayce and Arlo say in unison.

"There isn't a way for this to play out well," Oren says. "No matter what new information we learned, the outcome remains the same. This girl walks free while Piper's little sister remains locked in the Delmar dungeon. Twelve is awfully young to be held captive."

They were there to rescue a *little* girl? Panic pushes words out of my mouth before I remember that I need to stay silent.

"You've got to go back." My throat catches. I try to sit up, but my abdomen is stiff from the serum and knocks me back to the ground.

They all jump up like they were caught without their swords during an ambush. I turn away from them, fighting against the spots in my vision. Something sharp pokes against my right lung every time I try to breathe in deeply. Rayce's creased brow breaks through the dark spots.

"Yun's beard," Arlo curses from somewhere behind Rayce. "That kind of scare will stop the heart quicker than a stunner shot."

"You were trying to save a girl," I say, using my elbows to force myself up.

The three men look at each other, and I can almost see the question they're all asking themselves: How much did she hear?

"Don't worry about that now," Oren finally says, his eyes flicking to my face.

"Why didn't you let me go when you had the chance?" I ask Rayce, staring him down. "If you'd just listened to me, maybe everyone could have been freed tonight."

Rayce looks away from me, unhooking a brown leather water pouch from his belt.

"Right now you need water," he says, ignoring my outburst. "You must have ingested too much of that powder and it sucked up all the water in your body."

I push the pouch away.

"Please don't make us force it down your throat," Rayce says, waving the pouch in my direction.

"You can try, but it will be the last thing you do." I clench my jaw to emphasize my point.

"I already told you," Rayce says, shoving the pouch toward me again. "As long as you have no intention of harming us, we won't harm you."

Which means I'm safe, but only for now. I move to accept the drink, but my elbow gives out and my head slams onto the ground. I didn't think the pounding could get worse. I was mistaken.

I close my eyes against the pain and don't fight when someone places a hand on either side of my head and gently lifts it onto a soft surface. The smooth fabric cradles my cheek.

Opening my eyes, I find Rayce staring down at me. I realize I'm resting on a shirt bundled up on his knee, but before I can protest his closeness, he holds the water pouch to my mouth. The cool liquid trickles down my throat, but all I can think about is whether that girl they were supposed to rescue is dying of thirst in the dungeon. The water suddenly tastes like ash in my mouth, and I turn away from it, letting the rest dribble down my chin.

"Better?" Rayce says.

I keep silent, refusing to look away from the flames in front of me.

"Is that how they say thank-you in Varshan?"

His words kick me more than I care to admit.

Oren clears his throat. "Speaking of Varsha, do you have any family there?"

My gaze flicks to his face, and I work to keep my limbs perfectly still. My heart hammers against my chest. They're already getting too close to the thing no one can ever know about, especially since they could use it to accomplish whatever they're trying to do with their rebellion.

"You shouldn't feel afraid of the past, Rose," Oren says, misinterpreting my fear for shame. "Our history is what shapes us. We all make mistakes. Look at me. Just last year, I was on the Imperial Council advising Galon on the best way to handle rebellions, and now I'm helping lead one."

I can see Oren in that life, dressed in the grand blue-and-white robes of the council, walking around the palace with an armful of dusty scrolls. It suits him much more than sitting here in the middle of the forest with soot covering most of his brown robe.

"How long have you been gone?" Arlo asks.

When I don't respond, Rayce jostles me gently, so I look at him. "Remember what I said. Honesty will go a long way to us trusting you."

*Is that before or after you throw me in a cell?*

I roll my eyes, already knowing how this will go. If I remain silent, they'll try to piece together my past. Instead, I give them the bare-bones version I've rehearsed even more than my dance routine.

"I've lost count," I say. "I don't know, maybe eight years. It's hard to keep track where I came from."

I lied. The truth is it's been almost exactly ten years since I was ripped from my land. No matter how much I block out my life before the Garden, I can't erase that clock in my brain ticking out the days since I knew the gentleness of my father's touch. But locking all that away keeps me safe. Only the Gardener knows the truth about where I came from, and if anyone else found out, I'd become nothing more than a bargaining tool. To accept my past would mean accepting everything that comes with it, and I don't think I'll ever be ready for that.

"A lot has happened since then," Rayce says. "The Varshan throne has changed hands and the old king was killed."

I pretty much knew this, but hearing it hurts. The Gardener never let anyone talk about Varshan politics around me, his own personal brand of cruelty.

"His daughter, though," Oren says, stretching out the words. "The rightful heir to the Varshan throne? She was never found. Many believe she was killed, too."

I keep my face straight. That life, that girl. She's dead. But even if I knew she was still alive somewhere, what would the rebellion do with that kind of information? They owe me nothing, so why wouldn't they use me as a pawn? The Gardener did. How quickly could they reach a truce with the emperor if they had a rose with a crown to barter?

"I couldn't help but notice those odd markings on your heels," Oren says. "How long have you had them?"

"I don't know what you mean." Another lie. "The Garden left lots of scars." They just usually weren't on me.

I flutter my eyes and go limp, hoping they think I passed out.

"Rose?" Rayce's voice comes from above me. With my eyes closed, it almost sounds like he's concerned.

"She's probably still weak from overheating and the excitement of our escape," Oren says. "Let her be."

Only when Rayce's retreating footsteps fill my ears do I let the tears for everyone I've let down tonight water the forest floor.

Sometime later, I hear leaves crunching as someone picks their way toward me. I squint one eye open long enough to see Oren's long black beard before closing it again. The footsteps stop, and the edge of Oren's robe brushes across my hand as he sits on the ground next to me. He clears his throat. Though I keep my eyes shut and give absolutely no indication I'm awake, he speaks anyway.

"I don't believe Piper's sister was in as much need of a rescue as you were," he says as if it's fact. As if he's not trying to ease my guilty heart.

My mind recalls every girl I've let down in one spectacularly disastrous night.

"Her capture is for leverage," he continues. "A card the emperor can play anytime to bend us to his mercy. As long as she isn't used for this purpose, I don't believe she'll be harmed. On the other hand, if your true goal was to escape that show, then you made the only logical choice by escaping while the performance was happening. Had you not created your own release, it would have never come."

He pauses, waiting for my response. The thing I should say, the thing I might even want to say—"thank you"—lodges in my throat.

He doesn't stay to see the single unwanted tear that leaks out of my eye. But his words make me feel something I haven't dared feel in a long time. Hope for my own freedom grows in my chest like a weed, and I'm too terrified someone will notice to move.

# Chapter Nine

The next day Rayce gently shakes me awake as the sun begins its ascent into the sky. We head west toward the mountains. Arlo leads the way with steady steps through the never-ending trees. The bed of dead leaves coating the ground makes for soft terrain, but even though I pick carefully through the forest floor, cuts litter the bottoms of my bare feet. Toward the end of the day, the thin white tree trunks grow thicker and turn brown, their limbs twisting out in wild directions.

We stop as the stars awaken. Each of the men takes out what's left of their rations, piling a few scoops of old rice and dried meat from each of their portions on a dinted tin plate, and Rayce hands me the result. I blink back my surprise and accept their food, not digging into the rice until after they begin to eat.

Though the fire warms us, we don't talk much. Rayce keeps one eye pinned the way we've come, like he's expecting to see someone following us. Oren *tsks* over my battered feet and rips off a couple strips of his robe to tie around my feet tomorrow.

Their unexpected kindness almost makes me sorry I'm going to leave them, but the need to rescue my sisters could never be quelled by a few rations and makeshift shoes.

I peek through one open eye as Oren takes the first watch, followed by Rayce and then Arlo. All three have been annoyingly vigilant, but finally, Arlo slips behind a tree to relieve himself.

If I'm going to sneak away, it has to be now. In the brown light of dawn, I force myself up. My mind swirls with exhaustion, but my heart hammers against the idea of being locked away in another cage. I will not be someone's prisoner again.

I crawl over to Rayce, ignoring the sharp pain in my right lung. He's sleeping on his back, his arms threaded behind his head. From this angle, the scarred half of his face isn't visible. It's odd seeing him without it. He looks like he's been carved out of stone. Too perfect. His sword rests an arm's length away from his face, but I'm afraid to get close enough to take it, so I snatch the stunner by his feet instead. Hopefully I won't have to use it.

Lacing my hand through the strap of the water pouch, I snap upward and start moving in the direction I hope is east. Without the sun or moon, it's impossible to tell. When it's brighter, I'll climb a tree to find Delmar, but the best I can tell now is we're at least two days west of the Imperial City, very deep into the Shulin Forests. My only solace is I haven't begun to see mountains yet. Once I figure out how to get back, I'll find a way to save the others.

I step out of the clearing, diving just into the tree line.

"Get up!" Arlo shouts, his voice booming out behind me in the silence of dawn. "She's escaping!"

Against my better judgment, I turn at his voice in time to see Rayce and Oren spring upward. Oren's long hair is crinkled from slumber, and Rayce still has his boots off.

Almost as if Rayce can feel my gaze on them, he looks in my direction. He's on his feet and leaping for me quicker than I can blink.

"Rose, wait!" he yells from much closer than I'd like.

I didn't want it to come to this. Slithering off like a cobra in the grass. But if you corner a snake, it strikes. Raising my stolen weapon to eye level, I take aim and pull the trigger at the person who taught me how it works. But instead of kicking back like an angry horse, nothing blasts out from the barrel.

*But why?* Then I remember he warned me not to turn the stunner on him when he gave it to me to protect myself from the soldiers. He said it didn't work on them.

No time for questions. I don't waste another second.

I drop the stunner and plunge into the forest, dodging the nearest tree trunk. Dead leaves crunch out my flight and the morning air dampens my bare skin as I race through the forest. Tree trunks and bushes rush past me in a blur as I push myself faster. I feel like something wild, hair flying out behind me and bare toes touching the earth. Like a real woods spirit come to life. My feet are spurred on by the rising need to save my sisters. They're probably waiting for me, wondering why I left them. I duck under a low branch. Worse yet, they might think I died. I was in the tent when it went up in flames.

"Come back!" Rayce's voice chases after me.

But he won't catch me. He can't.

I burst through the trees into a meadow, surprised by the clear view of white clouds overhead.

I look behind me and catch a glimpse of ivory, the color of Rayce's shirt, striking through the tree trunks, heading in my direction. How can he keep sensing where I am?

I rush into the middle of the clearing, the long emerald grass tickling my calves.

One minute my feet connect with solid ground and the next I'm falling through the air. My body slams into rock ten feet below, knocking the wind from my lungs. Morning light pours in from an opening above me, illuminating the dust and dirt in the air. I've taken a halo of dead leaves with me into some kind of underground passageway. Its narrow walls are crudely hacked out of stone and look just big enough to fit two people walking shoulder to shoulder. A moldy mix of dirt and stagnant water fills my nose, and darkness stretches out so far it looks endless. If I head into it, I might never find my way back. On the other hand, if Rayce gets a hold of me, I won't find my way back home, either.

I push myself up and hobble out of the beam of light just as Rayce's voice fills the air.

"Are you hurt?" he yells.

Nice try. I'm not about to give up where I am now that I'm almost free. Not now that I know they plan to lock me up as soon as we reach Zareen and prod me for information I don't have. Besides, my sisters need me.

I don't stick around to hear what he says next. I wade into the darkness and finally figure out why it was so easy for him to follow me. My entire body casts a dim green glow on the cave walls. Probably another side effect from that awful powder. I'm like a dull lantern, lighting up the grayness in front of me. Behind me, I can still see the beam of light marking the hole I fell through. As long as they don't cover it back up, I should be able to find it when I come back.

After what feels like twenty feet, the passage widens and forks. No markings indicate where either tunnel leads. Stepping into the right passage, I notice that the floor gently slants down. I definitely don't want to go deeper into the earth, so I head left instead, where this passage remains level.

A loud whistle rings out in the dark, and I drop to my knees. Bright light fills my head as Fern's scream joins the snaking notes of the flute. I cover my ears as it echoes all around me, but it's too late.

*The sticky heat of my cage creeps up my back; the stale air chokes its way down my throat. Fern's black hair shines in the sun as she reaches out with a shaky hand, pleading for her life. Her begging morphs into screams. Shears walks forward, his blades shining in the daylight, but Fern's head whips around. Her brown eyes lock onto mine, glinting harder than when she used to talk about her father selling her to the Garden.*

*"Why didn't you help me?" she yells. "You promised!"*

*The anger in her gaze sears my flesh.*

I cower on my knees and shut my eyes tight to escape the memory, but she follows me behind my eyelids. I let her die. No matter how many times I relive it, I know. I let her die.

*My nostrils fill with the rancid scent of the Gardener's breath hot on my cheek as he explains the rules to me. Nine years old and alone in the world for the first time. Dance until your feet give out, never talk back, and don't ever disobey an order, or your Wilted pays the price.*

*The Gardener's fingers tickle my neck like a spider's legs as he unhooks my mother's ruby and then clasps it around his own neck.*

*His touch lingers, but it feels uncharacteristically soft on my back...*

"Child, you're going to be fine," Oren says.

My ghosts vanish in the warmth of Oren's gaze. What just happened to me? How could I have gone back there, even in my mind?

My mouth feels like I chewed on sand, and my head hangs heavy. I run my hands along my middle to make sure I'm intact. I've seen things that aren't real after starving in my cart for a few days, but never as vivid as that. Have I gone soft like Tulip the first time she combed the air, insisting it was her dolly's hair?

I blink back the last of the false sunlight from my vision and notice Oren's hand lightly touching my shoulder.

His fingertips burn into my skin, and I crawl to get away from him, but my mind is still dizzy from the hallucination of the Garden.

"Please, just let me go," I say.

He frowns and shakes his head like I've given the wrong answer to a question he never asked.

"Why are you so keen to run back to your captor?"

"Because I need to save the other girls," I say, the words catching in my throat.

"The girls from the Garden?"

I clench my fists at the word. It grates against my skin, because it sounds so beautiful when people say it. Like something that springs life from the ground. But if they felt the reality, knew what it was like to be powerless...they wouldn't say it like that. They'd know it was all an illusion made by their god of death, Yun.

Oren's brow furrows deeper, creating a little $M$ at the bridge of his nose, and the wrinkles stay there so effortlessly, I get the impression it's a mask he wears often. For a moment, I even think he might understand why I can't stay here.

"I need to rescue them and make sure the Gardener can never steal another life."

He rubs his beard, considering my words. "They're your family."

There's no question in his voice. I nod at his assumption, even though "family" doesn't express how deeply I care for them. How much it kills me every time the lackeys hold Violet down to color her hair purple and it leaves burn marks all over her scalp. "I know you have no reason to trust us," Oren says, "but that kind of abuse is part of the reason we started the rebellion."

"Of course I can't trust you," I say, searching his smooth face for a reaction. "I heard everything you said by the fire. I'm your prisoner, and I wish you'd stop pretending I'm anything different."

He takes a step toward me.

I recoil, slamming against the rocky wall. The moment my back presses against the stone, bright green light explodes from the surface, bathing my skin in its odd glow.

"What have you done to me?" I shout, stumbling away from him.

When I separate from the stone, the light disappears.

"No need for concern," he says in a soothing tone. "It's just the Zarenite in the wall reacting to the Zarenite powder still left in your body."

My arms and legs won't stop trembling, but it's unclear whether the tremors are from fear or exhaustion. My predicament weighs down on me, heavier than the rock above our heads.

"Look, see, it happens to me, too." He presses his palm to the wall.

Green veins burst from the stone, brightest where his skin comes into contact with it. But unlike when I touched it, the light spreads from the wall down his arm in a strange spiraling pattern, like what the wind might look like if it could be seen, shining bright even through his clothes. The odd light emanating from the rock feels familiar, but I can't place it.

"It's the same reason you're glowing slightly," he says, letting his palm fall away. The moment he does, the green light in the rock surface and his skin fades. "Though, since you only ingested it, the effects won't last long. Another day or two and it will be out of your system."

I stare at the spot that was glowing a moment ago and remember where I saw it before. It looks like the large hunk of rock in the Gardener's collection, but I keep that bit of information to myself. I want to ask him more about it, but I can't decide if I should. In the end, my curiosity wins.

"It's the powder that makes the walls glow?" I ask.

"No, it's the mineral in the wall, Zarenite," he says. "That's mostly what the powder is made of. It reacts to itself and begins to glow. It's the same mineral that allows our stunners to work and why we glow when we use them. When Zarenite is heated up by our bodies and comes into contact with more of the same mineral, it causes it to glow. That's the wonderful thing about our base—even when you are lost in the dark, you can always find light in the stone."

So that's why a dull glow has emanated from my skin ever since I woke up, like a beacon leading my captors right to me. Not only did they ensure I wouldn't be able to escape by causing me to black out, but they also made sure I couldn't slip away in the darkness. I clench my fists, a scream crawling its way up my throat, but it's silenced by a high-pitched whistle that peals through the air. My eyes snap shut and I throw my hands over my ears, telling myself over and over again to stay in the present.

"We're over here," Oren says, his voice muffled through my fingers.

My eyes open at his words, and I cower under his intense gaze. I watch him reaching out, my heart hammering as he places his hand on the ceiling. As he explained, the Zarenite in his body reacts with a system of Zarenite lining the top of the cave. It continues to light up the corridor overhead, down the way I wandered, bathing the cave in a glow like what the sunlight might look like if it caught a fever.

Rayce and Arlo are illuminated about thirty feet from our spot.

"You could have told us you found her," Rayce shouts as they rush toward us.

So, Oren kept me talking until the others grew closer and used the connecting Zarenite clusters to signal our location. At every turn, these men are showing me their true colors. My younger self would have missed the signs, but thanks to *him*,

I'm able to see a man's true colors much quicker now. The anger I felt a moment ago bubbles over, and I jump back from Oren, the man I thought might have understood me.

Rayce catches me by the wrist, his large hand dwarfing it.

"Are you hurt?" he asks, his words clipped.

I shake my head.

"Then you can walk on your own," he snaps. "Don't test us again."

His words drip menace, but before he lets go of me, his gentle grip reveals his worry underneath.

"Oren, do you think you can navigate the tunnels based on where we are?" Arlo asks. "I've never been this far out."

"You definitely found a new entrance to the mines," Rayce says.

"I've studied enough of the maps to reasonably lead the way," Oren says, stepping around us. He leans in as he passes by and whispers, "Don't worry, we'll make it just fine. Adventuring is good for this old soul."

His kindness isn't unnoticed, but all I can think about as Oren ducks in the tight space is that in my panic to get away from them, I've brought myself even closer to the cage they want to throw me in. The irony escapes my lips as a chuckle. Rayce raises an eyebrow but doesn't comment as Arlo and Oren head back out to the forked passage. He motions for me to follow.

Only our footfalls break the stillness as we walk. I'm not sure about the others, but my sleepless night weighs down my eyelids. A deep ache pulses in both of my feet as the bottoms scrape against the scratchy stone.

We walk until the moments blur together, stuck between my heavy eyelids. The tunnels keep winding, the rock growing rougher the farther we go.

Every so often Oren presses his hand to the wall, bathing the entire tunnel with that unnatural green light. The air becomes cooler with every step, biting into my lungs, and I'm grateful again for the dirty white robe Rayce gave me.

Halfway down this tunnel, Arlo touches three long scratches carved in the stone and smiles.

"This is part of the fourth passageway we made," he says. "I know where we are now."

We walk for another endless stretch of time until we reach yet another fork in the road, and my three captors take a right. I follow Arlo inside then nearly crash into him when he stops. Rayce squeezes in next to me, and Oren moves to reveal a solid wall in front of us.

They've led me to a dead end. My heartbeat picks up, picturing the three of them spinning around with their weapons drawn, murdering me where no one will hear my screams.

Rayce lays his hand on the small of my back, pushing me to the side as he walks up to the dead end.

"When we return, you remember your duties?" Rayce asks.

Oren and Arlo nod. Rayce's gaze falls onto me.

"I'm letting you enter my base without restraints, even though you tried to escape once already, because of your previous circumstances." He doesn't meet my eyes. "But if you show even the slightest hint of aggression toward my people, there will be consequences, understood?"

I glare at him but nod.

Satisfied with my answer, he turns around and presses his free hand to the rock. It bursts to life, obliterating the darkness.

Green light cracks up the middle of the rock like a vein. As it grows brighter, the markings on Rayce's skin dim. The stone wall rumbles like the earth is shaking, and I hold my arm up against the light like a shield, as if the rock might explode.

"Arlo, I think I'm going dark," Rayce says. "Care to lend

me a hand?"

"The rebellion's own leader can't even get into the base." Arlo tuts at Rayce.

He steps beside him and places his hand next to Rayce's on the wall. It flashes brighter, the rumbling growing so loud it feels like my chest will burst. Rayce and Arlo begin pushing on it, parting the thick slabs of stone to reveal a hidden passage behind it.

At one time, I might have stood in awe at such a trick, but right now, all I can wonder is what the insides of their base will hold for me. Another cage to rot in? This one buried so deep that no light will leak through? Chilly fear pumps through my limbs.

Rayce's eyes meet mine, and that same smirk he wore when he asked me to run away with him at the Garden plays on his face.

"Welcome to Zareen, Rose," he says.

# Chapter Ten

My first impression of Zareen is the barrel of a stunner shoved in my face. The woman clutching it stares intently at me, her mouth in a thin, no-nonsense line and her brown eyes staring hard through the green light. She'd be imposing even without the weapon, standing at just about Arlo's height with her dark hair tucked back in a low bun on her neck.

"Were you followed?" she asks, her stern gaze sliding from me to Rayce.

"No."

She lowers the weapon, allowing us to step through the hidden passageway into one with a lower ceiling. I remain completely still, my feet unwilling to cooperate. Rayce places his hand on the middle of my back and nudges me forward into the base.

Oren steps in after us, the top of his head grazing the low ceiling, and he takes up most of the hallway with his wide shoulders. He pulls an ivory pipe in the shape of a dragon from the folds of his cloak and runs his fingers over the bumpy scales on the long stem that makes up the dragon's tail.

The female guard's eyes burn holes in my face as I walk past her, and I'm acutely aware of how her skin also glows with Zareeni markings. It's a sharp reminder that I'm an outsider here. The icy chill of the stone floor seeps into the bottoms of my feet, and bumps prickle down my arms. No sound reaches us, almost as if we're the only five people crazy enough to be underground. But that can't be right. Last I heard the rebellion had recruited more than a thousand to their cause.

Rayce's hand still rests on my back like he's afraid I might run again, even though I gave him my word I wouldn't. Besides, I wouldn't get far in a place like this, where they can easily find me with their magic mineral in the walls.

"I'm glad you made it back safely, Shogun," the guard says to Rayce. I'm surprised to hear her use such a formal name for him, since Oren and Arlo have been referring to him by his first name. They must both be high in rank.

She helps Arlo yank the wall back in place. The two pieces of stone meet with a rumble, sealing me into whatever fate they have in store for me.

When she turns back to face us, her eyes are downcast. "Unfortunately, I don't have good news for you. There's been an incident."

Rayce's grip on my robe tightens. "Report, Suki."

She holsters her stunner. The light radiating in her skin dies as soon as she lets go of the handle.

Her gaze remains fixated on the tops of her boots. "The food supply cart heading to Dongsu was ambushed."

I glance at Rayce. The color drains from his face, and his grip slackens on my back, pulling the fabric away from my skin. The chilly mine air slips down my robe, attacking every inch of my skin.

"How many died?" he whispers.

Anxiety swirls around us, laced in every breath I take. Rayce and Arlo wait for an answer, suspended in place, and

Suki frowns, unwilling to give them the answer I can already tell is coming by the defeated way she grips her hands. The news of death has a certain way of clinging to people. Only Oren looks on with a calm face.

"All of them," she says.

Rayce swings around and kicks the wall not an inch away from where I'm standing. I stumble back from him, desperate to put distance between me and his fury. Where I come from, a man's anger means my pain.

"All of them?" Rayce yells, his voice bouncing off the cavern walls.

Arlo runs a hand through his hair and looks down.

"By Yun," Oren says. His pipe nearly slips from his mouth. For a religion with five gods, Delmarions seem to concern themselves mostly with only one. I could never understand why they honor their other gods with temples until Fern explained that the fifth onyx temple was destroyed out of defiance by one of the first emperors after his beloved wife passed away. Even to this day, nothing will grow in the place where it used to stand.

Rayce rubs his eyes and lets out a sigh, his scar appearing to twist like a snake from the shadows. After taking a few deep breaths through his nose, he looks up at his traveling companions, all sign of his anger gone.

"Arlo, gather the others for a meeting," he says. "Oren, collect the maps and all the intel from the past month. Two failed operations in two days isn't coincidence. We have to figure out what went wrong."

"What about her?" Arlo asks, pulling all eyes to me.

"I'll take care of her then meet you in my office," Rayce says.

"Are you sure you don't need assistance?"

Rayce shakes his head and touches the stunner hooked to his belt, turning his glowing face to me. "Don't test me. Are we clear?"

I clench my jaw and nod.

"This way, then."

His clipped instructions leave no room for debate, and my feet instinctively follow him. His fingers slide around my wrist, and I pull back like his body heat burned me.

"I can walk," I snap.

"Fine," he says. "But fair warning, the ground is uneven in parts here."

He spins on his boot and heads down the nearest tunnel. The ground slants downward, leading us farther into the belly of the rebel camp. He keeps a quick pace, and his face remains blank, but I can feel his rage rolling off him. Suki's declaration of the failed mission and the fact that not a single Zareeni guard made it back sticks to my skin like the grime of travel. I've been so trapped in the Garden that I forgot sometimes the outside world can be just as harsh. Every time Rayce's eyes flicker my way, my feet stutter and I wrap my arms tighter around my middle.

The tunnel snakes and forks the farther down we go, and every step makes the ceiling sink heavier above me. The walls grow narrower, and the air begins to taste stale, like it's been breathed in and out a hundred times before it reaches us. I catch the murmurings of daily life as we pass by openings in the rock, snippets of people walking together as if in the middle of the market instead of deep underground, but we pass by them so quickly it's hard to keep them straight.

My head feels light, and my vision dims at the edges, from lack of either sleep or air. Small clusters of Zarenite suspended in jars all along the floor distort our shadows in their green light, allowing me to avoid the uneven dips in the floor.

Rayce stops in front of me and places his hand on the tunnel once more, lighting the sleeping Zarenite in the rocks and probably signaling to anyone up ahead that he's on his way. The fact that I can't decipher his intent makes me uneasy, and my mind wanders back to how intensely he questioned me back in the alley. I want to ask him what Zareen wants from me, but I won't let him see signs of the fear swelling inside my gut. Fear breeds power, and power leads to abuse.

Park taught me that lesson. Just thinking his name brings up his soft brown eyes and infectious smile. His face used to come to me every time I fell asleep, but over the years I learned to push it away. He taught me about fear, about the broken words of men, before the Gardener ever laid a chubby finger on my flesh. His deceit was the first root to ever take hold in my heart and the one that strengthened long after I could no longer hear the sound of his silver-tongued words.

After a few more minutes of complete silence, a figure appears in the darkness up ahead, standing in front of a barred metal gate attached to the wall with rusty hinges. Hearing our footsteps, the man salutes as Rayce approaches then wrenches the door open. The old hinges squeak in protest.

Rayce scoots to the side and motions for me to go ahead. "Get in," he says.

My feet stay rooted as my heart hammers against my chest. Watching Fern butchered before my eyes, my desperate attempt to escape the Garden, running for my life from the Delmarion soldiers—all of it flashes in my mind. All my efforts can't have been to wind back up in a cage. The opening looms dark like the mouth of a giant beast.

I lick my dry lips. "And if I don't?"

His fingers wrap around my forearm—commanding but not so hard as to hurt. The cage opening grows larger.

"I don't have time to argue with you," he says, his voice edged with annoyance. "I have forty different families to inform that their loved ones won't be returning home."

"Why are *you* going to tell them? Why not one of your—"

"Because they gave their lives under my orders. Hearing

it from the person responsible is the least their families deserve."

He's going to *personally deliver* that horrible message? He tilts his head toward the cage, rousing me from my shock, and I remember what I'm fighting for.

"Wait," I say, grabbing his hand.

Our eyes meet, and I wonder if he can see the fear streaming through mine. Something soft sparkles just underneath the surface of his dark eyes.

"What are you going to do to me?" I ask, my voice sounding meek even to my own ears.

His grip loosens for a moment, and he presses his eyes closed like whatever he's thinking might flash before them.

"Please," I say, seizing this momentary break in his resolve. I remember him whispering that he didn't have a choice about taking me as his prisoner back at the Garden, and I hope he might waver. "Please don't throw me back in a cage."

His gaze flickers to the robe he gave me, still hanging loosely around my middle. The shoulder of my Garden outfit glitters red in the strange light.

"I wish that I didn't—" Whatever he wanted to say gets lodged in his throat.

He shakes his head, his next words sounding hollow and rehearsed. "You are a prisoner of Zareen and will remain here until we can conclude whether or not you're a threat. Now please go in, or we'll have to use force."

Before I can speak again, he spins away from me, waiting for me to walk into the dark unknown. I take a step forward, my eyes snapping shut as the great beast of an entrance swallows me whole. I trip on the uneven ground and tumble forward, my hands colliding with the chilly rock. For a moment the terrifying silence overwhelms me, until the slow *drip-drip* of a water leak fills my ears.

Slowly, I open my eyes and see the cage they've chosen is a

cavern many times taller than the hallways we'd been walking through before. Water drips from a hole about a hundred feet above, expanding a puddle near the door. A soft beam of blue light streams down from the opening, throwing enough light to make out a crudely cut wooden table in the middle of the room. A red quilt sits folded at the foot of what must pass for a bed carved into the stone wall. Overall, it's a step up from what I had in the Garden, but a cage is a cage.

The door squeals shut behind me, and I spin around, my last second of freedom slamming with the metal as it locks.

Rayce turns to the man guarding my door. "Don't speak to her unless she tells you she's ready to talk to me. Someone will relieve you later."

The man nods his understanding.

"Thank you," Rayce says, then turns to me. He presses himself against the metal bars, his face shrouded in darkness.

"You've got a day." He takes the key from the door and slides it into his pocket. "Figure out a way to convince us you aren't an assassin, and you have my word that we'll let you go."

Rage burns through me like fire, and I cut a glare at him. At least the Gardener knows what he is. Rayce pretends to want change, to oppose those that would lock us up, and yet, here he's doing the exact same thing.

"I don't have anything to tell you," I say. "Whether you keep me in here for a day or the rest of my life, I can't give you what you want."

He takes a step back, completely swallowed in darkness. The slightest glow of his tattoos swirls from the black depths like a beautiful trap set for moths.

"Remember, Rose, your cooperation is what will get you out of this," he says before the tapping of his boots on stone signifies his retreat.

And once again, I'm all alone in the dark, and the hole in my cage teases me with a world I can never have.

# Chapter Eleven

The light fades from the hole in the sky, growing weaker with each passing minute. A deep darkness rolls into my prison like a fog. If I'd known while running through the great open field above that it would be the last time the sunlight might touch my face, I'd have appreciated it more.

Now the chill of the base has buried itself within me, slipping through my eyes and mouth to freeze me from the inside. A flower can't grow when every breath is visible.

Rayce's parting words echo in my mind like a drum. How can I convince him I'm not an assassin and that I know nothing about whatever treaty the Gardener and the emperor were trying to make? They're approaching this situation like the Gardener viewed us as people instead of pets. The only thing I have is my secret. It's what Fern whispered before we were ripped from each other. But they can't have that. The Gardener has always been right about one thing: if anyone finds out who I am, I'll never be safe.

Even though Fern confirmed my past was part of the treaty between the Gardener and Delmar, I can't let them know that. So what can I trade for my freedom?

I know what the Gardener would want in return—to have his show sanctioned and a premium spot in the middle of Imperial City, but that seems like common knowledge. I throw a pebble into the puddle, hoping the ripples might reveal something I'm not seeing, but it holds no answers. If Fern were here, she'd know exactly what to do. What else do I know? How can I convince them?

I bite my lip, searching through any scrap of information I overheard, but the cries of my sisters begin building over my thoughts. They must be so scared now… First Fern's death and then my disappearance. Do they think I was killed in the fire? Did Calla and Lily see my attempted escape? If they did, I hope they know I'm coming for them. Nothing can keep me from freeing them all, not the rock surrounding me or a thousand of those stunners pointed in my direction.

Calla's and Lily's faces swirl in the darkness, so close I could reach out and touch their pale cheeks.

A sharp whistle echoes through the air, slicing through the illusion.

Before I can determine the source, Fern's shriek rises up with the pitch, two warring entities that fill my head. My breath catches as the picture in front of me changes. The twins dissipate like smoke parting, and ice shoots down my back as a familiar laugh rolls through the room. The smell of his breath—like rotten meat—surrounds me, ripping the air from my lungs. The Gardener appears in the darkness, his long open robe turning to smoke at the edges, and his mouth splits into a cracked smile.

My hands tremble as I try to scoot backward, but I can't stop staring into his dark, soulless eyes. The sound of Fern's screams plays behind us. His clothing and skin burst into flame, and he continues to laugh, clenching his fists like he's gained power from the fire.

He reaches out a burning hand and wraps it around my neck. A scream pours out of my lips as my hair catches on fire, but it's sucked up by the darkness. He lifts me by the neck until I'm eye level with his face, my flesh bubbling underneath his fingers.

"You are mine again, lovlee," he says, his words dousing me in an icy chill. "You will always be mine."

I twist away from him, stumbling backward. My back slams into stone, and bright green light bursts from behind me, slashing through his flaming body, banishing him back into the darkness. I blink against the light and freeze. I watch as it races up the wall, swirling around the round room as it rushes to meet the top in a thousand tiny rivers. And I realize as I'm standing there with my mouth hanging open that the whistling stopped.

*"That is the wonderful thing about our base—even when you are lost in the dark, you can always find light in the stone."*

Oren's words echo in my mind. It's almost like he was trying to prepare me for this moment.

I step away from the wall, and the light vanishes as fast as it appeared, leaving me alone in the emptiness.

It's so dark I question if the green glow was actually real. I reach out my trembling palm, bracing myself for the feel of the cool stone.

A loud squeal echoes through the chamber as the metal-bar door swings open, and I pull my hand back before it touches the wall. I scuttle back into my bed.

"Why's it so dark in here?" asks a female voice not nearly as far away as I'd like. "Hang on, there's a trick to this."

I clench my teeth as a *click* like stone hitting stone sounds out, and I wonder what type of weapon could produce it. The sound reminds me of when I was new in the Garden and Shears would circle my cart at night, slowly opening and closing his scissors. The *tick, tick, tick* still makes my stomach roll.

"Here we go," the female voice says. As she finishes speaking, the walls burst to life, light crawling up the cavern.

I blink against the brightness, forcing my eyes to adjust. But instead of light reflecting back from some sort of blade like I feared, I see a girl crouched in the corner. She holds a hand over her forehead to shield her eyes and touches a glowing green stone with her other hand.

She scans the room until our gazes meet, and I blink back my surprise at noting she can't be much older than I am. Her soft brown eyes resemble a doll's, round and hooded, and hold a rare joy among all the jagged rocks surrounding us. Though her skin is the color of the white sand on the beaches of the Lao Lin Ocean back home, her long, bushy light brown hair and pointed jawline suggest she isn't exactly Delmarion. As she heads toward me, she carries her lithe frame with the jaunty steps of someone who hasn't seen a lot of fighting.

"Stay back!" I sink farther into my bed.

"There you are," she says, letting out a little chuckle. "It was too dark to see you from the door, and you were so quiet I was beginning to wonder whether you'd found a way to escape or hurt yourself."

She runs her hands through her pile of curly hair, pulling it off her face. So she's even more out of place in Delmar than I am. Varshans are rare in Delmar since the emperor shut down the border, but a Varshan and Delmarion getting along well enough to have children is almost unheard of.

"You should try keeping the Zarenite active so you don't have to sit in the dark," she says. "The trick is to keep the stones touching." She motions to a few glowing stones pressed up against the wall, where she was just squatting. "That way you don't have to sit against the wall if you want light. I can give you a few extras if you want."

She takes a step toward me, and I scoot back, the coolness

of the stone leaking through my borrowed robe.

The girl frowns, tucking her outstretched hand into the long sleeve of her crisp green tunic. "Sorry," she says. "Didn't mean to frighten you. I just brought you some food."

Instead of trying for me again, she leans down and picks up a small plate of bread, cheese, steaming rice, and a slice of some sort of meat and sets it on the rickety table in the middle of the room, her curls bouncing with every move. The toe of her boot catches on the uneven flooring. So she must be new to this particular room. I'm not sure why, but that puts me a little at ease.

"I'm Marin, by the way." She looks up from the plate she just set down and gives me a toothy smile that reminds me of someone, though I can't place whom. "In case you need anything else."

I continue to stare at her the way I always stared at Shears, somewhere between distrust and disgust. When I don't move or say anything, the grin slips from her face and she tucks both of her hands into her sleeves. I fight to keep my eyes on her instead of the food.

My stomach rolls with hunger. I haven't eaten anything since Rayce and the others split up their rations for me.

"Well, I guess I'll leave you to it."

She spins around, putting her back to me as she walks to the door. She clearly hasn't had this position long enough to know better. All I'd need to do is rush her and I'd be out. I'm willing to bet my years in the Garden have made me quick, and if I've got momentum, she wouldn't stand chance against me. My gaze falls on the stunner contraption holstered to her hip, and I think better of the reckless plan. It isn't like I could find my way out of the base undetected anyway.

She pauses, almost at the door.

"Are the rumors going around the base really true?" she asks, turning back toward me. She wrings her hands together, and her voice softens. "Are you really from the Garden?"

I tilt my head up slightly, rebuffing her sympathy, but keep my mouth shut. Her brow furrows, obviously distraught by my silence. Something about the hurt expression on her face reminds me of Juniper every time one of the lackeys would stomp on her scrap of bread before she could get to it.

My dry lips crack as I croak out a single word. "Yes."

The sound of my voice slides across the room like a draft, sending ripples in the chilly air.

She places a hand on the metal bars keeping me locked in and gives me a small half smile. "I'm sorry you were stuck in a filthy place like that. You'll have to tell me more about it sometime."

My curiosity gets the better of me. "Why should I?"

She cocks her head to the side like she'd never considered I'd question her.

"Because," she says. "You and I are going to be friends."

She punctuates her ridiculous statement by slipping through the door and slamming it shut, the sound reverberating through my head.

With prying eyes finally gone, I lunge for the food she left behind, knocking the bread onto the floor in my haste. I snatch it up and stuff a flaky piece into my mouth, scoffing at Marin's final statement. Why she thinks I'd ever be friends with the people holding me captive is ridiculous.

I stuff another piece of bread into my mouth and look around. My eyes fall onto the small pile of rocks she left to light the room and I smile, an idea blooming in my mind. Maybe the girl was onto something, because only a friend would leave me everything I need to escape.

. . .

I wait for what feels like an eternity, not daring to move.

Sunlight creeps back into my cage, fighting off the gloom. When my bones ache from sitting at attention for so long, I dart over to the pile of rocks and grab the longest piece, the cool mineral sending a shiver down my body as it glows faintly under my touch. Rushing back to the comfort of my bed, I stick the piece of Zarenite underneath my red blanket. Then I wait, expecting to hear footsteps, for someone to shout at me not to move, but the only sound to greet me is the water dripping from above.

I pull the rock out and flick it against the wall several times, a point taking shape with each small movement. Sparks fly, and I'm brought back to the moment the first firework exploded in the Garden.

The mesmerizing way the weapon forms under my hands blocks out all other distractions. I don't hear the bars to my cage open or the footfalls of someone approaching. All that alerts me to someone else's presence is a throat clearing.

I jump, the nearly completed blade slipping from my grasp and slicing open my palm. A hiss escapes my lips as a pool of blood blossoms from a long slice running across my hand, and pain shoots up my arm.

I turn to the newcomer, and Rayce appears in the beam of light. Our time apart has been far kinder to him than to me. While I've lost more sleep than I've managed to gain, the bags under his eyes have lightened and he's changed into a fresh ivory tunic. Thick stubble peppers his chin in a very Varshan fashion.

"You cut yourself with that stone you were sharpening." He *tsks*. "Tell me, what exactly where you planning to do with that thing once you finished making it?"

Light pours down on him, streaking his dark hair into a thousand shades of black. He drops the sack he was carrying onto the table.

"Did you come to threaten me for information I don't

have?" I ask, pressing my hand closed. Blood trickles down my arm.

"I came with a peace offering," he replies, pulling out a woven basket with a top on it, a few smaller steaming pots, a water jug, and a cloth napkin. "But instead, I'm going to clean that wound. Lucky for you, I brought a first-aid kit, too."

"That won't be necessary." I wipe my bloodied hand on my dirty robe.

He turns to look at me, his brow furrowed in frustration, and grabs a small brown vial, the water jug, and fresh bandages.

"Do you have to make everything difficult?" he asks. "I'm coming over there."

He doesn't wait for my response, dipping into the darkness of my side of the cell without a second thought. I push my feet out, trying to slide farther back into my crawl space, but my back is already pressed against the cold stone. There is no escaping his closeness, and he doesn't seem to care that I don't want him near.

He sits on the opposite edge of my bed, placing the clean bandages between us. This close, I realize his gaze isn't nearly as hard as I imagined. He looks nothing like the man who locked me in here yesterday.

"You're going to have to promise not to make another one," he says, picking up the makeshift knife.

I straighten. "How did you know I had anything?"

He gives me a lopsided grin and sets the bottle down. "We've had people watching you day and night. We know exactly what you've been up to. Now, let me see that hand."

I press my bleeding hand against my chest.

"Come on, what good is refusing going to do? I'm trying to help you."

"I've had plenty of your help," I say, meeting his gaze. "Your need to 'keep me safe' is why I'm in here in the first place."

"You could be back in the Garden," he says.

"Or I could be free," I counter.

"Or you could be dead—and I wasn't going to let that happen. Ensuring your safety is the only thing I was able to get right over the past few days."

The conviction in his voice catches me off guard, and no matter how hard I squeeze my hand, I can't stop the bleeding. Pain surges from the wound, nearly bringing tears to my eyes.

"Fine," I say, holding my palm out.

He takes my hand in both of his, his warmth enveloping my skin. Though his hands dwarf mine, his touch remains light, his thumbs ghosting over my open palm.

"That," he says, motioning to the knife, "was a test. And you failed."

I pull my hand away from him, and he laughs as he grabs the brown bottle and tips it over a clean scrap of cloth. He waves for me to return my hand, but I don't.

"Don't you have anything better to do with your time than test a single captive?" I ask, annoyance coloring my voice. "Didn't you say you have families to notify?"

He stiffens at my words, the smile dropping from his face. I look down at my bleeding hand, see the bandages sitting between us and the way his shoulders slump, and for some stupid reason guilt washes over me. Though I haven't agreed with any of his methods, he has done his best to keep me out of harm's way. I swallow the lump forming in my throat.

"How did that go?" I ask, holding my hand back out to him. "It couldn't have been easy."

He takes a deep breath and looks down at my outstretched hand, an unreadable look on his face. He picks up a clean cloth and presses it to my cut, holding it and my hand tightly in between both of his.

"It wasn't," he whispers. "It's the worst part about leading." He looks up, meeting my gaze with eyes on fire.

"But it's also one of the most important things I can do. I'm not like my uncle; I don't view people as insects. Those men and women that died for our cause deserve to be honored, and their families deserve to know of their sacrifice from their leader."

Who is this guy? I look past the long scar twisting down one side of his face and the dark hair falling onto his forehead and really peer into the dark eyes of this person...this person who refused to let me go and might have saved my life at the same time. Is what he's saying true? He really cares about those he's responsible for?

It would be the first time a man actually did since I passed through the Blue Gate.

"I'm not sure I can believe you," I say. I expect him to protest, but silence stretches between us, and I search for something else. Fern's face comes unbidden into my mind, and before I can stop myself, I speak. "But if I were in your position, I'd want to do the same thing. The Gardener killed the girl I grew up with the night I escaped, but she doesn't have any family to tell."

His grip loosens on my hand, and his lips part slightly.

"I promised I'd protect her, but it turns out I couldn't." Her face, distorted in anger as she yells at me, fills my head, but then I can feel her warm fingers rubbing circles on my back right before a performance and the panic in my chest fades into something worse. "I...miss her."

My hand in Rayce's is a strange sight, so I study the shape they make rather than looking at his face. Even though everything I said was true, saying it out loud to someone who didn't even know Fern is embarrassing.

"What was her name?" Rayce asks.

"What?"

"Her name," he repeats.

"Fern."

He runs his free hand through his hair before dropping it back over mine gently.

"I can't take back her death," he says, and even though I get the feeling these are words he's practiced, the sincerity on his face holds me captive, like he's feeling her loss with me. "But I'm sorry that it happened."

I pull my hand back from him and turn away, clearing my throat.

"That's why you were so desperate to escape," he says, all of my actions apparently connecting in his head. "You said you grew up with her."

"She took my beatings," I say, turning back to him. I watch his face, unflinching, so he understands what kind of monster he forced me to leave my family with. "That's how the Garden works. We're assigned another girl who sleeps in our cages with us, who we bond with, to share our life stories and secrets and hopes and fears with, and then one of us is chosen to dance and the other takes our punishments. The dancers are responsible for their flesh, our misstep becomes their pain, and we have to watch, have to sleep next to them while they lie broken and bleeding."

He stills, listening. This time I hope the silence is uncomfortable for him.

His voice is hoarse when he finally responds. "That must be a pain too horrible to name. No one should have to suffer that way. I wish there was something we could do to ease that suffering. All I can offer now is that's something the rebellion will not allow to exist in the new world we're going to create."

He picks up the cloth and scoots closer to me. I stiffen as he pulls my hand back to him and places it gently on his lap. His callused fingers trailing along my flesh make me want to pull away, but I need to have this wound treated or it could become infected. Sensing my discomfort, he moves slowly, like he's afraid he'll frighten me, and presses the rag against my wound.

Whatever he used from the vial stings, and I suck in a breath through my teeth.

"That bad?" he asks, his eyes soft as he inspects my wound.

"A little," I answer through clenched teeth.

"Here." He leans forward and puckers his lips a few inches from my broken flesh.

My heart reacts like I've been running, and my entire world focuses on the point where our skin touches. He blows on my stinging cut, the whisper of butterfly wings against skin. The cool air is the perfect balm for a pain I can't even feel anymore.

I blink back my surprise and yank my arm away from him.

"Aren't we touchy," he says, but the corner of his mouth quirks up. "It's better anyway. I'm not really fond of blood."

"Then why not just give me the cloth and let me clean the wound myself?"

He stands up and stretches, turning an inch away from me so I can't see his face. "Because it's my responsibility as a leader to forgo my own fears for the sake of my people. If I shied away every time I saw a little blood, what kind of warrior would I be?"

A bitter chuckle escapes my lips, and he turns his head back to face me.

"Something funny?" he asks.

"Like a man would ever put anyone before himself."

He studies me for a long moment. "I can see why you'd think that way, coming from the Garden."

"How do you think I wound up in the Garden?" I don't hide the contempt shaking my voice. "Another boy wanted me to put my faith in him once, too, and that turned out so well for me."

He places his hand lightly over mine that still clutches the cloth to my wound, and his eyes never leave mine.

"I'm sorry about what happened to you in the past, but I *will* prove you wrong now. I'm going to make you believe in me, not because I want you to, but because that's what you need."

Maybe it's the restless nights or my intense need to get out of this cage, but for a second, my breath catches. We stare at each other, two tiny sparks in the darkness with nothing to do but burn. Then he clears his throat, removes his hand, and looks away, snapping me out of the stillness of the moment.

"Anyway, you should bandage that now, since it's clean. Don't want it getting infected. Besides, you're expecting company."

I take the white bandage still sitting on the bed and wrap it around my clean wound. A creaking sound bounces off the walls as the iron door swings open. I shoot up like we've been caught doing something inappropriate, even though Rayce was already standing. He tosses a curious glance my way then walks over to the wooden table in the middle of the room as a stream of people flow into the cage.

"What's this?" I ask Rayce.

Even though I don't trust him, the feeling of betrayal sinks into my stomach. For the briefest second, it felt like we understood each other, and now it seems his whole act was a setup.

"This," he says, holding out his hands, "is the Zareen council, and we're here to decide if we can let you go free."

Frustration surges through me as I stare him down, and my hands curl into fists. The fresh white bandage stains red as blood releases from the wound. An irreversible mark not unlike the one Rayce just made on my heart.

# Chapter Twelve

Seven people crowd into my cell, shrinking the area considerably. Rayce sits on one of the stools in front of the table, crossing his arms over his chest as he stares at me. Arlo stands a few feet behind Rayce, his hand resting on the hilt of his stunner, and Oren, his arms full with a rolled parchment, a pot of ink, and a quill, sits on another stool next to Rayce. Marin guards the door in the back, and a girl with black hair chopped off just below her ears walks toward me, two people scuttling around behind her, all dressed in crisp brown robes with thick black bands tied around their waists.

The girl leading them stops in front of me, and her long fingers wrap around my chin before I can blink. Her skin chills mine more than the constant cold in the air, and her nails dig into my cheeks.

"Don't touch me!" I snap, jerking away from her claws.

"Let her look you over," Rayce says. "She's checking to make sure you're okay since you passed out from the Zarenite. It's only a safety precaution."

I clench my jaw and take a step backward. As the girl

stares at me with her cold eyes, I'm reminded of the emperor sizing me up the night I escaped, and my stomach rolls.

"She doesn't have to grab her without asking," Marin says, and I'm grateful for her input. Her prying might have been frustrating before, but she's the only one here now who hasn't tried to force her way into my personal space.

"You aren't to interrupt, Shing," the black-haired girl says, her voice completely devoid of any pitch. There's no rise and fall, no cadence, and somehow that makes her even more intimidating than if she were yelling.

"And you aren't my commanding officer, Piper," Marin says.

That name shakes me. This is the girl Rayce and the others were talking about over the fire pit. They were trying to rescue her sister before I interrupted their plans by trying to take Rayce hostage. I wonder if she knows what happened and is angry with me. I turn back to her, searching for any trace of what she might be feeling, but her soulless eyes don't reflect anything. The corner of her mouth finally turns down an inch, like I'm a bug that she can't decide whether to pin or squash.

"Take this down," Piper says, snapping her fingers.

The man and woman standing behind her with parchment each begin to scratch away as she speaks.

"Body heat elevated, obvious signs of sleep deprivation and dehydration, but whether they are directly related to ingestion of Zarenite remains to be seen." Piper taps her finger on her chin for a moment, her eyes drilling into my face. "This girl is the reason Kyra is still locked up. What a waste."

Her comment answers my previous question, though I gather from the snarl on Marin's face that her rudeness isn't an unusual occurrence. I press my lips together, forcing down the rising need to pummel this girl. I won't ever get them to trust me if I attack her.

"That's enough now," Oren says. "Rose couldn't have planned to interrupt the rescue of your sister if she didn't know about it."

"Unless she did know about it," Piper says, walking back to stand near Arlo. She tucks her hands into her long sleeves and stares directly at me. "It's entirely possible the emperor had prior knowledge of Zareeni presence that night and her act was an assassination attempt on our leader's life."

Her accusation presses down on me as if she had her foot planted on my back, but I resist the urge to look away. Instead, I stare straight back into her dead eyes.

"That's what we're here to figure out," Rayce says.

The quietness that washes over the room is so complete the constant drip of water sounds like a waterfall. Every eye on the room focuses on me clinging to the dirty robe that still hides what's left of my sparkling Garden outfit. I feel more exposed now than when I perform. At least then they're all faceless bodies in the crowd, passing judgment on me without the added pressure of knowing their names, the way their voices sound.

"Why don't you come sit?" Rayce asks, but the firmness in his voice doesn't really give me a choice. He's completely morphed from the man who just cleaned my wound. In front of the council, he really is the leader of the rebellion, and I can see why the Imperial City is so frightened of him.

He tilts his head toward the stool across the table, directly in the patch of light.

My every step feels like I'm walking into the open jaws of a cobra, the splash of light momentarily blinding me. I slide onto the stool, the rough edge of the wood sticking through my thin white robe. Suddenly, I'm onstage again, the burning spotlight focused on me as I drop from the sky. But this time I don't have my rope to catch me.

Even though my breath comes out in ragged puffs, I stare into Rayce's dark eyes, unwilling to waver. I place my hands on my knees, and Oren leans over the table, his stool squeaking under his enormous body.

"You cut yourself?" Oren asks, breaking the tension. "Are you all right?"

Rayce and I share a glance, both remembering the moments before the council came pouring in.

"I'm fine," I say. "Thank you for your concern."

Rayce places his palms on the table in front of him, showing me he has nothing to hide, and leans back an inch. "I asked you to convince Zareen you aren't an assassin," he says. "That you weren't sent by my uncle to crush or divide us. And I need you to do it now. We're responsible for every soul in the rebellion, and we won't let you out of here until we know without a doubt that we can trust you. So, please, convince us."

He raises a hand toward me, signaling that I should begin. I take a deep breath and grip the edge of my stool with shaking hands.

"I don't know how you want me to do that," I say.

Piper lets out an annoyed snicker at my words.

I level her with a glare. "I've told you numerous times that I chose you randomly. The room was full of elite soldiers and Rayce looked the most unassuming."

"Thanks for that," Rayce says, humor leaking into his voice.

"You expect us to believe you selected the rebellion leader by coincidence?" Piper asks. "The odds of that are preposterous when you calculate how many people were in attendance. Besides, if you wanted an easy target, why not one of the women?"

"Are you implying women are incapable of fighting back?" Marin asks, touching the hilt of her sword.

"In a crowd filled with the emperor's soldiers, the likelihood is far higher that a woman would be a more favorable target."

"Even I know the emperor won't allow women to serve in the imperial army," I say, cutting off their debate. "And I needed someone with a weapon for my plan to work."

"See, she had a good reason," Marin says and sticks her tongue out at Piper.

I work hard to keep a straight face when Marin gives me a quick wink.

"That's fine," Arlo says from behind Rayce. "But the way you can prove to us that you aren't a threat is to tell us what you know about the treaty between the emperor and your former master."

I stiffen at Arlo's mention of the Gardener. I knew from the beginning that information would be how I got myself out of this cage, but all I have is gossip, and I'm not sure that'll be strong enough. The Gardener's portion of the deal is fairly easy to guess—legalization has always been the key to sustaining his horror show long-term—but what he's giving in return is a far more terrifying topic.

Fern's warning that it has to do with one of my secrets rings in my ears. I can feel her hands warm on my cheeks as she pleads with me not to let the Gardener go through with the deal.

I was supposed to save my sisters. Fern gave her life for this purpose, and I failed.

"Cooperation, Rose," Rayce says, cutting into my thoughts.

But I can't tell them about my part in the deal without revealing everything about my past, and if I do that, I'll never get a chance to save my family. No, I'll have to give them something else. Something less dangerous.

"You have to understand," I say, picking my words

carefully. "Flowers are lower than the dirt underneath the Gardener's feet."

"She doesn't know anything," Piper snorts.

"I didn't say that," I snap. "I just wanted to be clear that whatever I tell you is just speculation. Things I've been able to gather by overhearing conversations and talking with the others."

"Go on, child." Oren gives me an encouraging nod.

"The Gardener has always wanted to be deemed a legal business by the emperor," I say. "And he's been determined to set up a permanent business in Imperial City, since that's where the majority of coin lives and where most of the soldiers report back to."

"It stands to reason that if Galon was able to strike a deal with the Garden," Oren says, writing something down on a fresh sheet of parchment, "he would get a cut of any coin coming in."

"Which would mean more gold for the imperial bank," Rayce says.

"Not to mention a new form of entertainment," Arlo adds, scratching his chin. "Which, coupled with the first festival in ten years, would make the emperor appear to be listening to the people's demands."

"Weakening the rebellion's stance in Imperial City," Oren says. "And strengthening the emperor's reach."

"Plus, the Gardener is in possession of some of the most deadly men in Delmar," I add. "He employs a lot of dangerous ones in his troupe. Those the army passed up or who were discharged for their murderous tendencies."

Shears's face comes to mind.

"We've already inferred this," Piper says. "Speculation is as meaningless as her attempt to save her own life."

I narrow my eyes at Piper.

"She's *confirming* what we speculated," Rayce says.

"True," Arlo says, straightening. "But Piper's also correct."

I get the sense by how quickly Arlo agrees with both of them that he often plays the role of moderator between them.

"What we need to know," Arlo says, "is what the Gardener is trading for his permanent residency."

All eyes turn toward me as the question lingers in the chilly air. I keep my expression blank, because my entire life depends on this performance. I know my past is involved; Fern confirmed it. But they can't know.

*What else did she say?*

My mind revolts against the idea, but I close my eyes and picture the cage where I spent the good part of ten years. I can feel the straw poking through my thin traveling sack, can hear Fern's breathing filling up the space, can feel the helplessness of our promise as she was murdered just outside those wooden walls.

She said the deal had to do with something about me and that glowing rock…

My eyes flit to the Zarenite still lighting up the space. That's why it looked so familiar the first time I saw it! I know how I'm going to convince them without having to reveal anything about myself. Sending a little thanks to Fern, I turn to Rayce.

"The Gardener has a chunk of your Zarenite," I say.

The scratching of Oren's quill ceases as my sentence settles in the air. Rayce shifts on his stool, and Arlo lets go of the hilt of his stunner.

"He stole it from a man back in Nan Zun a few weeks ago," I say.

"That town is very close to us," Oren says, sifting through his parchments until he finds the one he's looking for. He flattens it out on the table, and I see a roughly drawn map of Delmar in black ink.

Rayce leans in, peering at the place Oren points to, and

Marin stands on her tiptoes, trying to see over him.

"Do you know if the Gardener has any information on where the Zarenite was found?" Arlo asks.

I bow my head. "No, I don't."

"This is troublesome," Oren says. "But also very useful information. Thank you for sharing it with us, Rose. You might have just saved us from a surprise attack."

Despite my best effort, the hint of a smile finds its way onto my lips at Oren's praise. I keep my head lowered so no one can witness that slip.

"She may have," Piper agrees. "But how can we assume the information is credible? We've already made it clear that her freedom is on the line, and it's been my experience that people will say almost anything when something precious is at stake."

*Give me a moment to breathe!* I open my mouth to argue but realize I don't know how to answer her question. I don't have any proof besides my own words.

"That's easy to fix," Marin says. "Where'd you find that information out from?"

"I saw the Zarenite myself. And I found out it was part of the deal from another girl. From Fern."

Rayce looks up, recognizing the name, and I meet his dark eyes.

"Fern lost her life for talking to someone from the rebellion about this," I say, my gaze flicking to Piper. "I wouldn't lie about it."

Arlo leans over, a hand on Rayce's shoulder. "You said she was speaking to someone from the rebellion? Was it Bái?"

"I didn't get a name," I say. "I only saw—"

"Was he well?" Arlo asks, cutting in. "Or did he get captured? We lost contact with him about a week ago."

"If it was him, he's dead," I say. "I only saw the head of a man the Gardener threw at Fern before he killed her, too."

The silence in the room echoes louder than the creak of the door to my cage. Even Piper's usual blank demeanor looks shaken by my last statement.

Oren straightens to his full sitting height and puts a hand out, clutching mine in his. His movement is so quick I don't have time to pull away before my hand disappears under his bear claw.

"Child, I'm so sorry for the things you've been through," he says. "Thank you again for the information you know. It must have been horrific, but at least we can finally tell Bái's family the fate of their loved one, and they can have some comfort in that knowledge."

The dripping water in my cell suddenly becomes the most interesting thing in the world. Anything not to look at Oren, because I don't think I could hold back the tears threatening to spill if I saw his face.

"I think we've heard enough." Rayce rises to his feet.

And this is where all his pretty words crumble and turn to ash. He has what he wants from me now, so there's no need to pretend anymore. I expect him to keep walking, tell the guard at the door to lock it up tight after the council has left, and leave me to rot underneath the ground.

Instead, he turns to every face in the room and back to me. "I don't believe Rose poses a threat to the rebellion, and I'm confident we can release her into the rest of our base under supervision."

*What?*

"I'm...free?" I blink, the concept sounding foreign to my ears. Did he really just keep his word and let me go after I told him everything I was able to piece together? A half grin slips onto his face as he studies my dazed reaction.

"That's an expeditious decision," Piper says.

"I second his decision," Oren says, letting go of my palm.

"Third it," Marin says, throwing her hand up in the air.

"You're not a member of this council, guard," Piper snaps.

"And yet I'm still smart enough to realize she isn't a threat. Maybe I should take your place."

"Shing," Arlo says, his voice full of warning. Marin rolls her eyes and bows her head. Arlo turns to Piper. "I'm in agreement with the shogun. Rose gave us solid information."

Piper blinks at him, but if she feels betrayed by Arlo's vote against her, she doesn't show it.

"It's settled then," Rayce says, turning on his boot to head toward the iron barred door. "Marin, show Rose to a room."

He kept his word. The rest of the group begins to follow Rayce to the exit, and as I see their backs turning on me, my mind pauses in its shock long enough for me to realize something. Something so important that it causes me to stand, the stool I was sitting on crashing behind me in my haste.

"Wait!" I say, my voice loud in the small room. "I have something I want to say."

Hand touching the iron bar, Rayce turns back to me, an eyebrow cocked in curiosity.

"You stopped me from saving the other dancers in the Garden because you thought I was a threat." I close my mouth, not wanting to say the next thing I know I have to say. I take a deep breath. "I know that you probably also stopped me from getting captured that night. And it's made me realize that I can't fight against the Garden alone. I want to know... will Zareen help me rescue the other girls still trapped there?"

I can see my sisters' faces as clearly as if they're in the room with us: Calla and Lily and Juniper and Star and Sickle, painting the room in a familiar glow. The fact they're still stuck in that horrid place kills me, and the indecision that passes over Rayce's expression is a close second. Especially since admitting I could use their help leaves me so exposed.

Rayce's brow furrows, and I can see a war raging behind his eyes. The gentle way he touched my hand while he cleaned my wound comes unbidden to my mind, and I pray to whatever Delmarion god is listening that I get that tender side of Rayce to listen now instead of the stern man that judged me a few moments ago.

"I think—" Rayce begins.

"I would exercise extreme caution," Piper interrupts. "The troops are already distributed thinly and with the recent reports from Dongsu..."

"Piper's right," Arlo says. "We're barely surviving here, but if we keep fractioning our forces, we might give the emperor the advantage he needs."

Rayce's grip on the iron bar tightens, and a pained look passes over his face. He takes a moment to smooth his features.

"I don't agree with anything to do with the Garden," Rayce says. His eyes cut me in two. "And I sympathize with your need to help those you love. However, I can't spare any of my forces for a separate mission at the moment. Not yet. If you stay and can prove yourself worthy of Zareen, we will revisit this discussion. You have my word."

The word of a man has burned far too many Flowers for it to mean anything to me, even if Rayce did decide to keep it once.

He pauses at the edge of the door, scratching the back of his neck. He doesn't look back as he says, "You've made it clear that my word doesn't mean much to you right now, but it will. I'll keep this promise, too."

I clench my fists as they file out of the room. When I escaped, I never saw myself asking for another man's help, and yet I resorted to that very thing, as if I were still a captive in the Garden, begging on my knees. I've heard all of these promises before from another's lips. Park made me believe in him only to betray me in the worst way possible.

"Have some faith in our young leader," Oren says, standing. "It'll all work out. I have a good feeling about it."

He gathers up the parchments and quills spread out on the table but leaves a small dark blue book. He nods toward it. "I selected that for you from my library. I believe you'll enjoy it, when you get a moment to read."

The urge to ask him if I look like someone who would waste my time reading rises up, but I push it away and turn as he shuffles out the door.

Rayce's words stung more than I'd like to admit, but I have to believe he meant it when he said he would reconsider my request later. It isn't like I haven't seen proof they're struggling in the short time I've been here, I remind myself, between their failure to save Piper's sister and the food supply cart that resulted in the rebellion force being wiped out.

I just hope by the time Zareen can help me, there's something left to save.

# Chapter Thirteen

I turn away from the door until the sound of retreating feet stops, preferring to stay in my cage instead of following them around like a begging puppy. I understand Rayce's decision, why he said they need to wait, but it doesn't make it hurt any less.

I gather up the cherry-colored blanket on my bed and spin around, surprised to see Marin still in the cage with me. She flips through the book Oren left for me with only a marginal interest then snaps it shut.

"Looks like we're going to be sharing a room from now on," she says, tucking a curl behind her ear. "Hope you don't mind too much, but I've been told I snore. Of course, that was from Arlo, so who really knows if it's true."

I raise an eyebrow at her statement, and she tilts her head, trying to figure out what I don't understand.

"Oh, the Arlo thing!" she says, snapping her fingers. "Most people around here already know, so I forget sometimes. Arlo's my brother."

Now that she's told me, it's a wonder I didn't guess it from the moment I saw them in the same room together. Both have the same hair color that stands out in the rebellion, almost as much as mine does, and the exact same nose. On Arlo it looks masculine, but on Marin it's slightly too big to be considered pretty by Delmarion standards.

"Anyway, why don't we get going?" Marin flips the book in her hand and tucks it at her side. "I'm sure you want to be out of here as much as I do."

She walks over to the gate, and for a moment my gut drops as I imagine her slamming it shut on me. It's something the Gardener liked to do—promise me time out in the sun just to throw the door closed in my face.

I walk over on shaky feet and hold my breath as I walk past the bars and into a small, crudely carved tunnel. Marin gives me a little smile, leaving the door ajar, and motions for me to follow her.

"I think you're going to like it here," she says as she leads me up.

The farther we walk, the warmer the air becomes. The constant chill that's slept with me since I stepped foot in the rebel base lifts from my shoulders. The tunnel walls smooth out, and large jars filled with Zarenite light up as we walk under them, showing the way.

Marin talks all through the maze of halls, turning left and then right like she has a map drawn on the back of her arm. She answers her own questions before I can respond. She's so distracted by her own conversation she doesn't notice I've stopped listening.

Her fingers grip my forearm. "Did you hear me?"

Apparently she did notice.

"No," I say. "I've been trying to figure out where we're going."

"There's no need," she says, nodding to a sheet of blue fabric covering an opening in the hall. "We're here."

Maybe the maze is another way to make sure I don't run.

She holds back the curtain and lets me walk in first.

Though it's a little smaller than the cell I was locked in, the tension drops from my bones as I enter the bedroom. Everything from the cheery blue quilts covering the beds to the wobbly little desk and refurbished stool tucked up next to it screams recycled furniture. It looks like each piece was pulled from different people's homes as they were leaving in a hurry. The three-drawer dresser has more nicks and chips in the wood than I can count. Every mismatched piece has been touched by many hands; it all has history, a past it's not running from.

Marin points to the bed on the right farthest from the entrance. "That'll be yours. I've been using this one."

I walk over to it and smooth out the ruffled quilt before sitting on the edge. The woolly fabric is soft against my bare legs, and I run my good hand over it.

"Anyway," Marin says, plopping down onto her bed, "I was saying that I've never seen the shogun look at anyone the way he looked at you during the council meeting."

I make myself busy folding the red quilt I brought up from my cage, careful not to show her my blushing face.

"I have no idea what you mean," I say.

"What were you two doing before we came in there?" she asks.

My wound stings in response, and I turn over my hand to see that the bleeding seems to have stopped.

"I cut myself accidently," I say. "Rayce was just helping me clean it."

She snorts. "That sounds like him." She flips over onto her stomach. "Have you eaten yet? We had supper about an hour ago, but I could go for another portion."

With all the stress of the impromptu interrogation, I hadn't thought about food, but now that Marin's mentioned it, my stomach growls angrily.

"I could definitely eat," I say.

"Great!" She rolls off the bed. "I'll grab us some food. Why don't you change while I'm out? There are some fresh clothes in the top dresser, and I've got a spare set of boots you can borrow if we're the same size." She motions to a pair of worn brown shoes sitting next to the dresser. "Oh, and don't forget about this!"

She tosses the book Oren left for me onto my bed on her way out then disappears behind the curtain. I wonder what she meant about the way Rayce looked at me. The feeling of his breath cooling my stinging cut floats through me, and my cheeks heat again.

I walk to the dresser and run my hand over its marked wood. Sitting on top of it in the middle is a tall statue of Yun carved out of onyx on a bed of pine needles and dried berries. An offering meant to keep death out. As if that would work.

I scoff at the statue, picking it up by the bulbous head, and turn it around so its eyes face the wall. Satisfied, I open the top drawer and find a fresh pair of clothes. I shed both the soiled robe Rayce gave me and my costume, throwing the last bit of the Garden onto the floor. I slide into a fresh white under robe and pull over it a yellow cotton robe embroidered with cranes. Marin's boots are a hair too big but they'll do for now.

Heading back to my bed, I trip over the dirty clothes on the floor. Unsure what to do with them, I stuff the tattered robe underneath the bed. My fingers catch on the sequined chiffon skirt of my Garden costume, and I clench my jaw. Before I can dwell too much, I rip a strip of fabric off and shove the costume with the nasty robe where it belongs.

Plopping back on the bed with the thin piece of fabric in my hand, I watch as the glitter dances in the Zarenite-fueled light. I notice the book Marin tossed on my bed and pick it up.

Printed on the dark front in silver letters, like stars in the night sky, are the words *A Collection of Essays on the Rise and Fall of Varsha.*

With a shaking finger, I reach out to trace the name of my home, anticipating the slightly rough texture of the cover.

Why would Oren give me this?

I open the cover and slide the scrap of fabric into the first page like a bookmark.

His questioning about the star-shaped scars on my feet—a brand given to me at birth—his insistence on telling me about the current state of Varsha, and now this book all swirl in my mind. Even if he believes I might know more than I'm letting on about what happened the night Varsha fell to that traitor's hands, what's he trying to say?

The feeling of his large hand cupping mine when he found out about Fern and the honest ache in his dark eyes mixes with the pit forming in my stomach. I don't want to believe such a kind man might betray me, but I've learned that *no one* can be trusted.

A cold sweat trickles down my back.

No matter what message this book was meant to send, one thing is certain: I have to find out what Oren knows, or everything I've been working for could be gone in a flash.

• • •

I haven't slept on something this soft in as long as I can remember, and still I toss and turn all night, thinking about the book Oren gave me that I shoved under my pillow. It remains there, a thick lump underneath the fluffy surface, seeping into my thoughts.

Marin wakes sometime later and motions for me to follow her. She leads me through another maze of tunnels on the way to breakfast.

"I have drills this morning." She pats the hilt of her sword.

"Maybe you could come with me."

"Do I have a choice?" I ask. "You're supposed to watch me at all times, right?"

She frowns, her brow crinkling as she thinks about my statement.

"Well, you could go back to the room," she says, her finger on her chin. "I guess I could station someone to sit with you, but wouldn't you rather learn how to fight? That way, next time you put a knife to someone's throat they'll have a harder time disarming you."

"And I'll have an even harder time convincing the next group of rebels that catch me that I'm not an assassin."

She giggles, a high-pitched sound that reminds me of bells, and I instinctively step in front of her to shield her in case a lackey might have overheard us laughing, but then I remember where I am.

We walk down one of the larger tunnels I've been in, wide enough to fit about ten people shoulder to shoulder, and judging by the sea of people filtering through the large space I realize it must be one of the main walkways.

Women pass us, huddled in little groups carrying fresh laundry, jars of Zarenite, and sewing kits, while others carry swords. A man bumps into me, curving to avoid a small group of children tossing around a ball.

Every time I saw Rayce's wanted parchment, I imagined the rebels were like the lackeys in the Garden, but now that I'm among them, I realize Rayce is fighting to protect not only his guards but also their families.

"This is the dining hall," Marin says, pulling me from my thoughts. "It's my favorite place besides the training room."

The low, slanting hallway breaks into a room twice as big as the inside of the Garden's show tent, with soaring ceilings. It does something very few things have ever accomplished since my tenure in captivity: it makes me feel small.

Sloping wooden bridges are suspended high above our heads, connecting passageways from one side of the room to the other at varying heights. They look like a piece of stitching Tulip's broken mind might have attempted, crisscrossing through the cavernous room in no apparent pattern.

The entire room curves like a beehive, and rivets dug into the stone wall spiral down from the dome ceiling like spiderwebs, directing water from somewhere on the surface to wooden troughs on the ground. The same bright green glow from Zarenite saturates the walls, pooling on the floor and showering everything in an emerald tinge, like prisms bouncing through a crystal.

"We're on the second breakfast rotation," Marin says, diving into the crowded room.

The buzz of voices, plates clinking, and chairs scraping all blends together into a symphony of pleasant noise. Almost every seat tucked into five long tables is occupied as people go about their day.

Three younger girls giggle to each other as they walk down the main aisle toward us, their plates filled with eggs, warm rice, bright red apples, and thinly sliced vegetables. My stomach feels like a squeezed orange as the smell of cooked eggs and ginger saturates the air.

"I like it better that way," Marin continues, cutting around a man carrying a bowl of steaming clear soup. "We get to eat all the leftovers."

She heads toward the back of the room where three large openings have been carved into the stone, revealing a room about half the size of this one, with low ceilings, where fifty people buzz around cooking for the rush.

As we line up to pick through the buffet, I catch sight of a familiar tall figure among the many women in aprons. Rayce stands over a steaming pot, wielding wooden chopsticks with more confidence than a sword as he flips steamed buns over on a wire rack suspended on the pot's lid. He fishes one out and blows on it before popping it into his mouth. A smile finds its way to his lips as he closes his eyes to savor the taste.

An older woman comes up behind him, saying something, and he nods before pulling the pot off the stove to serve his food to the next person in line.

Whatever he says as he plops two buns onto a man's plate makes him laugh, and I'm surprised by the genuine happiness on the man's face.

"You're certainly staring pretty hard," Marin says, her voice singsonging through my daze.

I blink twice, turning my head back to my plate, which I've haphazardly loaded up with more rice than any one person could ever dream of eating.

"I'm just hungry," I say, moving along the line, careful to avoid looking at the steamed buns.

"Looks like you're hungry for something hot and steamy," Marin says, laughing.

We make our way through the line, Marin filling my plate with all the things she wants me to try, but she must sense my hesitance to approach Rayce and doesn't insist we grab what he made. Even though I'm relieved at not having to speak with him after being caught staring, nothing I wind up with looks half as appetizing as the food he made.

We head back to the main dining area, which is now half empty, leaving plenty of seats to choose from. My gaze stops on a very tall man hunched over the table, eating his breakfast. I recognize Oren's neat black ponytail and unusually thick build, but I'm surprised to find he's eating alone.

Now that I've spotted him, I wonder if now is a good time to mention the book to Marin without sounding too suspicious.

"Marin," I say as she leads me in his direction. "Does Oren often lend books to people?"

She tilts her head at my question, nearly dropping the cup of water in her hand.

"Not really," she says. "I've tried to borrow a few before and he shooed me out of his office."

"I wonder why he gave me one, then," I say.

She shrugs. "You should go ask him. He's sitting right over there."

"I guess I could."

Marin nods, tipping her head to a group of two men and a woman dressed in the same deep green tunic uniform she wears. "I'll be right over there if you need anything."

She waves with her free index finger then heads in their direction.

Walking on the points of my toes to keep my heels from clicking, I walk past Oren, leaning over to see what he's doing. Tucked between his nearly empty plate of fish and rice is an open hardcover book and a piece of parchment that he's using to take notes.

In looped handwriting far too delicate for his large hand, he scribbles, "Deception wins wars with the least amount of casualties."

He doesn't look up as I pass him, so I sit a few chairs away and dig my chopsticks into the mountain of rice like I'm not interested in what he's doing. While his nose stays planted in the book he's reading, I take my time studying his face, trying to pick up any detail that will reveal his intentions.

Apart from the fact he has a small mole on the top of his left cheek, I don't learn anything new. I jab my chopsticks into the rice again and take a huge, unsatisfying mouthful.

"If you have a question for me, child, just ask," Oren says.

I jump, nearly choking on the rice sticking in my throat. I take a large gulp of water. "How long have you known I was here?"

He pats the seat by his side without looking up from his

book. "Since you came out from the food line."

I frown, shoving my plate across the table and then plopping down next to him. I'm acting like a child, but I don't care.

The hint of a smile touches his mouth.

"What can I do for you?" he asks, snapping his book shut.

I pick up a grain of rice, balancing it between both chopsticks.

"I guess—" I stop, not sure how much I should reveal. Oren lays his large hand on the table, and the memory of it enveloping mine when he found out about Fern gives me the courage to continue. "I wanted to know why you gave me that book on Varshan history."

He raises a bushy eyebrow, and my gut drops.

"I mean, it isn't like my family was important enough to be in there," I say. "So it wouldn't really be relevant to me anyway."

Our gazes meet, his brown eyes partially obscured by a comically small set of round spectacles on the tip of his nose. I want to laugh, but the way he's staring at me feels just as intense as the way the emperor did. Not harsh but purposeful.

He's waiting for me to fill the silence. That's what the guilty do. I've seen it countless times when the Gardener would confront a lackey who'd bragged about stealing when he was drunk the night before.

"Just because your family might not be recorded between the pages doesn't mean you shouldn't be interested in the state of your home. When Varsha was taken by force, it changed everything."

I stare at my plate, no longer hungry.

"Is it true the man on the throne now was the previous king's general?" I ask, careful that my voice doesn't change tone.

"Yes," Oren says, pulling out his ornate dragon pipe. "It's a shame, too. Varsha was very impressive under the old king's regime. I quite enjoyed my time there."

Oren visited Varsha and knew the old king? I wonder when he was there, if I ever passed by him on the sandy streets of the large marketplace without knowing. He pulls out a small metal contraption and lights the tip of his pipe.

"I was given this by the previous ruler," he says, tapping the tip of the dragon's mouth. "I imagine it's one of the only remaining artifacts from his collection."

The dragon's jeweled blue eye stares me down, captivating me in its deep gaze. My fingers twitch at my side, longing to feel the cool ivory against my skin. Its beauty is unmatched and almost as enchanting as the thought of the man who gave it to him. Oren's smile widens, and he pulls the tip from his mouth, holding the heavy-looking device toward me.

"Would you like to touch it?" he asks. "I promise he won't bite."

He chuckles at his own joke.

I look away. "No, that's okay."

If he's suspicious of anything, he's clearly not going to clue me in through conversation. I grab my plate and stand up.

"I'd better hurry to practice with Marin," I say, still unable to look at him. "I appreciate you answering my questions."

Oren catches my wrist before I can move, his fingers gently wrapping around it. "Take care of yourself, Rose. I'm looking forward to watching you thrive here."

He lets go, turning back to his notes. I blink slowly and walk over to Marin, who rises with her group, her plate completely clean. My mind circles through the conversation I just had with Oren, trying to find a place where he slipped up but always coming back to his last words. After so many years in the Garden, I never thought I'd see any man show concern for me the way Oren has. Almost like a father.

I push the thought from my head.

But I can't fight against the smile that slips onto my mouth as I head with Marin into the training room.

# Chapter Fourteen

Training with the Zareeni guards pushes any thoughts of not sleeping tonight out of my head. By the time Marin and I crawl back to our room, I have aches in muscles I didn't even know existed. My eyes refuse to remain open even before my head hits the pillow.

The piercing peal of a flute stretches out into the night, wrenching me from a deep sleep. I jump up, the chill of the rock floor seeping into my bare feet. The world around me swirls, all gray stone and blackness. In the dreariness, the only thing that stands out is the stark white bandage wrapped around my hand. I press my eyes closed to stop my churning stomach and grit my teeth against the sound of Fern's scream rising to meet the flute.

I force my eyes open to stare at the bandage, willing myself to stay in the present. But I'm slipping, crumbling to the floor, knees hitting cold stone, and I only vaguely register it. I'm being pulled back. Back to the night the Gardener captured me and my life changed forever.

*My caretaker, Hanna, leads me back to that dark room*

*where the family that hid me let me stay with their daughter, Zara. It's so small it barely fits a rickety, old armoire and the bed Zara and I share. The scratchy cream sheet is pulled up past my nose, and Zara's deep breathing fills the night. Something slamming in the next room wakes us, and we both sit up. The screaming that follows sends my fingers underneath the pillow for the knife I'd stashed there.*

*Zara dives under the bed, but I tuck myself under the armoire. We both stay still, staring at each other while the screaming continues.*

*Footsteps on the wooden floor. The creak of the door opening on rusty hinges. And then I see him. The man that would become my tormentor stands in the doorway, but just in front of his bulbous belly is Park, the boy next door.*

The first time we spoke had only been through scraps of paper pushed back and forth across a clothesline the buildings shared. He was three years older than me, about the same age difference as Zara and me, but he never treated me like a child. Those secret scribblings had grown quickly into hide-and-seek and sneaking sweets and dreams of a future I thought I wasn't allowed to have anymore.

"I'm afraid they'll find me," I whispered up into the stars one night.

"Who?" he asked, and because he'd kissed my knee when I'd fallen yesterday, I knew I could trust him.

"The people who want this," I said and showed him the ruby I'd stolen from Hanna the night before just to have a piece of my mother near me.

He turned to me, took my hand in his. "Don't worry. I won't let anyone hurt you. I promise."

And for the first time since I left the safety of my father's arms, I felt safe.

*But his words turn to ash now, standing in the doorway of Zara's room as he nods toward the bed.*

*"They sleep there," he says.*

*Two lackeys move around him then stop in front of the bed. I lock eyes with Zara, still terrified from her mother's dying screams. Then she's ripped from under the bed by her ankle. Dangled in the air by one of the lackeys.*

*"That's not her," Park says.*

*She's found wanting. Throat sliced. Blood. Dripping.* Plop, plop, plop *on the floor.*

*A tiny gasp escapes my mouth as I stare transfixed into the deep crimson puddle.*

*I turn back toward Park, sure he'd be horrified at what he just witnessed, but when I meet his gaze, his eyes are no longer soft.*

*"There," he says, pointing to me.*

*A hand reaching for me. I swipe the blade at it, but I've forgotten my training.*

*I scream out* why? *Why would he betray me? But he doesn't answer.*

Only when we returned to that tiny town years later did I manage to convince one of the men that attended our show to reveal that Park's father was in debt. There was no doubt that the murder of four innocent people and my enslavement was the reason his family could afford to move into a much larger home a few days later. *I struggle in the lackey's grasp, kicking out. But I know I'll die, too. Until I meet the eyes of the man who will be my captor for the next ten years, and I realize there are things much worse than death—*

Arms wrap around my shoulders, restraining me, and I flail, trying to break free. Maybe they'll drop me and I can escape.

"Rose, calm down," comes a raspy voice from behind me. Rayce?

My eyes snap open, and I try to force my arms apart, but strong hands keep me fixed in place.

"What's wrong? Are you hurt?" Rayce's hands slide halfway down my arms, checking for wounds.

"Let me go," I snap between heavy breaths. "It's all lies."

He immediately releases me, and I shuffle away from him, sweat dripping into my eyes as I push myself against the bed. The warmth of his touch smothers me. I pull my hair away from my neck, trying to cool down.

"What are lies?" he asks.

"Everything." I lock my gaze onto his, hoping he understands I'm including him in that statement. "Where's Marin?"

Rayce remains on his knees, his hand outstretched like he's waiting to catch me if I fall. He doesn't even have the decency to look smug that he's seen me so weak. His brow furrows at my mood, and his eyes show the worst kind of sin—pity.

"Marin reported with the others for our mission," he says. "She's probably checking in with her platoon now."

"Oh." Relief washes over me. At least she didn't see me cowering on the floor.

After a moment of silence, he clears his throat. "What were you thinking about? You didn't seem…here, exactly."

My cheeks burn from embarrassment, but a crippling fear of being alone in the middle of the darkness scares me worse than talking. Even if it is to him.

"About the night I was taken into the Garden," I say.

He rubs his face, the scratchy sound of his fingers dancing over the stubble filling the air. It takes me a second to realize he's hiding his shock, but whether it's at the fact that I even answered him or over what I was thinking about, I don't really know.

"There was word of little girls going missing in the town I was passing through with my guardi—" I stop then correct myself. "With my mother. Not that the warnings mattered.

Not when someone you thought you could trust betrays you. Besides, when the Gardener wants something, he gets it."

"You're still scared of that night, even now?"

I swallow the knot in my throat and look away, to the rumpled red blanket on my bed flowing down to touch the floor like blood.

"It's mostly their screams," I say. "I've heard so many since I came to Delmar."

His face freezes, and his hands flicker out like he wants to touch me, but he catches himself.

"What did you just say?" he asks, shock radiating from his eyes. He shakes his head, seeming to think better of his question. "Never mind. Don't answer that."

He takes a breath and clears his throat, leaving me to wonder why he didn't want me to answer him. "Does this happen often?"

"Why do you care?" I ask.

His brow knits at my retort. "Because while you're staying here, you're my responsibility. I just want to understand you a little better."

I sit back, wrapping my arms around my knees and study him. One second he's swinging an iron-barred door in my face, and the next he's trying to understand me. Though there is something honest about the way he looks at me and his simple explanation that I can't deny.

I take a deep breath. He wants to know me better, fine. "Every time I close my eyes since I escaped, I can't blink without seeing one of my sisters' faces. That's why I have to save them."

My instinct to ask him for help again hangs on the tip of my tongue, but I bite my lip, keeping it locked inside. Oren's suggestion to have a little faith in Rayce repeats in my head. I look over the leader of the rebellion, the man I saw happily cooking and serving his people yesterday morning, and my cheeks color for an entirely different reason.

He rubs both hands over his eyes and pulls in a deep breath.

"You should use that," he says.

"Use what?"

"That innocence." He rises and dusts himself off. "It makes people want to do things for you even when they know they shouldn't. If you ever get yourself caught in a tight situation, that'll be your best chance at survival, since we both know fighting isn't a strong point for you."

I'm not certain, but I think he's complimenting me. In a very roundabout way.

He holds his palm out. "Anyway, time to get up now. We're leaving."

His words lull me into a false sense of security, his open hand the snake waiting to strike.

"What do you mean?" I ask.

"Exactly what I said before. I want you to come on this mission with us. I think it'll go a long way in convincing the council to sway toward your case to help the other dancers." He half smiles, shaking his head. "Not that I should be telling you this."

He scoops up my arm before I can protest and pulls me to my feet. He's much more put together than the last time I saw him. Every black knot hook on his dark green shirt is fastened, and his long black sleeveless vest stops at the perfect height above his freshly polished boots. He looks more like the young prince he's supposed to be than any other time I've seen him.

"You'll need to put this on," he says, handing me a neatly folded pile of clothing.

I take the clothes from him, and we stare at each other for what feels like a long time.

"Are you going to leave so I can…?" I shake the pile of

clothes in front of me.

"Oh, right, yes, of course," he says, and I notice a faint blush before he swings around on his boot and nearly runs out past the curtain.

I press my nose to the pile of clothes he handed me, the scents of lavender and grass greeting me. I shake out the brown pants and glance up. Rayce's sturdy outline is silhouetted against the airy curtain, a breath away from being in the same room as I am. Not that I'm unaccustomed to men seeing my body, but the idea that *he* could stirs my stomach. I slide into the pants quickly. The deep green shirt matches the one I always see Marin wearing. My fingers fumble over the brown knot hooks, but I make sure to fasten each one.

"Can you tell me where we're heading on this mission?" I ask.

"Dongsu," he answers, his voice pressing in on me.

That name sounds familiar. I remember something about a failed food supply mission there and wonder for a moment what I'm getting myself into.

I let the final piece to the uniform out, a long brown vest, and run my fingers over the Zareeni crest sewn in white and silver thread. The intricate pattern creates a blazing sun surrounded by a tangle of knots in a diamond shape. It looks far more beautiful than anything I could have created, and I'm conflicted about putting it on.

If I wear this, does it mean I'm part of the Zareeni rebellion, supporting the same people who imprisoned me?

But what choice do I have? Rayce seems pretty certain that if I go on this mission with them, I can secure Zareen's help in rescuing my sisters, and that's far more important than my pride. The vest weighs heavily on my shoulders, but it takes away some of the chill from the air.

"Okay, I'm ready," I say.

Rayce pulls back the curtain and steps into the room.

"There's just one more thing to take care of," he says, pulling out a second sword and a stunner from his belt.

Even though he's made it clear he won't harm me, my heartbeat picks up as his fingers wrap around the sword's hilt. I have nothing to defend myself with.

"I wasn't sure which one you'd prefer," Rayce says, flipping the sword with a practiced hand so the hilt faces me. "Bear in mind, if you choose the stunner, you'll need to ingest another vial of Zarenite, and that didn't end so well last—"

"The sword," I interrupt. "Definitely the sword."

His mouth curves into a lopsided smile that I can't help but get tangled in, and he hands me the sword. The weight feels strange in my hands as the leather-wrapped hilt molds to my grip, much heavier than I remember, and I wish desperately it were the curved golden blade from my homeland.

"All right, follow me. We don't have much time."

Rayce heads for the curtain, holding it open so I can walk through. The narrow doorway feels impossibly small as I brush past Rayce's firm chest.

His eyes flicker over my face, and he pulls a piece of black ribbon out of his pocket.

"Tie your hair back," he says. "It'll get in the way of our mission."

Our fingers brush as he gives me the thick ribbon, and I can't help but wonder when he'd thought to set it aside for me. He doesn't wait for me to obey, and I get the sense from the easy way he walks down the hall that he just expects me to do whatever he says without question. My fingers fumble over one another as I quickly braid my hair and rush to stay by him in the maze of tunnels. As I secure the ribbon around the end, I remember the comforting feeling of Fern's adept fingers running through my hair.

Rayce turns at my quick footsteps, a crooked grin splitting his face. "Your hair looks good that way."

I toss the braid over my shoulder so it's no longer in sight and turn away from his gaze. He chuckles like he can hear my heart speed up from his compliment.

He walks with purpose, his feet stomping out a grueling pace for me to keep up with.

"So what exactly are we doing on this mission?" I ask.

"I'm sure you remember hearing about the food supply cart that went missing and that my entire squadron was wiped out."

I nod, not wanting to interrupt him.

"We have it on good authority that the city they were heading to has been occupied by Sun soldiers," he says. "And we can't have that. Not only is Dongsu a strategic point between the Imperial City and our base, but I can't let the townspeople come to harm because they've been assisting us. It's the rebellion's fault my uncle sent troops to occupy Dongsu, and we have an obligation to free them."

The determination behind his words leaves no room for questioning. He's clearly thought this mission through and believes it to be vital, even though it means putting his people in danger. I hate the tiny spark of admiration that flickers to life at hearing him speak and remind myself that no man can be trusted. Especially one in charge. "Why were you sending food supply carts to the town in the first place?" I ask.

"The recent drought has stretched far into this land," Rayce says. "Part of the rebellion's mission is to make sure all the people of Delmar have something on their plates at the end of each day. Piper's been working on more effective ways to farm, among many other projects, and since we have plenty, we need to share it."

Everything he says sounds beautiful. Like a dream. But I've learned far too many times that the most beautiful things are the most dangerous. I clutch the hilt of my sword.

As we move through the base, I catch glimpses of people

moving along their everyday lives through doorways and branches in the path, and I find myself wishing I could explore it more. Any time one of them notices Rayce, they pause in their work and bow their head, letting us pass unencumbered.

And he greets every person like they're part of his family, with a warm smile and most of the time by name.

I remember what he said about putting his people first, and my stomach twists. Was what he said actually the truth?

After ten minutes of sloping tunnels, we step through a doorway that opens into a large room. The quiet murmur of a crowd greets my ears.

Most of the men and women in the room wear uniforms identical to mine. Only a few people skirting the walls aren't in uniform, the vibrant colors of their shirts and long-sleeved dresses brightening the room. Mothers and fathers, sisters and brothers and other loved ones hug those in uniform with the ferocity of someone saying a final good-bye, and judging by the report I heard when I first got there, that isn't out of the realm of possibilities.

The crowd parts as Rayce steps through it, while I have to twist and turn to follow at his heels.

Marin catches sight of us and runs forward, her eyes bright.

"Are you coming on the mission?" she asks.

"It seems that way," I answer.

She lets out a squeal, clutching my free hand in both of hers.

"Then that training yesterday will come in handy!"

I look at her with uneasy eyes, the soreness in my muscles a reminder of how well the training went.

"Don't worry," she says. "I'm going to make sure you don't get into too much trouble."

"She shouldn't get into *any* trouble," Rayce corrects her.

"Right, no trouble at all," Marin says, winking at me.

Arlo stands at the front of the room, his long vest and knot buckles dyed a dark gray. As I search the room, I see some others in similar colors as Arlo, but no one wears black like Rayce. It must be a ranking system.

Back home, our military used colored cuffs to show rank, but all the colors could be found in precious metals — gold bracers were reserved for the king, chrome for the general, silver for the officers under him, following down the line to the black nickel bracers for the common foot soldiers. My father used to praise how practical the system was, since they could also be used for protection against incoming attacks to the wrists.

Arlo cracks a smile when he notices us and stands on the toes of his boots to look behind Rayce. "You were able to convince the Flower to come."

My skin crawls, hearing him use that word for me. Several people near Arlo turn at his remark, and their eyes land on me. I straighten my sleeves and avoid their gazes.

"I prefer the name Rose." I stare directly into Arlo's eyes. "*Just* Rose."

"I'm sorry," he says. "I meant no offense."

Keeping my face stern, I give him a quick nod.

"She didn't need to be convinced," Rayce says, breaking the awkward tension in the air. "She was eager to assist. Right?"

"Right," I agree, though my tone isn't nearly as convincing as Rayce's was.

Oren wades through the crowd, a head taller than everyone else in the room, smoke from his dragon pipe trailing behind him. He stops next to Arlo and pats Marin on the head.

"Be careful out there, child," he says, then turns to me. "That goes for you, too." He places his other large hand gently on the top of my head. My usual need to shrink away from touch doesn't come. "I'm praying to Yun that you both return safely."

"Thank you," I say, even though a prayer to his god will do nothing for me.

I used to believe in the Great Creatress, Fatima, the almighty Varshan goddess, but I decided after Fern received her second lashing—which nearly left her dead—that any deity who allows the Garden to exist isn't worth my prayers.

Rayce raises both his hands into the air, and all the guards fall silent, their attention locked on their leader.

"Thank you for gathering here," he says. "We'll be leaving in a few minutes, so please say your final farewells to your loved ones. I won't lie to any of you. I fully expect this mission to be dangerous, but you all have been tested in battle and proven yourselves more than capable. Those Delmarion soldiers think they can push us around—so let's go push 'em back!"

A cheer rises up at his words, and the energy in the room shifts into something electric.

"Is that even possible?" Arlo asks under his breath.

Rayce rubs his chin, his response muffled behind his hand. "I sure hope so."

His lack of confidence leaves a pit in my stomach that not even the comforting weight of the sword strapped to my side can fill. What awaits us in Dongsu, and will I be strong enough to face it?

# Chapter Fifteen

Rayce doesn't provide me with details about our mission, and I don't have time to ask. Marin stays next to me as we filter through a small opening in the tunnel Rayce made by pressing his hands against the stone, like the first time I came to the base. The narrow tunnel leads upward for what feels like hours, and with the fifty or so Zareeni rebels ahead of us, my lungs constrict.

We break aboveground just as sunlight paints the sky orange and move through thick forest. The twisting oak trunks grow in clusters, long branches reaching for the sky, and the ground is blanketed with dead leaves.

Besides the sound of feet crunching foliage, the group remains silent, leaving me to my worries. If I can't convince the rebellion to help rescue my sisters, will I stand a chance on my own? And what will I have to do at Dongsu to persuade them? My dry throat quivers as I swallow my unease before it spreads to my limbs.

After a few hours of trekking around trees, we stop in front of an opening. Standing on my tiptoes to see around a tall man in front of me, I catch sight of a patch of hard-trodden brown dirt in the form of a road.

On Rayce's signal, the large group of Zareeni guards spread into a formation that looks like a bird, flanking both sides of the road. About twenty guards move to the right and another twenty to the left, forming the wings. Rayce leads me and Marin, as well as the remaining ten people, into a pocket in the middle, keeping a good portion of his forces between us. He leans his head into Arlo, their whispers filling the morning air. Drops of dew that collected overnight sparkle on the tips of leaves like tiny crystals, the aboveground world reminding me why I longed to be free.

As we move west on the road, my eyes keep flicking toward Rayce, even though I should be scanning our surroundings, wondering what he and Arlo could be talking about and if that crease in his forehead means he's worried. By noon, sunlight filters through the green leaves above our heads and I lean my face toward it, welcoming the heat. Marin walks silently beside me, one hand resting comfortably on the hilt of her sword, humming quietly. Her curly hair bounces up and down in rhythm with her stride.

"Marin," I say, unable to stand the quiet any longer.

She turns to me, a smile on her lips.

"Why did you say we were going to be friends when we first met?"

"Because you looked like you could use a few," she says. "And besides, just because I'm tasked with guarding you doesn't mean we can't be friendly with each other, right?"

Despite my initial impression, I have to agree. I'm already starting to think of her as a friend.

"I want to ask you about the Garden," Marin continues. "But I think it might be rude."

A rueful smile slides onto my face despite my best effort to quell it.

"How about you tell me something about yourself first? Then it's just like we're sharing instead of you interrogating me."

"Okay!" she says, her tight curls bouncing up and down as she nods.

Her excitement fills me with warmth, and I realize living with Marin has been as seamless as living with Fern. The second I think her name, I can feel her fingers running through my hair. I clench my jaw against the overwhelming pain that comes with seeing her face in my mind.

"Something about me," Marin singsongs to herself. "Well, I hate my hair." She pulls a curl to emphasis her point, and we both watch it spring back up into place. "Really, I could do without all of my Varshan traits."

Her words snap my attention back to her face instead of her hair. "Why's that?"

She frowns, looking off into the tree line. "My entire life, I've never really fit in anywhere. The Delmarions only ever saw my thick jawline and light hair and thought me too Varshan to be friends with, and I'm sure the Varshans would hate my Delmarion upbringing. It's always felt like it's just been me and Arlo against the world."

"You seem to fit in well here, though."

She meets my eyes. "I adapted here. I learned at a young age that the only way to get along with people that were never going to like you is to kill them with kindness."

My fingers long to reach out and clutch her hand the way I'd comfort Fern when she was sad, but I keep them by my side.

"Did you join the rebellion because your brother did?"

"That's part of the reason," she says, her eyes somewhere faraway. "Arlo started meeting with Rayce and Oren to form the rebellion shortly after news came back that our parents' merchant ship was lost at sea. I think that's what made Arlo decide to go forward with it even though he was the one trying to talk Rayce out of starting it at first."

My brow furrows, trying to follow her logic. "I'm sorry to hear about your parents, but why did that change Arlo's view on the rebellion?"

Marin's grip tightens on her stunner. "Because there were rumors that the emperor was responsible for them not coming back. My family imported goods from Varsha. That's where my father met my mother. We were in competition with another family of merchants in Delmar. Unfortunately, the emperor married into our rival's family, and even though his wife died, he took over their business, and it was speculated that he didn't want any more competition."

I remember the feeling of the emperor's eyes digging into my skin as he paced around me, and I can picture him giving that order.

"Oren and Rayce tried to find proof before they split off to form the rebellion, but the emperor isn't known for leaving threads behind."

"That's horrible," I say, this time not fighting the urge to touch her lightly on the arm.

"Thanks." She pushes the hair off her forehead and looks into the sun. "Whew, I wasn't expecting to get into *this* conversation." She brings her fingers to her eyes in a wiping motion. "It's been a few years now, and revenge doesn't really sustain me."

"So then, why did you join the rebellion?"

She smiles, and it looks natural on her. "I remember slipping out of bed and tiptoeing down the hallways, sneaking past the guards and listening in as my brother and Rayce and Oren met late in the evenings to go over plans. I knew even then that I was going to be a part of the world they wanted to build."

"What did they say?" I ask, leaning closer to her. My

gaze darts around for eavesdroppers, but no one seems to be listening. Maybe they already know her story.

"Just what the rebellion would be fighting for. They want to bring a voice back to the people," Marin says. "For so long, we've been told by the emperor what jobs to do, whom to marry, what we can and can't say. There's no beauty, no art, no freedom to practice a religion other than his, no room for difference. No room for someone like me." She wraps her arm around my shoulders. "Or you, Varshan. But in the world we're fighting for, we'll all have a place. We'll all have the freedom of choice."

Her passion makes my world feel tiny. "And here all I want to do is free the Flowers and disappear."

Her eyes brighten with sincerity. "That's okay, too, Rose. You don't owe this empire anything. Not after what the Garden did to you. If I were you I'd ask Yun to curse us all."

"That's not what I meant."

Her hand tightens around the hilt of her sword. "It's what I would mean."

I turn away, trying to catch the breath that flew out of my lungs. Marin is the kind of girl who would have made it in the Garden—but if the rebellion helps me destroy the Garden, she'll never have to. No girl ever will again.

Without warning, the guards ahead halt, and I nearly slam into the man in front of me. Rayce marches to the front of our platoon and every head turns in his direction. In his crisp uniform, he looks the part of a shogun, dark eyes alert and sword at the ready.

"Dongsu is less than a mile out," Rayce says, shielding his eyes from the sunlight. "We're in dangerous territory now and need to use extreme caution. Sectors Sì and Wǔ, fan out and scout ahead. We'll wait for further intel before making any tactical moves."

Every hand forms into a fist and pounds on the right side

of the chest in response. Arlo makes his way across the road toward us as thirteen guards split off from the formation and divide into two sections.

"Shing, you're free to report to Wŭ," Arlo says to Marin. "The shogun and I will take responsibility for your charge."

Marin nods. "Yes, sir."

Her tone is brisk, but there's an echo of laughter behind her words. It must be strange being so formal with her brother. Giving me a wink, she turns on her heel and then heads to the left side of the road, making that group even with the section on the right.

Arlo rubs his fingers through his goatee, his eyes trained on Marin's retreating form.

"Shing," he calls out after her, the hint of a grimace touching his face. She turns at her name, and he says, "Be careful out there, okay? Remember your training, and at any sign of trouble—"

"I can do this." She gives him a reassuring smile. "I'll see you inside Dongsu, brother."

"Why did I let Rayce convince me to allow her to join our cause?" Arlo whispers, closing his eyes for a moment.

"She seems confident enough," I offer.

"That's what I worry about. She could have chosen to do anything in the rebellion; she had her pick. And she decided to be a scout."

Arlo and I watch as she connects with her unit and dives into the forest. The trees swallow her into their looming darkness like a beast's jaws.

Rayce walks up behind Arlo, and the smells of sugar and leather wash over me. "She'll be fine," he says, patting Arlo's shoulder. "Come on, we need to get off the road."

He gently tugs Arlo a few steps away from the spot Marin disappeared into, but I can't make my feet move. Seeing him up close again, with his neatly shaven face and well-fitting clothes, tramples any sense I had about me.

"You, too, Rose," he says, beckoning me backward. "We're responsible for you until Marin makes it back safely."

I follow them. We move with the remaining forty guards into the other side of the forest, stopping at a nearby clearing. The grass dotting the break in the trees lies broken and trampled, and the burned remnants of old fires dots the area. Someone must've used this as a base of operations before.

Twenty of the guards form a tight ring around the trees, each one holding a stunner at the ready as they scan the quiet forest for any sign of movement.

Rayce and Arlo stand on either side of me.

"I can't imagine the scouts will find much up ahead," Arlo says, looking to Rayce for confirmation. "The early reports detailed an unorganized force."

"That's right." Rayce nods.

Arlo shakes out his hands, shifting his weight to his left side and exhaling.

Rayce looks down at me. "But I would be prepared for some type of resistance when we breach the town."

"Thanks for the warning," I say, resting my hand on the warm hilt of the sword strapped to my side.

"If your skills with a sword aren't any better than with a knife, I'm not sure I'd rely on that too much," Rayce says, pulling a small cookie from a pouch at his side.

"That isn't very nice." I cross my arms over my middle.

Rayce chuckles at that. "You're kind of cute when you pout."

I swing away so he can't see my face, because the traitorous thing is suddenly on fire. Why should I care if he thinks I'm cute?

The sunlight bleeds through the thick treetops, casting bright yellow patches on the trampled grass. "Just stick by me if a scuffle breaks out," he says, then pops the morsel into his mouth. "If the forces are really as disorganized as the reports made them out to be, I can't imagine this taking more than an hour."

I furrow my brow as he talks around the cookie in his mouth. He closes his eyes for a second, relishing the taste, and looks so childlike I'm taken aback. He opens one eye, pulls another cookie from the pouch, and holds it out.

"It's sweet. You'll like it."

My growling stomach betrays me, and I snatch the cookie, trying hard to ignore the smug smile on his face — as if he thinks he's won some big battle instead of a silly argument. I throw the thing in my mouth, resolved to scarf it down with as little fanfare as possible, and a blast of syrupy honey explodes on my tongue. For such a small thing, it packs a flavorful punch, and despite my previous determination not to, I savor the taste.

"It's a honey crisp," Rayce says. "One of my earliest memories is of learning how to knead the dough under my mother's watchful eyes."

"Did you make this?" I ask.

"I did." He hands me another one. "I find cooking relaxing. Back in the palace, I wasn't permitted to cook. According to my uncle, it wasn't a skill fit for the throne. I don't bother with his nonsense now that I live at the base."

I run my fingers through the wavy end of my braid. "I saw you cooking breakfast yesterday," I admit.

He shrugs, popping another honey crisp into his mouth. "It's a small way I can give back, and I enjoy it. Being in the dining hall lets me meet with people I wouldn't normally get to see if I just stuck to the military."

"Well, your mother must be happy with your cooking skills now."

The smile he wore dies. "Probably not, since she wanted me to follow my uncle's succession and become the next emperor. I can't imagine she's happy with much of anything I do these days."

He rubs his face, his scar twisting as his brow furrows. Now that he's frowning, I find myself missing the way his lips looked when he smiled, and I wish we could go back to him teasing me. I'll take the smug look on his face over the sadness emanating from his dark eyes any day.

"That must be hard," I say.

He clears his throat. "Not nearly as difficult as trying to perfect her recipe without her input."

He offers me another cookie, and when I take it, my fingers brush his palm. It's callused, worn from years of sword training. My hands aren't smooth, either, but compared to his they must feel silky as petals.

"These really aren't bad," I say.

"Coming from you, I'll take that as the highest form of praise."

We take turns eating honey crisps as the moments drag on. He asks me what I think about Zareen and if I'm adjusting well. I can't tell if he actually cares or is trying to pass the time, but I find myself hoping it might be a little bit of both. As we talk, I'm acutely aware of the glances we receive from the rest of the troop and can't figure out whether they are looking to their leader for instruction or at the newcomer clinging to him.

With every ticking heartbeat, the panic in my chest spreads. How long do these scouting missions usually take? Did something go wrong?

Only when Arlo begins to pace back and forth do I realize my worry is justified. Looking up at the sky, I guess it's a few hours past noon at this point.

Sweat sticks the back of my uniform to my neck, and I pull my braid over my shoulder to let my skin breathe.

The lines under Rayce's eyes tighten. He stands and takes a step toward a man with long dark hair past his shoulders, but then the sound of twigs snapping to our left sends our attention that way.

An older man, in a uniform identical to the one I wear, stumbles through the woods, blood staining one of his pant legs.

Two of the guards in our circle formation break it, sheathing their stunners and running to help the injured man into the clearing.

Rayce breaks out in a sprint for the man, Arlo hot on his heels. I follow, my heart hammering in my chest.

The two guards lay the man down in a bed of dead leaves, and one of the women pulls a familiar-looking brown bottle and clean gauze from her pack.

"Report," Rayce says firmly.

The injured man nods, no longer paying attention to the other guards surrounding him.

"We walked into an ambush, Shogun." He winces as the woman presses a cloth to his wound. Rayce kneels next to him, and the man continues. "There was a Delmarion squadron waiting for us in the forest near town."

"The others?" Arlo says, his tone rising. "In Wŭ. Are they okay?"

The man shakes his head. "They were all captured. Your sister managed to convince them we were a lone group of intel scouts before they knocked her out. The only reason I slipped away was because the strange group of men didn't notice me."

Arlo presses his hands over his face. My stomach drops. *Marin.* I know better than anyone how harsh a cage can feel after tasting freedom. I hoped she'd never have to experience that. Now…

"What do you mean by strange?" I ask.

Rayce gives me a sideways glance and nods for the man to speak.

"They weren't Sun soldiers," he says, his voice shaking.

"They weren't even in uniform, but they definitely weren't friendly."

"Who would capture Zareeni rebels if not the emperor?" Arlo asks.

"Maybe soldiers in plain clothes," Rayce says, scratching his chin. "My uncle's done something like that before."

"We have to get them back," Arlo shouts over our conversation. "Now."

"We're going to," Rayce says. "But we need to act fast."

He stands, signaling for the rest of the guards to gather around. As they press into the clearing, space grows tighter, but even as I scoot closer to Rayce, it doesn't feel like we have nearly enough people.

"We're throwing away our element of surprise for speed," Rayce says. "We'll take the road. Every second counts. Fèng, Yù, stay here and tend to Li's wound. The rest of you, follow my lead. Hand signals only from this moment out."

The guards don't salute this time, turning sharply on boot heels and running back toward the road, eyes strained and mouths grim. Arlo leads the way, unhooking a stunner from his belt as he runs.

I turn to go and Rayce catches my arm. "Remember what I said. Stay close, okay?"

Not trusting myself to speak, I nod. He levels me with a stare like he's expecting something more from me. After a long moment, too long for the little time we have, he clenches his jaw and motions for me to follow him.

We sprint through the woods on reckless feet, branches scratching against my uniform as I jump over roots. All I can think about is Marin putting her arm around me the way Fern used to. She's the first friend I've made outside the Garden, and all of this feels terrifyingly familiar. I promised Fern that I would always have her back, no matter what.

But the last time I was in a dire situation, I let her die.

# Chapter Sixteen

The hard-packed dirt grinding under my boots as we sprint toward Dongsu feels a lot less friendly without Marin next to me. The troop was packed in four to a line by the time Rayce and I broke through the trees, and Rayce took his place in the middle, pointing for me to stand a row back. The moment I fell in line, Arlo held his palm out and all forty-something boots began to move in unison.

Twenty minutes into our trek, my lungs burn with exertion. The trees pass in a dizzying blur, and I push onward, even though my body screams to stop. I pin my gaze on Rayce's broad shoulders, forcing myself to keep moving through the exhaustion.

A few minutes more, and the road begins to slant upward. Unable to pick my footing well any longer, I stumble but keep moving, Marin's face pushing me forward. Arlo holds up a palm to halt as my vision blurs, and the entire troop stops a few feet from the top of the hill.

Water pouches unhook almost in unison as everyone works to catch their breath.

An eerie quiet clings over us like a veil. Rayce motions for me to follow him, and we head to the front of the group.

Arlo tips his head forward, and we crest the hill, Dongsu spreading out beneath us like a wagon wheel. A break in the rooftops in the middle of town must be some sort of square serving as the hub, and the dusty roads and alleys snaking out from there make the spokes. Houses and shops fill the spaces between the streets. The whole town would only take up half of the market district in Delmar. The forest stops about fifty feet from the town, like some invisible barrier bars it from growing any farther.

"Notice anything off?" Rayce whispers, his voice piercing after such a long stretch of silence.

"No people," Arlo says, finishing a gulp of water. "Not good."

I put my hand to my forehead, shielding my eyes from the sun, and look for any sign of life. All I see is a tiny shed at the edge of town. It looks like it sprouted up from the ground, fully formed and older than the dirt it came out of. The hands that built it are nowhere in sight.

"We're going to save her, Arlo," Rayce says, his voice hard with determination.

Arlo rubs his face, covering whatever worry his mouth might betray.

"We have to," I say.

Rayce flashes me a grim smile and nods.

The lump in my gut tightens, and I curl my hands into fists, letting my nails bite into the exposed flesh of my palms.

Rayce holds up his pointer and middle fingers pressed together and swirls them around in a tight circle. The troop responds immediately, marching forward to meet us at the top of the hill. We start our descent at a slow pace. Every stunner remains trained ahead, though there's no sign of movement.

I wipe my clammy palms on the scratchy fabric of my

pants as we near the bottom of the hill. The dirt becomes soft like sugar grains, and our feet sink, slowing us to a crawl. Almost like Lin, the earth goddess, is warning us not to go any farther.

Since there are no trees we can use for cover, Rayce opts to cut a direct path across the knee-length yellow grass. I fall in line right behind him, mimicking the way he scans left to right as we move forward. I'm not sure what I'm supposed to be looking for, so I keep scanning the shed and the areas around it for movement. My instincts scream to run, but I force every footstep steady. Sweat slicks my palm, making it hard to keep a secure grip on my sword.

The hair on the back of my neck prickles. Are we walking into a trap? My skin burns with the feeling of eyes on it, even though I'm not sure anyone is watching. We approach the shed at a snail's pace. Now that I'm closer, the white paint looks more like patches of snow, and the waterlogged roof sags from years of disuse. The shed is one strong breeze away from collapsing. Still, nothing stirs in the town just ahead. The deafening quiet of the empty streets sends a chill down my spine. No town would be completely dead during the middle of the day.

We step underneath the sunken roof of the shed, and the temperature drops. Cobwebs hang like streamers from the ceiling, and dust particles dance across sunbeams peeking in from the cracks in the roof. From where I stand, I have a clear view into town, but I still don't spot a single soul.

Rayce holds up a palm to pause the troop inside the shed. Though none of them speak, fear echoes out of each pair of eyes. No one likes what we've walked into. The sword strapped to my side feels woefully useless.

I rub my hand across my forehead and am surprised at how sweaty I am, when all I really feel is cool, sharp dread.

"What's going on?" Rayce whispers to Arlo. "We had no

reports of this."

I study Rayce's face. All traces of calm have left him, his mouth clenched in a tight line.

"I've never seen anything like it," Arlo says.

"I'm not sure whether we should stay here or infiltrate the town," Rayce says, scratching his chin.

"I'm not even sure there is anything here to infiltrate," Arlo adds. "Or anyone."

A look passes between the two men, and it frightens me almost as much as the abandoned town. Even when we had a pack of Delmarion soldiers pursuing us, they never seemed at a loss for what to do.

I turn back to the town and take in the eerie scene—the abandoned cobblestone roads, doors hanging open on their hinges, chairs flipped over, and the empty tan-stone houses. My gaze lingers on the building as an idea sprouts in my mind.

"What if you're looking at it from the wrong vantage point?" I suggest.

Both pairs of worried eyes turn toward me. Arlo blinks like he forgot I was here.

"What do you mean?" Rayce asks.

"Can you spot me?" I say, ignoring his question. "I want to go into the edge of town."

"I'm not sure that's wise."

"Cooperation, Rayce," I say, then plow forward. If ever there were a time to prove myself, it's now.

Their footsteps fall in line behind me as I run for the nearest building. Rayce hurries up alongside me, and Arlo appears at my other side, a stunner aimed in either hand.

Up close, the large stones of the building are even better for climbing than I'd originally guessed. I reach up, searching every cranny until my hand finds a little nook between a pair of stones. I pull myself, the toe of my boot finding purchase a few feet off the ground.

"Oh, Rose," Rayce says, doubt coloring his voice. "That's going to take too long."

"Is it?" I counter, a smile touching my lips.

Arlo moves to the corner of the building and peers out into the empty street, stunners pointed forward.

My limbs awaken with the familiar movement of climbing, and my hands begin to pick out crevices automatically, without needing to see them first. I scale the wall in less than a minute, pulling myself onto the flat-topped roof, and duck down. The stone surface is empty, like all the others in the vicinity.

"Okay, okay," Rayce says from below, trying to keep his voice down to a loud whisper. "Do you see anything?"

I crawl toward the opposite edge of the roof and peek over it. The houses near me still have robes dangling on clotheslines, red doors hanging open on hinges, and the wind rocks unlit parchment lanterns, but there's no sign of the people that should be tending to them. Movement off to the right catches my eye, and my gaze snaps to it, my heart hammering in my ears.

A light blue flag with the imperial crest waves in the light breeze, but there's no motion underneath it. I throw a curse its way and walk back to the edge where I left Rayce and Arlo.

"No, I don't see anyone," I say. "I'm going into the town."

Rayce frowns, something unreadable passing across his face. "I don't think this is such a good—"

"Have a little faith in me," I say. "I used to do stunts like this almost every day in the Garden. If something is going on in this town, I can find out easily, without you having to risk any of your people. I *want* to help find Marin and the others."

Rayce and Arlo exchange a glance. The silence of the town feels heavier as I wait for him to decide. Arlo nods, jaw clenched, but Rayce doesn't budge. A tiny part of me wonders if he might be worried something is going to happen to me, not just the mission, but I squash that thought before it can grow.

"Okay," he says, like it hurts him. "Go in just a little farther. But at the first sign of trouble, report back. Do *not* engage by yourself, understand?"

"Yeah, I understand."

He pulls himself up on the wall. We're still about twenty feet apart, but his face is much closer than it was a moment ago, and I can see the urgency radiating out of his dark eyes.

"Promise me," he says, his hand reaching out for another stone that will support his weight but not finding one.

"I promise," I say. "I won't do anything stupid."

He clenches his jaw and nods. "Okay, report as soon as you can."

I linger on the image of Rayce's outstretched arm for a second, wishing he was reaching for me instead of a hold, and then I dig my feet into the rooftop and run.

The edge comes for me fast, and I instinctively grab for my fabric rope. My stomach drops when I grasp only air, and I leap across the first roof onto the next one without my safety net.

A smile finds its way onto my mouth as I run for the next roof, picking my way into the town. This is the movement my bones know, the short bursts of sprinting followed by cool air caressing my skin as height looms under my boots. Up here, I am fully free.

My mind turns to Marin, spurring my feet faster. Is she safe? Even though Rayce pushed us at a grueling pace, it already feels like so much time has passed. In the Garden, that would surely mean death.

But I'm not in the Garden. *She's* not in the Garden. That fact keeps my tiny seed of hope alive.

I check the street below me, but there's still no sign of life. I run for the next roof and leap through the air. As I'm coming down, I see an opening in the middle of town and what looks like a sea of black.

I land hard on the roof, my feet shuttering with the impact. Boots might be good for walking, but they aren't adept at flying.

The building I'm standing atop is twice as large as the others and has a thin wall jutting up to about my thigh. I race to the opposite ledge and pull myself up onto it, balancing my weight.

At this height, I can see them: all the missing people gathered in some sort of square in the very middle of town. Excitement shoots through me before I realize the cloud of silence that's followed us from the road spreads to the crowd of men, women, and children gathered. What are they doing?

My feet lock up as I move to jump onto the next roof to get a closer look.

Rayce's words repeat in my head. *Do* not *engage by yourself.*

I spin around on my boot and jump back down onto the roof.

If I get closer, I can potentially gather more information and improve our chances of finding Marin. That advantage seems important enough to go against his orders. The stone warms my palms as I go to lift myself back onto the ledge.

*Promise me.*

I rub my eyes as his voice echoes in my ears. Even when he isn't here, he's trying to win arguments. How annoying can one man be? But as I take my hand off the stone and swivel around, I can picture his hand reaching for me, and my heartbeat speeds up.

My promise to him wins out, and I rush back, hopping from rooftop to rooftop like a thief in the night. When I finally reach the edge of town, I wipe the sweat slicking my brow. I shimmy down the side of the building, my limbs shaking from exhaustion.

Rayce and Arlo run to meet me at the wall as I land on my feet.

"What were you able to ascertain?" Arlo asks, his voice calm even though panic has replaced the laughter in his eyes.

"The townspeople are here," I say. "For some reason, they're gathered in the town square. All of them."

Rayce and Arlo exchange a confused look.

Rayce opens his mouth to ask a question but is interrupted by a voice on the wind. A voice I've only heard in my darkest moments since I've escaped.

"What's that?" I ask, pushing past him.

"Rose, don't go in there!" he shouts.

But I ignore him, my feet already moving. I pass the building I just scaled, praying I'm wrong. I've hallucinated him before. And he wouldn't be here. Not this far east. Not in a town too small and insignificant to bring him any gain.

"People o' Dongsu, I think eet's time for a display of your great emperor's might," the voice says, turning my blood to razor blades.

It can't be. The Gardener *can't* be here. My feet speed up, and my boot catches on an uneven stone in the road. My knee absorbs the brunt of the fall, and I throw out my hands to catch myself. Using the wall for help, I pull myself up and come face-to-face with Rayce's wanted poster. And pinned up next to him is my own face, though, oddly, my nose tilts a little to the right.

Ignoring my stinging knee and the Gardener's voice, I walk toward the wanted poster. It's like wading through thick water. My feet are reluctant to move. Why would I be wanted by Delmar? The Gardener would want me back, sure, but what would the kingdom want with a girl they saw threaten the rebel leader?

Unless the Gardener told the emperor who I really am.

My gaze drops to the amount of gold promised under my

name, and I grip the side of the building to keep from swaying.

I'm wanted for questioning, and my ransom is more than Rayce's, Arlo's, and Oren's *combined*. If I had any doubts that my right to the Varshan throne would play a role in this war before, that seven-figure number erases them now.

I stagger, aiming to rip the poster off the wall, when a hand grabs my arm. Instinctively, I swing around, fumbling for my sword, until I see Rayce. He presses a finger to his lips and wraps a cloak around my shoulders before taking my hand.

I'm not sure if he saw my wanted poster. But I suppose, right now, it doesn't change what we have to do—save Marin and the others who were captured.

The sound of my own heart pounds in my ears, blocking out everything else.

He pulls me farther into the middle of the town, taking back alleys until we can peer into the square. People stand shoulder to shoulder in a circle, and in the middle of that circle is my nightmare sprung to life.

Rayce spins me so that I'm facing him instead of my former master. "Don't look at him," he orders, but his voice sounds kinder than usual. "Focus on anything else—keep your past in the past."

I don't protest his command, reduced to nothing more than a doll in his hands at the sound of the Gardener's voice.

He pulls up the hood on my cloak, covering my hair, and leans in close to my ear, the intoxicating scent of honey on his breath mixed with the leather of his uniform bringing me to my senses.

"Don't worry," he whispers, his words tickling my skin. "I've got you covered. Have a little faith in me now."

And with those final words echoing what I said to him earlier, he dives into the crowd.

# Chapter Seventeen

I plunge into the sea of people and elbow my way into the middle, keeping my eyes cast low since their violet hue exposes my heritage. The Gardener's voice scrapes across my skin like a sandstorm, and I have to remind myself to breathe.

Wedging myself between a tall man and a woman about my height with two small children clinging to her long gray skirt, I raise my eyes to the center. The Gardener turns his girth toward me, and my knees buckle. Eight lackeys dot the circle, keeping the crowd at a safe distance, armed with the same type of swords and crossbows I saw the Sun soldiers wielding.

"The emperor has given me full authority to enforce his rule until I find what is rightfully mine. He has sent me here to make sure ye understand the dangers o' lettin' Zareeni come into yer fine town."

Since when does the emperor trust the Gardener to do his dirty work? My stomach twists. Did the deal go through, even though I escaped?

The Gardener holds his short arms out to the crowd, his

plum silk shirt stretching thin across his belly like an overripe grape. In his mind, this is just another show, he the ringleader and these captive townspeople his audience. I *will not* get caught and become the main attraction again.

"It is known that yer town has been aidin' these Zareeni ratties, and I've been sent here to stress the importance of makin' sure you understand that you've been committin' treason."

He balls one of his baby hands into a tight fist. Sunlight sparkles on an array of colorful rings adorning his fingers. Ping, a dark-haired lackey with more fingers than teeth, breaks free from the circle and pushes through the crowd a few feet away from where I stand.

My heart pounds as he wades through people like water. He couldn't have seen me. The Gardener stands on his tiptoes and nearly tumbles over, but a smile peels his lips back to reveal a row of rotting teeth.

"Speaking of ratties, we have caught one for ya now," the Gardener says.

The other lackeys drag Marin through the crowd, her wrists and ankles bound in thick rope and a gag over her mouth. Blood from a gash in her hairline seeps down into her left eye. The two men throw her at the Gardener's tiny feet, and she hits the dirt with a solid *thud*. The sound causes the child next to me to cry. My hand twitches toward my sword hilt, and I push past the man in front of me.

The pieces fall together before my eyes. We met no opposition on the road, but the second Marin split off from the group, she was snagged. That's what he does—steals girls.

I knew we were walking into a trap. I just hadn't realized it was meant for me.

The Gardener's fat fingers disappear into Marin's curls, and she lets out a muffled cry as he picks her up off the ground. I wince, my own scalp feeling phantom pain. I push around another man and stop, two rows shy of the front of the circle.

"And if ye see more of these ratties, ye tell them they have a girl, one o' mine," he says, his eyes seeming to find my face in the crowd as he speaks. My fingers drop from my sword. "And if she does not find 'er way back to me within one week, I will clip a Wilted for every day she is gone."

Fern's blood coating the ground, sticky and congealed as I step over it, shines on the cobblestone. Her screams piercing the air as the three lackeys and Shears brutally attacked her, and how empty the world felt when she went quiet...all of it presses against my chest. My lungs are collapsing. How can I sentence Calla and Lily and Juniper, all of them, to death? The people who loved me in a place where love was skimpier than the clothing we were forced to wear.

"With a rattie," the Gardener says. "Ye have to chop off its head."

*No. He wouldn't. Not here, not with a girl who isn't his.*

A lackey with long hair pulls out a thick blade from his belt. It flashes wickedly in the bright sunlight. The crowd lets out a collective gasp as Marin's eyes grow wide. She wiggles around in her bindings, trying to swing her legs under her, but the Gardener just lifts her up higher.

I push around a woman in front of me, now just one person away from the man that held me captive most of my life.

The blade flashes again, and I stop. Marin's brown eyes fill with tears, and her body squirms around like a fish out of water. My brain screams to help her. To move through the ring of people and use the sword the rebellion gave me to protect innocent people. If I kill the Gardener, then he can't make good on any of his threats.

But as his kohl-lined eyes fall to the crowd and his rotten grin widens, my bones stop working. The lackey walks the sword over to the Gardener. All I keep thinking is go, *go*, but

I can't move. I can't defy the man who tormented me all those years. I might have escaped my cage, but my true prison is rooted much deeper than four walls.

The lackey presents the sword the way a normal person shows off a precious diamond.

I will my hand to wrap around the comforting leather of my sword hilt. The one thing that could help me save Marin.

It hangs stationary by my side.

The Gardener accepts the blade with his free hand, his fingers doing what mine can't. Panic claws up my throat, choking me, rooting me. How am I ever going to be able to look Arlo in the eye if Marin dies and I could have stopped it? Where is Arlo, anyway? And Rayce? He told me that he had me covered and then disappeared. Is *anyone* here? Are they seeing what I'm seeing?

It figures that the men in my life would disappear the moment they're needed. Just like Park.

It's up to me, then. I focus on my breathing. My vision darkens around the edges, and suddenly I can't feel my feet.

Anger burns a fiery trail down my throat, loosening my bones, and I break free of my roots. I remember Rayce saying warriors can't fight with fear, and I'm startled by how true his statement is. I push past the next man, my hand finding my sword hilt.

The Gardener brings the blade to Marin's creamy white throat. Her terrified face reflects in the shiny metal.

*I'm going to kill him. I'm going to kill the Gardener.*

A hand wraps around my wrist, the touch burning through my skin to my cold bones. I catch the end of a scar illuminated from his cheek as he passes in front of me. Rayce—he came back! *One second*, he mouths, his eyes scanning the crowd.

I nod, still wide-eyed that he didn't abandon me completely, and he squeezes my wrist gently before the corner of his mouth twists up. I follow his gaze and see the subtle waves in the sea around us as multiple Zareeni guards shift into place.

The Gardener's blade rises, unaware he's being surrounded.

Rayce releases me, pushing past the person in front of him. A green stunner bolt shoots out from the crowd, knocking the blade from the Gardener's hand. Arlo shrugs off his hood, smoke billowing from his stunner barrel.

In the time it takes for the lackeys to realize they're being attacked, Rayce has his stunner out and shoots the tall man nearest us.

Arlo and five of the nearest Zareeni guards break away from the congregation, their stunners blazing green as they let loose a wave of bolts. I unsheathe my sword, the blade singing as I free it.

"Delmeerions!" the Gardener orders, nursing his shot hand. "Kill them!"

I whip around in time to see a horde of Delmarion soldiers spilling from the nearby houses and colliding with the townspeople. My hood slips from my head. A woman lets out a cry as the soldiers trample over foot and child to get to the center. People dodge and jump to scramble out of the way, running for the safety of their homes.

"More are coming!" I shout out to Rayce.

The Gardener's gaze snaps to me, the only person not desperate to hide from the stampede of soldiers. Realization dawns in his dark eyes, like rot on an apple, just as Rayce shoves him away. The Gardener falls flat on his butt, and I expect the earth beneath to quake. My necklace slips out of his shirt, the ruby beckoning me. It's the only thing besides the Flowers I want to take from him.

I tighten my grip on my sword hilt and swing it between the first plates of shiny armor I see. Blood squirts out of the soldier's side as he falls to the ground. I look from the downed man and see at least fifty more clamoring to replace him.

"There're too many!" Rayce shouts over trampling feet. "Rose, get back here!"

I swing around at Rayce's voice and watch as a Zareeni woman gets tackled. A bright green bolt releases from the tip of her stunner, hurtling toward me. I jump to the left, forcing my body onto the ground, but the bolt nicks my shoulder. Electric pain blooms from the point of contact, jolting down my body in rippling waves. It's like blacking out from Zarenite but a million times worse. Instead of being lulled into the heat, it comes all at once, frying my blood and burning through my veins. By the time I hit the ground, my vision blooms gray.

Rayce yells something at me, but all I can see is the flash of his sword as he swings it.

My body convulses, and my skin burns. Torment rushes through every ounce of my core as my head collides with the ground.

Rayce's voice cuts through the fog descending on my brain. "Rose, get up!"

I blink through the pain, and a callused hand touches my cheek. My eyes connect with Rayce's.

"You shouldn't be stunned," he says, kneeling next to me. His tone almost sounds like he's pleading with me. "You were only grazed. Come on, stay with me."

*Stay with him?*

The idea sounds pleasant and soothing, something worth fighting for. I grit my teeth against the dizzying pain and push up on my elbow.

Rayce grabs my shoulder with gentle fingers and examines the place where the stunner bolt caught my skin. A chunk of fabric from my sleeve has been blasted off, leaving a burned brown outline on the remaining section. Smoke wafts from hole. Though my skin is pink and raw, as if I jumped into water that's too hot, it doesn't look like I'm bleeding.

His eyes dart upward, and I follow his gaze to see a soldier charging us. Rayce snaps to his feet, throwing his sword out to parry an oncoming attack, and then I remember where I am.

Reaching out with my other hand, I feel around the grass until I find my sword and use it to push myself up off the ground.

Rayce jumps backward, avoiding another attack, and shoots the Delmarion soldier in the fleshy part of his neck with his stunner. The man twitches and goes down, taking my place in the dirt.

All around us, the battle rages. A Zareeni man screams as a soldier cuts him through the middle, while a stunner bolt zips past them, finding its mark in another soldier. The sickening smell of sweat, dirt, and blood turns my stomach.

"Listen to me," Rayce says, grabbing my good shoulder so I focus on him. My head still spins from falling, but the world around us stops when I peer into his serious face. "Get Marin and get out of here."

"But I can help you fight." I tighten my grip on my sword hilt. The tip of my blade sags into the ground, the weight of it too much to bear. How did I carry it before?

His gaze flicks above my head, and I'm tempted to twist around to see what creases his brow. "Right now I'm worried about Marin. You said you'd stick by my side, and you have been. You've already done more for us than I expected. But please, I need you to help us one more time. Not for me but Marin. She's in no condition to fight right now, and I don't think she'll be able to survive this battle if she doesn't get some distance from the fighting."

I bite down on my lip, indecision slicing me through. We've already established that my skill with blades isn't nearly as sharp as it should be, and one day of training with the Zareeni forces isn't going to fix that. But I don't want to abandon him—I mean, this fight. With the Gardener here, it's personal.

Seeing my hesitance, Rayce points behind me. His finger leads my gaze to Arlo. Marin lies slumped by his boots, her face buried in the dirty cobblestone, and I can't tell if she's moving. My breathing stops. Arlo stands in front of his sister, blocking any incoming attacks with his own body, both stunners out and bolts blasting faster than I can count.

"Help her," Rayce says.

I open my mouth to tell him I will—how could I have put my needs over my friend's, even for a moment?—but he swings around and lashes out at a set of soldiers coming for him.

Though my legs ache and my shoulder feels like it's on fire, I sprint for Arlo and Marin. The farther I get from Rayce, the less confident I feel about this plan, and my heart squeezes, leaving him alone on the battlefield. If only I could be in two places at once. An arrow whizzes past my head, and I roll to the ground to avoid another.

With sweat pouring down my forehead, I crawl the last few feet toward Arlo.

"What are you doing?" he shouts over the noise, his eyes flashing to me as he lets loose another green bolt.

"We have to get Marin out of here!"

He nods, stepping aside from her. "I'll cover you both. Try to get her to the shed."

Grabbing her by the shoulders, I roll her onto her back. Her eyes blink open, and she thrashes against me, blood trickling from the wound on her neck where the Gardener left his mark.

"You're okay," I say, leaning over so she can see me clearer.

She takes in a shuddering breath and moves her bound hands to her neck.

"What's going on?" she asks, panic lacing her tone.

"Delmarion soldiers were waiting for us when we attacked," I say. "We're getting out of here, but first, I'm going to cut your wrists free."

She nods, holding her hands out for me.

"Hurry!" Arlo yells.

My attention snaps to him as a soldier slips past his last bolt then brings his blade down at Arlo. He juts out one of his stunners to block, metal colliding with metal, and stumbles back a few paces.

Careful with the large blade, I slip it in between the thick brown ropes binding Marin's hands and saw the strands apart. Her hands freed, Marin sits up, grimacing as her wounds bring on a whole new reality of pain.

"Can you walk?" I ask.

"I think so."

I hold a hand out to her, and she takes it without any hesitation. The moment we're both upright, she sways, nearly toppling over again. I wrap her arm around my neck to support some of her weight as Arlo shoves the barrel of his stunner in the soldier's face and pulls the trigger.

"Be careful," Arlo says, flipping his other stunner around to Marin. "Take this and get out of here."

Marin accepts the weapon, the inch of powder in the clear hilt glowing green as her fingers wrap around it.

With Marin's weight slowing me down, we hobble toward the alley nearest us on the south side. Exhaustion eats at my body as we weave around three Zareeni rebels fighting a pack of soldiers. Every step feels like agony, and if it weren't for Marin's body heat pressing down on me, the overwhelming pull to the ground would win.

I grit my teeth against the pain, blocking out the violent flashes of red blood and electric green bolts blooming every way I turn. I wasn't able to save Fern or the other Flowers the night I escaped the Garden, but I *will* save Marin.

We slip into the nearest alleyway, the large building blocking out the sun, and the sounds of war fade behind the brick.

"How far do we need to go?" Marin asks, her voice weak and her lips white.

Dried blood stains her face in rivulets, and her curly hair sticks to her head. I'm not sure how much longer she can fight passing out.

"Not too far," I lie, picking up our speed.

We struggle past the first building and into the alley of the next one, putting the horror of battle farther behind us. My mind wanders back to Rayce as I put one foot in front of the other.

His voice fills my head: *stay with me.*

And even though my body feels like it's a breath away from collapsing, and people were trying to kill each other, and there was blood and heat and terror surging all around us, I find myself wishing I could have stayed by his side.

# Chapter Eighteen

Every inch we move fills me with a hollow dread that weighs down my exhausted limbs. What horrors lie at our backs? Every time I blink, I see Arlo getting run through with a blade still trying to guard the spot where we slipped away, or Rayce surrounded by a circle of the emperor's soldiers, brought to his knees by a thousand sword tips. The ghost of his fingertips caressing my cheek haunts me as he pleads for me to stay awake...to stay with him.

Marin and I remain quiet, but I can tell by the way she keeps peeking over her shoulder that our fears are the same.

We stagger our way toward the peeling shed at the outskirts of town. Relief floods through my body seeing it as abandoned as when we left. I lay Marin down against the splintered wood backing before slumping next to her. Darkness fades in and out of my vision as the sunset bleeds the sky red.

Finally, the sounds of heavy boot falls rouse me, and I sit up, clutching my sword with weak hands as I scan the nearest street for any movement. The familiar green and brown uniforms of the Zareeni rebels nearly bring tears to my eyes. There are far fewer of them now than the impressive force we started with, but our numbers still look strong.

I pick through the crowd, searching for the faces I recognize, and silently curse myself for turning around the statue of Yun back in Zareen.

If Rayce doesn't come back... I can't even finish the thought. My heart hammers in my chest as the men and women stagger through the entrance of the shed.

I catch Arlo's lighter hair in the crowd and shake Marin awake.

*Stay with me*, I silently repeat over and over in my head like a prayer. He has to be somewhere among his guards. He *has* to be.

My weak grip tightens on the sword Rayce handed me this morning as the trail of guards nears the end.

And then I see him, helping a wounded guard in the rear of the pack. Rayce's once pristine long vest flares out behind him, the tattered ends bloodstained, but *he* is in one piece. His dark hair sticks to the side of his face, and every inch of him is slick with sweat.

But he's alive. My fingers slip from the hilt, and tears blur my vision. He's really safe. I press my dirt-smeared hand to my lips and realize I'm trembling.

Arlo catches sight of me and runs to us, clapping me on the shoulder before bending over to help his sister. His whispers are lost to my ears as Rayce turns my way.

One of the other guards takes the man Rayce was supporting and helps him over to the shed. Rayce rubs the back of his neck, taking in a deep breath before heading toward me. His footsteps on the cobblestone sound louder than stunner shots to my ears. One moment, he's a million miles away, and the next we're inches apart—and I am not prepared for the way my knees buckle as he stares down at me.

"I'm relieved to see you're both okay," he says, his voice low with exhaustion.

Marin gives him a drained smile before Arlo helps her into the shed, leaving us completely alone, encased in the orange glow of the sun.

"Thank you so much for your help today, Rose."

"Of course."

Dirt caked on with sweat smears across his face, and most of his shirt is stained with dark patches of dried blood. The aftermath of war looks wrong on him, and I remember how serene his face looked when he was cleaning my wound. I want that version of him back.

"You did great," he adds.

My hands long to embrace him, but I force the nearly overwhelming feeling aside and nod, not trusting myself to speak. It's just the stress from today getting to me. A trick of my faulty heart and nothing more.

I look down at my feet to keep from staring into his eyes, and a stray piece of hair falls into my face.

His long fingers brush against my hot cheek as he pushes the wavy strand behind my ear, and his touch hovers for a moment too long near my face. He pulls his hand back as our gazes lock.

He clears his throat. "We need to get the wounded back." He swings around and walks inside the shed.

The words I want to say—*I was so worried, I thought you might be dead, I don't know what I would have done if you didn't make it back*—stay lodged in my throat.

The trek back to the base crawls as a sliver of the moon streaks across the midnight sky. The stars don't reveal themselves, mourning the fallen that lie slain in the streets of Dongsu.

By the time we retreat underground, I welcome the cold

air licking my wounds, and the weight of earth above my head feels like protective arms wrapping around me. In the back of my mind, I hear the Gardener's warning, but weariness blocks out the worst of the trauma.

Arlo helps Marin to the infirmary to treat her wounds, and I wander back to the room we share, her empty bed hollowing out a pit in my stomach.

• • •

I wake up cocooned in my red quilt. Green light emanates off a bundle of Zarenite on the patchwork dresser, casting an eerie glow on an old bowl of rice, shriveled baby carrots, and a slimy pan-fried egg. I slap the plate away from my face as my stomach rolls, and I try to sit up. My head pounds harder than a drum.

"After sixteen hours of slumber, the subject rouses and rejects food," says a recognizably dull voice from the corner.

*Piper.* If Rayce hated me that much, why didn't he just leave me there for the Delmarion soldiers to finish me off? I peek open my other eye, and my nausea expands.

Piper sits rigid in the corner of the room, managing to appear more uptight than the stool she sits on. She only has one shadow behind her today, and as she makes observations, the swift brush of a quill scratching parchment fills the room. Piper leans forward, pushing down her long sleeve quickly so it covers her hand. Something about her skin looked off, but I couldn't figure it out in her quick movement.

"On a scale of one to ten," Piper says, "one being a bug bite and ten being excruciating pain, how would you describe getting hit with a stunner? Please take care with your answer; it's crucial for research on the stunner's effects on a Varshan."

I put my hand over my forehead to stop it from pounding. "Ten now that you're here."

She shoves herself off the stool, sending it wobbling against her aide behind her.

"Your humor is juvenile," she snaps, her voice tight. "Though frankly, I shouldn't be surprised that you were more helpful to us unconscious. Apparently cooperation is a concept too complex for your intellect. And to think, now the shogun is pushing to have the council agree to helping you after some unnecessary excursion."

"Excuse me?" I snap, sitting up the rest of the way. "People died on that 'unnecessary excursion.' Marin almost died."

"And yet, somehow, *you* survived," she says. "The least experienced fighter in the entire platoon. I wonder how many lives were lost just so Rayce could let you face your old captor."

My fingers fist around my blanket, and I say through clenched teeth, "You have no idea what you're talking about."

She walks closer, her movements clipped, and leans down so we're face-to-face. A chill creeps through the room, biting me under my blanket.

"Even though you didn't act to help your previous master—this time—people don't really change."

My grip slackens as her words rip through my flesh. A single thought keeps circling back, screaming in my head: *What if she's right?* What if I will always be the girl who hesitates, the girl who cowers in front of the man who stole her life? A sour taste builds in the back of my throat.

"No matter how much Rayce wanted to believe your reaction in seeing the Gardener would reveal your true intentions, I knew you'd hide them," Piper goes on. "And I'm still not convinced we should use our assets to help you on a personal mission when the entire populace would better benefit our attentions."

I meet her dead gaze, my heart skittering, trying to decipher all the information she throws at me. My mind gets stuck on one detail, everything else falling away from me. Rayce, the man who nearly broke my heart with worry when he didn't show up in the line of rebels until the very end. Rayce, who gently tucked my hair behind my ear.

Could that man really have known he was sending me into a trap?

"Are you implying Rayce knew the Gardener was in Dongsu and sent me there as a test?"

For the first time since I met her, Piper's thin lips curl up before she spins around, giving me all the confirmation I need.

"Come, Fàn," she says to the minion in the back. "We've seen more than enough here."

They both shuffle out of the room, leaving me to contend with the anger burning through my veins that Rayce would knowingly put me up against the man who abused me. He talked of loyalty, about this being a chance to prove myself to the council, all while knowing he was about to trick me into facing the things that leave me raw. And I was scared for him, didn't want to leave him on the battlefield. He asked for faith and trust, told me he'd prove that he was worth it, and threw it all away the second it was convenient for him, just like Park. My rage boils over and I jump out of bed, kicking off the blanket. My right shoulder screams in protest like someone hacked into it with a knife, but I grit my teeth and push the pain aside. I stomp out of the room, my bones shrieking at every movement, and I find the woman who first welcomed me into Delmar standing guard on the side of my door.

"Where's Rayce?" I snap.

She blinks at me with her unusually large dark eyes. "Good afternoon to you, too," she says. "Did you eat anything yet?"

I ignore her pointless question.

"Where's the shogun?" I ask again, the edge in my voice sharp. I take a deep breath through my nostrils. "Your name's

Suki, right?"

She nods, hesitance clouding her features.

"Please." I force my tone calm. "Take me to the shogun. I *have* to speak to him."

"I'm not really supposed to, but"—she stops, her expression softening—"this way."

She weaves me through a series of matching halls that wind upward. Zarenite-filled jars hanging from the ceiling flicker on and dissipate as we pass under them like a hidden spirit snuffing out the lanterns. After a few twists and turns, she stops at an open doorway.

Rayce leans over a piece of parchment behind a small wooden desk just inside the room. To his left is a bed barely big enough for him, covered by a meticulously folded green quilt. Above it, in a nook carved into the wall, rests a neat pile of hardcover books. Several more piles of books litter the floor around his desk. Besides the books and a wall of maps pinned up in the back, the rest of the room looks much like the one I was just in. Same size, same used furniture. Nothing that screams that this is where the rebel leader rests his head.

Rayce's tousled dark hair sits atop a furrowed brow, and only half of the golden knot hooks on his shirt are fastened, revealing the hard line where his chest muscles meet. His boot taps a hectic melody, and he flips a green-feathered quill around in his fingers as he scans a letter in front of him.

Suki knocks on the stone doorway, motions that I should go in, and retreats quickly.

Rayce's attention remains fixed on the parchment in front of him.

The fact that he doesn't even acknowledge my presence sends the anger I felt earlier shooting down my limbs. I stomp halfway into the room, ignoring the pile of books I knock over on my way.

"Did you know the Gardener was in Dongsu when you

sent me there?" I ask, trying to keep my voice steady.

Rayce doesn't move or speak. The only indication he even heard me is a pause in his quill twirling. The flowing green feather waves at me from his hand as if to mock me.

"Did you hear me?" I snap. "You made me believe I could trust you, you told me this was the way I could earn the rebellion's help in freeing the other Flowers, and then you sent me right into the arms of the man who tormented me for years. Was that funny to you?"

He doesn't react to my questions.

I cross the room in a few short strides and rip the quill from Rayce's grasp, bending back a few plumes in my haste.

Rayce finally looks up to meet my gaze, and I hope the fire of the betrayal I'm feeling sears him.

"Would you sign off on a document if you knew it would mean killing at least a hundred people you knew?" he asks, catching me off guard.

My grip on the quill loosens, and it falls onto the desk between us.

"Because that's what I'm dealing with here," he says, reaching for the quill. "So please excuse me if I can't find the focus to address something that doesn't affect that right now."

Every insult I wanted to hurl at him flies out of my head, and I open my mouth, but nothing comes out. The tip of his quill hovers over the bottom of the parchment, and the feather trembles from his shaking hand.

He lets out a frustrated growl and slams the quill down on the wooden desk, finally looking up at me.

"This is all my uncle's fault. If he hadn't decided to be greedy and close down the border to Varsha, none of this would have happened. But he had to have more—more gold, more control—and in doing so, he condemned the entire empire to this…this…war and *death*."

He runs a hand through his hair, pulling it away from

his eyes, and I notice the black bags that have gathered underneath them. It looks like he hasn't slept since the rescue mission at Dongsu. Every one of the sixteen hours I was asleep, recovering, he was dealing with this—and probably other things, too—instead of caring for himself. My resolve softens, remembering the way he rushed to my side when I was hit with the stunner bolt and protected me until I could get back on my feet.

"I'm sorry," he says, his voice hoarse. "I shouldn't have taken my frustration out on you. It's been a very long week." His gaze pierces me as he leans back in his wooden chair and looks me over. "I'm glad you're awake and seem to be well."

I smooth out my blue robe, keenly aware of every place his gaze touches. He clears his throat and leans down below his desk. Reappearing with a brown satchel, he plops it on his desk, and as he opens it, my nose tickles with the sweet scent of the honey crisps he shared with me on the way to Dongsu. The sadness that darkened his brow when he spoke about his mother rests there now as he sinks his hand into the bag.

"The answer to your question is yes," he says, popping a honey crisp in his mouth. "I had an inkling the Gardener had occupied Dongsu from previous reports. Since your departure, my uncle has given the Gardener full jurisdiction to command and lead his troops. Apparently the Gardener is looking for something for my uncle, but we haven't been able to figure out what that is. Clearly, your old master is using this newfound power to secure you also."

I keep a straight face as Rayce speaks, even though my stomach drops. At least he hasn't connected that his uncle and the Gardener are after the same thing.

"Why didn't you warn me about him?"

"You know why," he says, offering me a honey crisp. I just stare at his open palm, so he continues. "I needed concrete proof to convince everyone on the council that you can be trusted, and we got that. Of course, that wasn't the sole reason for the mission. Now Dongsu isn't occupied anymore, and we've kept our promise to the people."

*We got that*, he said. But did he never question the price I would have to pay for their trust? A wave of nausea rushes over me as I picture the Gardener standing in the middle of the square, his blade pressed against Marin's throat.

"Do you understand what it was like for me to see him again?" I slap the crisp out of his hand.

He sighs, rubbing his hands down his face. The silence that follows rests heavy in the air, like smoke.

"No, I don't," he says. "I couldn't possibly. But I could tell by the look on your face that it was terrifying, and when I saw how much it affected you, I regretted it. I meant what I said before. I truly hope you can find a way to keep the past in the past."

His brow wrinkles like he's trying picture what was going through my mind, and he crosses his arms over his chest. His linen shirt pulls tight over his biceps, revealing muscles that endless weapons training must have given him.

"It was excruciating," I say, as if that single word could do it justice.

I can still feel the sunlight burning my face as the Gardener ripped Marin's hair out in the middle of the square. I will my mind not to think of it, but the Gardener's words hurl toward me like daggers.

"And he said he was going to kill one of the Flowers every day until I came back," I whisper, barely louder than my own heartbeat. "I can't let that happen to them. Even if that means I have to—"

I lose my composure for a moment, but Rayce's expression remains smooth as the stone surrounding us.

"That's why, if you can't get the council to agree to help me, you have to release me," I say. "If I go back, he won't harm them."

"I understand," he says, rising to his feet. "Maybe more than I should." The ghost of a smile touches his lips. "But you aren't talking about just helping them anymore. You want to sacrifice yourself."

"You don't get it." I shake my head. "The Gardener wasn't bluffing. He's crazy enough to actually follow through on a threat like that. And besides, I promised Fern I'd rescue the others. I wasn't able to keep my original promise to her and save her life, but I have to keep this one."

Rayce walks around his desk, closing the space between us.

I grip my hands tight in front of me and bow my head, something I swore I'd never do for a man again. I'm trembling, and I know he can see my weakness, but I stand my ground. Tears blur my vision. All I can see are my sisters' lifeless bodies littering the ground at the feet of that horrible man.

"Please, let me go, so I can try to save them."

Instead of answering, Rayce's fingers wrap around my fists, and he pulls me close to him, guiding my hands around his back. I'm too shocked to fight him. His arms slide around my shoulders, and my face fits perfectly into the crook of his neck.

He presses me to him, his body conforming to fit neatly against mine, and he takes a deep breath like he's teaching me how to breathe again. We release our shared breath together and the tension of a thousand restless nights with it. I'm not sure which one of us craved the comfort more, and right now it doesn't matter. I stay motionless next to him, letting the heat from his skin thaw mine, and close my eyes. With his arms around me, all my ugly pieces feel whole and beautiful. Like I'm glowing. Like we are two stars chasing each other through the night sky.

"Zareen is going to help them," he whispers into my hair.

The stubble on his jaw tickles my skin. "Arlo and I decided it earlier today. You were invaluable during the Dongsu mission and have more than earned our support."

I pull away from his warmth ever so slightly and make the mistake of glancing up, right into his dark eyes.

His hand traces up my neck, his fingertips trailing down my jawline as light as a snowflake on my skin. His lips part, and I realize I want to touch them. I want him to take away the horrible weight of the girls I left behind, of the tormentor I can't defy.

This desperate need scares me in a way height never did, even when I was new to aerial dancing. I turn away from his hand before my body can betray me and stare at the stone wall, reminding myself that his words don't guarantee action.

He takes a step back and clears his throat.

"I told you to use your innocence to your advantage," he says with a halfhearted chuckle. "I just didn't think you'd use it against me."

His warmth still clings to me, a reminder that what just happened was real. That I let him get that close. That, for a moment, I *welcomed* it. I'm not sure which weighs heavier on me, that it happened or that I wish it would happen again.

"Zareen is about to strike Delmar on a separate assignment," Rayce says, folding his arms in front of him. Every trace of our exchange erases from his expression. "And I think in that confusion, we could also take the opportunity to finally end the Garden. I could assign you to the team that I'll put together to rescue your friends, but I'm hoping you'll choose an alternative."

I wrap my arms around my middle, unsure whether I'm trying to keep his warmth in or replace it with mine. His face gives no inclination whether he feels bad about asking me to give up the chance to rescue the others, and I've already learned the hard way that trusting him can be a double-edged sword.

"What alternative did you have in mind?"

He scratches the stubble on his chin.

"Do you remember when you overheard that we were trying to rescue Piper's sister the night of the Spring Ceremony?"

The knife in my stomach twists, recalling how awful I felt when I found out. Even though Piper is less than charming, her sister doesn't deserve to be imprisoned by the emperor.

I nod.

"Well, we think now would be a good time to try rescuing her. My uncle is a creature of extreme habit, and every year around this time, he and his elite forces make a trek to the Delmar–Varsha border to inspect the wall. He should be heavily distracted with preparations for his departure and not focused on much else."

I shift my weight. "Okay, but what does that have to do with me?"

He smiles at my question, and mischief glitters in his dark eyes.

"Arlo and I witnessed your...*talents* at Dongsu firsthand," he says. "And the rebellion needs someone like that to save Piper's sister, Kyra."

I raise an eyebrow at his words, but his lopsided grin reveals no explanation. "I'm almost scared to ask what you mean by that."

"How about I show you instead?" He holds out the same palm that touched my cheek a moment ago.

I frown at it, thinking of all the things he's hidden from me until after the fact, and wonder what I'm about to get myself into. The temperature in the room heats under his intense gaze. Sensing my hesitation, he tilts his head.

"Cooperation, right, Rose?"

I roll my eyes and take his hand before I can talk myself

out of it. Trusting Rayce has led me to experience more things than I ever would through my little peephole back in the Garden—scary, bloody things, sure, but I've also seen the love of a brother standing in front of his sister to protect her, the conviction of a girl who, despite being shunned for her differences, still wants to devote her life to a cause she believes in, and the kindness of a leader who can identify almost every one of his people by name.

# Chapter Nineteen

Rayce pulls me to the back of his desk and sits me in his chair. Just being in it, I feel the weight of his responsibilities. The quill he abandoned still lies atop the piece of parchment he was agonizing over. He leans down, rummaging through a drawer in his desk. His sack of honey crisps releases a pleasant scent in the air, sitting next to a tiny statue of Lin carved out of Zarenite. As he stands back up, the statue begins to glow a soft green.

Unfolding a piece of parchment, he smooths it out on his desk, and then he puts the quill and an ink pot on top of the curled corners. His warmth presses into my back as he shifts to stand directly behind me. As he leans over the map, he rests a hand on my shoulder, and the dim light accentuates the smoothness of his face, in stark contrast to the winding scar slicing down the other side. Tiny flecks of dark hair shadow his jawline, and I have to pin my hands at my sides to keep from touching him.

This desire to touch anyone is unnatural for me. Unnerving. But no matter how many times I force down the need, my resolve crumbles the second he gets near.

He points to the middle of the page. "This is a map of the dungeon Piper's sister is being held in."

My heart hammers in my chest, and I bite my lip, forcing my focus on the parchment. "I drew it from memory," he says, "so it isn't very good."

I touch the curled end closest to me, smiling down at the roughly drawn lines. The brittle paper crinkles under my fingertip. Rayce can cook, but he doesn't have much of an eye for drawing.

"What?" he asks, catching me smiling.

"Nothing." I clear my face. "So why is the rebellion going through so much trouble for a single girl?"

Rayce's brow furrows at my question, and I realize how heartless it sounds. But even I know it's probably not a good strategy to risk so much for a single person. I wanted to help the lives of almost fifty girls and had to prove myself before my request was considered, because of the danger of sending in more of his people. There has to be a reason, and I want to know why it's worth it to him before I risk my life.

"I didn't mean that you shouldn't," I clarify. "I'm just curious, since it's so dangerous going into the city."

Rayce frowns, turning away from me to face the map. It casts the top half of his face in shadow.

"Because if we don't, we might lose Piper," he says.

"I'm not sure that's such a bad thing."

He shakes his head.

"That would be the worst thing to happen to us. She was the one who discovered the properties of Zarenite, and without her genius of harnessing it and creating the stunners, we wouldn't stand a chance against Delmar. As it is, my uncle's army outnumbers ours twenty to one. Without the stunners leveling the playing field, my rebellion would've been crushed within a week. I owe everything to Piper's curiosity and Oren's strategic mind."

No matter how I try to picture it, I can't imagine Piper putting in all that effort for the cause. She doesn't seem like the type who would willingly do something for others.

"Her only condition for joining the rebellion was that no one she loved got hurt. We did our best and were able to keep her and her sister safe for the past five months, but then she took her sister on an expedition near Imperial City while testing a new weapon, and they were attacked. Piper made it out, but Sun soldiers captured her sister. It was a promise we shouldn't have made, because no one is truly safe at war, but I feel like I owe it to her to make it right."

"Is that why she was so against sending forces to help the Flowers?" I ask.

"Yes," he says. "She doesn't believe it's right to free others when we have already promised our army elsewhere. That's why I've been working on this new plan to free everyone. But I don't think it'll succeed without your help."

I trace my finger slowly around a compass at the bottom of the map while I think over his answer.

Rayce points to a dotted line on the eastern side of the castle. "That's the entrance that we need to get to. It's been blocked off, but Piper is figuring out a way around it."

"Okay."

"And this is what I need you for."

He unrolls a second piece of parchment. I lean over the crude map and breathe in the multiple layers of ink staining the page. A thousand little indents and fingerprints smudge most of the lines, but the gist remains.

The map details a large canyon with towers perched on both sides, one labeled "East Tower" and the other "West Tower." Two lines connect them, creating a wide, oval shape with tiny squares dotting it at even intervals. I furrow my brow, trying to interpret what's on the page.

"I'm not exactly sure what I'm looking at," I say.

"Clearly I'm not the best artist." He rubs the back of his neck. "Basically, there are two platforms here held up by the towers." He motions to the map. "These square things here are prisoner cells. They're suspended by heavy wires."

"So the prisoners are hanging?"

He nods.

"Over what?"

"About a five-hundred-foot drop."

"Oh."

The proper reaction would be nervousness. I know that. And yet, it feels like such a small price to pay in order to help the other Flowers. I'm more worried about the soldiers in Imperial City than the fall.

He clears his throat. "As soon as the soldiers see the rescue party, they'll freeze the levy system, which means Kyra will be stuck. If that happens, someone's going to have to walk across the wire to retrieve her."

"And you thought that with the unique skill set I used to perform for the Garden, I might be able to do that."

With a nod, he adds, "I won't lie to you, it'll be dangerous. But you'll only have to cross to get to her."

He reaches into his sack and pulls out a stunner, then hands it to me. Instead of the empty barrel where the Zarenite comes out, a spool of silver wire is rolled up in it. A sharp hook hangs out the bottom.

"Piper invented this after finding out where Delmar moved her sister. Arlo will shoot the end into the ceiling when you reach her cage, and you should be able to use the cable to slide down to him, as long as he keeps hold of the other end."

I purse my lips, thinking over his plan. There isn't even a remote chance I'd survive a drop like he described, but my fear of heights was forced out during years of training in the Garden. I could walk across a high wire with my eyes closed.

"What about the Garden?" I say.

He rubs his chin, considering his words before saying, "While you're with the first group down in the dungeon, I'll send a second smaller group to the Garden. With your previous master out searching the land for my uncle, I doubt there will be too much resistance. I'll hand select the best I can afford. I'll be leading up the final party that will act as a distraction so you can slip in unnoticed."

The Gardener's threat slithers around my brain, his toxic voice mixing with the pealing shrill of Fern's dying screams. I will not sentence another girl to die by Shears's cruel hands, and if helping the rebellion save Piper's sister will also help save the Flowers, then the choice is already made. Though laying some ground rules might make the process go a little smoother.

"I'll do it on two conditions," I say.

Rayce turns to look at me, our faces mere inches apart. "Go on."

"You have to let me see the soldiers you're sending, and you have to promise to be more forthcoming with information that will directly affect me."

His mouth curls up at the corners. "Still don't trust us?"

"Haven't given me much reason to," I return.

"I think both of your requests can be accommodated. So you have a deal."

"Don't you need to discuss it with your council first?" I tease.

My joke earns me a laugh.

"It'll be our little secret." His eyes dance around my face, and his warm, honey-scented breath tickles my cheek. I should look away, but I'm pinned under the nearness of him. My skin still hums from where he hugged me, where he made me whole for a tiny sliver in time. The girls in the Garden used to whisper about kisses, stolen sloppily in the darkness by unwanted men, and I could never understand why someone would want one. But as I stare at Rayce's lips, I wonder what it would be like to press mine against them. Would they be soft? What would they taste like—sweet like the cookies he eats or strong like the words he uses to command his troops?

As if he can hear my questions, he inches closer, ready to answer them.

A tinkling bell echoes down the hallway outside the room, dancing its way across the air. He startles at it, blinking twice.

"Is it that time already?" He straightens and presses his hand over his eyes, hiding his intentions from me. "Come on, I'll walk you back to your room. I've got a lot of work to do if we're going to be attempting dual missions in a few days."

It already looks like he hasn't rested since we've returned from the mission. I have no idea how he can run on no energy and expect to win.

"Shouldn't you get some sleep first?"

He pulls the chair out for me and I get up, aware of the absence of his warmth.

"Sleep? Who has time for that?"

Then he motions with his palm for me to exit first. But as we step into the hallway, disappointment blooms, knowing we'll be separated soon. I yank that weed before it can spread and move as close to the wall as the narrow tunnel will allow. He places his hand on the opposite wall, a green vein of Zarenite springing to life, and then leads me deeper into the base.

"You might want to consider getting a tattoo before we leave for this next mission," he says. "Of course, that would mean joining the rebellion. Officially."

The casual way he mentions it rubs me wrong, almost like the entire scene back in his office was just to convince me to join his cause. I haven't decided what I'll do once my sisters are freed, but *officially* joining the rebellion would be the most dangerous thing for me. I can only avoid them finding out about my past for so long.

"Why would I do that?" I ask.

Rayce clears his throat. "Well, it seemed like you were fitting in well here, and I know some people would miss you if you left—"

"Like?" My heartbeat picks up. Is he implying *he* might miss me?

"Like Marin," he finishes.

"Right." I turn away from him so my eyes don't reveal the disappointment lodged in my stomach like a stone.

He clears his throat. "Besides, you'll probably want to operate a stunner. They're much more compact than a sword, and since you'll need your mobility for the mission, it'll be an ideal weapon."

"I'm not so sure about that."

Rayce ducks under a low patch of ceiling, his face growing closer to mine.

"At the very least, I'll ask Arlo to train you in shooting one tomorrow," he says. "That way you'll be better able to defend yourself, and if you have some Zarenite in you and you get hit by a stunner again, it won't have such an adverse effect."

"Or it'll kill me."

"Then my suggestion is not to get hit," he counters.

There's no way I'm getting a tattoo. Even though I do like Marin, I won't be staying if the mission goes well. At the next right turn, Rayce stops, and I nearly run into his back. The sudden nearness of him sets my nerves on edge, and the faint scent of honey tickles my nose.

He stands in place, blocking the entire hallway.

"Are we here?" I ask, peeking around him to see the familiar light blue curtain of my quarters.

"I guess we are," he says, motioning forward. The Zarenite

that flickered on overhead just touches the opening of a doorway several yards away.

Rayce puts his hands in his pockets but doesn't move out of my way. He stares down at the tips of his boots and rubs his lips together slowly like he wants to speak.

"Rose." He whispers my name like a prayer. He looks up, his face drawn tight. "Do you ever think about what your life would have been like if you weren't captured by the Gardener?"

His question crashes through me, and silence clings to the air like mist as I take a moment to ponder it. He crosses the space between us in a single step and leans against the wall, staring up at the Zarenite. Our shoulders press together, radiating heat, but either he doesn't notice or doesn't care.

"No," I say, my voice firm. "Picturing a different future leads to hope, and hanging on to false hope is deadly in the Garden."

His rough fingers wrap around mine for a brief second, and he presses them together before letting go. That single touch says more than a thousand sorrys ever will.

"Maybe that's why I feel miserable so often," Rayce says, turning to look at me with a sad smile. "I can't stop myself from thinking about how different my life would have been if my uncle hadn't pushed the people to their breaking point. If things had worked out better when I was younger, I might not have been forced to fight him or disappoint my mother so thoroughly."

The hurt when he talks about his mother makes his tone waver, and a tiny piece of my heart aches for him. I've known pain that can't be washed away no matter how hard it's scrubbed.

"Doesn't she see the emperor for the monster he is?"

Rayce rubs the back of his neck, not meeting my eyes. "He isn't a monster to her. He's the one that secured their family name after their father nearly bankrupted the imperial treasury during his reign and brought some semblance of order back to Imperial City. My uncle gave our family stability, and for my mother, that's always been the most important thing. To her, I'm the one who broke everything by declaring war against him." He chuckles, a bitter thing that dies in his throat. "He can do no wrong. He even almost united Delmar and Varsha ten years back."

That last sentence hits me sharper than a sandstorm in the desert.

He pushes off the wall.

"But it's late, and I'm sure you don't want to hear about my family problems, so I'll let you sleep," he says and quickly turns back toward the way we came.

"Wait." I catch his arm. "What did you mean by that?"

He pauses, then turns to face me. "By what?" His voice is strained.

"About your uncle uniting both kingdoms."

He shakes his head. "If Varsha hadn't fallen, the negotiations my uncle and the old Varshan king were working through would have been settled, and I would have been married to their princess. Maybe in that future, Delmar wouldn't have been torn to pieces and the people would finally be at ease."

I open my mouth to speak, but nothing will come out.

"That dream died the same day the Varshan princess did." He bows his head, maybe at her memory or maybe at the death of the whole thing. "But I hope you know that doesn't mean we should stop dreaming. Otherwise, my uncle really will win."

He waves from behind him, not even bothering to look back as he leaves me. If he had, he would have seen my trembling hands and the way I have to lean against the wall to stay standing. And he would have read the truth written all over my face.

Strands of my father's long black beard tickle the top of my head as he leans over to kiss me good night, the blue silken covers of my bed tucked up to my chin.

"Daddy, you look tired," I say, yawning.

He turns on my favorite night-light, one of the last things I have of my mother. The ornate golden cylinder shoots jewel-colored lights all over the room, sending them dancing over the ceiling like rainbow stars.

Father sits next to me on the bed, and the weight is comforting. He pulls from his head the Jewel of the Sand, the crown passed down from generations of Varshan rulers, and places it carefully on his lap.

"It has been a long day, my sweet," he says. "Your father's been talking with an ambassador of Delmar since the morning."

I scrunch up my nose, remembering the lesson I'd just finished with Madame Patel about the barbarians of the west.

"Why would you do that?" I ask. "Madame Patel says they don't even believe in the Great Creatress."

"Don't be so quick to judge," Father says, tapping me gently on the nose. "Always remember to be kind. That is a princess's job. And a king's job is to try to maintain peace for his people. That's what I was doing today, and you get to help me with that. Would you like that?"

"Of course," I say, sitting up.

He smiles. "One day, when you're much older, you and the young prince of Delmar are going to unite this kingdom for the better."

He touches my cheek with gentle fingertips, and I fall asleep, one of the last nights I'd ever spend tucked in that bed with my father watching over me.

Ten days later, Varsha fell, just after my father made that deal with Galon, the emperor of Delmar. Rayce's uncle. Was my arranged marriage part of the reason why?

Surviving in the Garden forced me to forget who I was. And even though I knew from the beginning that Rayce was meant to take the throne after his uncle, I never connected him with the young prince of Delmar I was supposed to marry. Not this man with healing hands and mischief in his eyes.

My stomach rolls, but somehow I stay upright. I look down the tunnel where the man who might have been my husband in another life disappeared, taking with him a thousand possibilities that flicker into darkness like the Zarenite above me.

# Chapter Twenty

The night passes in a blur as I toss and turn over what would have been. The book Oren gave me feels like a rock underneath my pillow. The answers might be on those pages, but I'm too afraid to check after the secret Rayce revealed last night. What else will I find between that bound parchment that will shatter what I thought I knew about my life?

For the first time in years, I let myself dream big. Rayce carved out the missing pieces of a future I could have had with him by my side. Maybe in that world, I wouldn't shudder every time he drew near. What would he have done if I'd told him who I am last night? Who I *was*. And how is it that, even though I'm supposedly dead and he's no longer in line for the throne, we managed to find each other?

Not that it matters.

I clench my fist, feeling the way my nails bite into my palms to bring myself back to the present. Dreams won't help me now. After breakfast, I try to decipher Marin's directions to the training room for a third time but wonder if I took a wrong turn somewhere. Nothing about this newest hallway looks any different from the one before it.

"Stupid tunnels," I mumble under my breath, stopping.

The sharp *zap-zap* of a stunner reaches my ears from a little farther down the hall.

Sweat drips down my face as I stop in front of a doorway deep inside the mines of the rebellion.

I take a deep breath and enter before the shouting in my head can talk me out of it. After the maze of tunnels, I'm not in an ideal condition to focus on weapon training, but since we're leaving in a few days, I don't have time to be picky.

The last time I practiced sword fighting in the training room, it was a jumble of weapons and bodies crammed in the close quarters. But now that it's empty, I realize the ceiling is only a few inches higher than the hallway, and the room itself is only about ten times the size of my sleeping quarters. A cluster of swords, a few axes, a handful of crossbows, and a row of stunners hang neatly on the wall to my right, and four wooden targets line the back of the room. Arlo stands near the door, aiming his stunner at a human-shaped target in the back of the room. Black burn marks scour the wood on its chest.

Arlo's dark blue sleeves are rolled up to his elbows, and his boots sit discarded next to the door. His eyes narrow just before he lets off a shot.

It's beautiful the way his body makes a straight line, drawn tight like a crossbow string, and the tender way his fingers caress the stunner's hilt. A quick smile melts onto his lips as the bolt finds its target directly on the same burn mark.

I clear my throat.

He whirls around, aiming his stunner at my heart. Even though I don't think he'll shoot me, I throw my hands up to show him I'm unarmed. A bolt to the chest right now would squash any dreams of aiding with the rescue mission.

"You really shouldn't sneak up on a man with a weapon,"

Arlo says, lowering his stunner.

"Maybe you should be paying more attention to what's going on behind you," I reply, leaning against the doorframe.

He laughs, a full-throated thing, and waves me in. I wonder if he can sense my stress.

"Normally I'd ease into the training," Arlo says. "The art of long-distance accuracy is a delicate one, but we don't have time for that."

I stop a few feet from him. He rolls his eyes, bridging the gap I made, and offers me the stunner he was shooting with. I accept it, my hand dipping with the weight of the metal contraption.

"Not to mention I've already used a stunner before." I move my hand into the position Rayce showed me back in Imperial City.

He chuckles. "Not very well, though. But after today, you should be able to shoot a target if it's close range."

He pulls a second stunner from his holster, handling it with the same kind of ease that I would with silk strips. He flips it around so the butt of the handle faces upward and takes a step closer to me.

"This," he says, pushing down on the top of the hilt with his pointer finger, "is where you load the Zarenite powder."

The top comes off, revealing a hollow cylinder full of glittering dust.

"As you pull the trigger, the spring here"—he motions to a coil on the bottom of the lid—"moves the powder up. The trigger also creates a spark that ignites the Zarenite, which is what you see coming out of the barrel. That's about all I understand. Piper knows the rest."

He fishes inside his shirt and pulls out a vial of Zarenite, exactly like the one Rayce had me swallow when we escaped Imperial City. Just thinking his name conjures up the memory of what he revealed last night and…other things I can't seem to forget. I turn away to hide my blush. Arlo raises an eyebrow but doesn't comment, handing me the vial.

"We're all required to carry extra Zarenite in case we go dark," Arlo says.

"What does that mean?" I ask, trying to stay rooted in the present.

Arlo holds out his other arm, which is covered in dark green swirling arrows that snake up into the fabric of his shirt.

"If our tattoos become invisible when we're in contact with Zarenite, that means the mineral inside us has been used up and we need to get more fast," he says, pulling up his sleeve farther to reveal more of the tattoo. "The bigger the tattoo, the longer we can last without going dark. The extra vial is just a precaution, so we're almost never caught without it, because if we are, our stunners are basically useless."

I frown at the Zarenite in my hand. It's strange how to him it probably represents security, but all I can think of when I look at the green vial is the rocketing pain of a stunner blast.

"Take only a quarter of that vial, since it affects you more strongly than us."

Arlo ignores my sour face and waits patiently for me to swallow the Zarenite. A wave of heat races down my throat, like I've just downed an entire bottle of whiskey.

"It's hot," I say, passing him back the vial.

"Then it's working." He clears his throat. "While we have a moment, I wanted to thank you for helping save Marin back in Dongsu. And you might not be very good with a stunner, but you scaled that wall quicker than any trained soldier I've seen. It was impressive."

"You don't have to thank me for helping her," I say. "I really like your sister."

He directs me to plant my feet in line with my shoulders, keeping my knees bent. My body falls into line with the commands, used to being told what to do by someone other than myself. The stance, the flow it requires, reminds me of the setup before a dance.

"I always worried something like that would happen," Arlo says. "To be honest, that's the only reason it took me so long to join the rebellion."

"Yeah, Marin told me a little about how reluctant you were at first…and what changed your mind."

"Use both hands; it'll help you steady the shot." He pulls my right arm to meet my left then circles around me so I can't see his face. "The emperor pretty much ordering my parents to be killed had a lot to do with it. But back when it was just an idea, Rayce and Oren knew they'd need someone to do all of the actual work, since they were both being monitored in the palace. Rayce and I have known each other since we were children, and when his uncle closed the Varshan border, killing my family's business, he thought I might be interested in fighting with them. He brought me into the palace under the guise of instructing him on long-range weapons, since at the time I spent most of my days entering contests to win money and was well-known for placing decently. Even won a few."

He shot the sword right out from the Gardener's hand from at least a hundred feet back.

"I doubt it was just a few," I say.

He flashes me a wide grin. "I might have been downplaying my accomplishments a bit." He puts a hand on my shoulder to move it to the correct angle, and I clench my teeth, remembering the feel of Rayce's palms on my back last night when he held me. It was only to comfort me. We both needed it. But now that I know what he could have been, I can't get his touch out of my mind.

"At first, I wasn't interested in what Rayce had to say," Arlo says, pulling my straying mind back to his story. "If we had been caught before all the measures were in place, I would have put Marin at great risk."

"I'm sorry," I say and find that I mean it.

He takes a deep breath behind me. "There isn't any need to be. Instead of being sorry or mad, I did something about it. It was the only way to cope with the loss of my parents. Besides, I like what we're doing here, and I believe Rayce will be a great leader when all this fighting is done."

I turn away from him, lowering my weapon.

"Was Rayce always like he is now?" I ask, keeping my voice light.

"What do you mean?" Arlo asks, then interrupts himself. "No, your weak hand should steady the stunner." He pushes my hand back up.

"I don't know, he seems...intense," I say. "But you knew him growing up. Was he always so focused on leading?"

"No," Arlo says, laughing. "Before his uncle started coming to his training sessions periodically, I thought they would throw him out of the palace. He was always playing silly pranks on the palace staff and rarely ever took anything seriously. We used to sneak him out of the palace at night and watch all the girls shopping in Imperial City's market square."

"The girls must have loved him," I say, keeping my voice steady. "Both of you, probably."

Arlo's face splits into a smile that borders on arrogant.

"A fair few," he says, then lets a beat of silence draw out between us. "Of course, Rayce never seemed too interested in any of them. I've only ever seen him actively try to impress one or two. Especially since he started the rebellion. That's why I was so surprised by how hard he fought with the council on your behalf to help the others in the Garden."

Fire rushes to my cheeks, and I hear Arlo chuckle over my racing heart.

"I think you're about as ready as you can be to shoot," Arlo says. "Just align the little notch at the end of the barrel and pull the trigger when you're ready."

I figured my hands would stop trembling, but thinking about pulling the trigger makes them shake even worse. I close one eye, fighting to aim the stunner. I can fly through the air with only a piece of silk to catch me; I can stop my fall mere inches from the ground. If I can accomplish those things, a stunner should be easy.

"Remember to breathe," Arlo says.

My body reacts before my mind, and as I take in a breath, I pull the trigger. The gun kicks back, but because Arlo made me hold my arms out, it doesn't come near my face. The bolt of Zarenite flies from the tip of my gun, a blazing green blur, and nicks the side of the target.

"Not bad." Arlo nods his approval. "You wouldn't have knocked a soldier unconscious, but you'd have slowed them down. You might just be more than a liability yet."

"Thanks, I think."

"It was a compliment," Arlo says. He scratches the back of his head. "I do worry about Rayce, though. Leading this rebellion is definitely taking a toll on him. Intense, you called it...I see that more in him every day."

"What do you mean?" I ask, steadying my feet to take another shot.

"He has to make a lot of difficult choices. Usually that means choosing between what he wants and how he feels or what's best for the people he's leading. But he'll always choose his people over what he wants for himself. I don't think I could make the same choices in his shoes."

My finger hovers over the trigger, and I remember the shape of his lips just inches from mine before the bell saved us from ourselves. Thinking of that moment forces me to relive Rayce's parting words last night, and I wonder again what he would have done if I'd told him my secret. Would he betray me if he thought it would save his people?

"A lot of times it's little stuff, like helping the miners dig for Zarenite when he's tired or staying up all night interpreting the latest information provided by our spies, but sometimes it's much harder than that."

"What has he had to do?" I ask, cold dread seeping through my feet from the floor.

"When we originally started this rebellion, there were four of us. We don't talk about Wèn often, because it's still pretty painful for all of us. He was another childhood friend of both of ours, but we found out later that he was a spy for the emperor. We lost a battle that killed hundreds of our own because Wèn reported our location beforehand. We didn't want to believe it, but Rayce had him followed and it was confirmed."

Sweat slicks my hand, and I rub it on the back of my pant leg. "What happened to him?"

"We don't know," Arlo says. "Rayce left him wounded on the battlefield. He either died there or he was surrendered to the emperor's custody. Death would be kinder." Arlo shivers, shaking off his words. "But on to better things, like how to defend yourself. Take another shot."

Forgetting everything he taught me, I pull the trigger, but my mind isn't here anymore. I can't get rid of the gnawing sensation crawling up my body, because Arlo more than answered my question. Rayce will do anything for his people, even if that means sentencing someone he'd known his entire life to die. He can *never* find out about my heritage, then.

I take another shot and feel like I was the one struck with the Zarenite bolt as I remember all of Oren's little questions and observations.

I have to figure out what Oren knows. If I don't, I might end up the next hard decision that comes across Rayce's desk.

# Chapter Twenty-One

The second that Arlo decides the wall behind the target has had enough torture for the day, I race out of the training room, waving good-bye to him over my shoulder. Somewhere, crawling around the tunnels, is Oren. After a few minutes of aimlessly wandering, I realize I should have just asked Arlo to show me where Oren stays, but it takes me more than thirty minutes to get back to the training room, and by then, Arlo's disappeared.

I trace my steps back to my bedroom, thanks to Marin's map, keeping one eye up to scan the passing faces for Oren, but luck isn't on my side. The next few hours are a blur of exploring and retracing my steps. Every time I try to ask someone for directions, they scurry away or pointedly look down, like I've been shunned. Or they're afraid of me. I wonder what kind of rumors have circulated.

My growling stomach convinces me to give up the search. Following the twisting tunnel back the way I came, I head toward the dining hall from my room. My feet trace these familiar steps with ease.

As I swing my last right, I nearly run into Oren. Scrolls fall from his clasped arms as he jerks to avoid hitting me, raining paper onto the floor.

"You startled me, Rose!" he says, pushing up his small spectacles.

"Let me help you with those." I squat down to gather his fallen parchment.

I'd been looking for him all day, but I'm so surprised at nearly colliding with him that I forget why I wanted to find him.

"Are you all right, child?" Oren asks. "I didn't step on your toes, did I?"

I blink at his question, my mind racing to catch up with the conversation. "No, you didn't, and I'm fine." I pick up a few scrolls. "Just a little hungry."

He frowns at my answer. "I'm afraid the last round of supper ended a good hour ago." He tilts his head. "Although I do believe there might be a straggler left in the kitchen. We might be able to snag a scrap or two if we ask nicely. Why don't I walk you?"

Though I really want to pick his brain, I look at the mountain of scrolls we're picking up and hesitate.

"Are you sure it isn't a bother?" I ask.

"Of course," he says.

"I can I help you carry these until we get there."

He smiles and hands over half his stack. Most of them have a red wax seal of a dragon similar to the one on his pipe and are held shut with green ribbon. Oren turns around to head back the way he was coming from and ducks to clear the nearest hanging lantern filled with Zarenite. Living under all this rock in what must feel like tight spaces would probably annoy me if I were his size. I have no idea how he does it.

"Have you gotten a chance to read through that book I loaned you?" Oren asks, inadvertently pulling me back to my mission at hand.

"I haven't found the time yet," I say, which is half true.

"I know you've been very busy. I'm sure you will when you find a moment to breathe. I marked a passage in there that I thought might be of particular interest to you."

I fiddle with one of the ribbons on a bottom scroll, trying to work out how to broach the subject of Varsha with him again without sounding too suspicious.

"Speaking of that book," I start, keeping my voice light, "I was wondering if you knew any specifics about why Varsha fell."

He raises an eyebrow at my query. "Well," he says, taking a deep breath, "that's a loaded question. I suppose the leading grievance for the rebellion was the previous king's talks with the Delmarion ambassador."

"Oh?" I look down at my boots as we walk. "What were they trying to negotiate?"

"A treaty that would have united the kingdoms," Oren says, "and put an end to this pointless war once and for all."

My father's weary voice floats back to me. I remember the worry lines that deepened on his face in the days before Varsha fell. Ever since I let that one moment seep back into my consciousness, his face hovers in the back of my mind, attacking my composure every time I close my eyes.

"Why would the rebels see that as a bad thing? Isn't an end to the war supposed to be good for the people?"

"It is," Oren says. "That was the previous king's mind-set, too. He was a very kind man and he cared deeply for his people. I took many of the lessons I learned from him back with me and used them to teach Rayce. But the problem was, the Varshan rebels didn't believe the kingdoms should be united through treaty, but rather, by force."

I scoff. "That's ridiculous."

Oren and I reach the empty dining hall. All the chairs are

pushed neatly against the five long tables that line the room, and the quiet of the tall space feels overwhelming. As Oren walks in, the wall begins to glow green.

"I believe that was simply false propaganda spread by the usurper in order to spur enough of the people into a civil war," Oren says. "After all, since he has taken the throne, there have only been four attempts on the wall."

If what Oren believes is true, then the reason my father is dead is because he tried to unite the kingdoms through love. And even though Rayce had nothing to do with it, I can't keep myself from believing it was because of our arranged marriage that I lost everything and my father is dead. The pile of scrolls crunches in my arms, and I turn away from Oren in case anything in my face might betray me.

Oren marches us toward the back of the room and into the kitchen. Six ovens line the back wall, and long stone countertops cut through the space. Shiny metal bowls and a variety of utensils sit abandoned in the corners of the cooking stations, and the absence of the usual bubbling pots and people shouting gives the whole place a lonely feeling.

"Ah, here we are," Oren whispers, motioning to the far corner.

A single familiar figure breaks the flat loneliness of the room, his dark hair pulled back in a very short bun on top of his head. A few strands fall onto his forehead as he bends over the countertop.

*Rayce.*

He stares intently at a pile of dough, the muscles in his arms flexing every time he kneads it. His large hands and a good portion of his green shirt are peppered in white flour. Though his brow is furrowed in concentration, all the tension I saw on his face the night before has disappeared into a calm serenity.

He hums softly to himself, the slightly out-of-tune melody

of an old folk song floating through the stillness of the air.

"I've found a straggler hoping for dinner," Oren says.

Rayce startles at the interruption, his left hand flying for a sharp knife resting next to him. At seeing Oren, he lets it go, leaving the handle covered in white.

"You scared me," he says, laughing at himself. "How long have you been standing there?"

"Not too long," Oren says. "Do you think you can manage to find some supper for Rose, here?"

Rayce's gaze slides to me, and he wipes his brow with the back of his hand, leaving behind a smear of flour on his forehead. I remember how close I was to his face last night, how his lips hovered near mine, and heat rises up my neck to touch my cheeks.

"I think I can figure something out," he says.

"Well, then, I'll leave you to it." Oren scoops up the scrolls in my arms.

He gives me a pointed look and motions that I should head farther into the kitchen before he disappears back into the dining hall. All of that searching and I still didn't get the answers I need from him.

Silence stretches out as I turn back to Rayce, and Arlo's words from earlier flood my head. It's clear Rayce puts his people before everything, including what he wants. I can't let myself be tricked by his kindness, no matter how good it feels to stand next to him.

Rayce stares at me with curiosity coating his eyes.

"I'm afraid we don't have much left over from dinner tonight," he says. "There are a few whole apples, and we always have a good supply of jerky, but if you want to wait for a bit, I can pop these in the oven and you can have some honey crisps. I can't say they'll be the most nutritious meal, but they'll hold you over until breakfast."

"Okay," I say, clasping my hands in front of me.

Three long countertops separate us, and I feel every inch of distance in the large space. The low lighting casts shadows in all the corners, except for a lantern flickering warm light across his workstation.

His attention returns to the dough, and he clears his throat.

"Would you like me to teach you how to make them?" he asks. "I don't want to pressure you or anything, but this is a pretty big deal. This recipe is a family secret, so I can't let just anyone know how to do it."

Despite the nerves somersaulting in my stomach, a smile finds its way to my face. "I guess I can't say no, then."

He tips his head toward the place next to him, and I move forward, my feet feeling strangely heavy. Moving around the countertop, I stop a few inches from him. He pushes back a cluster of his hair.

"Go ahead and dip your hands in the bowl to wash them."

I plunge my hands into the large bowl full of water, sending ripples through the clear surface. The water still has a bit of heat to it as I rub my palms together.

"I heard from Arlo that your stunner training went well," Rayce says, giving me a white cloth from his shoulder.

"Liar," I say, patting my hands dry then placing the rag on the counter.

His mouth quirks up in a smile. "You still have a few days to get it down."

"How are plans going for the mission?" I ask.

"Well, I'm in here," he says. "Which generally isn't a good sign." He sighs, nodding at a sack of flour. "Now coat your hands in flour so the dough doesn't stick to them."

The flour rests on the other side of him, and I have to reach across to grab it. He doesn't bother moving, seeming comfortable with our nearness while my heart threatens to burst out of my chest.

"I'm sorry it isn't going well," I say.

"It's just the stress of trying to figure out so many different operations at once," he says. "Our strategy meeting ended just a few minutes ago, which is why I was so surprised to see Oren again."

I pull away from the flour.

"You're going to need more." His hands cover mine as he guides them back to the flour and gently sticks them into the powder until they're coated almost up to my wrists. "There."

He smiles at our joined hands but doesn't show any signs of letting go. Then he stands behind me, his hard edges pressing into my back. I can feel every ripple on his chest, and my breath catches. His warmth radiates through me, sending tiny sparks down to my toes.

"You have to knead with just the right amount of force," he says, his voice tickling my ear. "It's a bit tricky at first."

Cupping my hands in his, he places them on the dough, and the slightly squishy texture seeps between my fingers as he shows me how to knead it properly. The sticky-sweet scent of honey mixed with yeast permeates the air every time we apply pressure. His scratchy chin brushes my cheek as he leans in to watch our progress, and I fight against the tremble threatening to take hold of my body.

"Do you do this often?" I ask, trying to distract myself from the warmth of his touch.

"I wish I could," he says. "There have been a great number of things preoccupying my mind. I don't expect it to get any easier as this war progresses."

"Every time I try to rest, all I can think about are my sisters in the Garden, so I can only imagine what it's like for you, with so many more people counting on you."

He moves his hand up the length of my arm and turns my face toward him so we're staring at each other. The edge of the countertop presses into my hips, pinning us together. I'm helpless against the intensity in his eyes.

"Sometimes I wonder how you understand me so well." The throatiness of his voice vibrates against my spine, rippling outward from there to every nerve. "I guess it's because we both feel responsible for the people around us."

He reaches up with a flour-coated finger and pushes a strand of my hair behind my ear, dragging his finger down my cheek. My lips pulse next to his, our energy electric.

Rayce blinks, shaking his head like he's trying to get water out of his ears. He straightens, releasing me, and steps to the side.

"It's funny, though," he says, his tone suddenly clipped. "I find myself not having time for distractions anymore, whether it's doing the things I love or spending time with the people I care about. I have to stay focused."

Arlo's voice echoes in my head like alarm bells: *he will always choose his people over what he wants for himself.*

"It's getting late, so I'll just finish this quickly."

His face drawn tight, he takes the dough away from me and pounds down on it with quick, practiced movement. His hard gaze remains trained on his task. All of the heat I felt a moment ago dissipates, and I'm left with nothing but his pursed lips and emptiness in the pit of my stomach. His sudden indifference burns me far deeper than I imagined it would, and I wrap my arms around my middle.

"I just realized that it isn't good to eat this close to bedtime anyway," I say. "I'll wait for breakfast."

"That's probably for the best," Rayce answers, not bothering to look up from his work.

"I guess I'll see you tomorrow, then."

"Uh-huh."

Did I do something wrong? His entire demeanor flipped faster than the bolt of a stunner. My breath sticks to my rib cage, but I will my feet to stay measured most of the way across the room. As I near the exit, I dare a glance over my shoulder. Rayce runs his flour-streaked hands through his hair and then slams them both down, the dough he was carefully kneading probably ruined with such a fierce beating.

The moment I slip out of the dining hall, I press against the wall, trying to catch my breath. The cold stone seeps into my back, erasing the feeling of Rayce pressed up against me, but no matter how many times I lick my lips, they won't stop burning.

And neither will my heart.

# Chapter Twenty-Two

The next few days are crammed with stunner training. I see Rayce when he walks through the training room during a morning session, but his eyes slip over me like I'm invisible. My entire life, I wanted to be out of the spotlight, so why does it feel like my stomach falls to the floor when he passes me over without a second thought?

The rest of the training session is a blur of clumsy mistakes, my mind back in the kitchen while I try to figure out what I might have said or done to make him act this way.

Marin informs me that we'll be departing for the dual mission at first light, which means nothing in the constant darkness of underground, but I nod in agreement.

On the day of the mission, she gently shakes me awake, and I sit up, bleary-eyed, smoothing down the stray hairs on top of my head. The large pack of provisions we grabbed the night before sits neatly at the foot of my bed, sending a wave of panic through me as I remember this complex rescue we're about to attempt. Marin leans over her bed, rolling up her quilt with a large pack at her feet.

"How're you feeling today?" I ask.

She looks at me and smiles, the thick white bandage wrapped around her neck where the Gardener cut her peeking out over the collar of her uniform.

"Better now," she says. "Luckily, the wound wasn't too deep. It's just sore."

She touches her throat, and we both look away, picturing how the injury happened.

"Can I ask you something?" she says.

Her eyes are different. They understand what it means to be under the Gardener's rule, even if just for a minute, and my heart aches for her. Now Marin is more than a friend. She's one of my sisters.

"How did you do it?" she says. "How did you live in the Garden? How did you survive, because I can't imagine—"

"I just did," I interrupt. "Every day, I just survived."

She shakes her head, her curly hair bouncing with the movement, and stuffs her blue quilt into her open bag. A single drop of darker blue catches my eye. She must have looked down so I wouldn't see her cry.

"Do you want to know something funny?" I slide out of bed.

"What?" she asks the wall.

"You know that stupid accent the Gardener uses? It isn't even real."

"What?" she repeats, swinging around. "I wondered what dialect it was."

"He invented it. He thinks it makes him sound more exotic."

"That's so stupid," Marin says, the happy lilt back in her voice. She lifts up her pack.

"I know." I slip Oren's book into my pack, wondering if I'll ever have the time or presence of mind to read it, throw on my uniform, and pull the strap over my shoulder.

We both leave the room and walk through the tunnels, heading for the chorus of voices, until we enter a large room near the top of the base. A crowd of guards and their families are spread throughout the room in little pockets.

Marin points me toward my assigned group, gives me a quick hug, and heads to her appointed area. She's part of the team that will be the distraction, though she was placed in the perimeter ring, away from the highest risk.

I push through the crowd, trying to find my area. Everywhere I look feels like I'm eavesdropping on private moments, and it twists something deep in my gut that I thought didn't exist anymore. What would it be like to have a brother embracing me tightly or a mother handing me a loaf of lovingly baked bread while she kisses me good-bye? I reach into my pack and grab the book Oren lent me just to have some piece of my own family close to me.

The air around me feels cold without a body to keep it warm.

"You're looking awfully pensive," comes a deep voice from behind me.

I swing around and almost crash into Rayce, who leaned down to whisper in my ear. I jump back an inch, putting space between us. I expect to meet the hard expression he's given me since the night in the kitchen, but instead I'm swept away in that same mischief glinting from his eyes as the first time I met him. His tunic has been freshly pressed and his face shaven clean. While I've driven myself crazy wondering what I did wrong, he acts as if nothing transpired between us. Like he didn't practically throw me out of the kitchen a few nights ago and ignore me the past few days. I cross my arms over my chest and narrow my eyes at him.

He cocks an eyebrow.

My back tingles where he touched me that night. "Are we talking again now?" I ask, the tremor in my voice betraying me.

The air heats up with his nearness, and I hope it doesn't show on my face.

"We were always talking, Rose. I just got busy the past few days."

"It felt like you were avoiding me."

He puts his hands on my shoulders, bending down to look me squarely in the eyes.

"Are you angry with me?" he asks, his tone surprisingly light. "Because it seems like you're mad, and then I'd have to assume that's because you *enjoy* talking to me." A teasing smile plays on his lips. "Did you miss me?"

"That's not—it isn't like that!" I shake away from his grip. "Why would I miss you? You're impossible."

"And yet, you're blushing."

Before I can respond, Arlo and Oren walk up to us, saving me from continuing the awkward conversation. Clearly, adrenaline or something has put Rayce in a severely good mood and he's taking it out on me. I'll take his joking over him ignoring me. Even though I won't tell him, I *had* missed his company. But only a little.

"Piper's been updated on your orders, and we're ready to leave," Arlo says. "Here, Rose, I got you these."

He holds out a stunner and a leather cord with a vial of Zarenite that matches everyone else's here. I grab the stunner with my free hand and press the book Oren gave me behind my back before he can notice that I'm keeping it on me. If he found out it was here, he would just ask me again if I've read it yet, and I haven't come up with a good excuse why I haven't.

Before I can grab the leather cord, Rayce does. Using both hands he slips it over my neck, his fingers brushing my cheek as he lifts my braid to accommodate the makeshift necklace.

Oren clears his throat. "I've got to brief the small party you selected for the more delicate mission."

"He means breaking out your friends," Rayce clarifies.

"We'll do what we can," Oren says, smiling. "You leave that to me. All three of you, be safe out there."

He nods at the two men and places a hand on top of my head like I'm a child.

"Especially you," he says. "This is your first mission out in Imperial City, after all."

"I will," I say.

He ruffles the top of my hair with his bear-size hand.

"Very well then," he says, nodding. "I'll be off."

The small part of me that wished I had some sort of family here to see me off smiles, but I refuse to let it reach my lips.

"Watch where he goes," Rayce says.

"Why?"

He just motions for me to watch Oren as he walks over to a group of about twenty soldiers at the far end of the room.

"You asked me to show you the ones that'll be focusing their efforts on the Garden, so consider my end of the bargain fulfilled."

"Now we've just got to successfully complete ours," Arlo says.

There's an edge to his voice, barely distinguishable over the noise of the crowd. I nod, feeling my own gut swell up with nerves. If everything goes accordingly, I might be reunited with my sisters in two days.

*Calla, Lily, everyone. Please just hold on until then.*

Rayce walks to the nearest wall and places his palm on the stone. A secret door slides back, revealing another cave, which I now know will lead us out into the world above. He doesn't look back as the people nearest him file out. But I do. Just once. Because if my sisters really will be freed, I don't think I'll ever return to this little base underground again.

• • •

I'd hoped for sunshine, but instead, a chilly wind howls through the Shulin Forests. Leaves are ripped off branches, and dark gray clouds hang low in the sky. Even though the group moves forward, it's like there's a string trying to tug them back toward Zareen and their loved ones.

Fat raindrops splatter through the trees, coloring everything cold. Even the cloak Marin packed me can't keep the tricky little devils from lacing my hair, face, and arms. My boots squish out a depressing melody through the mud as we push onward, water soaking through the leather and attacking my toes.

We move in silence, huddled together to combat the drop in temperature. The mixture of exhaustion and my waterlogged bones magnifies my anxiety. Rain was never a good omen in the Garden, and the superstition stuck with me.

Rayce heads the front, pushing the group at a grueling pace. Arlo explained that a smaller portion of guards went ahead the night before to set up camp, and that even in this storm, we should reach it by tonight.

The only way I can tell we're moving forward is the reappearance of the thin trees that skirt Delmar. Their white trunks resemble ghosts peeking out of the downpour.

"How far are we going?" I yell over the pounding rain.

Arlo turns my way, his hair plastered to his forehead. "The camp's about twenty miles from the city. We're getting close."

The thunderstorm doesn't let up all day. Half the time I'm not sure if I'm actually walking or if my shivering makes me move.

Then the camp appears out of nowhere. One second I'm looking at a sheet of rain so thick I could swim through it, and the next I stumble over the rope of a brown tent sinking into the mud. Squinting into the rain, I catch the shadows of more tents springing out from the downpour like tombstones.

A guard runs over to us, a black hood sagging over his

eyes as water streams off it. He gives a quick salute, flinging water in Arlo's face.

"I'm sorry, sir!" he shouts, shoving his guilty hand behind his back.

"Don't worry about it," Arlo says. "I'm already soaked."

"Please, let me show you to your tent so you can get out of the rain."

Arlo nods. "And make sure this lot gets some help putting up their tents, too."

"Sir, yes, sir." The guard salutes again.

Arlo blinks back the fresh water in his eyes and holds up his hand before the guard can stammer out another apology.

He turns to me. "Come on, Rose, you're with us tonight."

We follow the guard through the campsite, but I can't see much besides the back of the man's cloak. He stops near a tall tent and peels open the flap, stepping out of the way so that we can enter. Arlo motions for me to go first.

As soon as I'm underneath, the pelting rain softens into a snapping sound as it hits the fabric. The moist air follows me in, but at least the rain isn't stinging my eyes anymore. Two cots are set up at the back with blankets folded neatly at their bases. A flap separates a small portion of the left side of the tent from the rest of the large space.

Arlo heads toward the cot without the bag already sitting on it, instructing me to put my things on the empty one behind the flap. I plop my own bag down, and water oozes out, dashing any hope of dry clothing.

"Where'd the shogun go?" Arlo asks, turning back to the guard.

*Good question.* Glad I didn't have to ask it.

"He's, um—" The guard blinks and turns to look into the downpour. "Ah, he's there."

Arlo and I walk to the edge of the tent and follow the guard's finger. Rayce is barely visible through the rain, helping a woman unfold what will soon become her shelter from the storm. He walks backward, spreading out the water-resistant fabric. Arlo and I glance at each other, and he smirks, shaking his head.

"He just can't help himself," he says, walking back to his pack.

I watch as Rayce rushes over to grab the first pole, and I take a step toward him. The way the water runs through his hair, dripping down the deep ridges of his scar and sticking the fabric of his white shirt onto his skin captivates me. I wonder what it would be like to run my hands through his wet hair and press my lips against his drenched skin. Would he taste like the rain?

"Don't bother offering to help," Arlo says, making me jump. I blink and turn away from Rayce. "He'll just make you come back here if he sees you, since we've been traveling through this downpour."

"Oh." I step back into the tent. "Right, thanks."

"Anyway, sorry for putting you in here," Arlo says. "Rayce had you with Marin, but I thought she needed to focus on her portion of the mission without having to also watch out for you. I hope you don't mind."

"No, that's fine."

Arlo lights lanterns, the closest to a fire we'll get tonight. I walk into my small section of the tent and pull the flap that separates me from the rest of the tent closed tight. I listen for Arlo on the other side of the curtain, and as soon as I hear a pot clang, I peel off my wet clothes and spread them out to let them dry.

I unpack my bag, in search of something halfway dry to change into. My quilt squashes underneath my fingers, but it protected Oren's book from getting wet. I grab it by the spine and shove it under the pillow on my cot. Maybe tonight I can face those words, but even imagining cracking open the pages and letting more secrets spill onto the floor causes my heart to thud against my chest. As Rayce suggested, I should keep the past where it belongs. Dreaming of a dead future won't keep me alive in the present, and right now I can't afford to fall apart.

And still, the need to find out what Oren wants me to see pulls my hand near the pillow.

As I brush the sharp corner of the book, Arlo shouts from behind the tent flap that dinner is ready, shattering the last of my nerve. I leave the book tucked away, relief and disappointment warring within me, as I head back into the main portion of the tent.

# Chapter Twenty-Three

Rayce, Arlo, and I gather around one of the lanterns in the main section of the tent for a dinner of cold rice, grapes, and day-old fish. Neither Rayce nor Arlo attempts to make conversation, with the threat of tomorrow's mission looming over our heads. While I pick at my food, my mind wanders back to the book resting under my pillow and whether I should read it.

After excusing myself, I pull the flaps to my section of the tent closed and dim the lantern to almost nothing. I cloak the dry blanket around my shoulders and sit in the middle of the cot, crossing my legs. Outside, the rain still falls, but it's lightened up to a soft pattering.

Oren said he marked a passage in the book. He wants me to know something. Maybe I could just peek.

I scratch an imaginary itch behind my ear and reach under my pillow before I can talk myself out of it. The cloth cover is bumpy against my fingertips. I place the book on my lap and stare at the cover that resembles the night sky, the silver title gleaming like cold stars in the lamplight.

I should open it now before I risk my life tomorrow. Wouldn't it be better to know what Oren knows? Especially if something goes wrong, and the list of things that could go wrong is endless—Rayce's distraction doesn't work, someone else gets captured, I fall trying to walk across a rope I've never seen, or the girl isn't where she's supposed to be.

I run my finger along the book's spine, and the yellowing, beveled pages call out to me. My eyes find a folded corner near the middle of the book.

If I do this now, am I already accepting that something will go wrong tomorrow? Giving up before the fight?

"Rose, are you awake?" Rayce whispers.

I shove the book back underneath the pillow while turning to the flap that separates me from him and the rest of the tent.

Rayce appears just inside my portion of the tent, illuminated by the lamplight in a white shirt that hugs the line of his shoulders, his hair flattened on one side from lying on it. His dark eyes glow in the warm yellow pool of light, and tiny nicks and scars covering his arms catch the shadows.

"Oh, good, you are," he says, sleep coloring his voice husky.

I avert my eyes quickly. I would have seen Rayce like this every night if my father hadn't lost his kingdom. This would have been normal for us, but now it feels anything but.

"What's wrong?" I ask, pulling the covers tight around my middle.

"I couldn't sleep." He combs his fingers through his hair. "I never can the night before a mission. I'd like some company...if you don't mind?"

I want to ask him why he isn't talking to Arlo instead, but then I'm afraid that will make him think better of asking me and he'll leave. If I'm being honest with myself, I'd like some company, too.

"I don't mind." I scoot over on the cot. "Did you want to sit?"

I hope my cheeks aren't glowing. This is the first time we've been alone since he was teaching me how to knead dough.

"Sure," he says and settles beside me.

Even with the warm blanket wrapped around my body, I can feel heat radiating off him. Every inch of my skin is aware of his hands as he places them in his lap. Cold from the rain still sticks between my bones, but his nearness chases it away.

Why is my heart beating like I've been running?

This is the man who took me prisoner and threw me in a cell to interrogate me. But he's also the man who helped a random soldier put up her tent in the pouring rain, who gets up early in the morning to cook and serve his people breakfast, who always carries around sweets and cleaned my wound when he's afraid of blood. He kept his word and freed me when he believed I didn't try to assassinate him.

I shake off my last thought, and the blanket slips from my shoulders. A small smile plays on his lips, and he reaches over to slide the blanket back up. "You're shivering," he says.

*Yes, but it isn't from the cold.*

His fingertip blazes a trail across my bare shoulder, and I hold my breath. Our eyes meet. Only a few inches separate us, but the space is so foreign it might as well be miles. I wonder if in our other life I would have fit into those inches, welcomed them. Would we have been in love? Or just playing the part of a happily married couple for political gain?

Rayce clears his throat and breaks eye contact first.

"I'm worried about tomorrow," he starts. "We've never attempted three separate missions at once. It'll hedge our chances of *everything* going wrong, but it also increases the odds that something will fail."

My heart aches at his words. I know people in every

mission. If mine fails, I'll be in trouble and so will Arlo. If Rayce's distraction fails, he and Marin will be caught. And if Oren's attempt to free the Flowers goes awry… My sisters flash through my mind, and I grip the blanket.

"That has to be a lot of pressure on you," I offer.

"It always is," he says through a sigh. "Sometimes more than I can take. I want to help you and Piper, but all those men and women out there are counting on me to get them back to their families, too."

"So why do it, then?" I ask, looking up at him.

His brow furrows and he frowns. "Why wouldn't I help if I could?"

"Because helping is tough. Being responsible for so many people. Sometimes I don't even think I can be responsible for myself."

"Yet the only thing you've done since leaving the Garden is to try to figure out a way to help the others," he says. "The way you feel about them is the way I feel about all the people risking their lives under my orders. They're my family."

His eyes drip sadness. All I want to do is take it away from him, but I have no idea how. The confusing desire to touch him returns, and I start to reach for him, but my hand trembles, betraying my nerves. I let it fall back on my lap.

"What you do here is almost impossible," I say. "I can't imagine how hard. You have to make awful decisions and you hold yourself accountable for them, and I could never do that. I just want to know why you think it's worth it."

"Because…" He rubs the back of his neck. "War was imminent for Delmar. Oren and I knew it the moment Uncle Galon shut off the trade to Varsha and crippled most of the merchant class. And we decided that if I were ever going to earn the respect of my people, I needed to stand up to him."

"That's why you started the rebellion?"

"Partially," he says, letting out a deep breath. "There was

already talk of war that would rip Imperial City in half. But mostly…"

He cuts himself off and stares hard at his bare feet.

"Mostly what?" I prompt him.

"Mostly I couldn't stand who I was becoming under his watchful eye." He shakes his head at himself. "Three years ago, when my uncle named me his heir and I was forced to move into the palace, you wouldn't have even recognized me. He appointed me captain of the Delmarion army by the time I was sixteen. I carried out his every order without question, because I wanted to prove to everyone that I earned my rank." He rubs his face. "But I was always conflicted about his orders. I think he wanted to make sure I kept myself unattached. Fit to rule in case he ever passed on."

"I can't imagine you being that way."

"I wish I never was," he says. "But I used to be. The most frustrating thing is that I used to believe my uncle wasn't a bad man. That deep down he had the capacity to be kind. But I was wrong, and it nearly cost me my soul. He's just too logical, all about numbers." He tilts his head the other way. "If there are more mouths to feed than food to go around, he eliminates them. He stopped seeing those numbers as people a long time ago."

"Any man willing to make a pact with the Gardener isn't a good leader."

"I know," Rayce whispers. "He's done a lot of things over the past few years that have made me realize there's no going back to his side, but I didn't decide to leave because of what he did. It was because of something *I* did."

His gaze flickers to my face, and he gives me a regretful smile that seems to drain the last bit of warmth from his eyes.

"You don't have to tell me—" I start, but he's already decided he's going to.

"There was this small town. Just a handful of people

lived there." He holds out a cupped palm like he can scoop up the people in his memory. "My uncle assigned me a small platoon. The mission was simple: eliminate the contaminants. People were sick, and Uncle Galon was afraid of the plague spreading. I viewed it as the mission that would validate my rank." The corner of his mouth twitches, twisting his scar. "The people, they were terrified that the Delmarion soldiers had been sent."

He folds his hands in his lap. "When we got there, I saw a little boy run through the streets and nearly trampled him with my horse. I stopped just short of him and he reached up, offering me a piece of his bread, even though food was already scarce at that time. Seeing such generosity from people who had so little to give, from a child...I knew then I couldn't go through with it. So I ordered my soldiers to stand down, but my uncle had already anticipated that I might bend. I tried to stop them, but I was outnumbered—" His voice catches. "I can still feel the heat of the fire on my skin as that town burned to the ground. And their screams." He squeezes his eyes closed for a moment. "Their screams don't ever go away."

He looks at me, pain etched into every part of his face. "That's why I was so shocked when you told me that screams haunt you. I've never heard anyone else put my nightmare into words."

My breath stops, trying to process what he's saying, one thing at a time. "So *all* of the people in the town were sick?"

"The orders were to eliminate the illness."

The fact that he didn't answer my question reveals everything.

"How many?" I breathe.

He closes his eyes again. "A hundred and twelve. All because I couldn't stop it. I was powerless."

His words sear the air. Those hands that have helped a thousand people are covered in innocent blood. Killing people like that would cripple me forever, not spur me into action. I'd hide from what I did—but he's accepted those deaths.

Suddenly, it makes perfect sense to me why the leader of the rebellion would stay in the rain to help a woman build her tent. He's trying to repent. He built an entire opposition—not only against the government but also against his own blood relative—to avenge those people he wronged. To make sure it never happens again.

Without hesitation this time, I place my trembling hand on top of his, the need to comfort him stronger than wanting to hide my nerves. "If you tried to stop the soldiers from murdering those people, then it isn't your fault."

"Like you not being able to rescue the Flowers isn't your fault," he says.

I purse my lips, because he's wrong. I only had one person holding me back. He had a whole army.

He takes a shuddering breath then continues. "The moment we got back, I went to my uncle and told him everything had to stop. That I wouldn't let him hurt anyone else. There had to be another way." He meets my eyes. "But I've never been able to beat him in a sword fight. Not a single time. He challenged me to a duel right then and there, and I fought him even though I knew I'd lose. No one questions Galon without consequences."

He winces, sending his scar dancing. And the truth dawns on me. With a single finger, I reach up and trace the puckered line running down his face.

"He did this to you?"

I feel his cheek push up into a smile underneath my fingertip.

"I think he wanted me to remember his absolute power every time I saw it." He runs his fingertips up my arm and cups my hand in his. "And I do, just not the way he intended. Every time I look in the mirror, I'm reminded of why I'm fighting. Of what and who I'm fighting for."

The tip of his thumb is rough as he rubs tiny circles across the back of my hand.

"I don't think any one man should have all that power," he says.

"Is that what you hope to accomplish with all this?" I ask. "To get him out of power?"

"That's part of the reason."

He lets go of my hand and rests his on his knee. Being this close and not touching is like a flower fighting its way back in the ground. It doesn't feel right.

"But what we really want," Rayce says, "is to create a system where no single man has all the control. Where an Imperial Council votes on issues together and that's how the law is created. I want people like Oren on it, people who aren't so out of touch with the rest of the population. I want to open up trade with Varsha again and let people practice art and make their own decisions. But first, we have to take my uncle out of power."

His voice speeds up, his fervor humming in the space between us. It's like his words paint a new future in the air, the passion he feels for what he's fighting for providing the red, the sorrow of past trespasses smearing blue, the life he wants to create bursting green, and I can finally start to see what Marin, or any of these folks, are willing to risk their lives for. He talks about equality, about turning life in Delmar around. About giving everyone a voice.

It lights a spark in my gut, like a piece of Zarenite beginning to glow.

And it dawns on me bright as the first rays of sunlight.

Rayce helps things shine.

"I'm sorry." He shakes his head and starts to rise. "I'm keeping you up. You should sleep. If everything goes well tomorrow, then you'll finally reunite with the others from the

Garden."

He rises, turning my little side of the tent to ice, and I realize that if what he says comes to pass, then this could be the last time we talk like this. Sadness wells up in my chest.

He makes for the flap, every step pulling us farther apart. The ghost of his warmth still lingers in the blankets next to me. I'm not ready to let him leave. Tomorrow I could plummet to my death. Tonight I want just want him near me.

"Wait." I reach out and wrap my fingers around his hand.

"Yes?" he whispers.

The idea of spending what could be my last night alive completely alone breaks me. I want to go back to the moment he pressed me against him and taught my body how to breathe, trapped in the safety of his arms where nothing else existed.

Rayce's eyes hold mine captive, stopping the world and my beating heart for a second.

Why can't I just say the words? They bubble up on my lips, beg to be released: *Stay. With. Me.*

"What is it?" he asks, a half grin splitting his face. "Do you want me to stay?"

"No!" I say, so surprised to hear him voice my exact thought that I drop my grip on his hand. "I just wanted to say, um, be safe tomorrow."

His mouth loosens, and I can't tell if it's relief or disappointment shining from his eyes.

"You, too, Rose." He gives me a weak smile, hand still gripping the tent fabric. "Before I go, I wanted to ask you about what happened to the man that turned you in to the Gardener."

"What do you mean?" I sit up straighter on the cot.

"Back at the base, you'd mentioned something about it being a man that turned you over to the Gardener when you were younger. Do you know what ever happened to him?"

A frown falls onto my lips. "Nothing happened to him.

He was someone I thought I could trust and he betrayed me. Why?"

Rayce shakes his head. "He must have been stupid, this coward. Clearly, he had no idea what a precious thing he was giving up."

Before I can respond, he pushes through the flaps, leaving me to unravel his last words.

I watch the fabric until it stops swaying, all signs that Rayce was ever here disappearing with the movement, and curl into myself. Even now, without a guard or a ton of rocks to trap me, I am not free to do as I really please. I can't seem to break the chains still tightening around my soul. If I could, my mouth would have obliged, and maybe Rayce would still be here to keep me warm.

# Chapter Twenty-Four

Morning brings the memory of Rayce's eyes as he waited by the tent flap for me to speak three little words: *stay with me.* My mouth betrayed me, though, fear rendering my body a prisoner. I held those words close for the rest of the night, wishing the darkness would end and dreading morning coming.

I sit up on my cot, a dull ache spreading from my back, and notice a tiny scrap of parchment resting on my pack. Pulling on my boots from the end of my cot, I plop down into the mud covering the ground and pad over to my bag, snatching the piece of parchment. It crinkles under my touch. The small, tight script looks like it was written in haste.

> *Stick close to Arlo. I've instructed him to keep an eye out for you. I'll see you soon, and please, just fare well today.*
>
> *— Rayce*

A blot of ink stains the page right before his name, but whatever else he wanted to say is lost between the lines.

The message he did write reminds me of what I'm about to do. Today we march on Imperial City, and if all goes well, I'll have a chance to help at least one girl take back her freedom.

I walk back to my cot and slip off my muddy boots.

My fingers struggle to pull the clingy gray pants, created specifically for this mission, over my hips. They fit like a second skin. I strap a harness to my waist and eye the corner of Oren's book peeking out from under my pillow. I grab it and then hold it over my bag to drop it in, but my fingers won't let go. It reminds me too much of the man who gifted it to me, and right now, I need to channel his calm.

I pull out the waistband of my gray pants and tuck the book against my back. Then I attach a leg holster to my left thigh, slip on a white silk under robe and a sky-blue one over it, drape a matching piece of white cloth over my head to cover my hair, slip back into my boots, and shoulder my pack.

Ready as I'll ever be.

Outside, the rain has bowed out, giving center stage to a blue sky and the large yellow-white spotlight of the sun. Every tent but ours and two others has disappeared while I slept.

"Ready to go?" Arlo asks, coming up behind me.

"No," I say. "But I guess I'm never going to be."

• • •

Being back in Imperial City, the place where my life outside the Garden started, is surreal. The upper-class marketplace looks just as I remember it when I passed through in my cart, but the air tastes fresher now that I'm not confined in a wooden cage. Cherry blossom petals litter the cobblestone. The four temples honoring each of Delmar's deities surround the square on all sides, in various states of disarray.

Arlo and I face the spring temple, the only one that's been restored to its former glory. Its freshly painted six-tiered green roofs wrap around the long, straight main tower. A serene pond brimming with lily pads and koi fish sits in front of the temple, a navy-colored bridge arching out of the water like the back of a sea serpent. Since it's the time of year to honor the goddess Lin, large paper lanterns in every color sway in the wind throughout the open temple, and small wooden boats sail the tranquil pond, candles burning day and night as an offering for good crops.

The palace walls spring up tall and imposing to my right, but there's no sign of the Garden's tent or any hint of me ever having been here. Somewhere locked inside, the emperor sits with no clue that his precious city is about to be thrown into chaos.

Arlo grabs my hand, pulling my attention away from my phantom past.

"What do you think, my love?" he asks, holding up a shiny red apple. "A bushel for thirteen silver? The price seems a little steep to me."

I frown at the fruit he presents. We're supposed to blend in by posing as husband and wife, but it's proving hard to concentrate, knowing what's about to happen. The crowd presses close together in the small marketplace looped around a fountain depicting a golden dragon snaking around lily pads. The air is saturated with the smells of fresh bread, ripe fruit, newly blooming flowers, and sweat—both human and animal. Hidden among the unfamiliar faces of women shopping for their family's next meal and Delmarion guards clad in full armor are Zareeni guards stationed in small clusters, awaiting a signal from their shogun to draw their weapons and fight.

"Do you think the price is worth it?" Arlo raises the apple to my face.

"I guess," I say.

I scan the crowd, searching for some sign of Rayce. Our conversation from last night replays in my head. What did he mean about me being precious? The fact that I didn't get to say good-bye to him this morning eats at me. What if something happens to one of us, or what if he's already been captured?

My breath catches thinking about him forced to his knees, blade at his throat. If something happened to him, I don't know what the rebellion would do. His face was so heavy with worry last night, illuminated by the warm light. My skin still feels raw where he touched it, and I keep imagining the sorrow plaguing his eyes as he talked about his uncle's men killing all those people. If they're willing to do that to innocents, what would they do to Rayce if they caught him?

Maybe trying to accomplish all these goals at once wasn't such a good idea. What if the Zareeni forces are spread too thin? Since I arrived, we've come up against the Delmarion soldiers several times and barely escaped to tell the tale. I can almost hear the thumping sound of their crossbows firing at our backs as we ran from the city the night I fled the Garden.

I pull the wrap of my robe closed tighter, trying to block out the chill that licks my skin even though the sun beats down high above our heads. Fear seizes my chest as I imagine all the horrible ways this day could go wrong.

The lady in the short red robe behind the booth raises an eyebrow at my lack of enthusiasm.

"Ah, the wife's a shy one." Arlo pats my cheek affectionately. It takes all my willpower not to wince at his touch. I know Arlo wouldn't hurt me, but after so many years of abuse, my instincts still need time to adjust.

"Stay focused," he whispers under his breath.

"How?" I whisper back. "There's so much that could go wrong."

A hint of a smile touches his lips as he reaches up and adjusts my wrap over my head, pulling it farther down to cover my face.

"Everything's going to work out," he says with a wink.

"I'll keep you safe, I swear it."

I'm surprised by the sincerity in his voice, and the knot in my stomach loosens.

He turns his charming smile toward the merchant. "You aren't shy, though, are you? And you're going to give me a great deal, right?"

"Oh, no, you don't," the lady says. "Flattery's going to get you nowhere with—hey, what's going on out there?" She points, and we follow her finger.

One of the Sun soldiers clutches a cloaked figure by the shoulder, in front of a large bronze dragon water fountain in the middle of the square. The man tries to pull away from the soldier's grasp, but the soldier swings him around, and the hood of the cloak falls from the man's face.

"Hey, you better—" The soldier's voice cuts off midthreat as he takes in the long scar twisting across the face plastered on every building in Delmar.

Rayce's lips split into a smile big enough to see from here.

"You look like you've been touched by Yun," he says to the shocked soldier.

"You're the—you're—Shogun Sun!" the soldier shouts, fumbling for his sword with his other hand while he tries to keep a good grasp on Rayce's cloak.

"Nothing gets past you," Rayce says, his voice far too cheery for the occasion. If I hadn't seen with my own eyes how all of this weighs so heavily on him, I'd think he was enjoying it. But it's all an act, and he's good at it. His part of this mission is to create distraction, chaos.

"Zareeni vermin!" the soldier shouts.

"You heard him, 'Zareeni vermin,'" Rayce says, raising his voice. "Attack!"

About eighty Zareeni guards drop their ruse as citizens at the same time, shedding their cloaks and jackets to reveal stunners and swords.

Their sudden appearance shakes the market square. A lady from the next booth lets out a piercing scream that grows into a chorus of voices and ignites a stampede. Zareeni guards rush to defend Rayce while citizens head for exits, only to find them clogged with soldiers rushing toward the commotion. Arlo grabs my hand and follows the flood of townspeople dashing for the nearest palace gate.

We head under the huge stone overpass and right into the center of the palace without so much as a glance from anyone. Arlo holds me close, shielding me from the brunt of the crowd, but one soldier rips between us, separating Arlo from me and slamming my shoulder into the gray stone wall of the palace.

Arlo fights his way over to me. "You okay?"

"Yeah, I'm fine."

I grit my teeth against the pain and roll my shoulder back as we rush down the little path just inside the palace. According to the map now burned into my brain, the secret entrance to the prison lies near the innermost eastern building. In order to encourage wealth, the first emperor had the palace constructed with two of every building and a gate that surrounds each set of structures.

As we're walking, eight more disguised Zareeni guards filter in behind us. Suki nods her head at me before she pulls her long hair back in a tie off her shoulders. We cross under another overpass and step into the courtyard lined with cherry trees in full bloom.

The melody of a lone flute winds into my ears from someone practicing nearby. I turn toward the music and stop cold. Remnants of the Garden's purple tent sit abandoned on the scorched grass, and snaking around it are the faces of the twelve girls I abandoned, painted on our cages. The Gardener must have left the Flowers and Wilteds safe within the city while he went out to search for me.

Two poles draw my eyes upward, and my stomach nearly spills its contents onto the ground. As the Gardener threatened, the heads of Star and Sickle sit fastened to the poles—a warning to anyone who passes by. A warning to *me*.

"No," I whisper, stretching my hand out.

I should turn myself in right now.

My feet are suddenly bare, covered in dried blood. Fern's blood. I have to run, but I've planted roots in this spot. I promised Fern, and I've let her down yet again.

A hand falls lightly on my shoulder. I follow the blue sleeve up to Arlo's face. His light brown eyes sparkle in the midday sunlight, full of concern.

"Rose, we have to keep moving," he whispers.

"I did that," I say, unable to peel my gaze away from the gruesome sight of Star and Sickle's dead stares. "They're dead because of me."

My hands shake at the thought of giving myself up. Rayce would never forgive me, and Piper might bust me out just to murder me herself. But I'd also save the rest of the girls from this fate. I wouldn't free them, but they wouldn't die because of me, either.

"You had nothing to do with it," Arlo says, placing a hand on my shoulder and forcing me to look at his face. Compared to the paintings of my family, he looks blurry and saturated, as if he isn't real. "You can't control a lunatic's actions. The Gardener did that."

"But I—"

"Repeat it with me," he interrupts. "The Gardener killed those girls."

"The Gardener—" I can only nod the rest, emotion clogging my throat.

"I know it's hard, but we have to stay focused," Arlo says. "Oren and the others will be here any minute, and they will put a stop to that horror show. Do you understand?"

I lick my chapped lips, still not finding my voice.

"Please," he says. "We can't help Kyra without you."

As he speaks, a man walks out from underneath the purple-and-white-striped tent set up in the middle of the carts. His quick steps and jerky movement shake me to my core.

*Shears.*

My fist feels like lead. He hasn't seen us yet, but if we don't move, it won't be long before he does.

*I can do this.*

Rayce put himself at risk in order to give us this chance to save the rest of my sisters and Kyra. I have to do my part. The wind changes suddenly, hurtling the noxious song of the flute away from us.

"You're right," I say, focusing on Arlo. "Let's go."

He nods, and we hurry through the courtyard, once again leaving the Garden at my back. The deeper we wade into the palace grounds, the less populated the areas become. We pass a blur of serenity ponds, large open pavilions honoring shrines that look like they've never been used, and buildings laden with lace woodwork growing more intricate with every step. We walk until the sun disappears behind the looming palace walls and my legs burn from exertion.

Finally, we reach the two innermost buildings. Both pale blue towers shoot up, almost like they aim to scrape the bottoms of the clouds, and eight silver roofs wrap around each level. Lurking on one of those floors is the man who started this war, who has been hunting me.

"I never thought I'd see these towers up close in my entire life," Suki says, shaking her head as she continues on with the rest of the small guard.

We head for the east tower, coming to a halt at the base. While Suki counts out paces with her feet, all I can focus on is whether Oren has led the attack on the Garden yet and if Rayce is okay in the middle of the courtyard. The last time I saw him, he was locked in a fight with a Sun soldier, his face twisted up in rage as he pushed him back with his sword.

Suki's pace count reaches eighty, and three guards rush to help her pry up several artfully placed stones. Every rock they uproot reveals the shiny metal surface of the long-forgotten entrance of Imperial City's dungeon.

I lean down and trail my finger along the cool surface that was sealed off ages ago. A thick metal chain with links as wide as my hand coils around the door handles.

Suki's shoulder brushes mine as she leans down next to me and yanks on the chains. The links are welded together, with no lock and no hope of ever coming apart.

"How are we supposed to get in?" I ask.

"With this." Arlo reaches into his pocket and pulls out a square-shaped metal contraption that fits in the palm of his hand. Pointing one end at the metal, he flicks a switch, and flame begins to eat away at the chain. The moment the halves clatter onto the metal doors, Arlo holds the device out to me. "You may as well keep it. You'll need it to cut the bars off Kyra's cage."

I study the device, turning it in my fingers until I find the small switch, and then I shove it into my pocket. Suki and I work on opposite ends of the chain, unlooping it from the handles.

"Thanks." I give her a grateful smile.

Two of the other guards grab the handles to the entrance we just unlocked and wrench the double doors open, revealing a dark hole in the ground, gaping wide like a mouth.

"We're going into that?" I ask, even though I already know the answer.

"Sadly," Arlo says.

"Why couldn't they have kept her in a field guarded by puppies?"

"That'd be worse." He shivers. "I don't trust puppies. Shifty eyes."

"You're very odd."

"Thank you."

Suki volunteers to go first, leading our group into the endless darkness. Once we're inside, I untie my sash and rip off my robes, revealing the skintight gray suit underneath.

I leave my robes on the first step and hurry to catch up with the others, who have already faded into the darkness. No one speaks, but the stale air fills with the constant *tap-tap* of our boots.

The farther we go, the heavier the rock feels above us. It's like my body can sense every inch we drop. After several minutes, a small orange flame bursts to life up ahead from a metal contraption that Arlo holds, illuminating the cave. I blink through the brightness, my shoulder brushing against the bumpy tunnel walls. Water oozes down the rock, staining the stone black. The air is damp, and every breath leaves a moldy taste on my tongue.

Before we came here, I didn't believe that any place could be more depressing than the inside of my cart, but the dungeon entrance proves me woefully wrong. Even with the light, the walk takes forever. My heart beats out the seconds, and the full magnitude of what we're attempting hits me hard.

A five-hundred-foot drop over stalagmites to rescue a little girl, guarded by who knows how many soldiers.

My stomach churns, my food threatening to come up for the second time today. I try to stanch the panic by recalling Kyra's face from the picture Piper gave me. She's counting on us.

A door comes into view, cutting off my thoughts. Arlo moves the meager light near the door, and my heart drops. A thick line runs down the metal doors where they've been welded shut.

Arlo turns, the light moving with him to illuminate his face. "All right," he whispers into the darkness. "Tāng, Shǐ, get to work on the door."

Suki and a young man step forward. She pulls a small tan

pouch from beneath her cloak and unhooks the drawstring, revealing black powder that sparkles in the minimal light. The other guard produces a paste-like green goop from a tube, and together they start to coat the wall.

Arlo catches me staring and leans in. "That's the same stuff we used to make the fireworks."

I nod and watch as Suki sprinkles the black powder into the green paste.

"Gather round," Arlo says, his voice harsh in the silence, and we all take a step closer to him. "Once the doors blow, we've got two missions." He holds up one finger. "The first is to rescue Kyra. Rose, that's up to you." He holds up a second finger. "As for the rest of us, our only goal is to provide cover for Rose, and above all else, we cannot let the soldiers reach the top of the tower and sound the alarm. But no matter what happens, Rose and Kyra get out, understood?"

Everyone nods except me. How am I supposed to locate Kyra in her cell, walk over a five-hundred-foot drop, open the cage, and get back before even a single soldier reaches the alarm?

We're doomed.

"All you need to do is to get to Kyra," Arlo whispers to me. "Put the harness around her, and I'll do the rest. You can do it."

"What happens if I just turn around now?"

"We fail," Arlo says. "And Piper probably figures out a way to paint you as a traitor."

Death beyond the door and death behind it. There's only one way to make it through this alive: don't fail.

"I can do this," I repeat under my breath.

"How are we doing over there, Tāng?" Arlo asks.

Suki looks over her shoulder, a wire still in her hand. "Almost done."

"Okay," he says, pulling a stunner out of each pocket. "I want you all to form a line. Rose, you're behind me, and now would be a good time to down some of that Zarenite. Don't hesitate once we're in, understood? And leave room for Shǐ and Tāng to fall in behind us."

Everyone tucks in tight together, with Arlo at the lead. Guards stand at either side of me, stunners poised straight ahead. My heart hammers in my chest. I pull on the cord tucked in my shirt and sprinkle a little of the Zarenite onto my tongue.

We're doing this. We're really doing this.

My hand fumbles for my own stunner strapped to my leg over my snug pants. When my fingers wrap around the grip, the Zarenite stuffed in the barrel glows. I stand on my tiptoes to peer over Arlo's shoulder and see Suki and the other guard run back toward us, their feet pounding the stone.

There are only seconds now.

Suki starts the countdown, her voice loud in the focused silence.

"Five."

"Four."

*Is this is really happening? This is really happening.*

"Three."

*Please let everything go okay. For us down here and for Oren above trying to save the girls in the Garden.*

"Two."

*And for Rayce. For the man I want to stay with, even if I can't say it aloud.*

I take a deep breath, hold it like I'm about to plunge underwater, and remind myself that I'm strong. I've survived the Garden and escaped it. Just because I couldn't help Fern doesn't mean I'll mess up again. My eyes snap shut as Suki's countdown ends.

"One."

*Boom!*

The explosion sends tremors down my body, and the metal doors cave.

# Chapter Twenty-Five

Heat from the blast rips through my body, blowing my hair back. The banging sound echoes in the small space, nearly knocking me off my feet. My ears fill with a heavy humming, and the loss of hearing throws off my balance.

"*Move out!*" Arlo shouts, but it sounds jumbled and slow. He swings his arm toward the hole.

Arlo and the two guards in front move through the opening we've just created, and I follow their movement without thought. My feet stumble over rubble from the blast, then I straighten up in a room so massive it makes Zareen look tiny.

The blend of mold and decay hits me first, and I fight the urge to hold my nose. We're standing on one side of a canyon made of dark gray stone. About one hundred yards away, a wooden tower sprouts up from the ground, about as tall as the highest point of the Garden's show tent. I can almost see Rayce's choppy writing sticking up from the base labeling it the East Tower.

Below us stretches the infamous five-hundred-foot

drop, torches revealing jagged stalagmites reaching out from the mouth of the cave. Above our heads, two rows of wooden cages hang suspended in the air from a thick metal cord attached to the tops of the towers. It reminds me of a really twisted laundry line, with the caged people replacing the drying clothes. And hanging in one of those cages is our target. Kyra.

Arlo doesn't waste a second, holding his right stunner up and shooting a bolt at the soldier in the tower. The Zarenite finds its mark, disabling the soldier nearest the alarm. He aims his other stunner toward the swarm of soldiers rushing from the tower. He lets off two more shots, burning the cavern green.

Other stunners go off, like Arlo's shot woke them, plunging the room into a kind of lightning storm. A handful of soldiers peek out from over the tower, their arrow tips pointed our way. The soldiers' first wave of arrows rains down on us in response. I aim my own stunner for a guard about halfway up the tower and pull the trigger. The kickback doesn't surprise me this time, and the bolt finds its mark. Arlo's lessons worked.

Cutting my eyes away from the war starting around me, I search the cages hanging over the drop, combing each one for a little girl.

*Man, older man, middle-aged woman, another guy.*

Precious seconds tick by. Any minute, one of the soldiers could reach the alarm and it'd be over for us. All the prisoners sit up in their cages to see what the commotion is, pale hands sliding through bars, but I ignore them, locating the girl dead center on the line closest to us.

My small group of Zareeni guards advances toward the tower. They use themselves as a human barricade so the other soldiers can't get to me. But once we reach our destination, I won't be able to rely on them.

I add my stunner to the mix, aiming for the soldiers with

crossbows. A tall Zareeni man standing in front of me falls to his knees, an arrow embedded in his shin.

He doesn't stop shooting even though he's on the ground. Suki takes his place, blocking me from the onslaught of soldiers charging for us with swords drawn.

The *thwap* of crossbows letting arrows loose booms through the cavernous space, accompanied by the *zap-zap* of our stunners. An arrow whizzes past my head, the air stirring from its momentum, and I duck as another one quickly follows.

"Time to charge!" Arlo commands.

Without a word, the entire party picks up their pace, stunner bolts colliding with arrow and soldier alike. Another Zareeni guard drops near me, and I pass him, noticing a pool of blood staining the dark stone red. I don't even know his name. Rayce would. Another family he'll have to tell—

I push the thought from my mind and plow forward with the other seven still standing. At the base of the tower, about nine soldiers charge us. Arlo disposes of two quickly, but before I can warn him, an arrow slices through his forearm, forcing him to drop his left stunner. He lets out a sharp hiss.

"Arlo!" I call over my shoulder, fighting the urge to double back to make sure he's okay.

Suki shoots the soldier closest to her. "Go, Rose!" she yells, narrowly avoiding a sword to the head.

I duck under the swing of an oncoming sword, and the soldier goes down, thanks to a well-timed stunner bolt from someone behind me. But it doesn't matter who. All that matters is that wooden tower in front of me. I reach the base of the wooden ramp and aim my own stunner for a soldier running toward me. The Zarenite explodes green on his neck, and he goes down. I jump over the body and keep going.

The wooden walkway zigzags its way up the looming tower. I run it like I'm fleeing the Gardener all over again.

Sweat drips down my forehead, and if I stop I'll probably throw up. The booming sound of stunners keeps my pace. I hold on to it, focus on it.

I have to save Kyra.

The platform is no bigger than my old cart, a square that you can only take five steps in. The soldier Arlo hit lies crumpled on the floor in a pool of leather and tiny metal links.

A huge gear that suspends the wire holding the prisoners' cages protrudes through the middle of the platform. The crank to reel the cages in looks like it would take two grown men to move it. No way that's an option for me.

At the back of the tower, a large bucket of water rests near a wooden trough that runs to the alarm Arlo warned us about. All it would take to end our cause is for this soldier to gain consciousness and tip the bucket over, sending the water down to power the alarm.

Over the edge, more soldiers pour in from the east entrance. The Zareeni guards have fanned out, defending the tower.

I shiver and turn back to the gear. Kicking off my boots, I run for the steel wire suspending the cages. The wood brushes my bare feet, rough and splintered, but I'm going to need to feel the wire under me to keep my balance.

All I have to do is get halfway across the chasm just once and free Kyra. Then Arlo will shoot the spiked cord into the ceiling, and we'll be able to ride it to safety. I take a deep breath and throw a prayer up to Yun, since he seems to be the only god paying attention.

Grabbing the thick wire, I heave myself up, causing the cable to shake. I wait for it to steady, pulling myself into a crouching position.

*Here goes nothing.*

I rise slowly and hold my hands out to balance my weight. Inhaling deeply, I take my first step, feeling the way the strands of woven metal twist under my bare feet.

My feet move with every breath released. An old trick from my time in the Garden. The sound of arrows whirling by threatens to break my concentration, so I tune them out and force myself to forget—about Piper counting on us to make this work, about Rayce risking his life to give us the small fraction of time we need, and about Arlo and Suki in the canyon, blocking arrows and swords with their bodies.

There is only Kyra, who gets a little closer with every step I take.

A scream rips through the open air and is silenced almost as quickly. I turn toward the noise instinctively, and my body tilts to the left. The pit stretches out underneath me, a hungry mouth with rows and rows of razor-sharp teeth.

Tightening my core to correct my balance, I take a second to catch my breath.

The gap between Kyra and me shrinks until, finally, I'm standing directly above her. Her round cage peters up to a wide point that hooks onto the metal cord. The cage is so narrow that if she were fully grown, she'd be obligated to stand, but since she's so small, she squats down in the enclosure, her arms wrapped around her bony knees. She's forced to balance her feet on a metal bar to keep them from sticking through the bottom of her cage, reminding me of a bird with a broken wing.

"Kyra?" I say. "I'm from Zareen. Your sister sent me."

"Piper?" Her weak voice drifts up from below.

"Yes." I squat. "Stay where you are. I'm going to get you out of there."

I grip the cord underneath my feet and let my left leg down until it touches the top of her cage. The cold air reaches out and tickles the bottom of my bare foot. My right foot follows, catching the first crossbar of her enclosure, and I use it to crawl down the slender metal cage. Sweat streams down my back and forehead. When I reach the bottom rim of Kyra's cell, I peer between the bars at the wide-eyed girl. She can't be more than twelve, judging by her pencil-thin frame and the way her pale green dress sags against her barely there chest.

The dirt and grime covering her skin doesn't look like it's a natural part of her yet, meaning she hasn't been in this condition long.

"All right, Kyra. I'm going to open your cage in just a moment. Then Arlo is going to shoot a rope across the cavern, and all you have to do is ride it down to him."

"Arlo's here?" she asks, sitting up from her slouched position.

"He sure is." Whether he's still in one piece…not so sure.

As if he heard us talking about him, the whizzing sound of the anchor echoes next to my ear. The spike embeds itself into the rock ceiling, and I follow the line back to Arlo at the edge of the canyon. He's okay!

He's wrapped the device around his left arm, and with his right hand he shoots at a soldier. He turns and yanks his end, throwing his full weight backward to test the security of the cord. A few rocks crumble off the ceiling, falling into the darkness below, but the spike doesn't budge. All I'll need to do is open Kyra's door and help her zip down the line into Arlo's waiting arms.

"See?" I put on my stage smile to hide my racing heart. "Nothing to worry about. Arlo's right there. We just need to get to him. Can you do that?"

"I think so," she says, her clenching jaw morphing her into a mini Piper.

Wedging my feet underneath the lowest bar in her cage, I unhook the metal harness coiled on my waist. Piper instructed the metalworker to weld the ends into loops for Kyra to stick her hands through.

"Just slip your hand through one end," I say, handing the

harness to her.

She holds out the metal cable and forces her shaking hand inside the left loop.

"Good. Now I'm going to get your cage open."

Trailing a few paces to the right, I find her cage door. Retrieving the flicker from inside my waistband, I bend down and flip the small button on the side, bringing the flame to life. The heat near my face steadies my breathing.

The small fire eats against the thick bar, dripping glowing red drops of steel into the cavernous pit below. The flicker slices the rest of the way through the bar, and the door pops open. My slippery fingers fumble as I go to tuck the flicker into my pocket, and it slips from my grasp.

A tiny gasp escapes Kyra's mouth as we watch the flicker plummet toward the ground. One wrong move and that could be us.

"It's all right," I say to her. "I'm finished with it anyway."

She nods, but her eyes don't leave the ominous fall.

I twist around to face Arlo. "Are we good to go?"

The remaining five guards have surrounded him. I can't tell if one of them is Suki, but I selfishly hope she is. Aside from welcoming me to Zareen with a stunner to the face, she's been good to me. The rest of the platform resembles a graveyard scattered with arrows, swords, slain rebels, and stunned soldiers.

"Ready!" Arlo yells, his voice bouncing off the walls.

My nerves squeeze my throat, threatening to choke me. Rising to my full height, I reach for the cord Arlo shot over and pull it toward me.

"Now, Kyra," I say. "All you need to do is wrap the end of your harness around this cord and stick your hand through the other end."

She doesn't move.

"This is going to work?" she asks, her voice shaking.

"I'm sure of it." Kind of.

She gulps down a breath of air and closes her eyes. Clasping her hands into tiny fists, she pushes to her feet. When she opens her eyes, I see the same determination that used to gleam from Clover right before a knife was thrown at her.

She walks over to the cord I'm holding and loops her harness around the wire with shaky hands.

"On three, push off, okay? Right into Arlo's arms."

"Right into Arlo's arms," she repeats.

"One."

"Two."

She looks at me one last time, weighing whether she should trust her life in my hands. I want to tell her that she isn't trusting me, she's trusting her sister, but there isn't time.

"Three!"

Kyra pushes off her enclosure with eyes shut tight and body rigid. I watch as she zips toward Arlo's waiting arms.

The sound of crashing metal draws my attention away from Kyra. My eyes shoot to the eastern entrance as a group of at least twenty soldiers race down the stairs. One of them near the front has a crossbow aimed directly at Arlo. Before I can call out, the crossbow fires and an arrow zips through the air, burying itself into Arlo's middle.

Kyra collides with him, pushing the arrow in farther. Arlo cries out sharply as he falls back with his arms wrapped around her. She's safe. But his end of the cord slips from his grasp, leaving me stranded over the chasm without an easy way to get down. I hold my breath, waiting to see if Arlo stirs.

"Get back over here, Rose!" Suki calls out, waving for me to go. "I'll make sure he's okay."

Her words spur my stagnant body into action. I pull myself back up the cage, reaching for the thick cord at the top.

Just as my fingers grab the wire, a piercing shrill rings out in the cavernous room, nearly causing me to lose my grip. I pull myself onto the wire, gritting my teeth against the earsplitting sound that rips through me.

One of the soldiers reached the alarm.

Suki supports Arlo with one arm and fires her stunner with the other hand. One of the other rebels tucks Kyra behind himself, and they retreat toward the hole we blew in the wall. Relief washes through me like cool water.

All I have to do is get to the tower and back through the makeshift door.

With the alarm ringing and my limbs shaking, I head back, ignoring everything around me. Just one foot in front of the other, until all of the wire disappears.

I jump onto the wooden platform, feeling it creak underneath my feet, and take in a deep gulp of cold air. Almost safe. Now I just have to get down to Arlo and the others. We didn't do it all before they sounded the alarm, but at least we got Kyra.

Tears spring to my eyes, blurring my vision. I swipe at them with the back of my hand to keep my view clear, but I can already feel the crushing weight that has smothered me since we blew through the wall lifting. Almost like I could accomplish anything. Like the world is mine. All I have to do is take it.

The hilt of my stunner cools my fingers as I rush to the wooden ramp, ready to make my way down.

A soldier blocks my way. I hold up my stunner, firing before it's even well aimed and scurry forward. The green bolt never comes. I look down in a panic and realize the stunner barrel is empty. I'm out of Zarenite.

From behind him, I see Arlo shoving Kyra into Suki's hands and aiming his stunner. Even injured, he refuses to give up on me. One of the other rebels grabs him before he can shoot, pulling him through the exit as a large cluster of Sun soldiers rush toward them.

"Rose, look out!" he yells, and then he's gone.

I glance up as the soldier's blade swings at my head, but I lunge back, tripping over the wood. Then the butt of his sword falls heavy on the top of my head, pain exploding from the impact like the bomb on the door. For a moment, all I can hear is the unrelenting squeal of the siren, mimicking the pain surging down my body, and then arms wrap around my middle. I throw my head back, trying to break the hold, but it tightens around me. Tiny rivets of his metal uniform dig into my back. Pain sparks all down my body, and white spots bloom in my vision.

"Nice try, Flower," the soldier says, his voice sliding around my neck like a noose. "I know who you are, and when the emperor gets here, he's going to give me a huge reward for finding you."

Icy dread floods my limbs, sending my head spinning. The emperor's eyes crawling up my skin as he judged me during the night of my last performance mingles with the stories Rayce told me.

"And here he comes now."

My body seizes up at the soldier's words, and I follow his gaze toward the stairs. At the very top of the stretching stone staircase, a tall figure descends, his arms tucked into the long sleeves of his sapphire robe and his train flaring unceremoniously behind him as he moves. His long iron-tinged hair is tied back at the base of his neck.

The emperor's sharp eyes flick my way, and I'm pulled under the weight of his gaze, recalling the wanted posters plastered in Dongsu. The steep reward. *He knows who I really am.* The sound of his measured footsteps echoes in the stilled air, drowning out the sound of my own racing heart.

A few moments pass as he takes his time down the staircase. Reaching the last step, he sweeps over the scene in front of him, the cold expression on his face unchanging as the stone. On the side of his robe, woven just over his heart, is the imperial emblem—a white dragon snaking around a blue sky. Three captured Zareeni guards are forced to their knees in front of him, blades digging into the backs of their necks.

The emperor parts his hands. "Kill them," he says in an uninterested voice. "Now that we have her, we have no use for any more captives."

"No!" I scream, thrashing against my captor.

But it's too late. The sound of metal slicing through flesh and bone fills the air.

The emperor meets my gaze, the sight of him blurred through tears, and all I can see is the jagged scar running down his nephew's face.

Rayce's lament echoes in my head: *I used to believe my uncle wasn't a bad man. But I was wrong, and it nearly cost me my soul.*

If this man will kill three people without a thought and permanently scar his own heir, what does he plan to do to *me*?

# Chapter Twenty-Six

Leaving the three lifeless bodies of my Zareeni comrades on the floor, the emperor turns to head back up the stairs. I stare down at their unseeing faces—a woman maybe only a few years older than I am and two men—and try to recall their names so I can tell Rayce whom he lost…if I even see him again. Blood pools from their wounds, staining the stone floor.

"Bring the girl," the emperor says without turning his head, and it's clear where Rayce got his knack for giving unquestioning orders. "Throw the others into the pit."

A short soldier twists rope around my wrists, pulling so tight that my hands turn pale as the scratchy strands dig into my flesh.

The soldier holding me slings me over his shoulder like I'm a sack of grain, and I come face-to-face with my reflection in one of the soldier's shiny armor plates.

He follows a few paces behind the emperor, my face bumping into his back every time he takes a step. I kick out at him, and using his other hand, he pins my legs to his chest, twisting them until I can feel my tendons straining against the resistance.

The sound of Arlo screaming my name bounces around in my head, the fact that they left me here appearing quickly after. What are they going to tell Rayce? Will they come back for me like they did for Piper's sister?

After everything I've learned about Rayce, I'm inclined to believe he won't. This mission was already too dangerous, and he made it clear his rebellion can't afford to risk losing people or assets. Every time I blink, I see him sitting next to me, his face bright as he describes what the rebellion wants to accomplish, and my gut twists. Will I ever be that near to him again?

As we walk, the walls change from crudely carved stone to lacquered wooden panels detailing ornate scenes of cherry trees dripping with delicately carved petals, of birds in flight and long, twisting dragon tails. Reflected from the glistening white tiles that line the floor like snake scales are exposed beams in the ceiling, painted in bold patterns in a myriad of colors with jewels dotting along the dizzying pattern like stars. Though the surroundings are elaborate, the paint looks sun worn, and each panel on the wall is in need of a thorough polishing.

Everything sparkles with cleanliness but lacks the love of something truly cared for, like a beautiful face without paint.

My thoughts wander back to the Garden and Oren. I hope they were successful and the others have been freed from the Gardener's rule.

My captor takes a sharp left and enters through a pair of large doors. We walk into a room lined in dark blue wallpaper dotted with clusters of yellow, red, and white flowers and intricate depictions of bugs. Large beams break up the room, the silvery length of a dragon carved into the wood to look like it's wrapped around them. Tucked in the corner is a small seasonal shrine, with the jade figure of the goddess

Lin clad only in leaves, surrounded by artfully placed stones. The sky-colored prayer pillow underneath it shows no knee indentations.

I wonder how many times Rayce stood in this very room when he lived at the palace. Is this where the emperor permanently scarred him?

"Set the girl down," the emperor says.

The soldier who's been carrying me grabs me by the hips and swings me onto a bench, slamming my knee into an oversized wooden desk on the way down.

"That's attached," I say, glaring up him.

He ignores me, placing his hands on my shoulders and proceeding to pat me down. I try to get away from him, but the back of the bench pins me in place as his hands grope. He removes the book Oren gave me, setting it and my stunner on the corner of the desk.

"Sir, I've placed the items recovered from her person on the de—"

"Cut her wrists free," the emperor snaps.

The soldier looks down at his helmet.

After a short pause, "That wasn't a request."

"Yes, sir."

The soldier produces a serrated knife from his boot. He yanks my hands up by the rope and shoves the blade through my bindings. A sharp prick pulses from my wrist as the knife nicks my skin, and blood trickles down my extended right arm.

"Now gather the instructions for the journey to the wall and get out," the emperor orders, pointing to a towering stack of parchment on the corner of his desk.

"But sir, are you sure it's safe to—"

The soldier's questioning finally warrants a turn from the emperor. The muscles in his jaw twitch beneath his impeccably trimmed goatee.

"Right away, sir," the soldier stammers, snatching up the papers and taking a step backward. He stumbles over the edge of a blue rug, nearly dropping the parchments.

The door behind us clicks shut, signaling that I'm now completely alone with the ruler of Delmar.

He moves away from me toward the left side of the room. I follow his movement, my eyes widening as I see what he's gazing at. Covering the entire wall is glass, blocking out the expensive wallpaper. Enclosed in the square cases of glass are over thirty different sections filled with white sand. Running through the grains are tiny rivulets, snaking all the way up the cages like branches on a tree, with red, brown, and black ants of varying sizes.

"Over here, Flower." He motions next to him.

I cross my arms over my chest and lean back on the bench.

"I'd like you to get one thing straight," he says, cracking his knuckles. "You're sitting here as a courtesy. I could just as easily be talking to you three days from now after you've had no food and plenty of time to reflect on your attitude. It would behoove you to be civil. Now, *come over here.*"

Gritting my teeth, I rise from the bench. My feet feel like rocks have been tied to them as I cross the room, standing as far from the emperor as I possibly can. He touches the hilt of his blade, and I wonder if it's the same one he used to carve into his nephew's face.

"Do you know what I appreciate about ants?" the emperor asks, leaning down to look into the nearest terrarium. He nods for me to follow his lead.

I don't oblige him with an answer, choosing instead to focus on the spot above his head.

"They're orderly," he says. "The workers work without question because that is what they were made to do. The soldiers defend their colony because that is what they were made to do, and they all understand that their place is underneath their queen. Ants have mastered the perfect social order. There is no argument, there is no disagreement. Just work that benefits everyone."

His explanation loosens my tongue, and I clench my hands into fists, blood dripping out from the nick on my wrist. The bodies of three Zareeni guards now lying broken in the bottom of the pit turn my blood cold.

"Does killing innocent people benefit everyone, too?"

Emperor Sun clicks his tongue. He turns and picks up a long, thin utensil from a table lined with strange-looking metallic instruments. For a moment, my heart stops as his finger trails over the pointed tip, and I wonder if those might be torture devices.

"Your answer lies here," he says, spinning around and pointing to a spot on the glass.

My gaze flickers to his finger, and I see a single ant splitting off from the steady stream of his brethren, heading up a different path on its own.

He sticks the wiry instrument into the sand, putting it in the way of the lone ant. It takes the bait, stepping onto the metal, and the emperor fishes it out.

"If the people are already ruined, yes," he answers, holding out the utensil between us. I can just make out the tiny ant crawling around on the stick. "Sometimes even ants don't fall in line, preferring to go on their own path."

He holds up his thumb and forefinger, smashing the ant on the wire.

"And if you don't eradicate the problem quickly, other ants will follow the scent."

Despite myself, my attention falls back on the ant farm in front of me. About ten others have broken from the path and are marching in the tunnel their now fallen comrade chose, forging their own way.

"Now the entire colony is ruined," the emperor says with

a sigh.

He takes a bucket of soapy water sitting on the edge of the table and pours it into the ant farm, flooding the sand routes as the ants scramble to move away from the water. After emptying the bucket, he wipes his hand clean on a silk towel and moves back across the room.

The ants squirm, trying to survive the flood, climbing on top of each other in their desperation, and I'm reminded of the twisting tunnels of Zareen filled with people who have fallen out of line. Is this the emperor's answer for them, too? A shiver jolts down my spine.

"Would you care for some tea?" the emperor asks, stepping behind his desk.

"No." I purse my lips. He can offer me the entire world and I still wouldn't accept anything, not from the man who allowed the Garden into his city. The man who nearly stole Rayce's soul... I fist my hands in my lap, happy to feel the bite of my fingernails on my palms.

"Sit." He nods toward the bench.

With stiff legs, I do as he says.

Emperor Sun takes a seat in a high-backed chair, and I have to squint against sunlight filtering in from the floor-to-ceiling windows behind him. The middle one hangs open to a marble balcony. A cool breeze blows in the scent of freshly cut grass. If only I could dive into that open space and disappear. Maybe...

My gaze falls from him to my stunner sitting on the edge of his desk.

"I wouldn't even consider it if you value your life," he says, taking a parchment from his desk and rolling it up.

He opens a drawer in his massive desk and drops the parchment inside. I can see from here that every spare quill, ink pot, and fresh piece of parchment is meticulously placed in its own spot. He pulls out another scroll and rolls it flat on the desk. I recognize my face on it and realize he's sliding a wanted poster between us.

"You're a hard girl to track down, Rose," Emperor Sun says.

"That wasn't by accident."

"And yet, here you are." He sits back in his chair and steeples his fingers. "I knew taking that child would convince my nephew to rescue her eventually." He drums his fingers together. "He's always been soft. What I didn't expect was for him to give me *you* in exchange."

I watch his face, waiting for some hint to help me figure out where this is leading.

He doesn't. His steely gray eyes bore into my face like twin blades.

"He didn't hand me over," I say. "I volunteered to come on this mission."

"He either placed too much confidence in your abilities or he didn't know who you really are." He leans forward. "So tell me…which mistake did he make?"

"I have no idea what you're talking about."

I force my gaze to stay locked on his, try to forget about the blue sky beckoning me from just beyond that open window. He's a trained warrior, with years of practice reading people. He can't know I'm planning to bolt until I'm already out of his reach.

"You can drop the act, Flower." He spits out the word like it's a weed. "I know your secret."

His declaration crawls up my skin like frost on a windowpane. The Gardener wouldn't have gotten so much help from Delmar without their leader knowing what I'm worth. All those wanted posters. Of course he knew—and I knew he knew—but to hear him admit it stuns me.

"I'm just a girl, a nobody," I say, keeping my voice flat.

He's up before I'm through speaking. He slams his palms

onto the hard wood of his desk, his mouth in a snarl. The parchment under his fingers crinkles.

"Don't you dare take me for a fool!" he snaps. "I know what that marking on your foot indicates. Why do you think you're sitting here right now instead of lying in pieces at the bottom of the pit with the others?"

He straightens, running his thick fingers down his robe to smooth out the wrinkles. Every bit of rage erases from the lines in his face, receding back into the fiery pit of his eyes. Back to blank. Back in control.

"I understand what you're running from," he says. "Your master showed me your little trinket and told me all about your secret past, *Princess*. Why do you think I even considered his proposal?"

"I know things, too," I snap. "I know why you need the Garden here in Imperial City."

"Have you bought into my nephew's rhetoric, too?" the emperor asks, his tone verging on amused. "Are you so quick to join a rebellion when it was that same thing that overthrew your father?"

The way his voice flips around like two sides of a gold piece sets my skin on edge, and his mention of my father knocks the wind out of me. Talking with him feels like negotiating with a tiger that hasn't decided if it's hungry or not.

"I'm betting my nephew didn't know what he was giving up or he never would have let you come near the city. Would you care to explain to me why you never told him about your birthright?"

I stare straight ahead. My claim to the Varshan throne is still legitimate, even though the usurper sits on it now, but I can't go back there. I can barely make decisions for myself. What qualifications do I have to lead an entire people? If I went back, it would be for revenge, not for power.

"Well?" the emperor presses.

He will not inspire fear in me. He can't. Not if I hold any hope of escaping.

My fingers itch to move, my feet begging to run, but I stay still.

"No?" he asks. "Fine. That isn't the important question, anyway." He pours himself a cup of oolong tea, the thick, woody aroma giving away the flavor. "What we need to discuss is a trade."

"I'm not interested in trading anything with you."

"Is that so?" He sets down his teacup. "Pay attention. You might find Delmar has a lot more to offer you than some half-thought-out rebellion."

I cross my arms over my chest.

"Think about it, Princess," he explains. "If you combine forces with us, your enemies become our enemies. My army becomes your army. And with your claim to the Varshan throne, we could finally unite the kingdoms. All you would need to do is agree to marriage."

"To who?" For a moment my heart skitters, thinking he means Rayce, but then I remember: Rayce cut himself off from the royal line of Delmar. That only leaves— "*You?*"

Emperor Sun nods.

"I'm not interested," I repeat, this time through gritted teeth.

"Not even if you can end the Garden and free those still trapped in it?"

His words cut through my resolve. I've been so focused on my own predicament, I almost forgot about the other two missions happening today. "What do you mean, *still*?"

A predatory smile spreads over his face. "You didn't think your little friends managed to bring down the Garden, did you? My nephew may have dreams of grandeur, but his rebellion is just a boy's attempt at filling a man's role."

My world shrinks. *What happened to the other girls? And*

*Oren? Marin? Was Rayce captured, too?*

"So there is your choice. Combine our two houses and take down your enemies with all the might Delmar has to offer…or stay blindly loyal to my nephew and risk your life and those of your friends."

Maybe this is the better choice. If what the emperor said is true, then the rebellion already failed. Rayce's scarred face flashes through my mind, a direct result of his uncle's anger at being disappointed. And with his face, I remember the heat of his body just inches from mine, the way he held me without reservation when I broke down, and yet he still trusted me. The rebellion might be smaller, but they care about each other. That's more than this man in front of me could say, damaging his own nephew's face for trying to present a new way of thinking.

Sensing my indecision, the emperor leans over his desk so we're eye level with each other. "So what will it be, Princess?"

*Now. It's time.*

I don't give him a second more to elaborate, don't even think about what a life with him would be like. I'm up before he can blink. My fingers wrap around the bumpy cover of Oren's book resting on the corner of the desk.

Emperor Sun's eyes widen just a fraction as my hand swings out. The weight of the heavy book comes down on his right temple, slamming the left side of his face into his desk with a loud *thwack*. One second our noses almost touch, and the next I'm crouching on top of his desk, the cool breeze from outside flowing through my hair. With the book still in my hand, I jump onto the high back of his chair and ride it like a wave as it crashes to the ground.

I don't know if he's reaching for me or if my blow knocked him out. All I can see is the sky beyond the balcony beckoning me toward freedom—and I run for it.

# Chapter Twenty-Seven

The spongy carpet turns to warm marble under my bare feet. It only takes a second to cross the small space. I run to the balcony ledge, placing my hands on the hot wooden rail that goes up to my hip and think through my options.

We're at least four stories high, so jumping is out of the question. Even if I angled my body to absorb the damage on a less vital section, I'd probably break something. I look up at the sky. It offers no answers. But the low overhanging roof of the next level does. If I can make myself a few feet taller, I can hoist myself onto the next level and keep climbing to the top.

I tuck Oren's book into my snug waistband and jump onto the narrow wood railing. Balancing on the edge, I grip the sharp silver tiles of the next story just as an angry cry rips out from the emperor's office.

A glance over my shoulder reveals a Sun soldier crashing through the office door. Sunlight glints off the metal plates protecting his chest, momentarily blinding me before I pull myself up and pray my tired arms will hold my weight.

My fingers struggle to hold me, but all I can think about

is getting back to Zareen. To the people who can help me, if they're still willing. Did Arlo make it out after he was hit back in the dungeon? And if the mission to liberate my sisters in the Garden went as badly as the emperor implied, is Oren safe? What about Marin? Or Rayce? Just thinking his name sends a wave of panic crashing through me.

I grit my teeth against the pain and pull up, my muscles remembering the familiar movement.

"Hey, you, get back here!" the soldier shouts.

He stretches out his hand in a desperate attempt to catch my ankle, but I lift my feet, sliding onto the hot roof tiles. Flecks of silver paint cover my sweaty palms. Shouts echo from below, but I block out the words.

I'm on the second-highest roof of the palace, and it slants upward. My bare feet slip on the tiles as I crawl toward a thick wooden beam supporting a silver dragon statue that's longer than I am.

Securing my footing, I head westward, scurrying across the rooftop with light steps. From this high up, the entire city spreads out like a quilt beyond the palace wall. The upper marketplace is easy to locate with its wide-open space and jewel-toned fabric tents, tucked between all four temple towers. The temple peaks shoot into the sky like points on a compass, the spring temple with its green roof, the fall red, the winter white, and the summer blue to match the palace. It's hard to believe that just this morning I stood down there with my arm linked in Arlo's, pretending to be a carefree shopper.

Out past the upper marketplace and the Changhe River slicing through the poor part of Imperial City, I can just make out the green tops of the Shulin Forests trees. If I can reach them, I'll become like a grain of sand in the desert, nearly untraceable. I round the sharp corner of the palace and stop, squatting next to one of the snarling dragon statues. I need to get to the ground.

Far below, soldiers flood the stone courtyard, coming out of three different entrances, like a river of bodies. The thundering of their collective footsteps reminds me of the fireworks Arlo set off in the Garden tent the night of my escape. Packs line the wall behind them, probably in preparation for the mission to the border wall that the emperor mentioned before.

I tuck myself farther into the shadow of the dragon and keep searching for a way down, thankful for my dark clothing.

My gaze catches a thick black cord coming from this dragon's mouth, sloping all the way over the courtyard to the palace gate. Green paper lanterns dangle from the line, part of the decorations for the recent Spring Ceremony. Maybe the goddess Lin actually did hear my prayer.

I crawl to the roof's edge and wrap my hands around the cord. As long as it's secured well on the other side, it should hold my weight. Catching myself will be tough on my hands, but if I can ignore the pain, I should be able to cross.

Sliding on my belly to the ledge, I angle myself so that the left side of my body hangs in the air, knowing that it will lighten the momentum of the initial impact, and reach out both hands to grip the cord.

*On three.*

"We're looking for a girl," shouts one of the soldiers below me.

*One.*

"She is considered extremely dangerous."

*Two.*

"Should you come in contact, maim but do not kill."

*Three.*

I tip all my weight to the left, like rolling over during sleep, and fall into the open air. Years of hanging from heights have robbed me of my fear, but as I catch myself, I bite into the side of my mouth to keep from crying out.

The cord snaps in my hands but holds my weight. No

shouts from the courtyard, so I don't think they've spotted me...yet.

I hang suspended in the air for a moment and then reach out, putting one hand in front of the other. Over and over. My feet hang awkwardly below me. It's the first time in a long time they haven't been able to help.

Sweat drips into my eyes, down my face, flavoring the inside of my mouth salty. I keep my eyes glued to the large gray wall in front of me. Halfway there. I take a deep breath. If I'm caught now, whatever type of twisted mercy the emperor thought he was granting me before will be gone, replaced by anger at my escape. The scar ripping across Rayce's cheek comes into sharp focus, and my hand loses its grip.

A tiny squeak, no louder than a bird's tweet, slides out of my mouth.

I squeeze my eyes tight, surprised to find a memory in the dark. Our flour-coated hands kneading dough together, the warmth of him pressing his weight against me, the sweet scent of honey on his breath—I have to get back to him.

"She's up there!" a voice shouts.

I can almost feel their helmet-clad heads turning toward the sky, gazes homing in on my exposed body. There's a whizzing sound near my ear, and my eyes snap open. Looking up, I spot an arrow arching into the air above me.

My right hand catches the cord, and I abandon caution in favor of speed. The aches in my arms and head disappear as I race forward, the muscles I haven't been able to use since leaving the Garden awakening after a long slumber.

Nothing else matters except for reaching the palace gates. I can't help anyone if I'm stuck here, and I can't do *anything* if I fall. Another arrow flies in front of me, and the sound of more at my back keeps me scrambling. One hand after the other until the end.

Warmth sinks into my palm as I grasp the stone wall,

digging my nails into the other side—then a sharp pain punctures my leg. I suck in air, and my vision blurs, but I manage to pull myself over the edge of the wall and land hard on the walkway below.

Boots pound toward me from both directions, but I can't move. I try to catch my breath while I study the arrow sticking halfway into the meat of my thigh. Blood spreads around the shaft, coloring my gray pants dark.

I crouch and grip the middle of the shaft. My leg begs for me to rip it out, but I take a deep breath and snap off the end instead. If I remove the arrow now, at worst I'll bleed out before I make it to the woods, and at best I'll leave a trail of blood for them to track me.

Turning away from my leg, I see a pair of soldiers blocking either side of the small walkway about fifty yards away. Both sets approach with brightly painted shields held up in front of them. Almost like the walls are closing in on me.

They break into a run, their feet clapping against the ground in time with the hectic rhythm of my heart. As they thunder closer, I jump onto the ledge on the other side of the palace wall and search the landscape.

About four feet away, a square green-tiled roof of a neighboring mansion beckons. A soldier to my left shouts for me to stop. He's scrambling for me, all reflective surfaces and reaching limbs, but he's too late. I squat, feeling the muscles tighten in my legs and pain tear through me where the arrow still sits embedded in my flesh, and jump, slipping through the soldier's grasp like a fox would from a hound.

For one glorious second, I'm flying through the air, the wind kissing my sweaty face and taking the sting from my wound. Just like when Rayce blew on my cut. Everything he's done, since the moment I met him, has been to help me— how could I have not seen it? The roof appears underneath me, and then my knees and palms collide against the rigid tiles. The impact sends a jolt of fresh pain pulsing through my entire body and rattles my teeth.

Perhaps I just needed a fresh perspective.

I jump up, my head still spinning, and scramble forward, forcing my toes into the grooves of the roof tiles.

The sunbaked surface burns through the fabric covering my knees and sears the skin of my palms and feet, but I keep pushing myself up. I pull a leg over the top point of the roof and twist my body so I'm facing the cityscape. There's a flat roof next to this one, but trying to climb down a slope like this would get me killed.

I could propel myself. Which could also result in death, but it's less likely that I'll slip. I point my toes toward the other roof, lie flat on my back, and push off. The edge comes racing toward me. I slap my palms down hard and stumble onto the next roof.

I turn and smile at the house behind me. My silent dare. Let them come after me now.

Adrenaline got me this far, but it's starting to wear off, and my leg stings like a nettle. I grit my teeth against the pain and take off at a run.

The rooftops open for me—my path out of the city lighting up like it's paved in Zarenite instead of shingles and stones. The soldiers swarm below, looking like ants as I weave and bob and jump high above their heads. They assumed I went down. It's what any rational person would do, but they don't realize the Garden takes the rationality out of anyone who stays there long enough. By the time I slide down near the river, the sun has sunk into the ground.

Using the shadows as my cloak, I dart across the empty bridge and into the poor part of Delmar without sight of a single soldier. I look over my shoulder and run straight into someone.

"I'm sorry," I say, keeping my head bowed.

"Watch where you're going," the man grumbles. Seeing another person turns my blood cold. I try to peek at his face, but a long straw hat covers most of it.

As I move to let him pass, he grabs my wrist, his fingers digging down to my bone.

"What's a girl like you doing in this part of town?" His voice reminds me of Shears.

I rip my hand from his grasp and grab his hat off his head. The man's wide eyes and bearded face are nothing like the wicked face with the sharp, beady eyes I was picturing. Being on my own has made me paranoid again.

I throw the hat on the ground and run before he can catch me again.

"Are you the one all these damn soldiers have been looking for?" the man shouts.

I pick up my pace as I rush for the woods. Almost there. I'm sure the soldiers won't risk searching the forest. They're probably expecting me to stay in the city, assuming I won't be able to get past the gates. Underestimating me.

Emperor Sun's face comes unbidden in my mind as his thin lips draw into a tight, predatory smile. My skin prickles now that I'm alone to reflect on what he was implying back in his office. The ugly pieces slide into place as I connect exactly how my title can help him. By us joining together. By me giving him everything, including myself.

I shiver into the cool night air and pull Oren's book from my waistband, replaying the sound it made when it slammed into the emperor's head.

He'll never underestimate me again.

# Chapter Twenty-Eight

A crescent moon hangs at the highest point in the sky by the time I stumble into the Shulin Forests. The moment I step under the treetops, the frosty white moonlight disappears. Dead leaves crunch under my toes and the earthy smell of dirt mixes with the scent of dried sweat coating my body.

I grip Oren's book against my chest to distract myself from the throbbing in my leg, but I know I have to take the arrow out soon and dress the wound. The longer I wait, the more likely it'll become infected.

As I bump my way through the trees, I'm drawn back to a certain cold gray room made a million times warmer by Rayce's presence as his hands worked to clean the cut on my hand. The feeling of him blowing cool air onto the stinging wound soaks through me. I was so angry he wouldn't let me take care of it myself. But relying on someone else isn't so bad every now and then.

Every bone in my body aches from the workout I put it through today, and I want nothing more than to head back into the direction of camp, especially since I still don't know if everyone made it through their missions safely. The pain of uncertainty hurts almost as much as my leg. But I can't go back to our camp. Not tonight. Not when there's a possibility I'm being tracked.

I collect twigs and start to rub two of them together, hoping to catch friction in the dark.

If Piper were here, the friction part wouldn't be a problem. Her presence can start a fire in any room.

Thinking of her and Zareen brings other, friendlier things to mind—Marin's curly hair, Oren's thick black beard, Suki's dark eyes, Arlo's wicked smile, and Rayce's patient hands. I never thought I'd miss them all like this—so much that it physically hurts.

A tiny fire bursts to life, eating away at the darkness.

Now, it's time for the really painful part. I huddle close to the fire and examine the arrow now covered with dried blood. Fitting my fingers near the arrowhead on the shaft, I take three deep breaths. My mind wanders back to Rayce. To his warm eyes and the patch of stubble coating his chin. Through his wavy black hair. Down to the delicious tilt of his mouth.

I yank hard. The arrow slides out with a spurt of fresh blood cast black by the firelight. *The pain will subside*, I tell myself. *Don't focus on the stabbing, white-sharp wave pulsing from your thigh or the black spots in your vision.*

Taking deep breaths, I use the tip of the arrowhead to cut through my pant leg, starting where it entered. I keep cutting until I get a piece that's relatively clean and wrap it tight around my thigh, right above the wound.

Ignoring my screaming leg, I scoot back and lean against the scratchy bark of a nearby tree. From this vantage point, the forest floor seems wide and ominous. Why can't these be the trees near the Zareeni base with their thick, spidery branches? Perfect for climbing and buckling down into for the night.

I shift to find a better position, and something bites into my back. Reaching behind me, my fingers brush something coarse: Oren's book. The moment I decide to read it, the crushing weight I'd been carry around pinches off like dead skin, and I can breathe.

The page Oren dog-eared is about halfway through the book. There's a portrait staring back at me—me, eight years old, with wild blond hair escaping a long braid, a missing front tooth, and an entire future I'll never have shining in my violet eyes.

Hanging around my neck on a thread of gold is my mother's ruby. My father used to tell me the story of how he gave it to my mother on their wedding day and how she'd hoped it would be passed along to me. That same necklace hangs around the Gardener's neck today.

Below the painting of me, of the girl I used to be, a small caption reads:

> *The heiress to the throne was never accounted for after Varsha changed rulers. Many believe the princess was beheaded—privately, unlike her father—though several historians suggest she may have escaped.*

Though I'd known all along that Oren suspected me, to have it confirmed shakes me. Why hasn't he done anything about it?

I flip to the title page of this article he marked for me.

### THE FALL OF THE EASTERN KINGDOM AND RISE OF A NEW VARSHA
#### *By Oren Whitlock*

Oren's known all along. Since before Marin was captured, before he even asked me about my heritage that first night, when he saw the mark on my heel.

I read farther down.

*It was upon my first walk through the palace that I overheard a whisper of rebellion from two of the king's own palace guards. Though it probably was in Delmar's best interest to keep quiet things that might help the Delmarion crown, I alerted the king of the unrest. Torn between my duties as an honest man and that of the Delmarion ambassador, I ultimately decided to leave the news out of my many letters to His Imperial Majesty, opting instead to assist the Varshan king in preparations against the upcoming rebellion.*

Oren was the *ambassador* sent there by Delmar. Meaning he was in charge of, among other things, arranging an agreement for marriage between Rayce and me...

Yet he's never once tried to use my past as a pawn, and he obviously hasn't told Rayce I'm his former betrothed. Like the emperor said, if Rayce knew, I doubt he'd have let me near the palace today. I thought my life in the Garden prepared me to be hard and allowed me to see the ugliness people hide behind their masks, but all it's really done is make me keep a distance from the people who really care about me.

It's made me into the exact person the Gardener wanted me to be—scared, desperate, obedient. I've spent the last ten years of my life cowering in a cage, terrified that if I look up into the sunlight, someone will see who I really am and use it against me. And yet, for as long as I've been around Oren, he hasn't once tried to force me to do anything against my will. Instead he gently guided me to the answers myself.

I've been such a fool.

I've risked everything, including Rayce's trust, by not telling the rebellion the truth because I've been too afraid of the mistakes in my past. Park might have betrayed me, but he isn't every man, and he *certainly* isn't Rayce. My position could give them exactly the leverage they need. Rayce would never turn me over to his uncle. He's fighting against him for a good reason, and my heritage could give Rayce a claim to the throne again. All I have to do is offer it to him. He helped me when he knew he shouldn't—now it's my turn to return the favor.

If Emperor Sun and Oren know who I am, then Rayce needs to know as well. I have to tell him everything when I get back.

*If* I get back.

• • •

The hours pass at a crawl, my time measured between heartbeats and crackling twigs. The red glow of the fire turns to embers, and my body pulses from the beating it took today, but still, sleep won't come.

The sound of a branch snapping breaks the silence. I jump up, pain surging through my leg, and turn to face the threat, willing my eyes to peel back the dark. Did the emperor's men catch up to me?

My heart hammers as I strain my ears, but no matter how hard I listen, I can't hear anything over the rapid beats.

I search for cover, but besides climbing the large tree, there isn't much to hide behind.

Footsteps grow closer. I grasp in the darkness until my fingers brush a thick tree branch and snatch it up, holding it out like a sword. Shifting, I inch up the tree, until I'm in a standing position. I'll only get one shot with this.

A figure pushes through the bushes, darkness clinging to it like bat wings. Before whoever it is can move toward me, I swing my stick as hard as I can at their head.

A hand shoots out and catches the branch, sending a *whap* noise echoing in the darkness.

The hood slips from the person's head. But I don't let them make another move, yanking hard on my end of the stick.

"Rose, it's me," a voice says—a man's. He puts his hands up in surrender, and I recognize a familiar scar running down his cheek. It's hard to believe that just hours before I stood in front of the man who gave it to him.

"Rayce?" I ask, my voice cracking.

All the fear and worry from today come rushing back. He stares at me, his eyes shining in the dim light like embers, and a lump swells in my throat. If I hadn't managed to escape the emperor today, I might never have seen Rayce again. A wave of panic washes over me just thinking about never seeing this man who somehow weaseled his way into my mind and took root.

"You're alive," he says. He reaches for me, his large hands trembling in the air, brow furrowed. Every trace of mischief has left his eyes, which comb over me now like I'm something precious that must be memorized before I disappear again. "Arlo said— I thought for sure if my uncle got a hold of you that you'd be—" His voice cracks, and he sucks in a deep breath. "I was coming for you. I never would have left you. I'm just— I'm so relieved you're okay."

He's holding me before I can even think of pushing him away. The warmth of his body spreads around me like a quilt as he pulls me to him, melting away the panic that burns in my stomach. My brain struggles to grasp that I'm in his arms again. *Is this real or another hallucination? Is he really here?* He buries his face against my neck and squeezes me tight. The pain in my leg disappears as his embrace lifts me off the ground. The moment I'm about to break, he holds me together.

I slide my hands over his wide shoulders and realize he's shaking. Or maybe I am. It's hard to tell where I end and he begins, and right now, I'm okay with that.

"How did you find me?" I ask.

"When we heard from Arlo that you were captured, I sent patrols into the forest," he says into my neck, his stubble sending shivers across my sensitive skin. "It was a long shot, but I couldn't bear the thought of not doing anything. One of them caught sight of you a few hours ago, running away from the city, so we focused our efforts in the surrounding area and tracked you here. Still, you weren't easy to catch."

"I'm sorry I worried you."

He twines his fingers gently through my hair.

"Don't be," he says. "I'm just happy you're okay and we found you before my uncle's soldiers could. I can't believe you were able to escape. But I should have known you'd find a way, because you're…well, you."

I can sense just how worried he was in the strength of his grip and the quiver in his tone, and it shreds me to the core. I never thought anyone but my sisters would care what happened to me.

Moonlight slips through the forest canopy, casting a dim glow on the grassy clearing, just big enough to hold us both. The moments we stay pressed together tick on. Finally, I let my arms slip from him and move to step back, but Rayce holds me tighter. He twists so that his next breath tickles my earlobe.

"Before we head back, I want to thank you. Arlo assured me that without you, our rescue mission would have failed. And thank you for finding your way back here to the—" His voice catches, and he pulls his head back, trapping me in his gaze. "Thank you for finding your way back to me. I didn't think there was anything I wouldn't be willing to give up in order to win this war, and then you came along, and suddenly, everything changed. I told myself I didn't have time for distractions, that I didn't have time for you, but I was wrong.

No matter what I do, Rose, you're here." He presses a hand to his head but never breaks his gaze.

Heat rushes to my cheeks, watching his lips paint pretty words in the air, and I turn away. His fingertips brush my chin as he guides my face back to meet his, his eyes asking permission for something I never even dared to dream about in my darkest hours in the Garden. He leans in, his face growing closer to mine with every heartbeat. Every inch of my body hums as he draws nearer, and my eyes close involuntarily. I wonder if I should allow this, if I should pull away, but I can't make myself move a single muscle.

*Because you want it.* The thought surrounds me. *You want him to—*

"Rayce, did you find anything?" a voice calls out from behind us.

My eyes snap open and meet Rayce's shocked gaze. The muscles in his jaw twitch, and he turns away from me.

"Y-yeah," he says, his voice rough. Then louder, more controlled, "She's over here."

He releases me, clearly trying to erase whatever spell the stress of today put him under, and I let out a sharp cry as my foot meets the ground. Pain surges through my leg, and I catch myself on Rayce's arm to keep from falling.

"You're hurt?" he says.

"A little."

I grit my teeth against the pain. Rayce leans over, inspecting my shoddily wrapped leg. "Why didn't you mention this earlier?"

"Sorry," I snap, suddenly defensive. "It slipped my mind when I thought I was being attacked. And then you…"

*Almost kissed me.* I didn't imagine that, did I?

He shakes his head and sweeps his arm under my legs, lifting me up once more. But after what almost transpired, I can't bear being this close to him. It's wonderful and at the same time confusing. I look up, ready to ask him to put me down, but he anticipates my protest and stops me.

"You're hurt," he says. "You can yell at me about this later. For now, just rest."

Fatigue rushes over my body, sending my head spinning, and everything I wanted to say slips out of my mind. I close my eyes, my head falling against Rayce's warm chest, listening to the steady *thump-thump* of his heartbeat, and remind myself that accepting help doesn't make me weak. Relying on the people who have helped me find myself outside the Garden makes me stronger. Maybe even strong enough to finally face my past.

# Chapter Twenty-Nine

After Rayce meets up with some of his men, he carries me back to our tent in the temporary camp. Even though my body shakes with exhaustion, I explain to him how I escaped the emperor, leaving out the part about why he wanted me alive in the first place, since there are seven others among us. Once I've answered their questions the best I can, they retreat and I fall asleep as soon as my head hits a pillow.

The next morning, Marin tells me Rayce wants to speak with me, so I make my way through the camp right after breakfast. I stand just outside his brown tent, his silhouette on the thin piece of fabric that separates us taunting me, and gather my nerves as I replay our last encounter in my head.

He was going to kiss me. And I was going to let him.

This perfectly stubborn man who thinks he knows everything, who teases me about my fighting skills, even though he knows I've been locked up most of my life, who offers me handmade cookies when I'm too busy to enjoy them, who helps people put up their tents in the rain, risking sickness the day before a mission he's supposed to lead, was going to kiss me. *And I wanted him to.*

My cheeks burn, and a smile spreads across my face. All that energy and worry back in Imperial City was worth it, knowing he missed me, too. This entire time we've been fighting each other, fighting these feelings welling up inside, but why?

My finger brushes the tent flap, and a tendril of fear curls in my stomach. What if we were both so worn down from stress and worry of the day that what happened last night wasn't real? That all our moment could ever be was a trick of the moonlight and too little sleep?

But I've seen the man behind the leader, seen the things that scare him, and I know he is good and kind and real. And so was the look in his eyes.

Besides, there are more important matters at hand right now. I have to figure out if the emperor was lying when he said the mission to rescue the Flowers failed, and I have to find the words to tell Rayce the truth about my heritage. My stomach twists at thinking about revealing my past, but then I remember the way he held me in his arms last night. We can overcome this. He has to know. I push aside the tent flap. Rayce sits behind a hastily made wooden table covered in maps and documents. He's wearing the same crinkled tan shirt he had on when he found me.

With his head down like that, poring over his paperwork, I'm taken aback by how much he resembles his uncle. He doesn't look up at my entrance. My gut twists.

I clear my throat, and he startles.

We stare at each other in silence, and I wonder if he's thinking about our almost kiss. My gaze falls to his lips, and that same treacherous smile reappears on my own face.

"You wanted to see me?" I ask.

The corner of his mouth quirks up even more. "Aren't we awfully happy today?"

I turn my head away from him and cross my arms. "I have no idea what you're talking about."

"Yes, you do, but it's cute to watch you pretend." He extends his hand. "Come in."

He rubs his eyes, revealing his fatigue, while I shuffle to a stool across the table from him and sit. The rough wood bites through my cotton pants and my back aches, but my heart pounds from his nearness.

"I'll get straight to the point," he says. "I didn't want to worry you last night, after everything you'd just gone through, but the mission to infiltrate and end the Garden was unsuccessful. While our distraction in the courtyard brought a good portion of Galon's forces to us, away from the Garden, Oren and his small unit slipped through the gates as planned, but we lost contact from there. It's likely they were caught by a stray battalion on their way to the courtyard. We have all our spies on high alert for news, but we haven't heard anything back yet."

My stomach drops at his words. I didn't get the sense that the emperor lied, but I was hanging onto the hope that maybe he had. I study the point on the map where his hand rests, trying to keep my face straight.

"And on top of that, Oren and his squad haven't returned yet," Rayce continues. "Did my uncle mention anything about holding them while he spoke with you?"

Oren, the only man who was truly kind to me from the beginning, might be in trouble because of a mission I asked Rayce to attempt. "No, he didn't," I say, keeping any emotion out of my voice.

Rayce nods but remains quiet for the moment, rolling his quill along the desk in thought.

"There's a chance they escaped, then," he says. "And maybe they just haven't been able to report back yet."

I sit up at his words. "Why do you say that?"

He doesn't blink. "Because if Galon had them and he thought it would hurt you, he would have mentioned it. He can't help but lord his power over people."

If what Rayce says is true, then Oren and the others could really be okay. Relief floods my limbs. Even though the Flowers aren't free, I'm glad no one else was captured, either.

"I just hope I'm correct about this. It seems too optimistic to think both you and Oren escaped Galon's grasp. When I found you last night, I could hardly believe my eyes..." He trails off, his gaze glassy, and I know exactly what he's thinking. But he doesn't have the decency to blush about it.

"I was happy to see you, too." The words stick in my throat, but the panic I felt when I thought I'd never get the chance to see him again rises up, outweighing my embarrassment. "I realized I didn't tell you last night how relieved I was that you were okay. You risked your own freedom to allow both of the other missions a chance of success. That was so brave. The whole time I was down in that dungeon, I couldn't help but wonder if you were hurt or got captured yourself. And when I thought I might not be able to see you again..."

I expect that cocky smile to fall across his lips, but as his gaze focuses, his dark eyes dart around my face with the same desperation as last night. Like I'm someplace far away from him and drifting farther.

He stands, and I follow his motion, too surprised by his sudden shift to question it.

"What would you have done if the Garden mission went successfully?" he asks, his brow furrowing. "Would you have gone away somewhere with the other girls, started a new life?"

His abrupt interest in my future startles me. When he locked me in a holding cell, I spent most of my time trying to figure out a way to leave the rebellion behind me. But after going on two missions with them, seeing how much they want to help shape this land into someplace worth living and feeling Rayce's concern for me when I returned, I'm not sure anymore. What *will* I do once they're free?

A lock of hair falls onto his forehead as he looks down at his nails.

It's strange seeing him like this. Almost like a lost little boy, not sure which way will lead him back home. Even when I had a knife to his neck, he remained calm. But right now, he shuffles his hands like they've grown too big and he isn't sure where to place them anymore.

"I don't know," I say, the words struggling to break free, even though I know I should probably keep them in. "I thought I would leave immediately, and we could make our way somewhere through the mountains—"

"The reason I asked," he interrupts, like he's afraid to hear the rest of my answer, or perhaps he heard enough of it to move on. "I realized yesterday when you didn't come back that I wanted you to. To come back, I mean. Rose...I want you to stay here with us...with me."

A strange sense of relief washes over me as he speaks. I've been yearning to hear him ask me to stay since the moment we parted the night before the mission. The length of his desk is the only thing separating us now, and I'm suddenly aware of every splintered inch of it.

"I shouldn't have been so consumed with rescuing you," he continues. "There were so many other things that also needed my attention, and yet I couldn't get you out of my head. I wasn't even prepared to try."

My heart feels like it's going to burst, hearing him say he wants me to stay. Those three little words kept me from all the things I wanted before, but now that I've faced a reality without Rayce, I know the horrors of that life, and I know it isn't what I want. My feet move on their own, around the desk, planting me right next to him. Where I know I want to be.

"I couldn't, either," I whisper.

It's usually his hands evaporating the space between us, mending me, but this time I don't hesitate as my fingertips glide along the ridge of his scar. This is it. He has to know who I am. I have to give him this final piece and trust that he won't use it the way the Gardener and his uncle tried to.

"So…you'll stay then?" he says.

I can't handle this raw honesty radiating between us right now. Not when I've been keeping something so huge from him. He deserves to know everything, though…about who I am and what that could mean for his cause. Maybe in a different life, if our paths had worked out the way they were planned, he would have whispered those words to me every day. But that's not the future we're dealing with now.

I take a deep breath. "Yes, I want to stay."

He doesn't give me a chance to speak, his arms wrapping around my waist and pinning me against him. I can feel his smile pressing against my neck, the steady rhythm of his pounding heart thudding against mine. And for a perfect moment, I can see the life we might build together and I lean into it, slipping my arms around his broad shoulders and letting the tips of his dark hair tickle my cheek.

We can be happy. I believe it. But…

I pull away from him and stare into his face. All the worry and pain there just a moment ago have been erased by my words, a promise I can't be sure he'll let me keep until he knows who I am. "But there's something I need to tell you first."

"Anything," he whispers, his fingers trailing down my cheek and pushing through my waves.

"I don't know how to say this," I say, my heart hammering in my chest. But he needs to know. "The thing is—"

"Sir!" a female guard shouts, rushing into the tent and cutting off my words. She quickly salutes Rayce, completely ignoring me.

Rayce drops his hand from my side, his gaze wavering from me to the guard, and I silently will him with everything I have to send her away. If I don't tell him now, I'm not sure I'll have the strength to try again.

*Please...*

If he notices my pleading, he doesn't give in to it. He frowns and focuses on her.

"Report," he says.

"Oren and his platoon have been sighted five hundred feet from camp—"

Rayce pulls away from me before she's even finished speaking and hurries toward the entrance of the tent. The tenderness emanating from his eyes when he asked me to stay is completely gone. How easily he shifts back into his role as leader, just like his uncle.

I reach out a shaky hand toward him then let it fall on the desk beside me, the fact that we might once have been wed hanging on the tip of my tongue.

He touches the tent flap and turns to me, his brow furrowed.

"Hold that thought," he says. "Once I've confirmed Oren's whereabouts, we can continue."

My fingers turn to a fist on the edge of the desk, and I nod for him to go.

"I'll let you know what Oren reports," he says, running out of the tent.

The woman rushes ahead of him, yelling for Rayce to follow her. The tent flap waves in the wind, signaling his exit, but I stay rooted in my spot. I've never spoken the truth about my past to anyone. Not to Fern or the other girls. Not even to people who know it anyway, like the emperor and the Gardener.

And I was about to tell Rayce.

My vision blurs. One more minute and everything I've been keeping inside for ten years would have been lain bare like the parchment covering the table in front of me.

I try to move. Electric pain shoots down my wrapped leg, and I embrace the searing agony, more familiar with it than the boulder of disappointment crushing my body. Pain is easy. Something I can understand.

Arlo's words circle in my head, and I cover my ears in an attempt to block them out: *Rayce will always choose his people before himself.*

But he asked me to stay with him.

The heat in the air sticks to my skin.

How can those two thoughts live in the same headspace? I don't doubt that he cares for me, and it's clear now that I have feelings for him. Why else would I want to tell him the truth about my past?

But I have no doubt the knowledge would kill him. He'd be forced to choose one more time between what he might want personally and what's best for the rebellion. And because of his kindness, because I've seen him call to every one of his people by name and seen him stand in the rain to help others before helping himself, I know the choice would break him. His tormented face the night he told me about burning down that village... I can still feel his sorrow weighing down his every action.

If he felt like it was for the good of his people to barter me away, even if it meant losing his own life, even if he'd never forgive himself, his sense of duty would force him to.

Why would I put him in that position?

I don't ever want to see him in that much pain because of me. Which only leaves me one option. I have to take away the temptation before he has the chance to act on it. I have to leave.

The tent flap rubs rough against my fingertips like the

warning alarms back in the imperial dungeon, and I run through the camp, pain shooting down my leg. I push past a man walking toward the middle of camp, keeping my head down as I go.

Even though it's my choice, it doesn't stop tears from brimming to the surface. I head for the tent I woke up in, knowing I'll need the cover of darkness in order to slip away unnoticed.

Ducking into my tent, I lie on my cot and watch as the day stretches on until light is smothered with darkness. I gather my knees up to my chest, fighting against the panic that threatens to overwhelm me and wishing desperately for the comfort of Fern's encouraging whispers. If only I'd known that was the last time I would see Rayce. Tomorrow and every day after that, all I'll have is his plea to stay with him to keep my flame alight in the darkest places.

# Chapter Thirty

Silence settles over the campsite after dark. Not finding me back in his makeshift office, Rayce came to look for me in the tent, but I pretended to be asleep, and eventually, he left. I remind myself that it's best for him and let that idea settle into my bones.

Besides, right now I need to focus. I must get to the Garden and find a way to free my sisters. The heads of Sickle and Star greet me every time I close my eyes, and I wonder which other Wilteds have paid that price for my continued disobedience. Every day, another one clipped.

The Gardener's threat falls over me again like cold water, and I snap upward on my cot. A few abandoned packs sit inside my tent, and after further inspection, I find they have enough food and water to get me back into Imperial City.

By now, the soldiers will have assumed I left the city and their search there will be less intensive. It's time to go back.

As I slip the pack onto my shoulder, I consider the emperor's offer as a possible option to end all of this. Though he'll be a lot less likely to negotiate, if I could find a way to pardon the entire rebellion and free the other Flowers, siding with Delmar might be the only way I can get everything I want.

Not everything, though. Not Rayce. No matter which option I choose—going to the emperor or trying to free the Flowers on my own—nothing gives him to me.

I rub my middle, trying to erase the feeling of Rayce's arms around me from the night before. His warmth still sears my body, running hot through my veins. But I can't let the way I feel about him affect what I must do to keep him from having to make another horrible choice that might destroy him.

I peek through the flap of my tent. The fire in the middle of the campsite burns bright, the smell of smoke clinging to the air, but there isn't anyone around to stop me. Everyone is asleep. I move before I can talk myself out of it, sending up a silent prayer to Lin, the same goddess I saw on Rayce's desk, that the rebellion doesn't catch me.

The night air sticks to my skin, heavy with moisture. I move as quickly as I can, trying to step on leaves carpeting the forest floor so they can't easily track my steps. My leg screams in pain, but I embrace the feeling. It keeps me alert.

Reaching the last of the tents, I look over my shoulder, back at the camp, my chest hurting. My freedom has dwindled down to a handful of hours, as fleeting as the last rays of moonlight before dawn.

I whisper a quick good-bye and hurry toward the tree line.

I'm so busy looking behind me that I don't see the person in front of me until I bump into him. The moment we collide, hot tea pours down my shoulder, and the person I ran into clicks his tongue.

"It's a little late for you to be out, isn't it?" Oren asks.

He straightens his round spectacles on his nose and peers down at me. His long black hair flows loose down his shoulders instead of the orderly ponytail he usually wears at the base of his neck. It makes him look less buttoned-up, even though he's dressed as impeccably as always in a brown robe.

I stand frozen in his kind gaze, the shock of seeing him thrumming through my limbs. A day ago, I thought he might be captured or dead.

The book he lent me burns a hole in my pack.

Before I can think better of it, I lean up and wrap my arms around Oren's neck, tears springing to my eyes. This is the man who tried to help my father, and even though he didn't succeed, I will never forget what he did. And he's tried to help me, too.

He chuckles, the tip of his beard tickling my forehead as he returns my embrace.

"What's this for?" he asks.

"I'm just relieved you're back," I say into his brown robe. The smoky scent of his pipe and the smell of ancient parchment waft up from the fabric of his robe.

His hand touches my stuffed pack.

"Nice night for a walk, isn't it?" he asks, even though it's obvious I'm not just going on a leisurely stroll. "Why don't you accompany me?"

I pull away, and he reaches in his pocket, revealing a red handkerchief. He hands it to me without comment on my watery eyes.

I nod, not trusting myself to speak.

To my surprise, he turns east, the way I was heading, leaving the camp behind. I force myself onward, struggling at first to keep up with Oren's long strides.

The moon peeks through the thin leaves, illuminating the white birch trunks like apparitions. The dusty white and blue world between the trees feels like magic personified. Oren doesn't speak for a long time, and his silence sets my nerves on edge.

We stop in a small clearing outside the camp, and Oren turns to me, the moonlight splashing brightly on his calm face. He seems different than usual, but I can't put my finger on how.

"You're leaving because Zareen couldn't keep our end of the bargain, correct?"

I open my mouth to protest but realize it won't do any good. I am leaving, even if it's not for the reason he believes. Besides, right now he seems content to let me go, and the less he knows, the better.

"And to that end, it's my fault," he says. "We fought hard to liberate those poor girls, but the emperor sent the majority of his forces on my platoon. We just couldn't gain enough momentum to break through the endless throngs of Sun soldiers."

His words send a chill down my spine, and his brow knits, his eyes tinged with sadness.

"I'm not leaving because of the failed mission," I say.

The rest of the words stick in my throat. Every thought I've had swirls in my head, and the reason I'm actually leaving feels too raw to say out loud. To admit my fear of Rayce using me, to let anyone in the world know that I could be so easily broken by a *feeling* starting to well up inside me sends my knees shaking.

"I read the book you gave me."

*There.*

I stand completely still, my body poised to sprint if he shows any sign of trying to hold me back.

"Ah," he says, his voice betraying nothing. "I did warn you the writing was a little dry."

Normally, I'd appreciate his humor, but I can't right now. Not when everything I've been running from lies unveiled in the moonlight. I feel like I'm caught in the middle of an ambush without a sword. Open, exposed.

"You've known the truth about me the entire time I've been here."

"Yes," he says, looking up into the leaves. "I had my suspicions the moment I met you, and they were confirmed when I saw that marking on your foot."

"Why didn't you tell Rayce?" I whisper, tears stinging my eyes again.

"Because it needs to come from you." He levels me with serious eyes, forcing my gaze instinctively downward to the tops of my boots.

"You were there in Varsha at the start of the uprising. You were the one negotiating the treaty with my father to join our two countries through marriage."

"I was, yes," Oren says. "I wish I could have done more to help your father then, but I made a promise to myself from the moment I found you that I would help you now. It won't make up for my failure in the past, but you deserve for me to try."

He scoops his large hand under my chin and guides my eyes to his.

"That's why I believe you need to stay," Oren says. "You have to face the thing you want to run from. Only then will you be free from it."

The tears spill over, running rivers down my cheeks as I remember the emperor drowning his precious ants and how much it reminded me of Zareen. I can picture Marin's face splashed in sunlight as she told me why the rebellion was worth putting her life at risk, and Arlo standing over her broken body, guarding her from the worst of the battle in Dongsu. These memories swirl around into the one thing my heart truly desires—bathing my skin in Rayce's heat. His plea for me to stay with him fills my ears.

And a pit even deeper than the one I faced in the imperial dungeon opens up in my chest. I don't want to leave.

But if I don't, Rayce might have to make a terrible choice.

"I can't stay," I whisper.

"Of course you can," he says.

Staring at Oren underneath the canopy of trees with my pack weighing down my shoulders, I can't keep in the darkest of my fears. They come festering up my throat, choking me.

"You don't understand," I say, another tear sliding down my cheek. "If I tell Rayce that I'm the lost Varshan princess, he'll have to choose between giving me to his uncle or helping his people. I've seen what this type of choice has cost him in the past, and I can't do that to him. I won't."

Oren's eyes widen, his spectacles nearly slipping off the tip of his nose. I rub the back of my hand across my cheek, erasing the proof of my weakness.

"When you first got here, you wanted us to trust you." Oren clears his throat. "And even though Rayce knew he shouldn't, based on your actions, he fought to believe in you anyway. But trust works both ways. You must give trust to receive it, and you never even gave Rayce the chance to prove that you can trust him with your secret."

My resolve shatters at his words.

"But everything in his past shows he'll choose his people first, no matter what."

Oren lifts his hand, his finger brushing across my cheek as he wipes a stray tear away.

"But he is also a man," Oren says. "He'll see you for who you are, not what you are, just as he saw you were more than a Flower when you first came to us."

Air sweeps through my lungs. It feels like I've been underwater this entire time and finally broke the surface. Oren brings me close to him one more time, wrapping me in his arms the way my father used to do when I was young.

"I have a feeling that before this war is over, you'll have a great part to play in it," he whispers, placing a hand on the back of my head. "And I do believe you'll be spectacular once you figure out what your role is. You're going to do great things, Rose, if you let yourself."

I press my eyes shut, falling back to a time when all I feared was a scraped knee. "Thank you," I say. "Thank you for believing in me."

Every step I've taken since the moment I escaped the Garden has felt like I was flailing, but under Oren's watchful gaze my feet have mastered a proper dance. Maybe this new girl will learn to understand love, can have faith in people even when it's hard. The gnawing panic that sent me fleeing from camp begins to dissipate like the night sky under the sun's watchful eye, and a new path begins to take shape. A path that leads me back to Rayce. I look up, meeting Oren's eyes.

Except his eyes aren't on me. They're intensely focused behind my shoulder.

"Here," he says, shoving something into my hand then pushing me aside.

The ground comes for me too fast. But the arrow hurling toward the place I was just standing misses me, embedding itself into Oren's gut. He crumples to the ground. In my hands now is a vial of Zarenite powder that he probably had around his neck.

"You've ruined my shot," comes a sickeningly familiar accent behind me. "That one was meant to maim my Flower."

The breath dissolves from my lungs. My mouth goes dry. Every hair on my body stands on end as I realize why he gave it to me. I shove the vial into my shirt.

The Gardener can't be here. Not now, not after everything I've done to escape. It has to be in my head, a physical manifestation of all my fears and panic bringing the voice from my subconscious. I convince myself that this is true, so I can force myself to turn around.

"I knew trailing that last troupee of rebels back would work out," the Gardener says.

I look up at his bulbous belly, an inch of hairy skin peeking out from under his green silk shirt. He's surrounded by eight lackeys, each with a crossbow aimed at my head.

"We caught ourselves a Flower and a pretty important rattie," he says.

"Oren!" I shout, crawling toward him. "Run!"

The sharp bite of an arrow tip threatening my back freezes my limbs and I clamp my mouth shut as the lackey holding the crossbow motions for me to stay quiet. Oren lies a few feet away, one hand clutching the shaft of the arrow sticking out of his side. Blood coats his hand as he winces.

Pain explodes through my head as I'm yanked to my knees by my hair. I open my mouth to scream, but the Gardener *tsks*, pointing a finger to his lips. He signals with his eyes for me to look back at Oren.

"I wouldn't do that, leetle Flower," he says.

One of the lackeys holds a blade to Oren's neck, though Oren's already grimacing as his other hand fumbles for the arrow.

"Now let's get going," the Gardener says, a wicked smile carving into his face, puffing out his cheeks like an overstuffed plum. "We've got to send word to the emperor of Delmar that we finally have what he's looking for." He runs a single finger across my cheek, his long, yellowing fingernail scrapping against my flesh. "I look forward to seeing what he decides to do to you."

The emperor doesn't give second chances. I can't imagine what punishment will fit my crime.

It takes three lackeys to pull Oren to his feet, and as he struggles up, his face turns paler than the moonlight. The long-haired man on Oren's left kicks him forward, and Oren stumbles over a tree root. I move to catch him when a pair of hands yanks me to my feet. I squirm against the lackey's touch as he clamps iron shackles on my wrists, the spikes lining the inside creating a familiar pain.

A serrated blade slips between my shoulder and the pack strap, and the comforting weight of my supplies from Zareen slides off my back.

As they push me forward, I look over my shoulder toward the camp. My heart bleeds knowing the horrors that lie ahead. I can feel Rayce's presence, warm and kind, from the direction of camp like a beacon in the dark. How much will he break in the morning when he finds the man who practically raised him and the girl he asked to stay with him have both disappeared? My gut twists.

Something shimmering in the moonlight catches my eyes, and my gaze snaps to my pack. Peeking out from the opened lid is the small book Oren lent me.

Marin will recognize the silvery lettering on the front, and that'll give them a clue.

I just hope we're both still breathing by the time they stumble upon it. I close my eyes, knowing our nightmare is just beginning.

# Chapter Thirty-One

It takes us two days to get out of the forest. We stop often under the pretense of Oren's injuries, but it's the Gardener who always lags behind, his long-sleeved silk shirt sticking to his body and sweat glistening on every inch of him from exertion. On the first night, one of the lackeys attaches a small note to the leg of a falcon and lets it loose. It flies west with a purpose that sets my skin on edge. That same night, they extract the arrow sticking out of Oren's side. His scream sticks with me as I try to lie comfortably on a bed of dead leaves near the Gardener's smelly feet.

The next day I glance behind my shoulder every few moments, the shackles eating into my flesh with the movement, hoping to see the telltale green and brown uniforms of the Zareeni rebellion peeking through the birch trees. And every time I look, a little piece of the hope I dared cultivate withers.

Maybe Rayce won't be able to justify coming after us.

When we break free from the trees, a familiar sight greets me, sending bile rising up my throat. Breaking the early-morning sunrise are the silhouettes of the traveling carts of

the Garden. Still suspended high above my cart are the heads
of Star and Sickle. Two other heads have joined them, though
we're too far away to decipher who else paid for my absence.

The Gardener pushes us faster. I wade through the tall
grass of the plain that separates Imperial City from its wall,
parting the thin blades like water. The sun beats down on my
chapped lips and unprotected head, and my vision blurs sharp
edges into a misty haze.

We arrive at the Garden with little fanfare. Only Shears
waits for us in the center of the half circle our carts form with
a small piece of parchment in hand. The moment he lays his
dead eyes on me, a smile splits his face.

"I was wondering when I'd see you again, pretty little
Flower," he says, holding out the parchment to the Gardener.
"Message for you, boss."

The Gardener slaps the parchment away. "Read it aloud
for me."

Oren stops next to me, his shallow breathing rocking his
entire body. Sweat sticks his long hair to his pale face, and
blood stains the hasty bandages thrown around his wound.
My hands long to reach out and steady him, but my long years
in the Garden still them. Any amount of kindness I show him
could be reflected in his skin. It's best if I seem detached.

Shears frowns at the order and unfurls the tiny scroll.
"Just says the big guy will meet us in two days' time on his
journey to the wall. He also gave a small map on where to
go. Oh..." Shears looks up from the paper, a smile returning
to his face. His eyes flit up, combing across Oren's tall frame.
"And we're to have an execution when he arrives."

I lunge out at him, straining against the manacles around
my wrists. Shears laughs, pushing a hand against my forehead.
The lack of water and sleep sends my brain spinning, and I
nearly topple over.

The Gardener looks me in the face and speaks in a

perfect Delmarion accent, not the fake exotic one he uses for show. "You're about to give me everything I ever wanted, my precious Rose." He turns to the lackeys standing behind us. "Lock them up. We have someplace we need to be."

White-hot anger sears my veins, and I narrow my eyes at the Gardener's back. He snatches the parchment from Shears like it's a piece of rare chocolate and waddles over to his cart, studying the map.

"See you in a few days, Flower," Shears says, waving his fingers slowly as a lackey tugs me backward.

The three lackeys that have kept watch over us lead me at sword point toward my old cage. Four streams of blood now coat the outside of my cart, and though I try to avert my gaze, all I can see are Star and Sickle's faces, fixed in shock. Now on pikes in the back are Holly and Thyme, adding to the gruesome scene in front of me.

The man in front wrenches open the door to my cage, the familiar squeaking sound embedding into my bones. Darkness opens up its deadly arms, waiting to devour me. The lackey on the left shoves Oren inside, and the one in front pushes me into the yawning mouth. The sharp wooden edge bites into my knees as I tumble forward. The stench of stale hay and years of desperation fills my lungs.

I swing around as the light fades from the slamming door, locking me back in the hovel I used to share with Fern. Crawling across the splintered wood, I slam my bound fists into the door. The hollow sound of my bones hitting wood fills the room as laughter echoes from outside.

*How are we going to escape?*

My mind searches through everything I know. It took me ten years to find a way to escape last time, and now I only have two days. I have no weapons unless I want to burn myself up with the vial of Zarenite Oren handed me.

Rayce flashes before my eyes in the darkness, stinging my

heart.

Zareen might be en route to help us, but there's no guarantee they'll come for us. Arlo's words haunt me in the dark as they have a thousand times before, teasing me about not being important enough to risk everything for. Besides, even if they are coming for us, we can't afford to wait for them, especially if Shears was telling the truth about an execution.

No time, no way to defend myself, and likely no help.

Oren's sputtering cough breaks through my hopeless thoughts.

I turn and narrow my eyes in the swirling darkness. In my absence, someone has covered up my peephole with a spare piece of wood, sealing us in this false night. In the right corner of the cart, the shadows seem a little thicker.

Crawling on all fours, the crunchy sound of hay the symphony to my stilted dance, I scurry to the corner.

Oren leans against the wooden wall of the cage, his long legs nearly touching the opposite wall. Leaves and hay stick out of his long, ruffled hair and beard. His hands lie slack by his sides, and beads of sweat cling to every patch of his skin that I can see.

I reach out and pull a leaf from the front of his beard. He winces.

"Are you okay?" I ask.

His voice nothing more than a whisper, he starts to say, "No," but a coughing fit cuts it off. The way those hacking noises rack his body makes me wince, and I push him up farther on the wall so he can catch his breath.

"Take it easy," I say. "I'm going to try to redress that wound."

Grimacing, he nods.

With trembling fingers, I pull at the knot holding together the shoddy wrapping around his middle. He sucks in air as I take my time unwinding the cloth. The closer I get to his wound, the stickier the dirty makeshift bandage becomes. Pulling it off, I find the puncture near the edge of his abdomen. The skin puckers up on the incision, and the wound hasn't started to scab over.

I yank the bottom of my long tunic out of my pants and rip off a piece. I place the clean fabric over Oren's wound, wishing for the stinging brown bottle Rayce had when he helped me with the cut on my palm, and wrap it so it stays shut.

I pull back my shaking hands, now smeared with Oren's blood, and stare down at them, tears stinging my eyes.

"What are we going to do?" I whisper aloud, no longer able to contain the fear pulsing through me. "I'm so sorry. This is all my fault. If I had just been strong enough to tell Rayce the truth, then we wouldn't be here. If I hadn't been leaving the camp, if you hadn't been out there to stop me, then you wouldn't be here and—"

Oren's large hand covers mine, stopping my tongue, and his grip is strong enough to pull me closer to him.

"No," he whispers. "It'll be okay. Tru—" Another cough interrupts him. "Trust in them."

"Okay, okay," I say, nodding through my tears to keep him quiet. I can't believe in his words. Hope died the moment the shackles were thrown around my wrists.

He coughs again, his head rolling to the side, but his grasp on me doesn't loosen.

"Trust…in…Rayce," he says, each word stunted, like he's pulling them out of the deepest places in his mind. "Faith."

He pats my hand and I lay my head on his chest, letting my tears soak his filthy brown robe. We sit like that as the cart lurches forward. I listen to the sound of his heart pounding faintly through his chest and pray to whatever Delmarion god that's listening to let it continue on that way.

In the silence, I hear Fern laughing, feel her hands

weaving through my hair as she spins tales of her life before the Garden. Her words were the only thing to get me through those long nights. The first day we were locked in this very cage together, she told me the only way we could remember what it was like to be alive was to talk. The moment we stopped talking, stopped believing, we let the Gardener win.

"Why don't I tell you a story?" I ask, shaking Oren to keep him awake.

He doesn't answer, so I close my eyes and start to talk as our cart bumps along, blocking out the sight of the four heads strung up just above us and the panic filling my lungs. The words bottled up inside for years come spilling out. The true story he'll never get to add to the pages of his book.

"The night before my father's kingdom fell, he kissed me on the forehead and sent me away with the woman who raised me after my mother died. We were to head for Delmar. My nanny told me everything would be okay once we got here. I was nine and I believed her."

All I remember about her are her soft hands and the way she screamed when the Gardener broke into the home where we were staying. Rain and darkness and small spaces have robbed me of her face and our shared jokes and her voice.

"We were staying in a small farmhouse on the border of Delmar the night we were attacked." I blink back fresh tears as Zara's sleeping face appears before me. "I trusted a boy a little older than me, and I shouldn't have. He told the Gardener where we were hiding. The girl I was sharing the room with was just a few years older than me. When the Gardener broke in, they found her first. She—she never stood a chance. They found me curled underneath a cabinet with my mother's necklace. When the Gardener came in to examine what they'd found, he recognized it. He knew I was a prize. Then he kept me hidden for four years while I practiced day and night to perfect my routine, and when I had finally blossomed, he made me his star.

"My birthright has kept me safe, but it's also kept me gagged. He told me people would use me to get what they want, and after the betrayal from that boy I thought I could trust, I believed him. That it'd be safer to keep it to myself."

Even though Oren doesn't have the strength to respond, I imagine what he would say. I can almost hear his rough voice asking, "Why on earth would you do that, child?"

"I know I was wrong now," I say. "But after so many years here, his reasoning had to be true. Otherwise, how could good, honest people let something like the Garden exist? Either everyone was bad or no one cared. And that's why I couldn't trust any of you at first. Especially Rayce. Last time I let a boy get close to me, I lost everything. But I was so wrong this time."

Oren would have the perfect thing to say to that, too. The thing that would blow back the walls and bust the top off this hellhole. I don't know those words, though. Could never even conjure them up.

With no more secrets to reveal, and too many problems to solve, we fall asleep to the jerky rocking of my old cage bumping its way toward an execution I'm powerless to stop.

• • •

The pounding in my head can't be real. It builds like the slow rise of a tightly wound drum, and each hit shoots a wave of pain down my body that vibrates to my fingers and toes. My field of vision has shrunken down to a tiny speck of white, glowing high and fuzzy above me like a pinprick through a black veil. I stare at the light, trying to figure out where I am. I pretend my head lies on a pillow and the breathing next to me is Marin's, but in my gut I already know. The dim lighting, the wooden walls adorned with scratches and smudged with dirt, the stale hay and heat pressing down on me like I'm baking in an oven...

It's the place I've been running from.

I'm back in the Garden.

That thought weighs on me as if the Gardener sits on my chest. I turn my head to the left and see Oren still leaning against the wooden wall. Sweat drips down his forehead, his pale lips cracking from lack of water. The only thing that brings a tendril of comfort to my heart is the way his body moves up and down with each breath.

Sometime during my restless slumber, the cart stopped moving.

The sound of wood grinding against metal echoes in the darkness. I scoot up as bright sunlight pours into the cart. A silhouette fills the opening, but it's too bright to see anything.

"They're up!" one of the lackeys calls out.

Oren's hand finds mine. His long fingers wrap weakly around my palm as if he's trying to comfort me. Trying to say things with his hands that his mouth can't utter.

We stay there, frozen, in this single second of solitude, tucked away in the darkest corner of the earth, and his touch tells me nothing can break us.

Several dark silhouettes block out the blinding light, their weight shaking the cage. Whatever else Oren wanted to say is cut short as two pairs of hands wrench us apart.

They drag Oren out into the blinding sunlight.

"Where are you taking him?" I rush for the opening, meeting the sharp end of a blade. My eyes fight to focus in the bright light, but I can't make out anything in the glare.

"Tell me!" I yell at the lackey holding me at bay.

He chuckles in response, pointing the end of his sword deeper into my cage before he slams the door in my face, locking me alone in the darkness. I lean my forehead against the rough wood, trying to calm my shaking limbs. I go over my options in my head once more: Rayce and the others are too far to reach. Oren is gone. There's only me.

Alone.

In the dark.

Without even a shred of deceiving light to give me hope.

# Chapter Thirty-Two

The sound of a hammer beating wood rouses me from sleep. My eyes flutter open, and I expect to be met with darkness, but a splash of white sunlight beams down a few inches from my head. I lie still, waiting for my vision to change. Surely this is a trick of my mind. My dry throat burns as I try to swallow, and my head swims.

Yet the light remains through the pain. Turning toward it, I see light pouring in from the old peephole Fern and I used to share. But how is it uncovered again?

I sit up on my hands and knees, the banging outside pounding through my small space.

Scooting to the peephole, I peer out. Light attacks my raw eyes, casting everything white. I blink, my vision slowly adjusting to the brightness.

The side of a crumbling white building greets me, a giant chunk of the wall propped up against it. Beams hang off the wooden ceiling, and dark holes loom where the wood has split and caved in from decay. Part of a rickety wooden fence stands next to the dilapidated building, and the remains of brown dirt where a road once stood have been claimed back by the tall grass of the plains. A rusty ax sits embedded in a pile of rotting chopped wood, waiting for someone to come by and claim it from its state of disarray. Whatever this place used to be, it has long since been abandoned.

The lack of people makes it even stranger to see the top of a grand dark blue tent peeking out from over the ruined houses. This is the type of place the Garden would never go. It's poor, dilapidated, abandoned. We aren't here for a show.

Our carts have been placed in their usual formation in semicircle around the large tent. *Bang!*

The sound that woke me echoes in the air again. I follow where the noise is coming from to a shirtless man slick with sweat, pounding a large hammer into a wooden platform he's erecting between two ruined houses. The newly chopped planks of the small platform are jarring white next to the rotting houses surrounding it.

*Bang!*

The hammer hits the wood.

*Bang!*

And I realize they're building a stage for the impending execution. My chest seizes.

*Oren!*

I can't stand by and let them hurt him. There has to be something I can do. I place my shaking hands against the wall to steady them and take a few deep breaths. It's hard to tell how many hours it's been since they took Oren. I pull my hand back and see his blood dried onto my skin and clench my fist.

*Please be okay.*

What can I use? I peek out the open slot again and come face-to-face with a dark brown eye peering inside my cage. My heart slams in my chest as I jump back.

Laughter assaults the air, crawling up my skin. *Shears.*

"Preparing for the big show, Flower?" he asks. "I thought you might want a room with a view as your friend paints the grass red, so I took down the patch for you."

I ball my hands into fists, grabbing onto the stale hay to steady them. Shears flashes a smile, showing his large white teeth. Everything inside me longs to punch his face until my hands are bloody and every one of his precious teeth falls out of his mouth. Even though I know I should keep my head down and stay silent, anger breaks my vow of silence.

"You aren't going to succeed," I say. "I'm going to stop whatever it is you're planning."

"And I'm going to enjoy watching you try, little Flower," he whispers into the cage.

The wistful note in his voice slithers up my limbs, slicing into my resolve. The heat from outside presses down on me like the ceiling is growing gradually lower.

"I can't promise you'll make it out in one piece, though," he says, banging on the side of my cart. "But how pretty will you be lying on the grass in chunks?"

His manic laughter floats away from my cart as he leaves me in the darkness to picture his last statement. The banging of the stage being built mixes with the sound of Fern's final screams in my crowded head. I throw my blood-soaked hands over my ears to block out the noise, but it follows me behind my eyelids.

Oren will die if I can't figure out a way to stop it.

. . .

The sunlight disappears from the floor of my cage, draining the last of my hope with its fleeting fingers. The emperor will meet with the Gardener tomorrow, and Oren will die. The sun might as well stay set, because if that happens there will be no light left in the world. Last I checked, the sliver of a moon was already high in the sky, casting the world in a sickly blue tinge.

I run my fingers through my hair, trying to mimic the way Fern used to, but I find no comfort in the jerky movements.

The construction of the platform stopped sometime around sunset. I thought the constant banging would drive me mad, but the silence cuts sharper. This deafening quiet means everything is prepared for the Gardener's sickening performance tomorrow.

I close my eyes, rocking back and forth in the darkness, my chest swelling with emptiness.

*Knock, knock, knock.*

My eyes snap open, and I reach instinctively for my sword. My fingers grasp hay instead. Has Shears come back to haunt me in the night like a ghost? I still, drowning in the silence that follows as I listen for some other movement.

"Rose?" comes a familiar whisper near the front of my cart.

I wrap my arms around my shoulders and shake my head. Have I finally lost my mind in the solitude of my cage? Because I almost recognized that voice, the same one that painted a future I wanted to live in, that brought me back to life after escaping the Garden the first time. I can almost feel the strength of Rayce's embrace surrounding me, the scents of honey and spice tickling my nose.

"Rose, are you in there?" comes the same voice again.

His words break through the fog in my mind.

I scurry across my cart, rustling the hay to the side, and press my ear to the splintered surface of my door. Placing a trembling hand where the voice came from, I take a deep breath.

I utter the name that's been stuck on my lips for the past two days. "Rayce?"

My heart slams in my chest, hope bursting through my veins, as I wait for a reply.

"Yes, it's me," he says, his voice muffled by the door. "Hang on, I'm going to get you out."

*He came back for me. Even though I left him, he came back.*

The realization floods my body, pumping blood back into my veins, and my lungs restart, filling with fresh air. Light explodes in my mind as bright as the green Zarenite cracking to life in the dull walls of the rebellion base.

"Okay," I whisper, my voice shaking.

I listen in the silence, each tinny sound of metal clinking sending a wave of panic swirling in my stomach. But when he grows quiet, I worry he might have given up—or worse, I imagined the whole thing. The seconds multiply.

Finally, it gives way underneath my cheek. I reach out and catch the widening opening before it can swing out too far.

Through the crack, I make out a strip of Rayce's scarred face. His dark eye meets mine, concern pooling through its depths. My fingers shake, longing to reach out and smooth the anxious crinkles of his forehead. A moment ago, I was sure the only things I'd ever have of him to hold to were memories, and now he's inches away.

"What's wrong?" he asks.

"The door squeaks," I say, sliding my legs out from underneath me.

He nods, stepping to the side, leaving nothing blocking my escape but a thin strip of night sky. Holding the door in place with one hand, I slide sideways through the opening, contorting my body until I'm in a *C* shape to slip through.

My bare feet touch the prickly grass, and I straighten, closing the door behind me. A slight breeze caresses my face, blowing away the stagnating heat that clung to my body inside the cart. From where I stand, I see the abandoned houses continue down the faded main road, debris and piles of rotted wood littering the streets.

And in front of them is the man I thought I needed to run from.

Tatters creep up the bottom of his long black vest like unruly vines, and his stubble has grown into a small black beard covering his chin. His dark hair hangs wild over his knitted forehead, and his lips are parted ever so slightly, like he can't quite believe what he's looking at. The moonlight cast him with a grayish-blue tone—every hard edge of him in perfect detail. He's so exquisite standing here in the middle of this horror show that it hurts, but I can't keep my hungry eyes off him.

"Are you injured?" he asks, his voice scratchy.

"Not too badly," I say. "Shaken but not really physically hur—"

Before I can finish my sentence, his strong arms embrace me, folding me into his chest. His beard tickles my neck as he pulls me closer, like his touch can erase all the pain and hopelessness that have plagued me since I left the camp.

Helpless against his warmth, I wrap my hands around his neck, his silky hair soft against my cheek, and lean into him, every hint of worry I had falling away as I fit into the flexed muscles of his chest. His hand makes a slow circle on the small of my back, and he lifts me an inch off the ground, the tips of the grass kissing the bottoms of my feet.

"I wasn't sure you'd be able to find me this time," I say.

"I will *always* find you," he whispers, nuzzling the tip of his nose into my exposed neck. "When we found your pack, I rounded up as many people as I could and tracked you into the plains. The moment I saw wagon tracks, I knew who had captured you, but I feared we might be too late."

At the mention of time, I stiffen in his embrace. Rayce pulls his head off my shoulder, setting me back on the ground, and frowns slightly at my sudden change in mood.

"What's wrong?" he asks.

"We have to find Oren and free my sisters. The Gardener said your uncle will be here in the morning, and they're going to execute him."

The relief shining in Rayce's eyes fades, and he lets go of me. The moment we part, my skin longs for his again. A week ago this need to be near him would've bothered me, but after believing I might not ever get to see the way his scar ripples over his skin when he's worried or to feel the weight of his kind eyes on mine, I welcome the need that rises in my chest.

We both look at the night sky, and my stomach drops. The stars have faded back in their blankets, and the moon has fallen from its perch in the sky. At best we have an hour until dawn.

"We saw two sets of footprints," Rayce says. "And Oren was missing in the morning, too, so we assumed both of you had been taken. I have others swarming the camp looking for him."

I twirl the end of my braid, looking down in thought.

"I *have* to free my sisters," I say, "but you should find Oren."

Glancing up, I see the indecision weighing the corner of Rayce's mouth down. He rubs a hand across his chin, the scratchy sound of his beard scraping against his palm filling the silence in the air.

"I trust my people," Rayce says, but his voice wavers with uncertainty. "They will find him and report back to me. I'm going to help *you* like I promised."

Knowing I won't have to run through the Garden by myself steadies my pounding heart, and the relief of not parting with Rayce after finding him again washes over me as tenderly as when he bandaged my wound. I know there are things I have to tell him, hard things that will test us both, but right now I'm just happy he's staying by my side.

"You forgot this back at camp," Rayce says, pulling the

sword I'd been using out of a second scabbard strapped to his side. "I figured I'd hold onto it until I could return it to you."

My fingers wrap around the familiar hilt, the leather squeaking its recognition underneath my grip. Power surges through my body like wind through a tunnel, and I grit my teeth, ready for whatever lies ahead.

I open my mouth to thank Rayce, but another voice cuts off my own.

"I see a snake's snuck into our little Garden," Shears says from behind me.

Rayce and I both spin to face him, toward the center of the small circle the Garden carts make. Shears walks forward, his hands tucked in his pockets and a pleasant smile on his face. His teeth practically glow in the dim light. Flanking him are four other lackeys brandishing moonlit swords, except for one in the back who aims a crossbow at Rayce's head.

I clutch my sword tighter, moving back until I touch the door of my cart.

"Be careful," I whisper to Rayce.

He takes a step in front of me, hand falling to the grip of his stunner.

"I didn't think I'd get to see blood until morning," Shears says, twisting to pull out his cutting blades.

His movements are methodical, ordinary, unafraid, like he's reaching down to tie his shoe instead of getting ready to fight for his life.

"Stand down and we might spare your lives," Rayce says, pulling out his sword instead. I already know Rayce's words will fall onto deaf ears, but he hasn't had the pleasure of meeting the very worst the Gardener has to offer. Shears will always choose blood.

As if he can hear my thoughts and wants to prove me wrong, Shears holds up his hands in front of him, his double blades hanging slack, like he's going to surrender. I blink back my surprise. The four lackeys behind him look at each other, wondering if they should follow suit.

Then Shears swings his hands back up and smiles. "I wonder what her scream will sound like this time when I cleave you in two, snake."

An arrow whizzes in the air next to Rayce's cheek, and he jerks out of the way to avoid it. Shears charges at the same time, blades aimed at Rayce's middle. I see the blade coming for Rayce, trying to take away the one person I've come to truly care for, and the fear in my heart vanishes. I wasn't able to keep my promise and save Fern, but Shears will not touch another person close to me.

I lash out in front of Rayce, my sword singing as it collides with Shears's double blades. His smile widens, seeing who he's caught.

"So you're going to fight me, huh, little Flower?" he asks, his hot breath washing over me.

He pushes against my blade, the muscles in his arms flexing, and I strain against him, throwing all my weight forward. My arm begins to buckle, and I jump back.

As I retreat, Rayce swings at one of the lackeys coming for him, his clean blade now slick with blood. The lackey falls to his knees behind Rayce as he hammers toward the crossbow shooting at him.

*Stay with me. Stay safe.*

Sensing my momentary shift in focus, Shears lunges after me, his hand catching my wrist. His fingers clamp down on my bone, and he yanks me toward him. I throw my weight behind me, but my bare feet slip against his might. With his other hand, he swings his shears at my waist.

I flick my sword up, catching the first blade.

The second blade frees itself, slicing through the back of my hand. I stumble back, blood sprouting from the gash, and suck in air through my teeth to keep a scream trapped in my throat.

I readjust my grip, pain shooting up my arm.

Shears brings the blades up to his face and touches the sharp edge, pulling back some of my blood on his fingertips.

"You certainly bleed a pretty color," he says. "Let's see how beautiful the rest of you bleeds."

He charges toward me, but this time I'm ready. I jump out of the way, throwing my fist into his face. The bones in his nose crunch against the back of my fingers, and for the first time in my life, I hear Shears howl in pain. Blood pours from his nostrils, streaking down his face and into his mouth.

Shears's muffled cries pump adrenaline through my body, and I pull back for another punch.

He drops his signature blades, his hand lashing out to wrap around my neck, then he yanks me to him, pinning my back to his chest. His fingernails dig into the side of my neck, and precious air slips out of my lungs.

My sword falls from my fingers as he lifts me off the ground. I kick out behind me, but I can't get enough thrust to make it hurt.

Shears twists us around as the sun begins to reveal its pink center over the horizon. I catch sight of Rayce's back bathed in the soft light as one of the two remaining lackeys nicks him on the shoulder.

"You sure you want to keep a Flower, pretty boy?" Shears asks, raising his voice, his grip around my neck tightening. "They're fragile."

Rayce swings around, his blade flashing in the air, and our eyes connect.

"And they die very easily," Shears continues, nuzzling his nose across my cheek.

My lungs scream for air. I reach up, using my fingernails to try to claw his hand off my vocal pipe, struggling to yank his hand down. Tears spring to my eyes as my vision begins to blur.

Rayce's mouth twists in worry, his hand sliding down to his belt. I see the barrel of a stunner as white dots float in front of me, my throat seizing up. He aims it down, near my feet.

Green fills my world as I choke, my limbs too heavy to hold up any longer.

And then I'm falling toward the ground, air flooding into my lungs. I throw out my hands to catch myself and suck in the cool air, letting it slide down my pained throat. Shears falls a few feet next to me, clutching his leg in pain.

A stunner skids across the ground, and I glance up to see Rayce nod before swinging around to attack the last standing lackey.

We're a team. He knows just what I need.

I reach into my shirt and pull out the vial Oren gave me right before we were captured. I down the Zarenite as a hand grips my hair and snatch the stunner off the ground. The handle reacts to my touch, the powder coming to life under my fingertips, and I pull the trigger. Shears falls back as the blast rockets through him, and I snatch my fallen sword from the ground.

"This Flower doesn't die easily," I say, glaring down at him. "She isn't fragile. Not anymore."

He looks up at me, his nose still pouring blood from my punch, but instead of fear, his mouth splits into a grin, crimson staining his white teeth.

"It's a shame I won't be able to watch you die," he says. "But I'll be seeing you real soon."

I slam the weapon down into his neck. The blade slides through the exposed skin, cutting out a crooked smile, but struggles against his bone, so I pull it out and swing harder.

His head comes off in a blink, and warm blood splatters my face, into my mouth, his bitterness mixing with my own.

All I can think as I look down at his detached head is that I've wasted ten years of my life living in terror of this man, and it took less than ten seconds to end his life. Ten more seconds than he would have afforded me.

A hand on my shoulder rouses me from my thoughts, and I look up from Shears's head into Rayce's eyes. He touches my cheek, wiping off the smear of blood and sweat coating my face.

His gaze dances over me, finally settling on my neck. I put my hands up to cover the red mark appearing in the dawning sunlight, but he catches them with his own.

"You fought well," he says, the hint of a smile playing at his lips. "We need to hurry in case anyone heard us."

I nod for too long, my gaze drifting back to the man I just killed.

"I'm just glad you're okay," he says, using the crook of his finger to tip my chin back in his direction. Warmth radiates out of his dark eyes, and I feel myself relaxing as we stare at each other.

"What about you?" I ask, standing on my tiptoes to check the cut on his shoulder. Blood stains his green shirt, but it doesn't look too deep.

"I'll be fine," he says, cupping my face in both his hands. "Not to worry."

He breaks contact first, turning to stare at the sky. My stomach twists as the bottom of the sun crests the horizon. Day is almost upon us and with it, the emperor's reinforcements.

"We have to rescue the others," I say.

He nods, his mouth drawn into a serious line. "And quickly. I'm not sure if I have enough Zareeni forces here to hold if my uncle shows up with Sun soldiers."

His words send an icy shard of dread into my heart. I move toward Shears's body and pat around his shirt, sticking my hands in his pockets. I touch cold metal and wrap my fingers around the circle, yanking it from him. Gleaming in the morning light are thirteen keys that will grant my sisters their freedom.

I turn to run for the nearest cart, but Rayce grabs my palm. Securing my fingers in his, he nods and we take off together—a flower and a snake fleeing from the impeding daylight.

# Chapter Thirty-Three

As the sun's rays touch down on the abandoned village where the Garden has set up, my legs pump to keep up with Rayce. He keeps his fingers locked with mine, our kissing palms giving me an extra boost of strength. We leave behind the bodies we laid to waste, and they look surprisingly natural among the patches of dead grass and houses falling into themselves.

Jumping over a large rotting beam in the road, we scurry to Juniper's cart.

I glance over my shoulder toward the entrance of town. In the morning light, the silhouette of a head peeking out from the roof of the nearest building catches my attention.

"Someone's over there," I say, pointing to the house.

As Rayce follows my finger, thirteen Zareeni uniforms crawl out of a large hole in the side of the building like butterflies from a cocoon and fly toward us.

We stop in front of the large door to Juniper's wooden cage, and Rayce holds me stationary.

The guard in the front pulls ahead of the pack, and I catch a patch of short, light brown hair. Arlo's face splits into a large grin, which is so unlike the last time I saw him—panic-stricken and being pulled through the hole in the dungeon while I was captured.

Arlo runs straight for me, his arms extended, and nearly knocks me off my feet in an embrace.

I stiffen in his arms but don't pull away. He isn't an enemy just because he's a man. He's been just as much a friend to me as Fern or Marin.

"I can't even tell you how happy I am to see you safe," Arlo says. "I don't think I'll ever forgive myself for not being able to help you in the imperial dungeon."

The sincerity in his voice reaches my heart, and I return his hug for a moment.

"It's okay," I say.

He kisses the top of my head and pulls away from me, straightening his vest. The glee on his face drains as he turns to Rayce. "Word came in that your uncle's forces aren't far away."

"Then we need to hurry," Rayce says. "The rest of you, split up in pairs and start breaking into the carts. If you get in, escort the girls you find to the edge of town and stay with them, no matter what. Arlo, I need *you* to find Oren."

Arlo and the others nod, spreading out on Rayce's words.

I pull out the set of keys I pilfered from Shears and start working through them on Juniper's lock. Every time a key doesn't fit, I hear Arlo's warning about the emperor drawing near in my head. My hands tremble as I flip through another key.

"We're going to get through this," Rayce says, placing a hand on my shoulder.

The sound of the lock clicking open is almost more relieving than hearing my own cage open earlier. Rayce swings open the door, not even bothering for stealth anymore, and we peer into the yawning darkness.

"Juniper?" I call out, my voice sounding small.

No answer.

My bones turn to lead as I move to step into the cage and I remind myself that Rayce holds the door open. He won't close it on me. I wade through the dirty straw of her cage, willing my eyes to adjust quicker but all I'm met with is empty space.

"No one's here," I say, jumping out of the cart.

"Is that normal?" Rayce asks.

I shake my head.

"Let's check the next one," Rayce says.

We run hand in hand to the next cart, calling out Violet's name.

Nothing.

Rayce's brow furrows, and he looks at the other guards on the opposite side of us. Following his gaze, I see a Zareeni woman shrugging to the other guard holding open the door to Lily's cart.

We both look at each other, and the same thought passes through our gazes: something is horribly wrong.

I turn back to my cart, the heads of the four Wilteds still shoved on pikes sticking out from the roof. Their dead eyes stare down at me, guilt swelling in my chest. I can almost hear their voices screaming to save my sisters, save who is left.

*What's the Gardener up to?*

We run past the next two carts, where another two pairs of Zareeni guards are working on locks, and head for the last cart on the row. Behind the crumbling house at our back, the silky blue tent of the Garden looms overhead. The rising sun casts the shadow of the huge monstrosity over us, bathing us in a false darkness like everything to do with the Garden.

We reach Daisy's cage, and I yell out to her, already knowing we won't find them.

Rayce holds his hand out to help me down, and as my feet

thud against the dead grass, my knees nearly give out. I look up at the five points on top of the tent, a large beam shooting up the middle. The fabric falls off the largest tip like the blue water of the sea, hiding the dangers that lurk below it.

My mind recoils at the thought of stepping inside that tent one more time. Everything about that vile place reminds me of the last ten years of my life. Besides Fern, it was the one constant in my life. My feet turn to stone at the thought of moving any closer. I know in my bones that is where my sisters are being held.

The Gardener's final cruel joke.

I tighten my grip on my sword and turn to Rayce. "The girls are inside the tent."

"It seems likely," Rayce says. "You know it's a trap, though, right?"

I nod, not trusting my voice.

"Can you do it?" he asks, his eyes flickering over my face.

Clenching my jaw, I slip my good hand in his, stealing some of his strength. He locks his fingers with mine, and our palms fit together like they were crafted with the same mold, though his are two times bigger than mine.

"I have to," I say.

"I'll follow your lead, then," he says, turning around to signal to a Zareeni man at Calla's cart.

The man nods his understanding and takes off running.

Rayce and I duck around the one-story house in front of the tent, the dirty white side of the long-abandoned building providing very little cover as we run past it. The wooden shutters are thrown back, and I peer inside as we move. Weeds poke through the wood lining the floor, and a table is thrown on its side. The remnants of a clay pot litter the floor, the shattered surfaces reflecting the rising sun.

I lead Rayce around the house, peeking out from the corner of the building for any sign of movement. A small patch of trampled grass leads up to the looming beast of a tent. The large flaps to the Garden are pulled back with golden ties, but the inside remains dark.

"We could try to sneak around the back," Rayce whispers in my ear. "But he's likely expecting something or he wouldn't have taken the others inside the tent. Time is of the essence, so I think we should just go through the front."

"I don't like this," I say, trying to articulate the panic flooding my system.

"Whatever happens, I'm with you."

Though his words bring a tiny smile to my lips, a tinge of guilt settles over me. I was going to leave him, not willing to even try to trust him, and here he is, willing to risk his life to help me. I will tell him who I am as soon as we rescue the other Flowers and Oren, when all this horror is behind us and we can move forward together. I can give him the same trust he's willing to give me.

The seven guards from before lean in, and Rayce updates them on our newest mission. They each pull out a stunner, positioning around us.

I touch the base of my own stunner, feeling heat slip into my cheeks.

We move across the open grass between the small house and the tent on heavy feet. Every step takes great effort, and my heart hammers against my rib cage. A bead of sweat drips down my forehead, and I swipe it away.

The opening of the Garden looms ahead of us, resembling the entrance to a cave filled with angry bears.

The sunlight fades as we step past the heavy curtains. White glass beads dangle in the entrance, swishing to give away our position as we push through them. The air inside the tent tastes stale and is infused with a musky, floral scent of burning incense and the smoke of torches.

Three beams of limelight shoot down from the top of

the tent like the beginning of my routine, all shining on the Gardener, who lounges on a specially made metal chair with a young Seedling on each side of him. A little blond Varshan girl, likely plucked as my replacement, struggles to wave a large plum fan to cool his plump form. I wonder where he was able to steal her. Was he given access to new girls, thanks to his deal with the emperor?

The other girl clasps a golden bowl spilling over with chocolates. A smear of melted chocolate already crusts the Gardener's chin, and his kohl-lined eyes are trained on us as we walk in.

Behind him stands a flock of at least forty lackeys all armed with swords and knives—one even clutches a wooden hammer. They don't move for us as we hold up our stunners. A muscle-bound lackey in the front flips his sword back and forth, his one good eye never leaving us.

And in the very back, tucked behind the Gardener and the men who torment them, are my sisters, huddled together. Calla and Lily sit in front, clinging to each other, but instead of shivering they remain upright. When our eyes meet, the intensity of their fury gives my feet courage.

"That's far enough," the Gardener says, tossing up his chocolate-smeared hand. "Come any closer and one of them dies."

The myriad of rings clinging to every available space on his fingers twinkles in the lights.

Rayce puts a hand down, signaling the small troop walking in our footsteps to stop. The odds don't look very promising—almost four to one, even with the stunners.

"Why don't you let them go?" Rayce asks. "If you do, I can guarantee—"

"I don't bargain with ratties," the Gardener cuts in.

Rayce's hand falls to the hilt of his bloodied sword. The seconds tick out long in the all-encompassing silence, and I worry he might attack, risking my sisters' lives in the process. But finally, he nods.

The Gardener's beady eyes slide to my face. "You've put us all in quite a position, my leetle Rose," the Gardener says. "Unfortunately, we can't both get what we want. But even you aren't stupid enough not to realize your ratties are outnumbered. If you bow to me now and plead for their lives, I might be persuaded to let them go."

Part of me knows he won't keep his word, and yet, my legs long to fall to the ground, my head already moving toward it. I glance at Rayce, his jaw clenched tight, like whatever he wants to say is burning him from the inside out. The knuckles around his stunner have turned white, and his hand shakes, ready to spill more blood.

If I bowed, maybe he could make a run for it. He could live. The girls would be spared.

The glow of Zarenite beaming through my fingers sends a surge of adrenaline through me.

No, I didn't want to trust Rayce back at camp, and that's what got us into this situation. I *have* to trust him now, as Oren told me. As Rayce has been telling me from the beginning. I have to have faith that we'll get through this, together. The warmth of his touch pulses in my skin.

I shoot my head back up and stare directly into the Gardener's empty eyes—a forbidden gesture.

I will never look away again.

"Odds didn't stop me and Rayce from killing Shears a few minutes ago," I say. "And they won't stop us from killing you, either."

The giant lackey at the lead takes a step forward, dragging the tip of his blade across the ground. The sound cuts through me.

The Gardener puts both hands on the sides of his chair and tries to lift himself out of it. He gets stuck about halfway and has to slide back down. With chocolate and spit still coating his fingers, he flicks them up to stop the approaching lackey.

"I'll give you one more chance," he says, sliding out one of his feet. "Bow down and kiss my shoe, or everyone here will suffer the consequences."

A ripple in the back curtain of the tent catches my eye. From my vantage point, I can just catch a halo of tight curls duck into the tent behind the Gardener and his lackeys. Marin! She stands on her tiptoes and waves, signaling for us to stay quiet.

"Well? We haven't got all day," the Gardener says. "The emperor will be joining us any minute."

Marin holds up the curtain, and about seventeen other Zareeni guards flood into the tent, not making a sound. Everyone's gaze holds on me and the Gardener. Fine--if he wants one final performance, I'll give it to him.

"If I do this," I say, bowing my head, "you have to promise to release the man you picked up with me and hand him back over to the Zareeni rebellion."

"You don't get to make demands," the Gardener says.

I relax my fingers, the stunner grip slipping from my grasp. The booming sound it makes hitting the hard-packed earth echoes in the cavernous space. I take a step forward.

Rayce catches my arm, and I turn to face him.

"Don't do this," he says, his voice strained. I tilt my head at him, and he gives me a subtle wink. "I won't let you."

"I have to," I say, following his lead. I yank my arm from him, his grip loosening as he plays along with me.

With every step I take toward the Gardner, my world shrinks down to the point of a knife. There is only me and the former master who haunted my every waking thought for ten years. A smile slides onto his face, his yellow teeth coated with chocolate. Even though I know Rayce watches my back, my heart still flip-flops in my chest with every movement I make.

Someone sneezes in the back—likely from the nauseating scent of incense—and the largest lackey's head snaps around.

"There's more of them!" he shouts, breaking up our fake display.

The Gardener's face twists into a snarl, and he points a shaky finger at me.

"Get her!" he yells, spittle flying through the air.

"Calla, Lily, everyone, fight now!" I shout out to my sisters. "Save yourselves!"

The tidy line between rebel and lackey shatters at our screaming. The thunderous sound of swords unsheathing fills the air. Half the lackeys turn toward Marin's group. Marin tosses her sword to Calla and shoots a nearby lackey in the same swift movement, filling the space with bright green light. Her jaw is set, determined. She won't be bested by the Gardener and his thugs again.

My sisters burst into action. Calla swings her sword for a younger lackey's neck while Lily jumps on his back.

Two men take this chance to charge me. I unsheathe the sword at my hip and dispatch the first one with a swift swing to the gut. The other takes advantage of my momentum and nicks my shoulder with a knife. I spin around, letting the knife dig deeper into my shoulder and turn my blade toward him, but he falls to the ground before I can swing, twitching from a stunner blast to the back.

Rayce appears in front of me, a grin on his face, and throws me the stunner I'd dropped on the ground before he rushes for his next target.

Above his head, I see a lackey running for him, and I raise my stunner. Rayce doesn't flinch at the barrel of my weapon pointing his way, not even when my finger pulls the trigger.

In the haze of battle, I've lost my real target. My eyes pick through the sea of men struggling, metal clinging with metal, and bright blossoms of red sprouting everywhere, until I find him.

He scrambles to pull himself out of his chair. I grit my teeth. Five lackeys have surrounded him, but they won't be nearly enough with the rage welling inside me.

I lunge for him, the sounds of my sisters fighting for their freedom all around me. Some part of me feels the blood pouring from my shoulder. But that part is very far away.

I shoot at a man charging for Juniper but can't react quickly enough to stop a blade from running through Dahlia's middle.

The two lackeys on the Gardener's right run for me. My stunner takes care of the first, but the other swings for me. Rayce parries his blade, kicking him away from me. Another lackey aims for Rayce, but I don't stick around to make sure he's okay. I've seen him in action and know he can take care of himself.

A few Zareeni guards attack the lackeys on the Gardener's left, leaving him completely unprotected, and I refuse to let the chance slip through my fingers. I walk up to the man who robbed me of everything with the practiced grace he beat into me.

The Gardener stumbles back, but the large wooden pole holding up the middle of the tent blocks his exit. His collision causes a white ribbon to drop from the top of the tent. If this were a normal night, that same piece of fabric would catch me as I fell, but today I push it aside with the tip of my sword blade.

Another scrawny lackey with straggly black hair tries to rush me, but I see his hand coming in my peripheral vision and duck, cutting out a piece of his side on my way down. The man grabs at his ribs and falls to the ground.

I point my sword at the Gardener's gut, the heady mixture of three different people's blood dripping onto his ivory silk shirt, and aim the stunner at his face.

The Gardener's beady eyes bulge as he picks through the crowd for someone to stop me.

"What are you trash doing?" he yells to his lackeys, losing his accent in his panic.

But he's yelling mostly to their bodies. A sea of fallen men lies at my feet, the Zareeni guards much better at fighting than the men who were only good at fighting when their prey couldn't fight back.

The Flowers, Wilteds, and Seedlings gather around me, our bond forged in blood, fear, and tears.

I have all the power.

My fingers tighten around the hilt of the stunner.

The Gardener reaches for two little knives strapped to his side, but as he tries to yank them free around his large belly, he trips himself, falling back into the pole and landing hard on the ground. He looks like an oversize baby as he rocks back and forth, trying to get to his feet.

"You bastard," I say, taking slow steps toward the man who has ruined a thousand lives. My voice sounds like it comes from everywhere at once, backed by a million souls he's silenced before me. "You took us away from our homes, from our lives, stole our futures, and ripped us from the people who loved us."

The buttery leather of the sword hilt feels like it's burning up in my hand, the anticipation of his blood running like a fever through me. "And now it's time to pay."

As I walk toward the Gardener, I realize these are the moments I will come back to: barefoot, broken, slight limp on the left side, and more powerful than I'll ever be again. It's this moment and these steps that define me.

"You can't!" the Gardener yells over and over again, finally forced to look up at me.

And all I can think as I stop at his feet is that *I can*. For once in my life, I can.

For my sisters behind me.

For Fern underneath me.

For the blade he held against Marin's neck.

With the Gardener's death, my struggle will finally be over. I will be able close my eyes without fearing his face, and when I lay my head down on the soft pillow in the Zareeni base, I will finally be able to rest.

# Chapter Thirty-Four

A slow smile spreads across my face as the Gardener trembles before me. The bright spotlight beams down hot on my face as if giving me permission to finally end this dance we've been performing for almost ten years.

"It's over," I say. "And there is nothing you can say to change that."

I raise the sword, watch its shadow cross the Gardener's body and the unbridled fear erasing every cruel wrinkle on his face. The fact that he can't defend himself should slow my hand, but somehow it just makes me feel stronger.

"Don't!" he screams.

I shove the tip of the blade lightly into the skin of his throat and watch as a thin line of blood trickles against his pale skin.

A glint of ruby catches my eye—the necklace he took from me years ago. I lean down and, using the tip of my blade, fish the necklace out from underneath his shirt. The large gem sparkles the color of blood in the spotlight. I rip the chain from his neck and wrap my fingers around the surface of my mother's necklace, the cool jewel a balm in my hot hands.

I rise, ready to feel the sharp edge bite through the Gardener's throat. All the years of abuse will end with this final swing.

He throws up his chubby hands to push the blade away.

"Wait, Rose!" Rayce shouts behind me. "Don't kill him."

The hairs on the back of my neck prickle as his familiar voice drips down my back. I look over my shoulder and see Rayce reaching for me. His forehead crinkles in panic as he takes a cautious step toward me.

Most of the other lackeys have been downed now, and many of the Zareeni guards and my sisters are watching us. I can almost hear the other Flowers' thoughts, shouting at me to avenge their stolen years.

"What?" I snap.

"We need him alive," Rayce says.

I clench my teeth and tighten my grip on the sword's handle. I have to keep the other girls safe, and the only way to ensure that the Garden doesn't sprout again is to chop it off at its very roots. He needs to be clipped. A drop of sweat drips into my eye, blurring my vision.

"He has to tell us where Oren is," Rayce says, taking another step toward me.

"Yes," the Gardener shouts. "Of course I'll tell you."

His voice ignites my fury, and I whirl around to face him, pushing my blade farther into his skin. He lets out a little moan and tries to press himself closer to the splintered wood of the pole behind him to escape the sharp bite of my hungry blade. Heat clings to my body, and I recognize the same intense buildup as the first time I ingested Zarenite.

"We should just kill him and find Oren ourselves," I say. "It's the only way I can be sure nothing like this happens again."

My hand shakes slightly, but I steady it. I can't give up this chance.

"We don't have time," Rayce says, his voice wavering. "I won't stop you if you feel you have to take revenge later, but right now, I need you to think this through. He'll be more use to us alive. Think about Oren."

Fern's dying screams well up inside my head.

Following on the heels of her death shrieks is Oren's rattled cough bouncing in the small space Fern and I used to share. I can still feel his shallow breathing underneath my cheek and the pit of emptiness I fell into the moment he was snatched away from me.

We have to save him.

Rayce's fingertips brush my good shoulder, his sudden nearness accentuating his words. The heat of Zarenite courses through my veins, burning me from the inside. The other Zareeni and my sisters are gathering around us. Calla and Lily have their arms looped around Dahlia, while Marin works at patching her middle.

Rayce is right. There is no one left to fight here. All that the Gardener ever had has been mowed down by the strength of our combined families. Now we have to save Oren.

"Okay," I whisper, closing my eyes against the revelation that I have to let him live a little longer. But that doesn't mean his life can't be filled with the pain he inflicted on us. I swing around, bringing the tip of my sword straight through his foot into the ground. He lets out a scream that pierces the quiet.

I leave my sword stuck in his foot, all the anger and strength evaporating from my body as my fingers slip from the hilt.

"Thank you," Rayce whispers, tucking a sticky strand of hair behind my ears before walking up to the Gardener.

He squats next to the trembling wreck of a man who used to be my master, sword extended at the Gardener's bulbous belly.

"Ready to talk to this rattie yet?" he asks, tilting his head to the left.

The Gardener trembles under Rayce's long shadow. "Of course. Yes, anything you ask."

"I'm going to be asking a lot of you, I'm afraid," Rayce says, touching the tip of his blade to his finger. "And I'd better like your answers."

While Rayce speaks, Calla dances up to me and wraps her arms around my middle, resting her head on my good shoulder.

"You came back for us," she says.

"I'm sorry it took me so long," I say.

"Don't worry," Juniper adds, following her. "We knew you would."

The other Flowers rush up, wrapping arms around arms, sharing in my trembling. We're all strung tight like strings on a lyre, humming the notes of our sadness, our rage, our exhaustion, and our elation into the air.

I just never imagined freedom tasting so bitter. How can I feel the warmth of my sisters again and yet, everywhere I turn, someone I love bleeds? Dahlia holds a hand over the cut in her belly, Violet has a deep cut over her forehead, and blood drips from Saffron's mouth.

"Yes," the Gardener says, pulling my attention back to him. His eyeliner runs down his chubby cheeks in streaks like he's crying tar.

"I'm only going to say this once," Rayce says, his words stilted. "Where did you hide Oren?"

The Gardener opens his mouth like he's going to answer, but a loud horn drowns out his voice from somewhere outside the tent. The blaring note skates over my body, sending goose bumps down my arms. All the remaining Zareeni guards glance at each other, the confusion on their faces mirroring my own.

My attention turns back to the Gardener as the fear on his face drains, replaced by the same pointed smile I've seen a million times before during his performances. He sits up against the pole and laughs, the chilling sound shaking me to my core.

"You're already too late, rattie," he says. "Do you think all of this was just for fun? I gathered everyone here to waste your time. I knew that Flower"—he looks at me and spits onto the ground—"wouldn't be able to resist saving the other girls, and all I needed was to keep you here long enough for the emperor to arrive. If your friend isn't already dead, he will be very shortly."

My breathing stops.

Rayce moves in a blur, whipping out a stunner from his belt and shooting the Gardener point-blank in the stomach, stopping him midlaugh. I wish his aim were higher. A shot to the heart or head would have killed him instead of knocking him out. Chocolate spittle drips out of the Gardener's mouth as his body goes slack against the pole, and he begins to slide back toward the earth.

"You four," Rayce says, pointing to the four nearest Zareeni guards, "bring the women we found back to camp. Don't stop until you get there, under any circumstance, am I clear?"

They nod their understanding as the *zap-zap* of stunner bolts outside the tent sounds in the cavernous space.

"Shing and Che you two stand guard over the prisoner," Rayce says, motioning to Marin and a short-haired man. "If he wakes up, blast him again."

Marin grabs her stunner, glaring at the unconscious Gardener. "With pleasure."

A stray arrow rips through the far side of the tent, rocketing over our heads. The sounds of metal clanging together mix with a woman screaming.

Rayce turns to me. "Help the others get your friends to safety."

"No," I say, shaking my head. "I'm staying with you."

He grimaces, turning back to the remaining unassigned guards. "The rest of you, you know what to do."

They salute and race out of the tent toward the sounds of war.

Rayce grabs me gently by the arm and pulls me away from the small crowd. His eyes flick over as the guards empty out of the tent, but he shakes his head and focuses on me. A lock of his dark hair covers the top of his scar, and his earthy eyes radiate an intensity I haven't seen from him before.

His blood-soaked hand on my arm trembles slightly.

He whispers so only I can hear him. "Please go with your sisters," he says, his voice catching. "If my uncle is really out there, I'm not sure..." He takes a breath. "I've never been able to best him in a fight, and with the meager amount of people I was able to gather for this mission, I don't think we can beat him."

My heart sinks as his words sting me. I reach up, clutching his hand. He was nervous the night before our last mission, but right now, he remains completely sober.

"Do you understand what I'm saying to you?" he asks, his eyes desperate. "If you stay, I'm not sure you'll survive to see through your goal, and I want that for you, Rose." His voice catches. "Even if I can't, I want you to live."

A few weeks ago, I would have sprung for the chance to stay with my sisters and live. All I dared to dream about was freedom for everyone in the Garden. But then Rayce burst into my life, assaulting my senses, tearing down my walls, filling me with light and awakening a piece of me that I never knew dwelled inside. What I want is to be with him, even if it's only for these last few minutes. As much as I know I should, I can't abandon him any more than I can quit breathing. He sent me away last time, but I *will* remain with him until the end. Now. Always.

"I'm staying by your side," I whisper. "And we are both going to live."

He rests his forehead against mine, closing his eyes. He winces, sadness at my willingness to die passing over his face, followed by a calm that comes from knowing I'll see this battle through with him until the end.

"Okay then," he says. "Let's go save Oren."

He shouts for the rest of the guards to move, and we run for the far end of the tent, jumping over bodies littering the floor. Somewhere in the back of my mind, the price of war screams as I trip over a dead man's hand, but I keep moving, trying not to think about what all this killing will cost my soul.

Rayce swings his sword, ripping a slit through the blue fabric of the tent so we can wiggle outside. As we bust through the tight space, it feels like we're stepping through a curtain to observe a reenactment of a famous war.

The sun hangs much higher overhead than we left it, burning the sky yellow and orange. The heat hits me instantly, followed by the earthy scent of dirt mixing with the iron tinge of blood. About seventy Sun soldiers twist and turn in the throes of battle, their scalelike plated armor gleaming in the morning sunlight like fish in a stream. Four blue and silver flags emblazoned with the Delmarion dragon crest snap furiously with the wind on the south side of the town like they're cheering on the violence ensuing below them.

Green light fights against the sea of blue flooding the crumbling town, Zareeni guards shooting and swinging and blasting for their lives. Though each face I find grits in determination, it's easy to gauge the numbers—and they aren't in our favor.

"Stay close to me," Rayce shouts.

He jabs the sharp edge of his sword through a nearby Sun

soldier, hitting him in the sliver of unprotected space between his chest and helmet. Red blood spurts out of the wound.

My attention flickers across the wreckage until I find the thing that kept me up last night.

The wooden stage still stands in the middle of the small clearing. A group of Sun soldiers surrounds the platform, swords drawn.

Above their heads, a figure looms over the carnage like the god of war. The emperor's cold stare sweeps over the battlefield as his hand rests on the decorated hilt of a large sword. His armor is crafted almost entirely out of silver, each plate rounded at the end to make perfect half-circle scales. They catch the light, shrouding his figure in a hazy glow that makes it hard to stare directly at him. Like the sun personified. Intricate swirling dragons adorn the middle chest piece, the two flaps of armor covering his shoulders and his bracers. His gleaming helmet wraps around his head, and two horrible mandibles conform to the sides of his face, covering most of his beard.

His free hand grips the back of Oren's robe, who's slumped near the emperor's feet.

My stomach drops, and I stumble toward them. A blade swings for my head, but Rayce jumps in front of me, parrying the attack.

"What are you doing?" he yells. "Stay focused."

His worry snaps me back to my right mind.

"Oren's over there!" I shout, pointing toward the stage.

Rayce follows my gaze, his eyes widening at the sight of his mentor held captive by his uncle. The muscles in Rayce's jaw clench, and a fire ignites in his eyes. "Let's go!"

We sprint forward, Rayce running a little ahead of me. He swings his sword at every man in his path, cutting his way through the struggling bodies blocking him from the stage. Aiming the best I can, I shoot at anything silver, praying my shots aren't wasted.

The farther we move, the thicker the fighting becomes. I catch Arlo as he shoves his stunner into a soldier's face and pulls the trigger before ducking to avoid an arrow.

A Zareeni woman next to me crumples to the ground, life slipping out of her eyes as I jump over her. I don't know her name, but I will learn them all when I go back, and I will follow Rayce as he meets with every single rebel's family.

Rayce moves even faster.

"Don't you dare, Uncle!" he screams over the sounds of men dying.

The emperor's gaze snaps toward Rayce's command, and he points at us with the tip of his sword.

The four Sun soldiers guarding the stage rush for us, surrounding Rayce. He shoots the first one and spins, guarding against an oncoming sword attack.

"Go!" he yells at me, spit flying from his exertion. "Save him!"

I shoot for one of the soldier's backs and turn away before I see if my bolt landed. My heart hammering in my chest, I dodge around a Zareeni guard pummeling into another soldier, heading straight for the platform.

The emperor's gaze turns to me, and even through his helmet, I can see his mouth tick up in a smile. He drops his hold on Oren's robe, letting him slam against the platform as I run for them.

Another horn blast echoes through the town, and the emperor raises his sword. I'm close enough now to see the crusted blood coating Oren's face, his long eyelashes touching his cheeks.

I'm razor focused on saving him. I will not let Oren down.

Even though I'm not a marksman, I pull out my stunner and aim at the emperor's hand like I saw Arlo do with the Gardener. I take a deep breath, letting Arlo's teachings flow through me, and my finger finds the trigger.

A whimpering man reaches up from the dirt, grabbing my leg with a blood-soaked hand.

The ground comes for me hard, the stunner tumbling out of my hands. My nose cracks on impact, and I taste blood. It's broken, but that doesn't matter now.

I snap up and kick the man's arm off my leg, crawling for the stage.

Just a few more feet. Oren's eyes snap open, processing everything. His gaze locks onto my face, his pupils as deep and solidly brown as the earth I'm crawling on, and the tips of his mouth crook up. Like the bright blue sky has come down already and whisked him up into the clouds.

I reach out to him, my hand a trembling plea to stay with me, and the emperor's sword falls. The sound of metal hitting sinew and muscle and veins and bone fills the air even as his words fill my head.

*"You are going to do great things, Rose, if you let yourself."*

The way he ducked as he walked through the halls of Zareen without a single complaint, the smell of parchment and smoke always trailing behind him, the feeling of his bear claw-size hand ruffling my head before each battle swirls in my head as Oren fades.

My body gives out underneath me, tears clouding my vision.

*"What's your name, girl?" Oren asked me the first time we met.*

*"Rose."*

*"After the rare Varshan desert rose," he mumbled to himself. "It'll do just fine."*

Does he approve of my *real* name? Does he like it? I never got to hear the way it sounds coming from his mouth. And now, I never will.

# Chapter Thirty-Five

A soul-shattering roar rings out behind me, guttural, primal, deadly.

Rayce appears in my peripheral vision, his long, tattered black vest flowing out behind him, the scarred side of his face caked in blood. His knuckles are white, straining against the crippling grip on his sword.

His mood darkens the sky.

Maybe it's all the blood gushing from Oren's severed head, or the fact that I couldn't save him, that sends a wave of crippling anger searing through my veins. The sight of his headless body lying still on the platform mends my fractures and heals all the scrapes and bruises covering my body.

The moment Oren's soul left this world, pain and reasoning and logic left me. Even the complete devastation of watching him slaughtered like an animal evaporates in the fiery rage that rushes to my head. The only thing that matters now is making the emperor hurt the way Oren hurt, the way I've hurt for years.

Oren's words suddenly make perfect sense. I will play a

part in the war, just not in the way he thought. All the things I've accomplished since leaving here were pieces building me new. I am not the same submissive little Flower. I will make them suffer.

I jump up, wiping the blood and snot from my nose.

My gaze narrows to the man in silver, the man whose sword is coated with Oren's blood.

*I will kill the emperor.*

Rayce clearly has the same thought, because we charge at the same time, my feet pumping to keep up with his.

The emperor jumps off the platform to meet us, carefully wiping his blade clean with his light blue cape. The battle rages on either side of him, but he seems wholly unconcerned. A Zareeni guard runs for him, but he cuts him down without even looking. The swift way his blade moves as if it's one with his arm, striking fear like an arrow through my heart.

Rayce confessed he's never beaten his uncle in a sword fight. My feet slow, and for a moment a familiar sense of worry returns. But Rayce rushes his uncle with no thought for his own life, the fury of Oren's death fueling him. Will he be able to finally beat his uncle? Because I will *not* watch another person I love die.

My heart flutters at the thought. *I love him.* Somewhere among the pain and honey crisps and death and jokes and promises kept, I've fallen for this man who will freely give his life to save others. And I have to make sure it doesn't come to that.

Rayce reaches his uncle first, unleashing a flurry of attacks so fast I can barely follow them. His uncle parries each move as calmly as he studied his ant farms, meeting his nephew's speed blow for blow.

I run up behind Rayce and swing my sword as the emperor blocks Rayce's blade. The emperor throws up an armored forearm, and my blade skates across his metal armor, producing white sparks in the air.

"Are you going to need a woman to help you finally beat me, Nephew?" the emperor asks, shoving me back.

I skid to a stop just behind Rayce and grit my teeth.

"I don't need any help," he growls, his eyes hazed over as he slams his sword down on the emperor's again. "But Rose wants vengeance for Oren as much as I do."

"And I will gladly help him succeed," I say, squaring my shoulders.

The emperor jolts forward, his thick blade arching toward Rayce's head. Rayce jumps back, leaning to keep out of the way of the sharp tip coming for his neck.

"Stupid boy," the emperor says. "Feelings don't belong on the battlefield. Have you retained nothing I taught you?"

While he's distracted, I lunge, aiming for the slip of skin exposed on his neck, but the emperor easily parries my attack like he's batting away a fly.

"I don't need any of the training you gave me," Rayce spits, returning his uncle's attack.

The emperor jumps back, putting space between us. We stand in a triangle, swords drawn to make the points of the shape. Rayce's eyes burn with an unquenchable fire, his hands barely able to contain the rage welling through him.

The sun behind the emperor's back glows bright, and the reflection off his shiny armor nearly blinds me.

"Your insolence has gone on long enough," the emperor says. "You spout out nonsense about the value of human life, and yet, you continue to fight, claiming the lives of hundreds on both sides. How many people will you sacrifice before you've finished your temper tantrum?"

Rayce swings at his uncle but misses, nearly feeling the edge of the emperor's blade instead.

"How many will you sacrifice because they don't think the same way you do?" I ask. "Including your own flesh and blood."

The emperor's eyes slide to my face, and I fight not to crumple under the weight of them.

"As many as need be," he snaps.

The ant farm he drowned...how many of his precious pets did he exterminate because one moved out of turn? I know in that second that he wouldn't hesitate to throw his entire empire at Rayce if it meant righting the world in his mind. And I also understand why Rayce feels like he must press on through all the heartache. How he can justify every sacrifice he's forced to make, and why I find him up late into the night.

"Then we'll keep fighting," Rayce says.

"Wrong," the emperor says, glancing at Oren. "You'll die just like this traitor did."

When Rayce attacks again, something changes about the way he moves. He's more measured, his steps sure as he dodges and hacks, fighting with a different sort of fury. The emperor's words reach through his rage into a place deeper than his fury. For the first time, the emperor's movements become stilted as he wades backward.

I trail behind them, but I can barely keep up with their blurred attacks, jumping out of the way as their blades clash over and over again.

Rayce's sword slips through his uncle's defenses, slicing through the leather holding up his chest plate. Blood spurts out as Rayce pulls back his sword.

In that moment, the emperor rips out a small knife sheathed behind him.

"Rayce!" I scream.

But my warning comes a moment too late. The emperor jams the short blade deep into Rayce's gut.

Rayce's beautiful eyes widen, his expression frozen in shock and pain as he stumbles backward, dropping his blade to clutch the knife hilt sticking out of his stomach. My entire world shakes, and I reach out an utterly useless hand as he wobbles away from me, blood staining his shirt.

He trips over a fallen Zareeni guard and goes down, landing with a thud on his back. No! Rayce can't die. He has to stay with me. His uncle can't have him. There's still so much he doesn't know.

The emperor raises his weapon high with both hands planted on the hilt, aiming to kill.

I run up and shoot my blade out, my knee hitting the dirt hard in front of Rayce. The emperor's sword carves into the back of my ear as I break its trajectory away from Rayce's heart.

Everything in me wants to drop my weapon and check to make sure Rayce is okay, but if I do that, the emperor will kill him, and I will not let that happen. He'll have to administer the final blow over my dead body.

*Please be okay.*

My mind fills with the blood crawling up Rayce's shirt, but I push it away. There is no room for distractions if I'm going to have any hope of protecting Rayce.

"Are you going to fight me, girl?" the emperor asks, the hint of a smile on his lips. "Do you think you stand a chance when you just saw my nephew fall to my blade?"

"I don't know," I say, rising. My limbs tremble from the effort. Blood coats my face and runs sticky down the back of my neck.

"But I do know that you won't touch Rayce ever again."

I slide my left hand to the bottom of my sword hilt, readjusting my grip, and hold the blade out between Rayce and his uncle. Since he can't fight, I will be Rayce's shield the same way he has protected me up until this point.

"How many days did you practice with the sword, Flower?" he asks, amusement shaking his voice. "Did they teach you how to wield a weapon while learning how to dance?"

"No," I say, taking a step forward. My lungs burn, my muscles ache, but I remind them that together we killed Shears and stopped the Gardener. Luck will just have to be on my side one last time. "But you still won't win."

The emperor's eyes flicker above my head for a moment, and I use it, swinging my blade with everything I have at his shoulder.

His weapon meets mine, and my arms shake with the impact.

"Clumsy footwork," he says, pushing me backward.

"At least I don't have to cheat to win," I say, jabbing out at him.

"There is no cheating in war, girl," the emperor says. He jams his blade against mine, this time meeting my strength with his until our faces are an inch apart. As my muscles strain under his might, I remind myself that I bested him once. He underestimated me then, but I was able to slip through his fingers. I can do it again.

He gives a final shove, and I stumble back.

Instead of advancing, he whips around and takes a few paces backward. I follow him and notice again that he's looking around me, his focus someplace other than our fight.

I dare a quick glance to my left and see a Zareeni guard downing a Sun soldier with a zap of their stunner. Everywhere my eyes dart, I notice there's a lot less blue than when Rayce and I burst onto the scene a few moments ago.

I lick my lips, tasting sweat and blood, and turn back to the emperor. He comes at me with another blow, but the strength isn't behind his attack.

"Tell me something," the emperor says. "Do you really think my nephew will care about you after he finds out you've been lying to him this whole time?"

His words cut into the deepest roots of my fear, and the tip of my sword lowers. Maybe Rayce won't be able to forgive my lie, maybe this secret I've been harboring my entire life will be too big for the two of us to bear. Maybe we will crumple under the weight of it. Or worse, maybe he will fade from the decision he'll be forced to make.

Sword still out, the emperor takes a few steps back.

"He is my protégé, after all," he says, his eyes flicking above my head. "My teachings will always affect him, whether he will admit it or not."

Oren's final words to me about trust ring through my head, and I set my jaw. He believed Rayce is strong enough to shoulder the weight of my heritage, and I have to honor Oren's belief. I owe it to him and to Rayce and even to myself.

"Rayce won't abandon me," I say, lunging forward.

The emperor parries my attack with a lazy flick of his wrist, my blade slicing through his cape.

He continues stepping backward. I release a flurry of blows, dodging left and right, aiming for any sliver of skin I can see, but every time I move, his sword is already there, ready to deflect mine.

Sweat pours off my brow; my arms shriek with every movement. Our swords collide, and my muscles scream out in protest. Every bit of me wants to give up as the emperor keeps moving us away from Rayce's crumpled form.

But then I remember Oren, and my fury reignites, sparking through my tired limbs.

I spin around, putting all the force I can into my sword swing, and the emperor jumps back, twisting on his foot to retreat. I rush after him, dodging the clusters of Delmarions and Zareeni rebels fighting.

The emperor races through the crowd, breaking through the battle to jump onto a gigantic white warhorse. I rush after him, sword drawn, but the horse rears up at my approach, and I have dodge out from under its heavy hooves.

The emperor steadies the beast with a hand on its head

and peers down at me.

"Know this, girl," he says. "I won't wait forever for you decide to stop dawdling around with my inferior nephew to take back what is rightfully yours. You will not be able to free your people without the might of my army by your side. Remember that, and remember it well. Your time marches on without you, *Princess*, and soon you will be forgotten even by those that were once loyal."

He says my title in a mocking tone, his eyes alight with frustration.

"I will never surrender to you," I say. "I'd rather die."

At my statement, the emperor shrugs. "My war will be easier with you, but your death wouldn't pain me, either." His eyes scan our surroundings. "It seems we have worn out our welcome."

He raises two fingers, spinning them in a circle. "I'm sure this isn't the last time we'll meet." He clicks the horse's reins, and it begins to move.

"The next time we do, it'll be your head on the chopping block," I snap.

The blare of that blasted horn sounds out in three quick sessions. The Sun soldiers look up and begin to backtrack, fighting off stunner bolts as they move toward the emperor and their horses.

He's calling for a retreat.

I glance across the battlefield, picking through the carnage and blood painting everything red and see the relieved look on the Zareeni rebels' faces as the Sun soldiers begin to swarm their emperor. My mind can't quite process the information that stands in plain sight.

Rayce said there was a good chance he wouldn't have enough people, but it seems like with the help of the stunners, we might have…

We won?

A cheer swells through the crowd, the rebels picking up the sound and sending it with force at the retreating hooves of the army that should have bested us. Arlo screams louder than the rest a few feet ahead of me, the barrels of his twin stunners still shooting after the soldiers.

But all I can think as I see the emperor retreating toward the blue sky is that Rayce is still among the bodies littering the ground.

My feet pound against the packed dirt and trampled grass as I carve a straight path for the raised platform, careful not to look at Oren's body still lying there.

A figure struggles to sit up, crawling over a soldier's body. I catch the long black vest before I see his face.

I skid to a stop next to Rayce and drop to my knees. He holds his abdomen where the knife used to sit. Blood peeks through his fingers, and he breathes deeply through his nostrils.

"Rayce, are you okay?" I ask.

He grimaces and removes his hand for me to assess the damage. I peel back his blood-soaked shirt. A clean, deep wound pierces the lower left side of his stomach, blood oozing out. I place my hands on his stomach, feeling his warmth trickle through my fingers.

"I've been better," he says, placing a bloody hand on my forearm. "Where did my uncle go?"

I look down at the cut I'm holding closed.

"He got away," I say.

His hand moves up my arm, resting on my cheek, and though his eyes are shut tight, he rubs his thumb along my jawline.

"Don't worry," he says. "We've won this battle, and the Garden has been crushed. That's more than I could ask for." He takes another pained breath through his nose. "Thank you, by the way. For blocking my uncle's final shot and fending him off."

"I wasn't going to let him hurt you anymore," I say.

A small smile finds its way to his pale face.

"If I didn't know any better, I'd think you liked me," he says, his shaking hand going weak.

I look up, still applying pressure to the wound on his stomach, and scan the area. "Someone, please help!" I shout.

My eyes find Arlo's lighter-colored hair in the crowd. He turns at my voice, takes one look at the pain that must paint my face ugly, and sprints over.

"The emperor wounded him," I yell to Arlo and turn back to Rayce, pressing my hands over his wound. "You're going to be okay. Everything going's to be okay."

His eyes dart around my face, and a weak smile pulls on his lips.

"Don't worry," Rayce says, his voice nearly a whisper. "It only hurts when I breathe."

Arlo takes one look at my bloodied hands holding Rayce's stomach and starts shouting orders at the remaining Zareeni guards. They move with an ease that only comes through hours of practice, picking through the battlefield for survivors, constructing a bed out of the tent fabric from the Garden to carry Rayce and securing the Gardener for the trek back to the rebel base. I look away when three men walk to the platform to gather Oren's remains, a lump lodging in my throat.

While they work, Suki leans down next to Rayce and begins pulling out supplies from a small green pack. I see the same brown bottle Rayce used on my cut and look at his tense face, knowing his pain is just beginning. Suki cleans the wound, instructing me on what to hold and what to prepare, and together we help Rayce sit up and wrap it.

I hold Rayce's hand until they load him on the makeshift stretcher.

Arlo stands next to me as I watch the two men begin to

move out of the little town.

"You did amazing, Rose," Arlo says, clapping a hand around my shoulder. The weight feels friendly, like how I imagine Marin feels when he comforts her. "We lost a lot here—" His voice cuts out, and he clenches his jaw. "But we also accomplished a lot."

"I'm sorry," I whisper. "All of this is my fault."

Arlo pulls me closer to his side. "No, it isn't. It needed to be done, with or without you pushing us into action. We couldn't allow the Garden to exist in our new world, and this display of might definitely spooked the emperor."

I force the protest welling up inside me to stay pressed against my tongue and look at the tops of my feet, filthy from the muck and blood now staining the abandoned town. The grotesque view of slain or stunned soldiers and guards in front of me somehow completes the story of this site.

"What I need to know from you is what you'd like to do with all of this," Arlo says, motioning to the cages that used to hold me and my sisters captive and the looming tent now filled with holes. Sunlight floods through the fabric, burning dots on the ground like the edges of a diamond.

I recall the moment I fled the Garden for the first time.

"Burn it," I say, my voice strong in the afternoon sun. "Burn it to the ground."

As we begin the long trek back to camp, carrying the wounded, a plume of smoke billows in the blue sky at our back. The scent of smoke and tiny sparks of red ash rise in the wind, a reminder that today is the day the Garden had its final curtain call in Delmar. Tomorrow when I wake up, it will be only a memory, no longer part of this world, and my sisters will be able to stand next to me, free.

The victory sours in my mouth.

For tomorrow will also be the first day Oren will no longer be in this world.

# Chapter Thirty-Six

Three days later, I awake in the room I share with Marin, tucked safely underground in Zareen. The artificial light unable to chase away the darkness feels fitting as the previous days' events replay over and over in my mind. I stare into the bucket of water in front of me that's stained red from the dried blood still clinging to my hands. Even now, I can't get all of it off, like a permanent reminder of the lives I took. The water dyes a deeper color every second I leave my hands in it, and still, all I can think is a single thought. It keeps pumping through my veins, making my vision teary.

*Oren is dead.*

*I couldn't save him.*

*I almost lost Rayce…*

As it rushes over me again, I'm kneeling back in that field, the scratchy blades of grass poking through the fabric of my pants as I crawl forward. I'm reaching for Oren, and he looks at me with such serenity. Then the blade comes down, robbing me of his wisdom and kindness forever with one swift motion.

A gentle rapping on the door brings me back to the

present. I look up at Rayce leaning against the opening, his arms crossed over his chest. A white bandage pokes out above the collar of his tan shirt, and his dark hair is slicked back in a short ponytail from his face.

"You're looking worse for the wear," he says.

"You're not looking your best, either."

He chuckles at my response.

"I thought you'd want to know that the other girls have all been assigned rooms close to yours and are resting," he says. "And the Gardener has been locked up. We'll be questioning him soon."

I nod and turn back to the tainted water in front of me. Part of me heard him, but I can't bring myself to respond. Even though I accomplished my goal and my sisters are safe, I can't feel any joy, knowing what their freedom cost. I can't shake the feeling that Oren was vital to changing this land for the better, and now that he's gone, I'm not sure how Zareen will achieve that dream.

Rayce clears his throat. "Rose, I've been wanting to ask you something."

The change in his tone sends chills down my spine, but I keep staring at my distorted reflection. His presence reminds me of the things still left unsaid between us. The tops of Rayce's shined boots come into view, but still Oren's lifeless body won't go away, swirling in the bloody surface of the water.

He moves the bucket and kneels next to me, grimacing from pain as he hovers inches from my face.

"Why did you leave my tent the day you returned to us?" he asks. "When we saw a loaded pack, I got the feeling you might have been trying to sneak away in the night."

So Rayce must realize that I'm to blame for Oren's death.

I press my wet hands against my forehead, cutting off his view of my face. I've perfected the art of keeping my emotions from showing, but right now, I couldn't even if I wanted to. Too much has happened.

He places a hand on my knee, the warmth from his touch blooming on my undeserving skin.

"I was trying to leave," I whisper. "It's my fault Oren was killed."

Rayce's grip on my knee slackens. A lock of hair falls onto his face. He looks perfect, even in his sorrow. Even with that scar and those wounds. *Especially* with that scar reminding him who he fights against and those wounds still fresh from keeping his promise to me.

"What?" he asks.

I don't move. Can't even wiggle my fingers. I sit here staring at the man who was like a son to Oren and take responsibility. No more running away. If Oren had never told me I deserved to be saved, I never would've gotten as far as I did.

"I'm sorry. If I hadn't been trying to run away then—"

"Oren's death isn't your fault," Rayce says, his voice firm. He cups my chin, pulling my face so close to his I can see my own reflection in his pupils. "Listen to me, because it's time you started blaming the right people. *You* didn't capture Oren. The Gardener did. And *you* didn't kill him. The emperor did. It doesn't matter how much harder you should have fought or what you might have said differently. You, of all people, know that it wouldn't have mattered to a piece of trash like the Gardener or my uncle."

"Like you weren't responsible for killing those people on your uncle's orders?"

He looks away at my question.

It was a cruel thing to bring up, but he knows what it feels like to have screams play over and over in the quiet spaces. If I had just decided to trust Rayce instead of trying to make his choice for him and run away, then none of this would have happened.

"You're right," Rayce says, returning my gaze. "Those people's deaths aren't my fault the way Oren's death isn't yours."

"But I left the camp."

"Then it was my fault for asking you to be out there in the first place," he says. "Or maybe it was Oren's fault for finding you as you were trying to leave."

I blink back my surprise. He slides his hand up to my cheek, rubbing circles on my skin with his thumb.

"I should've trusted you," I say.

"Maybe, but that still might not have made a difference. The point is, we can't keep blaming ourselves for other people's actions," he says. "It's something we both need to work on."

I can see him bent over his desk, agonizing over signing a piece of parchment he believed could kill almost a hundred of his people.

Rayce sighs and drops his hand from my face, clutching at the wound in his stomach. "I still can't believe Oren's really gone," he says, his voice low.

If it'd been me in his position, I wouldn't have been able to say anything. I wouldn't have trusted myself enough to talk, and my sorrow would have paralyzed me.

"Me neither," I say. "He was—" I stop, overwhelmed by all the things Oren probably did for the rebellion.

"The heart of this entire operation," Rayce fills in for me, finally turning to look at me.

Even in the darkness of this little room, I see the sorrow pooling out of his dark eyes. Right now, we're two pieces of the same torn fabric. Our sorrow makes us twins.

Rayce runs a hand through his hair, letting it fall loose. "He always said it was up to the young to lead this revolution. He refused to accept that, without him, Arlo and I would just be two boys playing pretend at defying my uncle. But the truth is—" His voice catches, and he rubs at his eyes. "Rose, I don't think I can do this without him. The only reason I could even fathom leading was because I knew he'd be there to catch me if I fell." He shakes his head. "Now he isn't here and—"

"Hey," I say, touching his cheek.

So far, words have failed me, but this time they don't. What I need to say feels like it's been growing in me all along.

"You're going to be fantastic, do you understand me? I only got a few weeks with Oren, and I'm a completely different person. But you are his protégé. Everything that is good and kind about you are the things Oren cultivated in you, and you can continue to use them. You can do this."

Indecision colors his dark eyes, but there's a tiny spark of belief.

"One thing your rebellion has taught me is that you aren't alone," I say. "When Marin's scouting party didn't return, none under your command even considered abandoning her. Same goes for when I was captured by the emperor or when Oren and I were taken by the Gardener. Zareen always came. And they will be there for you, too. You've got Arlo and Marin and Suki and even Piper." I take a deep breath and look away. "And you have me, if you'll allow it."

Heat rises to my cheeks hearing what I just offered.

"But I thought you were going to leave when you rescued the other girls from the Garden?"

"I'd planned on it, but after fighting by your side," I say to the wall, unable to look him in the eye, "I decided I might stay."

"I'm sorry, but I can't allow that."

His hand slips from my leg, letting the cool air attack it. I stiffen, never expecting a refusal from the man who begged me to stay when we were alone.

His fingers twine gently through my hair, sending shivers down my entire body. He turns my head so I meet his gaze. His eyes suck me in, deeper than the darkest parts of my old cage.

I'm completely unprepared to fight against the gentleness radiating from them, and my breath catches.

"You have to be honest with me," he says, his voice rough.

My heart hammers against my chest as my face heats up. I'm trapped in this moment, in his gaze, and like a moth drawn to flame, it will be the death of me. This is the thing I've been fighting against since I met Rayce, since I was imprisoned in the Garden, since I crossed the border from my homeland. The person I never wanted to be.

My eyes flick to the open door, waiting to see someone walk through and break up this moment, but it remains empty, as if the gods and goddesses suspended this tiny slice of time for only us.

"I'm going to ask you a single question," he says.

"W-what is it?"

He shifts forward, the sides of his stomach brushing against the insides of my legs as he moves even closer. I see each ridge and bump on the long scar twisting down his face, and the soft scent of leather from his holster and honey tickles my nose. His free hand brushes my burning cheek.

"When we first met, I asked you this same thing," he says. "I need to know your real name, Rose. Not your stage name, but the one you hide from. I can't really know you until I know who you are."

He moves even closer, our lips a mere inch away from each other. The thing I've been longing for since he showed up on my side of the tent is now within reach, and this time I'm ready. I hold onto his shoulders, balling the fabric of his sleeves in my fingers. I rub my lips together and steel myself for the thing I already know I have to give him. To this man I might have once been married to.

"My real name is Arianna Vasile," I say. "And I'm the true heir to the Varshan throne."

Every bone in my body tenses as the words escape my lips,

as if their freedom has unlocked a piece of myself that doesn't fit anymore. I watch his face, not even daring to breathe. I'm as helpless to it as a leaf falling from a tree.

I wait. Wait for him to say something. To move. To do anything besides sit here and stare at me like I've just sprouted wings.

"Arianna," he says finally, his voice rough in his throat. "Now *that* name suits you."

His words echo Oren's. I wonder if he even knows he did it.

"Okay." I hesitate. "But you heard the part abou—"

He puts his finger to my lips, cutting me off.

"I heard everything, and your title changes nothing." He tilts his head to the side. "It does, however, answer the question as to why my uncle wanted you desperately enough to line the streets with your wanted poster. But it doesn't change anything for me."

My stomach drops. What does that mean? Because he's no longer an heir of Delmar? Or…what? I want to ask, but he keeps talking before I can get another word out.

"Arianna, right now, all you need to know is you're safe. And there will always be a place for you here in the rebellion." His hand tightens on my chin and his eyes search mine. "Here with me."

I can't fight the tricky smile that slides up my lips.

"I love that," I say.

He cocks his head in question.

"The way you say my real name."

He leans in, closing the space between us, sealing our words with something deeper than promises, stronger than steel. I tilt up my face, my own mouth tingling as I meet him inch by slow inch, breath by breath, heartbeat for heartbeat.

Our mouths meet, as hesitant as he looked when he first walked in, his stubble scratchy against my face. But as he pulls me closer, crushing me against his hard chest, our bodies begin to form their own language. Our skin forms our words in the places that touch and the ones that don't. Our lips create the cadence, rising up and down as he gently bites my bottom lip, and our shared breath provides the pauses.

For once in my life I don't measure time passing with the sound of our breathing. There aren't any heartbeats ticking out seconds or stories to weave into the empty space. Right now there are only little nicks and scars covering Rayce's skin and the knowledge that I've finally told him everything. And even more amazing, he's accepted the real me.

Our lips finally part, and it feels like my world has been doused in color. Rayce's eyes still remain closed, and a peaceful expression dominates his face.

"Your lips taste sweet, delicate, like a flower," he says.

"Don't call me that." I bury my face in his neck.

He runs his hands through my hair, creating slow circles on the back of my head, lulling my tired limbs into relaxing in one circle and sparking them to life in the next.

"Why not?"

"Because that word is ugly." My voice catches. "It represents all that has been wrong with my world."

He pulls away so that he can look at me, creases back in his forehead, and I regret speaking.

"No," he says, his finger trailing over my lip. "Flowers are beautiful, delicate, artful. Each one a painting from Lin. They're unique. They come in every color imaginable, grow even in the hardest of places with just a little sun and water and…" He peers into my eyes. "And love. With love, their colors deepen, their soft petals withstand rainstorms, and when they blossom, they take your breath away."

Is he…is he saying he…does he love me, too?

His lips brush mine, removing any question I might have had. This man who knows all his people by name, who carefully kneads dough and expertly wields a sword with the same hand, who can steal my breath with a single glance, loves me. I wrap my arms around his neck and lean into our kiss, pulling him near, whispering my love back with every second our mouths touch.

But I know one other way to show him.

"Rayce?"

"Hmm?"

"There's one more thing I have to do."

He opens his eyes, and I greet him with a smile.

• • •

Rayce leads me deeper into the tunnels of his base than I've ever been before. The air grows warmer as the hall slopes gently downward, and my heart hammers my eardrums. When I'd asked him for this one thing, I thought it might take a few days, but the second the request left my lips, he already had my hand in his and was halfway out the door. All it took was a single command from Rayce and suddenly everything fell into place.

He pauses at a fork in the tunnel, holding out a hand to block my path.

"Are you sure this is what you really want?" he asks.

I nod, not trusting myself to speak.

"All right, then. No going back now."

He takes a left and leads me into a large, open room. Piper leans over a low table laden with an array of strange tools—long ivory needles, several pieces of cloth, vials filled with black ink, a mortar and pestle, and a basket filled with Zarenite. The mortar holds a fine, glowing green powder.

Kyra sits next to her older sister, her long black hair pulled back into a loose ponytail and a fresh pink robe clinging to her thin frame. She rolls a chunk of Zarenite in her hands, watching her sister measure out ink into a vial.

Arlo stands behind Piper, looking over the tools of her trade with his arms behind his back, and Marin waves from the back of the room as we walk in.

"In order to take the oath, you need two witnesses to it," Rayce says. "I figured you'd want people you already know."

"Okay," I say, my voice small in the big room.

"Don't worry," Marin says. "It only hurts for the first few minutes. Then it's just like sunburn."

Only a few short weeks ago, I wouldn't have remembered what that felt like, having the sun kiss your skin so hard it left a mark. Now that I do, it reconfirms why I want to join the rebellion. I want to help Rayce and the rest of his people fight for a brighter tomorrow.

"I imagine it will hurt significantly more for the Varshan," Piper says, setting the ink down in front of her. "Considering the powder has countless adverse effects on her."

"Nice to see you, too, Piper," I say.

Kyra waves at me while her sister isn't looking, and I smile back at her. One sister dark and gloomy, the other light and bright.

"Anyway," Arlo says. "Why don't you have a seat?"

He motions to the only other stool in the room. I walk over and sit. The surface of the wood forces my posture straight. I wiggle around, but no matter how I slide, it remains uncomfortable. A perfect representation of how I feel.

Arlo and Marin move so they stand behind me, one over each shoulder. Rayce walks up right in front of me and remains standing. Arlo holds out an official-looking piece of parchment with a green ribbon holding it shut, but Rayce shakes his head. He steadies his gaze on me and speaks, his words filling the huge room.

"Do you swear to remain loyal to the Zareeni cause for the rest of your days and to uphold our belief that only through kindness will the seeds of change grow?"

His gaze bores into me, waiting for my answer. I swallow, the words burning my throat, and I remind myself of the panic I felt at not being able to use a stunner at Dongsu.

"Yes."

"Will you promise to always be truthful and to only use the abilities afforded to you by the Zarenite for the good of those who can't fight for themselves?"

That sounds more like what I'm aiming for.

"I will."

"And will you swear that your every action from here on out will be for the good of the people of this land, even if that means forsaking your own life?"

I understand that sacrifice means Fern taking a beating for my perceived mistakes the Gardener accused me of making and risking my fingers to steal another scrap of bread for Blossom when she looked too skinny. Or Oren giving up his own life so that my sisters could be free.

The thought is like an explosion in my mind, and by the time the dust settles, I understand what the tattoo means, too. It's more than just joining their cause. It's adopting a way of life that's bigger than any one person. Every single person who bears the Zareeni mark tells the world they will fight to stand up for those who can't, even if they won't live to see that wish come true.

"I swear it on my life."

The air shifts with my promise, almost as if my last words broke a spell.

Rayce smiles, his eyes gentle, and he cups my cheek in his hand. I'm so enraptured by the simple gesture that I don't notice Piper coming at me with a tool until I feel the bite of her needle. I keep my body still, my face completely straight. I expected the pain of a broken finger, but instead, I'm greeted with the slow burn of sun-kissed skin.

The metallic scent of blood mixes with the bitter ink,

clogging my nostrils. I focus on Piper's tremor-like movements, watching as her hand scrapes starlight into my flesh. When she gets through with the first line, she wipes away the excess ink and blood before sticking the needle point back in the ink cup on her finger.

The longer I sit, the warmer the air turns. The prickles all over my body smooth, and the tips of my hair begin to press against my neck.

Rayce never leaves my side, his large hand lending mine endless support.

The Zarenite burns through my veins like downing an entire bottle of whiskey. Sweat leaks from every pore, sticking the hair to the back of my neck as Piper carves the pattern of a beautiful bouquet onto my arm, filling my blood with the mineral that will help Zareen change the world. I look up at Rayce, and he smiles encouragingly at me. He knows everything now, the little bits I've tried to hide for so long, and he hasn't turned away from me.

It's like the Garden is being burned out of me with every line etched into my skin. A Flower on fire.

Piper pulls back, examining her work for a long moment before nodding.

"It's beautiful," Kyra says to her sister.

"You're done," Rayce says, leaning down to kiss the tip of my nose.

I smile at the delicate lines blossoming across my left arm, glowing just on top of the skin. It signifies that I'm now wholly part of something bigger than myself.

I am no longer just a Flower or a lost princess. Now, I am imbued with fire. A splash of sunlight falls onto the ground in front of me from a hole in the ceiling, stretching hundreds of feet underground to find me like a beacon of hope. But I turn away from it, because now I am my own hope—and with this oath, I make my own light.

# Acknowledgments

Writing acknowledgements has always been one of the most exciting and terrifying parts of the publishing process for me. I'm so thrilled to finally be thanking everyone who had a hand in making my book into the novel it has become but I'm also scared that I'll forget someone. So if you are reading this and you don't see your name here, please know that I am eternally grateful to you.

I'd like to thank my agent, Nikki Terpilowski, for her tireless work on my behalf. You were my first champion, and your guidance and steadfast belief in me as a writer have given me the confidence to persevere. I will never be able to fully express my gratitude.

To Lydia Sharp, editor extraordinaire. You took my novel and elevated it into something I could never even conceive when I first wrote it. Thank you so much for understanding my characters, believing in me, and the endless hours you put in to making my novel shine (and making sure Rayce doesn't wink).

My gratitude to assistant editors Naomi Hughes,

whose amazing input helped strengthen Rayce and Rose's relationship, and Judi Weiss, whose feedback on my novel was invaluable.

To Crystal Havens and the rest of the team at Entangled Teen, thank you so much for believing in my story and your incredible effort to help my novel grow.

I would like to thank my high school teacher, Bernie Bleske, for spending his lunch breaks explaining to me how a plot works in detail and spending his nights reading the first chapter of a story I wrote over and over. Thank you to my other teacher, Gary Miller, for instilling in me the importance of perseverance, especially when you don't first succeed.

Before my book was cultivated, there were several people who waded through its thorns and gave me vital feedback. To all the beta readers of my book, Andi, Kassidy, Jackie, Annie, Joanne, and any others along the way, thank you! Also, to Katie, I can't begin to express my gratitude for helping me navigate the world of publication. We met as bloggers and you have been there through every step of the publishing process. You are the best!

I'd like to extend my warmest thanks to my dad and stepmother for encouraging me to pursue my passions. And a huge thank you to my mom for being there for me no matter what. I may not be able to say "my mother loves my book" (yet), but without your love and support, this book would have never been made.

I can't imagine my life without my group of friends who reminded me that magic can exist outside the pages of a book or computer screen if I just take the time to look up (and roll). A huge thanks to Rebecca, Zach, Erica, Chad, Mindy, and in memory of Jon. All of you are so dear to me and I want to thank each of you for your encouragement and creativity. Some of you are wrestling with creative pursuits of your own and to that, I say, reach for the stars, the fall is scary but the view from above is worth the risk.

To Ashley, who I've been whispering stories back and forth to since we were old enough to talk. I have no doubt that without your excitement, nourishment, and hours spent talking about my confusing new ideas, I would have never made it this far. I'd like to thank you but there aren't enough ways in the world to repay you for your love.

Finally, to my husband, Brian, who has worked hard so that I can accomplish my dreams. Your willingness to believe in me when I couldn't find the will to believe in myself, the endless nights you've stayed up helping me figuring out how magic could work scientifically, and the love and support you've shown me since we were young adults, ourselves, has made this all possible. Thank you for showing me that love is real and can truly make you whole.

And to you, the readers and bloggers, who have taken the time to sit down and read this book that I've poured my love in to. As a reader myself, I know the time and effort it takes to commit to a book and I can't thank you enough for spending your precious time on me.

# About the Author

Amber Mitchell graduated from the University of South Florida with a BA in Creative Writing. When she isn't putting words on paper, she is using cut sheets of cardstock to craft artwork or exploring new places with her husband Brian. They live a small town in Florida with their four cats where she is still waiting for a madman in a blue box to show up on her doorstep.

## Discover more Entangled Teen books...

### FANNING THE FLAMES
a *Going Down in Flames* novel by Chris Cannon

Being a shape-shifting dragon has its perks, but being forced into an arranged marriage isn't one of them. If Bryn McKenna doesn't say "I do," she'll lose everything. Good-bye flying. Good-bye best friends. Good-bye magic. But if she bends to her grandparents' will and agrees to marry Jaxon Westgate she'll lose the love of her life—her knight.

### BEFORE TOMORROW
a *Forget Tomorrow* novella by Pintip Dunn

In a world where all seventeen-year-olds receive a memory from their future selves, Logan Russell's vision is exactly as he expects—and exactly not. Soon enough, he learns that his old friend Callie is in trouble. She's received an atypical memory, one where she commits a crime in the future. According to the law, she must be imprisoned, even though she's done nothing wrong. Now, Logan must decide if he'll give up his future as a gold-star swimmer and rescue the literal girl of his dreams. All he'll have to do is defy Fate.

### GRETA AND THE LOST ARMY
a *Mylena Chronicles* novel by Chloe Jacobs

After spending four years trapped in a place of monsters and magick, the last thing Greta expected was to be back on Earth. And now that she's there, she's not sure if she wants to leave, though that means giving up the boy she loves. But a powerful enemy won't stop at anything to defeat her. Even if it means following her to Earth and forcing her to face a fate as unavoidable as love itself.